Light, Descending

Also by Octavia Randolph

The Circle of Ceridwen Saga
The Circle of Ceridwen
Ceridwen of Kilton
The Claiming
The Hall of Tyr

The Tale of Melkorka: A Novella
Ride: A Novella

Light, Descending

Octavia Randolph

This novel employs the 19th century British English spelling and usage common to the writings of John Ruskin.

Contents

Light, Descending

The book (John Ruskin's *Unto This Last*) was impossible to lay aside, once I had begun it…I could not get any sleep that night. I determined to change my life in accordance with the ideals of the book. — Mohandas Gandhi *The Story of My Experiments with Truth,* 1929

How mightily this dead man lives. — Marcel Proust on hearing of Ruskin's death, 1900

In fact it becomes clearer to the world than ever that there is but one Ruskin in the world; an unguidable man, but with quantities of lightning in the interior of him, which are strange and probably dangerous to behold. — Thomas Carlyle, 1874

I think he is the finest writer living. — George Eliot, 1856

How things bind and blend themselves together!
— from the last published paragraph of John Ruskin, *Praeterita III,* 1889

Chapter One

The Lamp of Obedience

London: 8 February 1832

Even with the snow the boy knew his father would not be late, and he saw Mr. Telford's carriage roll up to the door at Herne Hill just before four o'clock. His father came into the house, stamping the snow off, and called out hello to him. He passed a package to his son's hands as the maid took his great coat and hat.

"From Mr. Telford, John, with his compliments of the day," his father said. John James Ruskin's pride in his sole offspring was such that he concealed with difficulty his satisfaction in the distinction implied by the gift. He was a man who was beginning to know his own value, and felt this recognition from his gentleman business partner as a shared one.

The package was heavy and squarish and wrapped round in stiff blue paper. "Please Papa, may I open it?" John asked.

Mrs. Ruskin had just appeared from her parlour, wearing her everyday white lace cap over her grey hair. A gift from Mr. Telford! she thought. Everything concerning her son conjured in Margaret Ruskin that mixture of pleasure and dismay peculiar to her. She did not hold with presents being lavished on children. It was kind that he recognized her son's special abilities, but to spoil him with gifts—! "No, John," she answered, "you may not; it must wait until after supper." She took the package from him and lay it on the hall table. "Good of Mr. Telford to remember you, John," she reminded.

1

"Yes, Mother." His mother had always been "Mother" to John, but his father was "Papa"; he did not know why he called them thus, only that it seemed right. He paused a moment to look at Mr. Telford's birthday gift, without touching the thick blue paper.

Mr. Telford was the Telford of Telford Ruskin & Domecq, Wine Merchants, and John knew from visiting the offices and the conversation of his father that Mr. Telford had had the money to start the concern, his father did the selling, and Mr. Domecq produced the sherry.

Mr. Telford liked John and gave him interesting things; John knew he had no boy of his own. Mr. Telford lent the Ruskins his own carriage for the family to use when he did not need it, and they had taken long summer trips to the Lakes in it, his father stopping at inns and the houses of rich men to sell them wines. John loved the Lakes and hills and wrote poems about them; two had been published. His parents paid him a penny for every twenty lines he wrote.

Cook had made a pudding with plums and walnuts in it for the occasion, and after the table was cleared John James Ruskin took down two little stemmed sherry glasses from the crowded highboy and filled them half-full. He handed one glass to his son. It was Telford Ruskin & Domecq's best stock. In the cellar sat a case of it, and with Ruskin senior's continual application to his work, the prospect of many more such good things to come. He eyed his boy, standing there holding the thin stem a little tremulously. John James laboured in Trade in order to make his son a Gentleman, and his expectations were nothing short of stupendous. With young John's brain, the boy would end a bishop, or Prime Minister. He would get him there, he and the boy's mother; he to teach him application, and his mother to teach him to be good. He touched the rim of his glass to his son's; his wife did not imbibe.

Light, Descending

From his twelfth birthday last year John had been allowed sherry, but he did not much like it. He took a small sip and tried to smile. He was wearing the watch and chain his father had given him in the morning, and he again thanked him for it.

His mother brought him the gift from Mr. Telford, and he unfolded the blue paper.

It was a book, a brown leather-bound copy of Samuel Rogers' poem, *Italy*.

"What pretty drawings!" said his mother. The book was of obvious value, a choice for a collector, and if John would be spoilt with such things, she could take comfort that they were worthy of him.

"They are engravings, Mother," John said, "and fine ones." He had explained the difference to her several times in the past, and did so again in a patient voice. Each page of the book had a verse or two of Rogers' poem headed by an illustration of a picturesque view of cypress trees, ruins, or cathedrals. John liked to draw, and every day he drew things––clouds, and flowers, and rocks—to understand them better. He looked more closely at the engravings. Some were signed 'Stothard' but many were signed 'JWM Turner.'

He looked at one by the Turner artist, a vignette of Lake Como. Boats were in the foreground, and jagged mountains in the background, and noble architecture to one side, all the things he liked. But what struck him was the way the sun was reflected in water, and how it lit the sky. He did not understand how Mr. Turner could so perfectly convey warm sunlight using only black and white lines. He would study the engraving and then draw it.

After he said goodnight to his parents John went up the stairs with *Italy* in his hands.

Light, Descending

He passed the painting of himself as a baby in the stairwell. He was shown wearing a long white dress with a blue sash, and holding the blue lead to a spaniel he could not remember who was also in the painting. His parents had told him that he had asked the artist to put blue hills in the picture and Mr. Northcote had put them in behind him.

The snow was still falling and the house was entirely quiet. He wished he could hear the muffled sound of his parents talking beneath him, or that one of them was musical and could play the piano so he might fall asleep to it. He wished the old house cat had not died; she used to nose her way into his room at night and nudge him. Most of all he wished his cousin George was still with them; George who was older and the only person who made him laugh. He had come to visit over Christmas but now was back in Croydon, readying to join his brother who was prospering in Australia. John feared he would never see him again; and indeed, in four months George would be drowned still within sight of England.

John said his prayers, feelingly, with something approaching ardour, and got into bed. Despite the watch and chain and the sherry he felt almost like the three year old on the landing, except in the painting he looked ready to smile. He thought perhaps he had been happier then.

He looked up at the shadows dancing on the ceiling from his candle, which he had not yet blown out.

"I have nothing to love," he said aloud.

He thought he might start to blubber but he knew he was too old for that. To make himself stop he pushed himself up in his bed and pulled the Rogers *Italy* from his night table. He opened it to the Como scene and brought the candle closer.

Chapter Two

The Lamp of Memory: 1836-1843

London: 1836

The two young people had met first in Paris, but that was two years ago. Now John Ruskin was almost seventeen and Adèle-Clothilde Domecq was fifteen. Her sisters called her Clothilde, but at this second meeting John thought of her, and called her, Adèle. It rhymed with *shell*, *spell*, and *knell* and thus served his poetry, and Clothilde rhymed with nothing. Adèle had blonde hair and light eyes. She and three of her sisters had been staying at Herne Hill, and in four days the heart of young John had been reduced to a heap of ashes.

She had been born in Cadiz, in the shadow of her father's vast vineyards—Pedro Domecq was the elder Ruskin's partner in the sherry-trade; the growing partner. But the Domecq daughters had been raised in France; the eldest was soon to marry a count. The four younger now gaily descended upon the Ruskin household and upended it. They had bouncing curls with ribbons at the root, from Adèle on down to the youngest, Caroline.

Adèle's frocks were from Paris, and her manners as well. She shrugged off her fur trimmed travelling cloak into John's hands, and he tried not to goggle at her dress, short and with bewildering pantalettes. She turned to smile at him with small, brilliant teeth. She was like a heroine out of a novel or stepped down from a painting. Her face was oval, her nose upturned. Her complexion reminded John of fresh-poured cream. Her eyes glinted blue fire as she laughed, and they met his for one steady moment. He thought he might combust spontaneously.

5

The girls' French maid was with them, and that night his mother's Scots maid Anne grumbled about the disdaining way the woman looked at the family's accommodations. His sweetly quiet, brown-haired, newly-orphaned cousin Mary Richardson, who now lived with the Ruskins, suddenly seemed another, inferior species altogether. She faded into irrelevance around the Domecq sisters.

"But we cannot eat such things!" Adèle would laugh at breakfast, her little sisters smiling too. The sideboard was laid with oatmeal, black pudding, and stewed fruit. They must have the bread, so, and the fruit fresh and a comfit, and *oui*, they were allowed coffee, very strong and with much sweet milk, *merci*.

When John excused himself after breakfast to sit down to his daily Bible reading with his mother, Adèle followed them into the little side parlour to watch.

"You are like—what—a child to her, a little child, who cannot read *sa bible* in private, for fear he will not do it himself," she told him later. She was laughing; she was always laughing. Her English sounded sung to him.

He invited her into his room to look at his minerals; she laughed and ran away. He realised too late he should have asked Adèle to bring her maid with her, and he looked around the house until he found the woman in her black bodice and frilled cap. She spoke no English, and his school-boy French failed him by degrees as she kept shrugging her shoulders and throwing up her hands at his stammering request.

And when Sunday came, the girls needed to be taken to Mass.

"I would be happy to accompany the Misses Domecq to Our Lady of Victories in the morning," John offered at supper Saturday night.

Light, Descending

Margaret Ruskin rarely spoke on any topic until her husband had made his pronouncement. This time she did. Mrs. Ruskin gasped, and followed this with a blink of both eyes across the table at her son. She was training John up as a devout evangelical Christian, and suddenly here in her own well-ordered household the glittering head of Popery had reared itself, ready to snatch her boy to perdition. John watched his mother lower her knife and fork as if to remove them from danger. "*You* will accomp—you will accompany—these girls—to a Roman service?" she asked him.

All the Domecq daughters were staring at him. Cousin Mary sat biting her lip, and lowered her head. His father cleared his throat and said he would send round to their Baptist minister's young clerk to go; he and the Domecq maid, joined by their coachman, would afford suitable protection. Adèle listened with cocked head and smiled at John as she cut into her lamb-chop. He felt himself to be in her plate. He imagined the firm thrust of her knife and graceful lift of her fork as a fragment of his flesh touched her lips.

If he could not escort her in public, he could yet woo her with words. He wrote a romance, *Leoni: a Legend of Italy*, and tried to read it to her.

"It is a tragedy, of how I might have been, if I had been born a bandit," he told her. She did not understand the term 'bandit', and when he attempted acting out the necessary behaviour for his hero's Robin-Hood-like career she dissolved in peals of laughter at his pantomime.

Labouring over his slight dictionary he composed, in French, a nine page declaration of devotion. He kissed the envelope and slid it under her bedroom door at midnight, and lay awake in a fever of expectation.

Coming early down to breakfast he saw on his plate his letter transformed into a little paper boat, with one of the costly Covent Garden *fraises* the girls had demanded as cargo. He snatched it up before Adèle arrived, tossing her bouncing hair, laughing at him.

Every attempt at conversation yielded disaster. Struggling to find subjects in common, John found himself lecturing his Spanish-born, French-raised, and Catholic-believing mistress of his heart about the flawed naval strategies that brought about the destruction of the Spanish Armada, then went on to Napoleon's debacle at Waterloo, and found himself burbling his decided views on Transubstantiation. Adèle listened, hands in lap, smiling, and one agonizing afternoon ruffled his hair with her hand before she jumped up, laughing.

He went out into the garden and wrote poems to her. He placed her in the Alpine mountains he loved, and saw how they now paled in his affections next to Adèle. It was then he began to weep.

When the Domecq daughters left, John spent months in a haze. He could not write to Adèle, now back in Paris, without permission from his parents, and hers, and he was afraid to ask for it. Hoping to somehow gain her attention, he gave his poems to his father to read, who promptly had them published in the annual gift-book *Friendship's Offering*. Heartened by his son's increased versifying and insensate to the poignant juvenile yearnings expressed therein, John James Ruskin saw in his boy the makings of a great poet. John listlessly turned the pages of his own crisp copy, unable to imagine the homely British production finding its way to a book-seller's on the Champs-Elysees. He began attending lectures on literature at King's College in the Strand; soon he would be going up to Oxford.

Whether writing poetry to a hopeless love object or devising a colour wheel to measure the exact blue of the skies, for young Ruskin it was impossible to do, feel, or believe anything by halves. On any given morning he might awaken with almost manic physical and intellectual energies, and the next dawn be wholly and silently absorbed in reflection. He wrote torrents of poetry, hewed firmly to his study of Scripture (for Margaret Ruskin had repeatedly confided to him that at his birth she had solemnly dedicated him to the service of God), and kept up his collecting of minerals and botanical specimens. His natural passion for, and satisfaction in, writing and study was well noted by his parents, and the elder Ruskins, deeming these worthy occupations, unwittingly but irreclaimably blurred the distinction between Love and Labour by rewarding him monetarily for his creative output. Nothing escaped parental attention; all he did and said was worthy of praise, comment, and correction. The joys of discovery, of close observation, of musing, and drawing conclusions—however fanciful these latter might be while he was yet a child—were not left as random seeds for germination by the Ruskins; they must be potted up, nurtured, pinched and pruned to flourishment. The producing of work by the younger Ruskin became equated with the preferment of affection and approval by the elder two. One was loved through one's work, and as the link between the two ossified in John's mind, one *loved* through one's work, as well. Holding his cyanascope to the heavens, rotating the circles of hand-coloured paper until one precisely matched the blue of the sky, he would then keep turning until he found one that recalled the eyes of Adèle.

That autumn John occupied himself by re-cataloguing and arranging all his mineral specimens, and in the creation of rhyme-charts to aid his poetry. Then he read a review of three Turner paintings on view at the Royal Academy. The critic for *Blackwood's Edinburgh Magazine* decried both the artist's moving the action of 'Juliet and her Nurse' from Verona to Venice, and the work's execution as childish. For Turner's painting of 'Mercury and Argus' the writer declared that the god referenced had no cause to put out the eyes of Argus; merely looking at the glare produced in the painting would have blinded him.

John had seen those paintings, and was incensed. Not only was the reviewer—a Scottish Presbyterian minister—ignorant of fine art, his flippancy was nothing short of vulgar. John had stood in awed wonder before Turner's pastoral scene of the god Mercury lulling the shepherd Argus to sleep so he could abduct the lovely Io. Turner had painted the landscape with infinitely and suggestively subtle variations; the pale and vaporous blue of the heated sky was striated with grey and pearly white, the whole melding into glowing and aerial space. As to 'Juliet', her small ebullient figure anchored the foreground of a Venetian sky phosphorescent with fireworks, a scene imbued with the transitive beauty of uncertain light.

He thought he would write a letter to the editors of Blackwood's "Maga," as its readers called it, and enlighten Rev. Eagles. Turner, John Ruskin wrote, was as an artist just as free as Shakespeare to re-imagine his settings; his imagination was in fact Shakespearean in its mightiness.

"This is powerfully put, my boy," said his father as he held the draught. John had come into his father's velvet-draped study to show him his rebuttal, and the old man had begun reading it at his desk. John James had risen slowly from his chair and now stood before his son with the expanse of the carved mahogany desk between them. "'He is a meteor, dashing on in a path of glory which all may admire, but which none may follow; and his imitators must be, and always have been, moths fluttering about the lights, into which if they enter they are destroyed.'"

John James Ruskin lowered the papers and pulled his spectacles down his nose. Fluttering moths! Of course it was beautifully expressed, and showed off the boy's facility with the language, but the passion of it, the declaration of Turner's supremacy, struck him as a bit rich for the blood. He looked up at John, who watched all expectancy, his fair skin colouring as he studied him. "Quite a lot of heat in there," he told his son. "It's perhaps, too warm."

"How can I let him call Mr. Turner's Venice 'thrown higgledy-piggedly together,' and 'thrown into a flour tub'? My descriptions tell what Turner really painted!"

His father removed his reading spectacles and lay them upon the blotter as he considered. It wouldn't do to have the youngster embarrass himself. "Why not let Mr. Turner make that decision? I might send him your letter in care of his agent and see what he thinks. If he approves you may send it on to *Blackwood's*."

The great painter wanted none of it.

My dear Sir,

I beg to thank you for your zeal, kindness, and trouble you have taken on my behalf, in respect to the criticism of Blackwood's Magazine for October, respecting my works; but I never move in these matters, they are of no import save mischief and the meal-tub, which Maga fears for by my having invaded the flour tub.

JMW Turner

P.S. If you wish to have the manuscript returned, have the goodness to let me know. If not, with your sanction, I will send it on to the possessor of the picture of Juliet.

In January John left for Oxford. His mother came with him, with an assumption of the correctness in her accompanying her child to university that went unquestioned in the family circle. John's health, in all their eyes, was delicate; he was given to colds and stomach-upsets. She and Mr. Ruskin had been their boy's almost sole tutors, and knew him best. Mrs. Ruskin had given him all the Latin she could, and Mr. Ruskin insisted on only the best verse for the boy, Shakespeare and Pope and of course that luminary of every Scottish family, Sir Walter Scott. John James enrolled his son as a Gentleman-Commoner at Christ Church, a sort of purchased rank. The fees were higher, the lodgings better, and it allowed John in without an examination, which, given the sketchiness of his home-schooling, his father suspected the boy might not pass even granted his natural brilliance.

The Gentlemen-Commoners sat apart at separate tables to dine. John's fellow scholars were a sporting crowd of horse-race-mad young lords. A trunk of new clothes had been made for his going up, and he had as well his Gentleman-Commoner gold-tasselled mortar-board and silk gown. John was sandy-haired, blue-eyed, tall and straight; he presented well. His brown-velvet-collared greatcoat was each day set off by a bright blue stock about his neck.

Mrs. Ruskin, with cousin Mary as companion, took lodgings on the Oxford High Street, and expected John for tea every evening, of which expectation he did not disappoint her unless he must. His father joined them on weekends as his business travelling allowed. The family came home briefly to London to celebrate John's 18th birthday, and it was then his father presented him with an actual Turner watercolour. It was a summery, sunlit view of London's Richmond Bridge, the round-arched stone bridge in the middle distance, genteelly dressed picnickers in the foreground. He had hoped for some time for such a gift, and though it was not what he would have chosen for himself—he would have asked for a mountain, any mountain, by the great man—it was a specimen of his work.

Late at night in his rooms at Peckwater Quad he thought about Beauty, of what constituted it, of the almost physical pleasure it gave him to stand before a lovely prospect in the woods, or before Turner's glowing Richmond Bridge view. He had been forbidden to bring it back to Oxford with him, but he had drawn a little sketch of it to help him in his recalling. He wrote poems to Adèle, away in France, which she would never see. He drew flowers and branches in the Physic Garden, and considered a treatise on the philosophy of architecture he might write.

Virgil bored him, and Milton he found parasitical. Sophocles was dismal and Tacitus too hard. Terence was simply dull. Plato he loved, from the first line. The great theme of Thucydides—the suicide of Greece—he felt with ringing sympathy of heart and brain. His father paid for tutors to help lift his Latin and Greek, with whom he worked long into the dim Oxfordshire afternoons puzzling out the finer points of grammar.

The chief activities of the other Gentlemen-Commoners were drinking, gaming, and horse-racing, rounded out by cock-fighting, badger-baiting, and boating. The ability to scale the heights of brick walls after the college gates had been locked each evening was also highly prized. They did no work and paid scouts to write the most cursory of essays for them. Nevertheless they treated John with amused benevolence, born, he assumed, of curiosity. He had shown them the first week that he could hold his liquor; that counted for something. The swells had sounded him out by inviting him to one of their rooms for an informal party. The daily drinking of sherry at home, coupled with his discreetly choosing one of the smaller glasses, alternated with draughts of cold water, allowed him to match his hosts, toast for toast. Yet they ragged him for his nightly visits to his mother, for the very fact that she had followed him to Oxford, and that nearly every Sunday his father came up too. His parents so wanted him to "get on" with the new crowd that he forced himself to find reasons to be in their company merely to satisfy their desire for fresh stories of his aristocratic neighbours.

After a day spent drawing the venerable buildings of his academic setting, John returned to Peckwater Quad to learn, to his disgust, that two of the Gentlemen-Commoners, having waged a day-long race against each other from Oxford to London and back, had killed three horses between them in doing so. But his mother was delighted because one day young Lord March asked to borrow a pencil of him.

Each week the undergraduates were required to write an essay on a philosophical subject, the finest to be read aloud in hall by its author on Saturday afternoon. John worked at these, and when one week his tutor told him that his piece on Juvenal had been selected, felt proud to be able to publicly represent his fellow Gentlemen-Commoners to the rest of the Christ Church student body. He was sitting between lounging Lords Desart and Emlyn when his name was called. He sensed, more than saw, their recoil—of pleased surprise, he imagined—as he stood, pulled down on his jacket to straighten it, and made his way to the rostrum. He delivered his piece with confidence and even, he hoped, élan. He returned to their tables expecting the jovial congratulations of the other Gentlemen-Commoners.

Light, Descending

Winding back through the blackened oak trestles, he found every man of them scowlingly alert and glaring at him. Some were hissing, and a few were pounding the stone pavers with their boots in protest. He felt the blood rushing to his face but forced himself not to hasten back to his seat. By actual application to his studies, he had committed the grossest lèse-majesté against the order of Gentlemen-Commoners. A foot darted out from beneath a bench as he neared his table, and tripped him. He saved himself from a complete fall only by ramming his hands upon the shoulders of Lord Kildare, one of the number who had formerly shown particular tolerance of the tradesman's son. The pages of his essay fluttered over the table. John swept his hands together with clawed fingers and drew the papers into a crumpled mass.

Late that night a remonstrative bonfire was lit outside his window. The glare of flames woke him, and as he stood at the casement watching the scouts and porters hastening to put it out he wished he had not already consigned his Juvenal essay to his room's fire-grate. He would have liked to have been able to toss it gracefully from his window into the flames where his fellow matriculants, watching from the shadows of the arcades, could have witnessed his embarrassed admission of innocence.

But he won them over, all and for good, the following night. Already asleep behind his closed bedroom door, he was awakened by drunken shouts, laughter, and the stamping of feet up the stairwell. He rose and tied on his dressing-gown as the party stormed his small parlour. It sounded as though his furniture was being hurled about the room; he heard pottery crash. "Come out, you little donkey," cried the voice of the ringleader. He took a breath and opened his bedroom door. His table had been upset, chairs overturned, his papers scattered, and his books freed from their now-splintered cases. Five Gentlemen-Commoners stood reeling in the wreckage.

15

John gave his waist tie an extra tug and came forward smiling. "Gentlemen, I am sorry that this evening I am not quite prepared to entertain you as you might wish, but as you know, my father is in the sherry trade, and he has put it in my power to invite you all to wine tomorrow evening. Will you come?"

More congenial was the small group of scientific men he met in other Oxford circles. The first he found was Henry Acland, a medical student who shared his interests in geology and natural science. After this his circle expanded greatly through the offices of an unexpected benefactor. One autumn afternoon he was drawing poppy seed pods in the walled enclosures of the Physic Garden when a shadow fell over his sketch pad. John craned his neck over his shoulder.

"An excellent representation," said an elderly gentlemen with a fringe of white hair upon his bald head. "Mind you see the pods of *Papaver somniferum* in the next bed; they are nearly ripe for opium-cutting!"

John stood to face his onlooker. The old man was gowned, and he recognized him as the famed mineralogist and fossil-hunter who also served as Canon of Christ Church.

"Dr. Buckland," said John. "John Ruskin, sir, of Christ College."

Buckland smiled and nodded. He reached for John's sketch pad, which he willingly surrendered. After flipping through a few pages he handed it back.

"I give a dinner, first Friday of each month. I'd like you to come."

Light, Descending

"I would be honoured, sir."

The old man laughed. "Don't be honoured. Be hungry. See you at seven, then."

A week later John presented himself at the stone house in the corner of Tom Quad. The door was opened by a curtsying maid. John stepped into a dark-panelled reception hall lined with horns and hats. Directly in front of him hung the mounted head of a rhinoceros, impressively vast, with tiny glass eyes peering from the thick folds of the heavy hide. A soft felt hat was hanging jauntily from its horn. Racks of antlers of deer, elk, moose, and the long spiral horns of some beast he could not name—an antelope from the depths of Africa, he imagined—were fastened on all three other walls. Men's hats hung from many of the appendages. There was even a grey silk woman's bonnet, ribbons trailing, stuck on the tip of a twelve-pointer. Instead of taking his hat, the maid gestured to the possibilities. "If you'd be so kind to choose a prong to your liking, sir," she said, and then vanished for the remainder of the evening.

He could hear voices, which grew loud when a door opened onto the hall. Buckland stuck his head out. "Mr. Ruskin. Come in and meet the rest of the party."

John stepped over the threshold and paused. A crocodile grinned at him, gigantic jaws gaping, exactly at eye level. It was hanging over the dining table, suspended from the coffered ceiling by slender wire cables. It was also covered with dust, a dust that coated much but not all of the room's extraordinary contents. John's nose was assailed by the mingled aromas of that same dust, combined with a pronounced animal muskiness, leavened by sweet briar pipe tobacco and cedar wood. No dining room could have been more distinct from that at Herne Hill and his mother's scrupulously exacting standards of cleanliness and decorum. He stood there mutely, blinking, his eyes fastened on the

17

fearsomely fascinating teeth of the crocodile, and found himself smiling back at it. A couple of men rose from chairs and came forward.

"Quite the reception, don't you think?" asked a tall, thin man a few years older than himself. "I'm Henry Liddell," he said as he extended his hand. John had seen him before; Liddell was a tutor at Christ Church.

"Liddell here has started on a Greek Lexicon, to be the most complete compendium of Greek to English ever attempted," said their host.

John shook Liddell's hand and said, "In that case, sir, my own tutors may soon have their considerable burdens lessened." Liddell laughed at this with a self-deprecating wave. John felt he had gained sudden admission not only to this curious scientific sanctum but its circle of convivial acolytes.

Dr. Buckland turned to a shorter man, also young, with brown hair and a heavy brow. "Ruskin, this is Charles Darwin. You would have thought he might have contributed to my collections here, but in sad fact, no. A few beetles was the most I could get out of him. I'll have to send him back around the world, just for my sake."

Buckland began riffling through a splaying stack of printed journals piled willy-nilly on the end of a sideboard. "Ruskin's of a like mind to we fellows. Ah—here you are, already represented in my collection." He looked over his spectacles at John before returning to the journal in his hand. "'*Remarks on the Present State of Meteorological Science*', by John Ruskin. And were you not the very young author of a paper on the colours of the Rhine, and another on the strata of Mont Blanc, which appeared a few years back in *Loudon's Magazine of Natural History?*"

John nodded. Darwin took the proffered issue in his hands. "You're another natural philosopher, then?" he asked, looking back at John. "I hope someday to do something meaningful in the sciences myself."

John had read the initial paper the naturalist had presented at the Geological Society of London about his voyages on the *Beagle*, returned less than a year ago. These two men were ten years his senior and already establishing themselves in their fields. Buckland was betting he'd be worthy company, and John felt keenly both the honour of the expectation and the pleasure of being suddenly surrounded by like-minded men.

Buckland passed glasses of claret. John had a chance to look about him; the delight he felt was akin to being eight years old again and set free in the laboratory of a playful sorcerer. One table by the window held an assortment of magnifying glasses, beakers, and a tiny still with writhing copper tubing. A stuffed hyaena with a snarling snout stood guard on a low bookshelf crammed with books. A hotchpotch of mounted owls, hawks, and sea birds in every attitude of flight or repose sat on tables and tall clocks or were hung from the ceiling. One long sideboard was covered with the skinned pelts of small animals pinned to drying boards, and another with dishes and trays holding fossils, minerals, sea shells, and unidentifiable lumps of earthen-coloured matter. Under all of this was an ancient and trailing table covering, which of a sudden moved. John watched as a high-domed tortoise, as large as a platter, lumbered out. Buckland took something from the dinner table and stooped and held it out to the creature. "*Aldabrachelys gigantea gigantea*," murmured Buckland. "The Aldrabra Giant Tortoise. Not as great as those Darwin noted in Galapagos, but worthy none the less of its appellation. This is a youngster, of course. She may live 200 years."

"If she can avoid the soup-pot," Darwin interjected. Buckland shrugged towards something to one side of Ruskin as the tortoise's beak chomped down on the offered greenery.

John looked at an old spinet which held an upside-down tortoiseshell, now empty of its occupant, and cradled in a silver ring. A long-handled silver ladle rested against the inside of the thick shell. "No punch tonight, Ruskin," Buckland told him, "we save that for Summer evenings, and of course use the bowl as well for turtle soup."

John nodded. A movement within a double rack of wire cages on the adjoining wall caught his eye. He stepped towards one and saw an odd, heavy-bodied, crescent-shaped animal with a long jaw and tail and something very much resembling armour covering its body. It turned slowly round as if to give its observer a better look. John raised his fingers to the wire cross-works and the animal closed its eyes meditatively.

"A North American armadillo, from the deserts of Arizona, and naturally needing indoor warmth," said Buckland. "Primitive creatures, and thus excellent for study. They make fine eating."

John hoped his smile covered his surprise. It was hard to picture a beast more unpalatable-looking than this armadillo, now performing the mesmerizing contortion of rounding itself into an armoured ball. His host watched with him. "Protection against predators," he explained, "but fortunately ineffective against the truly curious gourmand."

John felt at a loss to comment, and decided it might not be necessary.

It was not. Buckland straightened up and declared his intentions to the neophyte.

Light, Descending

"It is my goal to eat my way through the animal kingdom—mainly at these little dinners I give—and so far my efforts have proceeded admirably."

Liddell groaned a protest, which Buckland smilingly ignored. He took up a slender notebook from one of the sideboards and flipped through it. "Let's see, in the last few months we've enjoyed"—here Liddell coughed—"loin of horse, Icelandic style. Tail of beaver—also North American—poached in broth and Bordeaux." Their host sighed. "Poor Hardy. I really was fond of him. But he was growing old and going fast." He looked down at his list. "Yes—haunch of same, braised. And there is a great deal of good meat on a sixty-pound river rodent, I assure you."

"But where, sir—" began John. Buckland nodded towards the largest window. "Mostly right out there, in the garden. I have a series of little pools, a few kennels, and a large assortment of wire cages." He turned and pointed to the hyaena eternally snarling on the bookcase. "Bessie lived there for a while; I would have eaten her but I had already done so with her sister." He smiled brightly at John. "You do know they're all hermodrophites, don't you?"

"I did not," admitted John. He could not quite imagine a mammal possessing the reproductive characteristics of both sexes. He moved to one of the sideboards. The trays and baskets of specimens were guarded by a sign that read "Paws Off". Dust was very thick upon them. "Wonderful thing, dust," noted Dr. Buckland. "It is a nearly perfect preservative. It protects against the bleaching of the sun, absorbs errant moisture before it can stain, and lends a ghostly beauty to the surface of objects. Take care not to sneeze."

When they sat down, John, as initiate, was given the place of honour, directly facing the grinning jaws of the levitating crocodile. A few things were already upon the table, including plates of uncooked greens which he could only assume would be consumed in the same state as *Aldabrachelys gigantea* had enjoyed them, raw. A large Chinese pottery cup at each place setting held two each of what seemed to John to be shelled, boiled goose eggs. Buckland said a brief grace "for what we are about to receive" and John caught both Liddell and Darwin smiling. Then their host speared one of the eggs, and quartering it, popped a segment into his mouth. His guests followed. To John it tasted much like an ordinary vinegar-egg, perhaps stronger and chewier, but perfectly eatable. "Excellent, sir," John said.

"The pickled eggs of the caiman, a small South American crocodilian," Buckland explained. "Think of it as our friend's little brothers," he said, gesturing with his fork to the huge reptile suspended above. "Home-pickled, too. Mrs. Buckland, my most able assistant, and a fine collector in her own right, helped prepare them."

Wheels creaked outside the door, accompanied by the shudder of tinkling crockery, followed by a knock. Buckland rose and pulled a trolley inside and up to the table. He lifted a silver dome covering four small plates, and set one down before each of his guests and himself.

John looked appraisingly at his portion. It certainly smelled delicious. Before him was a thick slice of bread, delicately toasted, and streaming with butter. Atop the slice lay two small oval lumps of browned meat, which yielded easily to the pressure of his fork. He exchanged glances with Darwin and Liddell as he raised his fork to his mouth. He bit down and chewed. The meat was almost sweet, and reminded him of the very young calves' meat he had eaten in Italy. Darwin and Liddell knew that their host would not reveal what they had just partaken of until he was complimented upon it, and John quickly grasped the rule.

"Truly first rate," said Liddell, laying down his cutlery.

Light, Descending

"Tender to a fault," said Darwin.

"Quite delicate," offered John.

Buckland beamed at them and then took up another forkful. "So glad you are pleased, gentlemen. A very simple and domestic preparation. It is toast of mice."

Michaelmas term at Oxford was followed by Hilary term, and in late Spring by Trinity. These academic rhythms ebbed and flowed around John Ruskin. He applied himself with utmost rigour to his studies, staying cordial with the Gentlemen-Commoners for his parents' sake—and that of his own immediate peace while at Christ Church—and saw as much as he could of his new scientifically-minded friends. Yet regardless of the task or pleasure before him, always in the background of his mind was the image of blonde Adèle, away in Paris, living her life, and laughing.

He worked as hard as he could bear at Oxford. With his parents and cousin he went to Switzerland each summer, where he collected alpine plants and glacial rocks. He came of age and his father made over an income to him of £200 per year. He wrote letters to Adèle he couldn't send. He was made a Fellow of the Geological Society. He wrote his long essay 'The Poetry of Architecture', for the *Architectural Magazine*, urging the use of local materials in building, and signed it Kataphusin—Greek for 'according to nature'. *The Times* spoke kindly of it. His father gave him two more Turner watercolours, one of which he was allowed to bring back to his rooms at Christ Church. He worked for weeks at a long poem on a set subject, the Christianisation of two islands off the coast of India, and won the Newdigate Prize. He read it aloud before two thousand listeners at Commemoration, speaking after Wordsworth. Mrs. Ruskin was too overcome by the honour to attend.

Then his father wrote to say Adèle had been wed to the Count Duquesne.

I have lost her, was all he could write in his diary. Too staggered to go down to dinner or leave his rooms, he sat through the night stunned and mute, working at problems from Euclid. Three weeks later, mired in misery and alone in his rooms, he felt a tickling in his throat and gave a cough. He reached for water but another taste came into his mouth. He touched his handkerchief to his lips and saw a trace of blood. He slipped on his coat, wrapped a shawl around his stock, and walked to his mother's rooms on the High Street.

Chapter Three

The Lamp of Memory

Chamonix: Summer 1842

John's fingers were cramping and his cuff spotted with ink. His hand could not keep up with his thoughts, and his anger outstripped them both. Two days ago, in Geneva, he and his father had opened the thick parcel of English newspapers that had been forwarded to them. His father addressed the political and commercial news; his mother did not look at papers.

John turned first to the literary features and reviews, read a series of indifferent poems, and then found the review detailing a few of the offerings on view at the Royal Academy Summer Exhibition. Turner was being excoriated. Turner had five paintings in the exhibition this year, and John had spent long hours before three of them. He took up another newspaper. No mention of the exhibition. A third discussed Turner's entries in damning terms. The fourth was worst of all, a few lines dismissing the old artist as either half-blind or half-crocked. Turner's colours were outrageous. He was accused of smearing his canvas with cream, chocolate, yolk of egg, and currant-jelly. At times the subject of the painting itself—though attached to laughably long and descriptive titles— was indecipherable, lost in a swirling maelstrom of brushwork. His recent work was not True to Nature.

It had been Sunday; and twenty-two year old John Ruskin could do nothing but kneel during the evening Protestant service and pray to God to aid him in what he was about to undertake. They removed to Chamonix next day, to an inn with views to Mont Blanc and the Aiguille du Midi. John felt a reverential appropriateness in this majestic setting

25

for his task. By Tuesday morning at four a.m. he was seated at the wobbly desk in his room, looking across the still-dark valley at the ghostly peaks. Shaking his hands out before he took up his pen, he recalled his physical response when he stood before a fine Turner: a warming in the core of his being, every sense thrummingly alive. He would write a fitting defence of the greatest of landscape painters. He envisaged a pamphlet of some four or five thousand words; it would be finished by eight that morning.

By breakfast, writing as rapidly as his quills would allow, he had not even one sentence each on the points he felt he must touch upon. The viciousness and vapidity of the press, and the impressionability of its readers infuriated him.

Why do you blame Turner because he dazzles you?
Does not the falsehood rest with those who do not?

He wrote every morning beginning at dawn, stopped upon his mountain hikes to jot down thoughts, excused himself early from table at night. The torrent of words continued. He understood, and must convey, that the greatness of Turner's genius stood predicate on elemental ideas, ideas of truth, of beauty, of relation—and he would provide demonstrations of these ideas that, once understood, would stand as authoritatively as Euclidian proofs.

He must discuss the ways in which the ancient painters had shown water, hills, trees and sky, and look at the efforts of artists as varied in approach and result as Poussin and Vandevelde, Titian, Gorgione, and Claude. All major and many minor English landscape artists must be examined, held up to the light, their excellencies noted, and their inferiority to Turner explained.

But the vastness of his undertaking began to reveal itself to John. Everything is interconnected, he saw. He could not critique the depiction of mountains without discussing their actual geologic structure. To consider the painting of clouds without an examination of their formation and behaviour in the sky was impossible. The majority of people had *looked* at the natural world, but few had *seen*. Turner saw, and of all men living or dead came closest to the truth of God's magnificent creation. John realised that looking at a good painting was a religious act, and that the greatest works of Turner were themselves prayers.

The greatest picture is that which conveys to the mind of the spectator the greatest numbers of the greatest ideas.

Turner had never sacrificed a greater truth to a lesser, John saw; Turner's latest works, if they had fault at all, were the embodied passion of one who feels too much, knows too much. He did not know how he recognised this in the man, or what mirror he had found to hold to his own face and glimpse the same truth about himself.

He wrote all the way through the tour, thought all the way down the Rhine, spent hours gazing into the churning water or up to the castle-rimmed cliffs. He told no one but his father of his efforts, or his aims. For the first time on their annual tour he was eager to return home, free from the distractions of scenery and disruptions of travel.

But first there was the imposition of the removal from Herne Hill. John James Ruskin had in the spring bought the lease of a far grander Georgian house, and when the family returned to the south London suburbs, they and cousin Mary Richardson decamped with the servants to Denmark Hill.

"You'll have no hesitation in inviting your Christ Church friends there," John James Ruskin had told John when obtaining the place. Unbeknownst to his wife and son he had been looking about for almost two years for a large, solid, and quiet property, one which reflected both his mounting prosperity and dislike of fashion. "And your mother will have more staff to order about."

There were very few of his Oxford acquaintances John wished ever to see again, and those he did were the sort of men who were more or less unmoved by the trappings of worldly success.

John loved Herne Hill and was secretly pained that his parents did not share his affectionate association. Here, in his mother's little parlour, the two of them had five times read aloud the entirety of the Bible, from Genesis to Apocalypse, all the hard names sounded out and repeated until he had mastered them. Here in the brick enclosed garden he had studied the movements of ants for endless hours, and grieved silently when the gardener swept them away. Here his beloved Newfoundland dog had bitten him when he was five and left the scar on his lip.

"I would like to pet Lion," he had told Barkin, their coachman, who for a reason John could not now remember was carrying him in his arms across the stable yard. The odour of tobacco and horses surrounded John as the man lowered him to where the dog's great head was buried in his bowl. Barkin laughed as John reached down with both chubby arms to encircle the huge muzzle. Lion's possessive startle, and reactive snap at him was a blur. He cried out; and then his mother was before them all, scolding, holding her handkerchief to his streaming lip. He barely felt the lashing canine tooth. Most of all he remembered his surprise at being hurt by one he loved.

Here at Herne Hill he watched with delight the unfolding of the rose blossoms, tight bud to blown and spent petals to hard and unyielding rose hip. At seven he had, in secret, pulled a few of those tiny firm fruits from their thorned stems and crushed them between his teeth, to wonder how a flower so sweet could end in a fruit so bitter.

In Spring he would sit in the chair his mother brought him and observe from a safe distance the activity of bees in the peach blossoms, and in August it was the red and dripping Herne Hill peaches he was forbidden to eat for fear he disrupt his digestion. Adèle had slept here, walked here, laughed at him here. All his young delight, and many of his frustrations, lay enclosed in those brick walls.

But Denmark Hill was less than a mile away. His new study would be as large and comfortable as the rest of the place, with ample room for new cases to house his mineral specimens. The house stood in seven acres of meadow and garden, and they could keep cows and pigs and plan flower beds and orchards. And he could walk down the sloping fields to Dulwich Gallery, and take his fill of pictures every day.

John Ruskin was wandering through the yellowing meadows of Denmark Hill, found them too small to contain his thought, and strode across the downs towards Camberwell. Hands thrust into the recesses of his rear pockets, he waded through ripe grasses and nodding flower heads. He spoke aloud, as he sometimes had need of while describing natural phenomena. That morning he wished to describe a painting by Turner, the noblest seascape that great painter of waters had ever achieved, and therefore the greatest seascape ever attempted. He had seen it three years ago at the Academy show, and had stood before it so long his eyes had blurred. He had been forced by his looking to close his eyes a moment, and when he licked his lips was surprised there was not salt upon them. The great Master had taken him upon that violent sea and set him in another ship from which he watched the awful unfolding of the activity on the first. Now in the fading meadows he understood and could put words to Turner's accomplishment.

The painting was more than a masterful recording of elemental forces acting upon the puniness of a man-made vessel. The canvas conveyed heat and oppressive humidity of air. The sky, save for one small and retreating patch of pacific blue, was spasming with ivory, yellow, orange and red. The sea, broken as it was by wave, carried in it the ghosts of those shades upon a base of charry brown and lead gray. The ship being tossed upon that pitiless sea drove forward, stripped of all sail save the smallest foresail. Left in its wake was a quantity of its human freight, cast overboard, arm and leg chains still visible before the suck of water dragged limb and iron below. A phrenzy of fish swarmed the bodies.

...its thin masts written upon the sky in lines of blood, girded with condemnation in that fearful hue which signs the sky with horror, and mixes its flaming flood with the sunlight, and, cast far along the desolate heave of the sepulchral waves, incarnadines the multitudinous sea.

The intense and lurid splendour of it, the flakes of crimson and scarlet mirrored in jagged water peaks, the flaming clouds and white-hot shaft of setting sun, all transfixed John. Turner had light itself on his palette.

Turner called it 'Slavers throwing overboard the dead and dying—typhon coming on.' In his manuscript John would call it simply 'Slave Ship', not bothering to mention or correct Turner's spelling of the storm. He also named it the single work in which all of Turner's immortality could rest.

"It's in way of congratulations on the book—I know you've not yet done with it, but for its starting and near completion—and in way of a New Year's gift, of course."

With that his father had thrown back the green baize covering the display easel. There was Turner's 'Slave Ship.' His. The chiefest, the sublimest, the purest and most perfectly realised Truth ever painted.

John could not speak for a moment. His father was still standing by it, holding one end of the baize in his hand, and his mother, seated by the splayed legs of the easel, began gathering up the pooling covering. His father was grinning, his mother smiling uncertainly, wanting the baize up off the floor.

"You showed me what you wrote of it—the choice was simple. Turner still had the painting and Griffith was for once not a sharper."

John stepped forward to touch the frame, assuring himself.

"'Two hundred and fifty guineas," his father was saying.

It was worth kingdoms.

He turned to his father and extended his hand. His father took it and covered them both with his other. Here was his son before him positively glowing at his gift, and John James almost winced thinking that he might have refused the price asked for it. "A happy new year to you, my boy."

They had a glass of sherry and spoke of where it should hang. John did not think it right to take it to his study with the Turner watercolours that had been past birthday gifts; his father, and all who entered the house, should have the pleasure of looking upon it. The breakfast room was covered over in delicate watercolours of roosting doves by William Henry Hunt, and a growing number of Turner lake scenes. They agreed that as subject for a dining room it was not the right choice. And it was so large.

They left his father's ground floor study, and John pointed to the wall near the stair. "Here, in the entrance hall, don't you think?" he asked his father. "We shall all of us have enjoyment of it there, and as I come down every morning it will greet me, just as I will pass it each time I go up to my study to work."

"Some thoughts it will give you!" said his father with a laugh.

Come February John invited Turner to his birthday dinner. He had met him the first time just after he had got ill and left Oxford, at a dinner given by Griffith, Turner's sales agent, and since been given the signal honour of being allowed to call on Turner at home. Brushed up, dusted down, and swathed in a storm-blue greatcoat and moth-eaten top hat, the great man was happy and kind. He saw the prominent location given his 'Slave Ship' and leaned in on the canvas, his eye nearly touching the vivid surface.

"I don't like that fish," he growled. He pulled back, and tapped the offending pale-lipped monster so smartly with the tip of his battered walking stick that John feared it would puncture. "I'll come back and fix him." I devoutly hope you will not, thought John, as he steered his guest into the dining room. Following dinner the honouree invited Turner to his study to see the favoured positions given the artist's water-colour views of Richmond Bridge, Gosport, and Winchlesea. He did not reference the mass of manuscript papers over-covering his desk.

His father had a further presentation to make the next day. "I've hired George Richmond to paint your portrait, as a birthday gift," he told him. Richmond had been one of John's drawing masters, one that John still had a high opinion of. Richmond asked him how he wanted to be shown.

"Desk—outside too, if that makes sense—a pencil or crayon in my hand—or a pen—and in the background, Mont Blanc. Looking at my work—No, looking away."

"At what?" Richmond had asked.

"Infinity," he said.

The painting hung in a Royal Academy show. He laughed when he saw the placard: "John Raskin, Age 24, 1843." His father was furious and had the title corrected.

Modern Painters: Their Superiority in the Art of Landscape Painting to all the Ancient Masters, proved by examples of the True, the Beautiful, and the Intellectual, from the Works of Modern Artists, especially from those of J. M. W. Turner, Esq., R.A., by a Graduate of Oxford.

Signing himself thus, and only thus, was John Ruskin's half-ironic acknowledgement of the odd 'Double Fourth' Honours he had been granted at the conclusion of his interrupted education. And his father did not want him to risk his name until the reception to the work was gauged.

Five hundred copies were printed, and appeared in bookstores in May. It was four hundred and fifty pages and he knew it was just Volume I. A mere one hundred fifty copies were sold, but to the nation's most erudite and incisive intellects. It made its way into the hands of Wordsworth and Browning. Mrs. Gaskell read it with Charlotte Brontë. Tennyson, that model of thrift, borrowed a copy. They all puzzled over who the brilliant young Graduate could be. In private, George Eliot venerated the anonymous author as a prophet. Ruskin knew none of this.

The Tory magazine *Britannica*, his father's favoured journal, gave it a positive paragraph—but the reviewer was a family friend. John James scissored the piece out and contentedly pasted it in the scrap-book he had begun. The *Athenaeum* and *Blackwood's* failed to mention *Modern Painters*. Turner simply ignored it.

The silence did not matter. John Ruskin had not written it to flatter Turner, but to express the truth as he had discovered it.

Chapter Four

The Lamp of Life: 1848-1855

Perth: January 1848

Her hair was falling out by the brushful.

Euphemia Chalmers Gray was nineteen years old, and this was meant to be the happiest time of her life; a very great and good man had implored her to wed him. She loved him back and had, despite the sudden coolness of his parents, consented. *My Effie, my goddess, my enchantress, my own beloved,* his letters now opened. John Ruskin was mad with passion for her, rapturous in his letters, and they thrilled her so she dare show them to no one, but read them over and again and pressed them to her heart when she was done.

This morning Effie narrowed her eyes at her silver-headed brush, its boar hair bristles choking with her own auburn strands. What she had first noticed a fortnight past was now a daily occurrence—the quantity of hair on her pillow, after another night of bad sleep; the growing number of filaments which filled her comb, after even the most gentle run through.

It was the strain, thought Effie Gray, the strain of it all. The backdrop to her engagement had been fraught with anxiety. Her father, a respected and normally prosperous Perth attorney, had unhappily invested the larger portion of his family's funds in railway shares which now appeared worthless. As a result Effie's brother George, a young gentlemen, was suddenly thrust into looking for work in trade—any work to relieve the pressure on the Gray family fortunes. Effie herself faced the financial embarrassment of heading into marriage with not a penny to her name, nothing to bring to her beloved John and the elder Ruskins but her

pretty face and slender form and bright inquisitive mind. Mr.
Gray and had been perfectly frank about his investment losses
with Mr. Ruskin, with the result that the old man had himself
provided Effie's dowry. The Grays would keep no secrets
about their sudden financial reversal; John had made it rather
more than clear that he told his parents everything, and Effie
had resolved she would be no less than candid in return.

She set the brush down upon her bed. A brilliant life
awaited her at London, a future far beyond any she could
imagine here in Perth. John was twenty-eight, handsome and
well-knit, serious even to gravity about buildings and
paintings and trees, so good she felt a little in awe of his
dutifulness to his parents, so devout a Christian as to be an
exemplar, and a celebrated intellect and writer. His *Modern
Painters*, volumes one and two, were known to all of
intellectual Britain. And he was not without wit or charm,
but the way in which he used them sparingly made the
officers and engineers here trying to catch her eye look like
strutting peacocks.

> *My beloved Effie, you disrupt my work—I can
> scarce hold my pen—you are a complete man-trap—a
> siren on her rocks luring men to disaster—Mercy on
> me, to hear you ask once more "if I take sugar on my
> peaches?" —don't you recollect my being temporarily
> insane, for all the day afterwards, hearing you ask such
> a thing—I am utterly lost in longing for you—you are
> like a sweet forest glade into which a man might be
> tempted, searching for the heart of it, only to wander
> forever, enhemmed by thorns—you are like the soft
> swellings of an Alpine snow field—beautiful to the eye
> but hiding deep clefts that end in darkness where I
> might plummet and be gone, for-ever...*

She smiled at his extravagances, but they made her
catch her breath too.

Light, Descending

The young persons' fathers were friends—the Ruskins were Scottish at the bone, and had also lived at Perth. Effie had been born in Bowerswell, the rented Ruskin house where John's mad grandfather had died—born in fact, in that very same room. Margaret and John James were long-engaged cousins, and the unmarried thirty-seven year old Margaret had lived with the Ruskin family. She'd been alone in the house when John James' father, despairing of business losses and grieving the death of his wife, appeared spluttering in the drawing room doorway, his throat slashed through by his own straight razor. After the burial the cousins fled the house to wed, and set up at London. Not without reason Margaret Ruskin had been left with a holy horror of Perth, and of Bowerswell, especially.

The old Bowerswell was sold to Effie's newly-wed father, and after her birth her father had pulled it down, and the Grays lived in a new house on the same property and by the same name.

Effie—or 'Phemy' as she had been known then—had met John when she was twelve. She'd come to London to stay with the Ruskins before going on to her school near Stratford-on-Avon; an English school prudently chosen by her parents to dilute her Scot's accent. John had been twenty, and had amused her by taking her to the zoological gardens and describing the lives and habitats of the animals there.

The next summer she'd returned, sent away from Bowerswell where her three little sisters had just died from scarlet fever. She was sad and sorely in need of distraction. John, down from Oxford, wrote a faery tale for her, *The King of the Golden River*, the story of a neglected boy's goodness rewarded.

John and Phemy met again when she was fifteen, and returned to visit the Ruskins, this time at Denmark Hill. John had found her beautiful three years ago, and now noted that she no longer was. Phemy's face had lost its childhood roundness early. Her nose was long and narrow and her cheekbones high in her heart-shaped face. But a few days after her arrival he thought her in fact a striking girl, with lively eyes and quick conversation, and without a trace of shyness.

She was more than ordinarily skilled at the piano, devoted to practice, and John admired her dedication. She played each evening for the Ruskins, even playing Mrs. Ruskin to sleep; that old lady's eyes seeming to close of themselves not long after eight. John's parents were near to thirty years older than Phemy's—they looked more like grandparents than parents to her—and she could not remember a time when they were not both white-haired. Early in that visit she had glanced up from her keyboard at the rasping of Margaret Ruskin's snore, and she smiled at the slumped form in the wing chair before the fire. John was there and saw her smile, and smiled back at her; it formed a delicious first secret between the two.

The next morning he was writing up in his study, comparing actual cloud formation to the way in which artists depicted storm-clouds on canvas. The section was long and both subtle and technical, and he stood after a while and paced the floor, stretching his arms behind him. From below his feet he heard the faint strains of music. He paused for a moment, then thought he might go downstairs and see what Phemy was up to.

She was practicing Mendelssohn, alone. Her back was to him and he stood motionless on the crimson patterned rug as she played. He approached silently and obliquely. She saw him when she turned the page of her score, and then heard his voice, quite near.

"It's very cold in here, Phemy," he said. John thought she played well, played strongly; didn't plink away like most young ladies. He didn't like to think of her fingers hurting from striking the cold keys. She turned her head to look at him. It *was* cold, and her fingerless gloves afforded no warmth. But she laughed.

"No more than in Scotland, rather warmer, I should say," she answered, without stopping in her piece.

"Let me have a fire made up," he offered.

"A fire, for one person?" He watched her lift her eyes to the length of the drawing room. The purple draperies and ruby flocked wall-paper made the room no warmer.

"Two then, if you grudge the coal. I shall be your audience." He reached for a chair and drew it close to her instrument.

She went on with her playing as he sat watching her. She did play beautifully, and he thought the Mendelssohn she had chosen maudlin, and unworthy of her ability. He enjoyed music very much, but had no facility himself to produce it. Several times at parties he had seen young men and women play four-handed pieces at the keyboard, and he wished of a sudden that he could do so with her. Her concentration on her task fascinated and somehow in that cold room warmed him, and he sat next her and watched her still profile and swift hands.

"Phemy doesn't suit," John told her when she ended, rather than the customary compliment on her skill. Her name too was unworthy, maudlin and silly.

She looked at him and laughed. "I have been Phemy all my life. What else can one do with 'Euphemia'?"

"I shall call you Effie," he announced. "'Phemy' sounds nearly like Feeny, which is a kitten's name. Or a puppy's.

Effie you are," he ended, to her continuing laughter. Then he left her, back to his work.

She went on with more Mendelssohn after he'd gone. Effie, she said aloud. Effie. She repeated it silently as she went over a difficult left hand passage. She thought it did suit her. Effie. She liked it. John had named her.

What naughty thoughts your last night's letter gave me! You knocked all the philosopher straight out of me, and the art-man, and the man of letters too. That bit about your undressing—pray don't be angry— but how could I help myself–thinking of you cold, and knowing that in just a few weeks—don't be angry!— you might have my arms about you to keep you warm! And then I fancied us an old married couple, and out at the opera, and you sitting next me, and me just bending the crook of my finger into your hand, just so—where no one might see—and knowing all the men about were admiring you, and that I a King could think—Yes look all you like—but she is Mine All Mine!

She and John had been good friends, and she just another of the many young people coming to stay at Denmark Hill when at London. Margaret Ruskin never went to the theatre or concerts, but the male Ruskins enjoyed both, and Effie was an admired addition to the gentlemen's evenings out. Her vivacity contrasted pleasingly with the household's essential sobriety, and Effie did not take the Ruskins seriously. She found old Mrs. Ruskin wry and quaint, and Mr. Ruskin's brusque energy admirable. John himself was a study; grave and gay by rapid turns, always writing letters to newspapers or closeted with his cherished minerals.

Effie returned to London in the spring she turned nineteen. Mrs. Ruskin made a great point of telling her that John was on the verge of a brilliant match—a girl no less literary royalty than Sir Walter Scott's granddaughter. She

40

was glad for him, of course, although he never spoke of Miss Lockhart; oddly to her way of thinking, none of the Ruskins did. But an air of quiet assumption overtook Denmark Hill, with Mr. Ruskin composedly sanguine.

Their guest had as good a time as ever. John's cousin Mary had recently been wed and Denmark Hill seemed grateful for a young female presence. Following breakfast Effie practised at the keyboard while Mrs. Ruskin dusted her china figurines, an operation she refused to entrust to her parlour maid and which by Mrs. Ruskin's strictures of tidiness must be performed daily. John, in self-imposed exile up in his study, whiled away his morning drawing and writing. Dinner was at one o'clock, and after that it was John's habit to spend the afternoon alone walking, or driving into the country. By late afternoon Mr. Ruskin was home from his wine merchant's firm on Billiter Street, and the family took tea together at seven. Afterwards Effie would resume her place at the piano and play all the evening.

Effie and John were soon sharing long conversations about painting, and music, and architecture, and God—she realised there was nothing he couldn't speak on. She liked dancing and parties and Haydn, and he favoured geology and paintings and Bellini; he didn't like pink and it was her favourite colour. They chaffed and argued high-spiritedly. John began inviting Effie along for his afternoon walks and drives. He was as good as a married man in Effie's eyes, a sort of young uncle to her, and she felt perfectly free in his presence to laugh and teaze like siblings.

"I don't believe a word of John's entanglement with Miss Charlotte Lockhart," she wrote her mother not long after. "He scarcely knows her and really doesn't care to. He told me he's seen her but six times in his life, and that always at parties..."

Miss Lockhart's diffident suitor had in fact just received what was to be his first and only letter from that young lady, a decidedly tepid and laconic response to a poem about river currents he had hazarded sending her. The elder Ruskins knew, to their excitement, that letters had been exchanged, but as this was the rare instance in which John did not share the contents with them they remained ignorant of the lady's want of sympathy with their son's genius.

John began taking their young house guest down to tea each evening, knocking at Effie's bedroom door so that they might go down arm in arm. Margaret Ruskin had seen her son straighten his jacket in the hallway before knocking, and she had turned and hurried away. Soon after this Effie discerned the alteration in the elder Ruskins.

"John," announced Mrs. Ruskin at dinner. Mrs. Ruskin's voice was naturally high pitched; she also enunciated very carefully to cover her early Scot's accent. "I want you to read to me this afternoon; my eyes aren't strong today."

Both Effie and John looked at his mother. It was their custom to spend the afternoon together, and outdoors; Mrs. Ruskin knew he had ordered the brougham for 2 o'clock for their drive.

"It's Scott's *The Pirate*, so I know you'll enjoy it," Mrs. Ruskin finished.

It would be Scott, Effie thought. All the family read and reread Walter Scott endlessly. They did not drive out that day.

Over the next few days a growing reserve shadowed Miss Gray's relations with John's parents, and John too seem troubled, although he did not discuss it with her, and Effie was delicate enough not to ask. She had the creeping feeling that she was being *discussed* in the household, and it was a most uncomfortable sensation. She knew their fathers corresponded, but her family did not share the Ruskin habit of sharing letters from others for comment and opinion. Then one morning sitting at the piano, playing in an empty room, it struck her that perhaps John's engagement to Miss Lockhart had indeed been a fancy, more a desired coinage of the brain than reality, for all the Ruskins; and that now that her father was in financial crisis, the elder Ruskins thought her angling for a rich husband.

Effie was innocent, and she was angry. At one-o'clock dinner she took the reins.

"I really must return to Perth tomorrow," she announced to John and Mrs. Ruskin. The three of them had finished their soup and had started the fish. "Mama wrote me such a letter that made me know how much I'm missed. John, will you help with getting my rail ticket?"

Her voice was as light as she could make it. John's head snapped up in astonishment.

"Going? But—why?" he asked. Effie was easy for him to talk to; in fact she talked constantly. Over these last weeks he had gotten used to her being there, enlarging the constrictive family circle of the three Ruskins. Yet Effie was decidedly not part of the family. She was altogether more interesting than his cousin Mary had ever been; he had never taken her down to tea.

"Because Mama and Papa want me," she answered, and brought herself to smile at him. Mrs. Ruskin was bobbing her head.

"But so suddenly—" he said. "Mother, make her stay," he appealed.

"I'll not get in the way of any child's duty to their parents," Margaret Ruskin said, and speared her fish.

Now that Effie was clearing out, the family evening was as pleasant as before, at least for John's parents, who showed her quite their old warmth and familiarity. She was seething within, and John's mooniness and monosyllabic responses to his parents' remarks did nothing to cool her sense of insult.

She'd told him she'd go alone to the station, insisting a maid would be adequate chaperonage, but he dismissed the idea with something approaching vehemence. He handed her into the family carriage and she moved in so that when he was seated their arms did not touch. She kept her eyes fixed ahead, out the little isinglass window by the driver. As the carriage rolled forward John surprised himself by taking her hand. He was sorry that she wanted to go. She had been lively and fresh and now she was curt and brittle and he did not like the change. He'd reached for her hand to reassure himself that the affection and ease they had known could remain.

This may have been a moment for a declaration, and the young lady waited with pounding heart for the sudden action to translate to words. But her companion said nothing, merely held her hand with steady pressure. If he was going to let her be driven out of the house like this, Miss Gray was glad to go. She withdrew her hand, and he did not seek it again.

South suburban London's quiet gave way to increasingly busier streets. The iron-laced windows of Euston Station were filmed with grime, despite the unsparing efforts of a few boys at work with rags and pails. Once inside they were almost immediately engulfed by travellers clutching carpet bags, and hemmed by wheeled carts tottering with crates. Blasts of steam issued wheezily from waiting engines, temporarily obscuring their vision. Construction of a larger terminus surrounded them as they picked their way to the platform, the shouts of workers and driving of rivets adding to the din. Her locomotive stood steaming, poised North.

Light, Descending

"I despise railroads," John said, appalled at the noise and smoke. "No one with any sense of beauty should be forced to travel by them." But he was telling Effie nothing she did not already know. They parted after he had seen her to her rail carriage with little more than a brotherly embrace.

Alone with his parents that night John looked at the silent piano. Neither his mother nor father had mentioned Effie's name since his return from seeing her off. John James Ruskin was in fact gauging the amount of time required before it would be seemly to again mention Miss Charlotte Lockhart to his son.

John, sitting glumly across from the piano with a newspaper on his knee, was indeed thinking of that lady, but in briefest consideration. Miss Lockhart was nothing more than a shadow cast upon a wall, part of very short procession of such shadows. The shadow Adèle Domecq had cast had fallen across his heart. As a boy he'd had it so badly broken by her that as the years rolled on he wondered if he could ever wed. Then last year Charlotte Lockhart had swum into his ken, and because he knew it would make his father happy he tried to woo her. Miss Lockhart had never given him the faintest hope; during his recent visit to her in Scotland they had spent their time together sitting on a unyielding sofa while she asked his opinion of another man.

Now Effie, a girl he had known since her childhood, had come back into his life, active and bright and making him feel young again just as he was thinking himself old at twenty-eight. He wanted to love. He wanted a woman to say Yes to him.

Light, Descending

In October John made pilgrimage to Perth, asking to see
Miss Gray. She filled Bowerswell with her friends and
admirers for his visit. Chattering girls in their prettiest frocks
were flanked by dashingly uniformed Scots Guardsmen and
Dragoons, and Effie was at the centre of it. She wore a yellow
gown streaming with ribbons, and dressed her hair with little
Michaelmas daisies. Her brother George greeted John
warmly, but she was as cool and remote as if he had been a
stranger with a questionable reputation. How Effie suffered
that day! George played piano as she danced one mazurka
after another with every man there but John. It made her
miserable to see him so miserable, leaning up against the
arched doorway to the dining room, clutching his punch cup
on the fringe of the gaiety! But she had felt the sting of being
cast a fortune-hunter, and didn't mind wounding herself or
John, if that was what it took to persuade the Ruskins they
were wrong.

A week later came his letter from London, filled with
such ardent proclamations of love, and assurances of his
parents' support in pursuit of her that she felt the strain
would break her. She wrote back *Yes.*

Huddled over his crowded study desk John answered
with expressions of profound gratitude, which in his
innocence he did not recognize as a portent. Effusive thanks
were followed with a lover's declaration of eternal devotion.
He was not at all certain from what well these proclamations
were emanating, only that they must find utterance; and that
in Miss Gray he had at last an eager recipient. He realised
there was a fundamental variance in their natures. Before he
loved her he could recall watching her dance at parties or chat
at galleries and thinking her ideal future was as a diplomat's
wife, such was her ease of charm and manner. He did believe
her the bewitching figure he had accused her of being, but
being bewitched by a lady who seemed almost as devoted to
him as he was to her was a novel and most agreeable

experience. And she was very young, nineteen, quick and malleable; she would form around him.

After Effie accepted John she received a letter every day. His letters began with passages that left her blushing before devolving, sometimes abruptly, into practical matters. They ended in lengthy spiritual meditations which struck her with awe at the depth of his religious feeling, and his familiarity with Scripture. Despite their firmly held evangelical beliefs her future in-laws clung to the hope that John would enter the Anglican Church, and his mother now confided to Effie that she dreamt of her son as the Archbishop of Canterbury. Effie was grateful this intelligence had been conveyed to her in a letter, for she laughed aloud trying to picture John, equally fixed in his interests in art and natural philosophy, at Lambeth Palace.

He was planning their wedding trip. After a few days alone together, John wrote her, they would leave for the Continent, and as his parents would be joining them she must remember that her dresses ought not to be so wide as to make travel in a carriage for four uncomfortable. Effie had not quite imagined they would be travelling *à quatre* on their wedding trip, but the Ruskins always took their annual continental trip *en famille*, and John had made it clear this custom would continue.

Their first stop would be France, and he urged her to concentrate on her French language studies so as to be useful. They would then proceed to Switzerland to hike in the lower Alps. She had to laugh at his list of stipulations on her dress; he was so fearful of treading on her hem as they went along mountain paths. Didn't he know she'd been raised in an active household of younger children, and they'd romped and tramped long miles through the Highlands?

Sometimes he tried to imagine their life ahead.

Only six more weeks to wait! But who knows what we may be in six years! I haven't the slightest ideas of what will become of us—perhaps we shall get quite cool—and may have quarrelled so often that we shall do it as a matter of course—about everything—As to will I always love you as I do now—It will depend upon yourself and how you change—I can think of you or conceive of you as old—50 or sixty—and fancy myself a lover still—at 70—But to tell you the very truth—I cannot look fairly in the face of the Great Fact that you must one day—(God willing)—be Forty. It sounds very unpleasant indeed—to be sure—I shall be 50—if I see that day, and I don't know what of my views in general–and of you in particular, may be by that time. But for now my sweet I feel I should faint away for love of you—and become a mist or a smoke, like the Genie in the Arabian nights—Goodbye—Only about 45 more Goodbyes–

This word of warning went unrecognized by Effie. The warm exuberance of youth did not admit the chill attendant on her lover's fears for her maturity. She did pause however for a moment to consider her own mother, who at forty-two remained not only slender and attractive but, expecting her 13th child, highly fecund.

Despite their continued generosity in the manner of gifts, and the handsome settlement made over to her, Effie had not outgrown the nagging suspicion that she was a poor substitute in every sense of the word for the daughter-in-law the Ruskins truly wanted. As winter deepened so did her domestic responsibilities at Bowerswell; her mother had been heavily pregnant when she had returned home and now had a new son. Effie had charge of a household of young brothers and sisters who struggled with ear-aches, tummy upsets, and even the scarlet fever which in past years had carried off five of her siblings. Her brother George was reduced to seeking work as a clerk, and to her chagrin Mr. Ruskin, who she had hoped might procure him a position in trade at London, showed no inclination to do so. Worse than all was her dear father's deepening gloom over the financial morass he had driven the family into. His income from his law practice couldn't adequately provide for their large family, and his investments in the building of new railways had so far proved an almost dead loss. Effie lay tossing in her bed at night over all this. Now her hair was shedding at an alarming rate.

John wished to know how soon they might wed. At his urging she set a date for Spring, but not as early as his February birthday as he hoped. April 10th 1848, a Monday, was fixed as the date. All would be well, the prospective bride believed, once they were wed.

John James Ruskin need not knock upon his departing son's dressing room door. The panelled door was open to the bronze-striped papered walls within. Nonetheless he stood on the threshold and cleared his throat, and John turned from where he stood before his open trunk. His man, George Hobbs, was kneeling and fitting shoes into the trunk's compartmentalized interior.

"No need to stop, George," John James said at the man's rising. "Go on with your work."

His son still stood where he had turned, a smile on his face and a small notebook in his hand. The boy's piercing blue eyes seemed to have absorbed some extra depth and shine. If not for the pallor of his skin John James Ruskin would have suspected incipient fever, and he had to stop himself from lifting his hand to his son's brow. John was wearing a new bottle green coat, with a new and very blue stock wrapped round his neck. Even fully dressed he looked as slight as a boy to his father's eyes.

"A wedding gift for Phemy," John James said, and extended the flat leather jewel case he had in his own hand. Between the Gray and Ruskin families the girl had always been Phemy. John James saw no reason to adopt his son's fanciful moniker for her; it confused him in his letters to her father to have two names in currency for the same young woman.

John slipped his notebook into his pocket and took the case. "A wedding gift?" he repeated. "After all you have done for us?" The blue eyes glittered and John James feared his own might mist with tears. There had been entirely too much effort over this affair, the old man thought; it had disrupted the household and he was mightily glad it was nearly at an end. He cleared his throat, loudly, in response. Hobbs, an alert servant, rose and quit the room.

John snapped open the lid to reveal the garnet and gold necklace that lay within. It was his father's taste, the taste of an earlier generation, and a rich and costly piece. He could not imagine Effie caring for it, but he was moved nonetheless. "Most appropriate," he said, looking upon it. A moment passed before he lifted his gaze back to his father. He saw how old his father looked, and felt how unhappy he was making him.

John Ruskin did not know exactly *why* he had fallen in love with Euphemia Gray. Awakening in the cold light of various London mornings over these past weeks, he had wondered if simple propinquity had played a part: Effie happened to be there before him, and within reach. Lying in bed night after night he had fantasised her as the object of his pining, and long after she had accepted him he cast her in his imagination in the role of a dangerous and unattainable *fata morgana*. To remake her, and himself, to the extent that he could deem himself helpless against her charms had been an increasingly urgent desire. With Adèle he had been a force acted upon, and with Effie he felt he could act upon her. Love was never equal, not in Scott's romances at any rate, and he did not hope that the yearning he had found himself expressing to Effie could be equally returned by her. But he wanted to love, and the hope that she might indeed want that love made her tantalizing. He worked himself into a fever over her, and she had accepted him, and now he still felt tantalized but also that the fever had subsided.

The elder Ruskin was innocent of John's meditations. He'd felt forced to give his consent last year when he'd seen him sickening for love. Although the old man was loath to admit it, John's symptoms had been disturbingly close to the behaviour exhibited by John's grandfather, and that dark mental malady had deepened until it ended in madness and death. It was a loss of vitality combined with an unassuageable restlessness; lassitude one moment and frenetic yet unfocussed activity the next. If the boy wasn't watched carefully next thing he'd be spitting up blood again. The lack of appetite and snappishness sealed it; John James and Margaret Ruskin not only relented but urged the boy to press his suit at once in hopes of bringing the sufferings of all three to an end. And Miss Gray accepted John readily enough—it would have been insult if she had not—but John looked no better for that. He looked scarcely fit for the trip to Perth. But the sooner he was there and wed, the sooner out of danger.

John held the open box between them, and spoke. "Can you forgive me, father—for doing what is displeasing to you?"

John James did not expect this question, but John could get right to the point of the sabre when he wanted to, making it damnably awkward. What was he supposed to say? He and the boy's mother had always assumed a brilliant match for John; with his rising literary reputation and the social circles he was increasingly sought in, a Lord's daughter was not out of the question. More to his own taste would have been that Lockhart girl—what better match than marrying into Sir Walter Scott's line?

His son spared his father from answering.

"Effie will be, I know, the perfect help-mate," John was now saying. "She can draw well enough to help me in my architectural studies, and I mean to perfect her in that art. Her vision is sharp and she can save my own eyes by transcribing notes of the buildings I've measured."

These tasks were already performed by George Hobbs, who accompanied John everywhere, and John James might have scoffed to hear his son's bride spoken of as almost another paid assistant if the entire matter hadn't been so trying.

But now his son broached the more pressing particular surrounding his union with Phemy. "Her father's current circumstances are indeed unfortunate, but I need not tell you they in no way reflect his character, or even long-term prospects," he told his father.

John James grunted. A good man with a good solid law practice like Gray gone to smash—and all on the veritable lottery of railway shares! It was madness, he thought, this speculation on new lines that would be built, so-called investors staking their arduously gained money on the hopes that two points so connected via iron rails and belching smoke might win them ease! Half the time the lines never got finished, or the cotton manufacturer who had promised to build his odious factory at the end of it changed his mind, and the whole thing evaporated. He was ashamed that last year he himself had quietly lost £1000 on such shares. Gray's speculations had exceeded even the domestic lunacy running rampant today—he had sunk the bulk of the family's fortune into shares in Boulogne! And here was France in revolution instead, and everything gone to smash. It was all utter waste and gambling, trying to get rich without labouring for it.

The elder Ruskin had been astounded when Gray had written to tell him Phemy would be entering his family with no dowry at all, but at that point John was so close to going into a decline over the girl that he felt all he could do was offer his own settlement to give her a start in her married life. Britain had a seemingly unslakable thirst for his sherry; he could well afford the £10,000 he put on Phemy. To be sure, as a good man of business he stipulated that the interest be made over to John, and disbursed to Phemy quarterly in instalments of £25, but as she had been living on £30 per annum from her father this seemed more than handsome. Still, it confounded the old man that John had gotten into such a fix with a pauper's daughter. The boy had just refused the suit of his late Spanish partner's daughter Caroline—a lass who would have brought no less than £30,000 per annum with her. He'd refused even to meet with her, who he hadn't seen since she was a little child. John James suspected that he had never gotten over her sister Adèle, a flighty enough girl who never paid the slightest attention to John. If he was still pining for the older sister, how could one expect he would now settle for the younger? And true, Caroline Domecq had been raised in the Romanish church. John's mother had made it entirely clear to both male Ruskins that she'd be dead before she'd allow such a union; but the Domecqs had been keen enough on the match that the girl was willing to put aside her Papist superstitions.

And what the devil, John James wondered, had happened with the Lockhart girl? For someone whose stock in trade was words, John could be deucedly closed mouthed when he chose to. Had there been an offer made, or no? He couldn't bear to ask and learn that his son had been rejected, so ask he did not. He turned his attention back to the Gray's financial difficulties.

"Mark my words, my boy, a man can live more happily on £500 a year than £5000, and that the Grays will soon discover. There is no slavery like the slavery of fashion and society—all comes at the expense of domestic comfort."

The old man said this despite already having taken a town house for the newlyweds in Park Street, fast by Lady Davy's, and having made them the gift of their own new brougham and pair. He'd bought the right to a coat of arms— it featured a tusked boar—and had it and his personal motto painted on the door. *Age quod agis*— 'keep your mind on your work' it reminded all.

"Of course," John James went on, "you know I want you to have the advantages you need, the right house in the right part of town where you might entertain all the best men. And Phemy's so pretty she'd show to advantage dressed as a Quakeress, but she needs frocks and gauds when you go out. And a good cook, and staff, for the dinner parties you'll be hosting."

He wasn't pleased to see the barely concealed flinch from John.

"I want—I need—none of that, father, but only time and quiet to do my work. But it is yours to give, and my duty to respond to such generosity with a grateful heart." His father was lading them with gifts, almost, it seemed to John, in inverse proportion to his initial opposition to the match. And John hadn't anticipated the additional public exposure a marriage would subject him to. If he fell prey to Effie's and his father's myriad expectations his intellectual life would be overwhelmed by social duties.

John James' grunt came out almost a sigh. Everything he'd worked for had been for John. His own father had faltered so badly in trade that John James had as a young man worked nine years straight, without a single holiday, to extricate the family from his father's debts. It had meant giving up his dream to enter law. It had meant, too, a nine year engagement to his son's mother; they had been middle aged before they could set up their household and produce their child. 'Keep your mind on your work', indeed. For forty years he'd crisscrossed the length and breadth of the island kingdom selling his sherry, establishing accounts with public houses, squires, and clergymen, cornering all the best business, and with the finest quality goods to be had out of Jerez. How many endless miles in jolting, filthy coaches had he endured? And he had prospered mightily, yes; but it was all for John, every red copper of it, and the boy had a way of standing here accepting all of it while claiming he liked or needed none of it.

He looked down and pretended interest in the contents of his son's travelling trunk. "Your mother and I had no Ruskins at our own wedding, and you'll have none at yours," he observed, studying the brass knobs on the numerous little drawers. It was out of the question for Mrs. Ruskin to travel back to Perth; the idea of stepping foot on that property sent her into hysterics. Nor did John James have any desire to revisit the scene of his father's final horrible act. Their presence would be extraneous to a happy wedding party, a marplot and a nuisance to all. But he felt he was sending John up there—well, unsupported, and he had never not been at the ready for his boy.

He snorted again. "I'm glad you're leaving early, ahead of this mob thronging to march on Westminster," he added. "Better to be well clear of London in case of troubles, but I daresay old Wellington will quell the ruffians if any can. The People's Charter! Rubbish! They demand the vote, and with no property to their names. It's all madness."

Mr. Ruskin was an old school Tory, and John right behind him, but they'd had a few recent disagreements about just how far government's ear should be bent by the dissidents. Now his son's mouth twisted as if in pain, and he realised with a pang that almost everything he said these days elicited some measure of distress from the boy.

"Madness? Yes," John said, "for I, who have industry and brains to spend—or to squander—on cataloguing the work of mediaeval stone-carvers, do so when the men of my own day are reduced to human cogs in the gears of Manufactory."

John James nodded, sorry he'd ever touched upon it. But what was a man of business to do? Mobs and the fear of lawlessness were everywhere these days, what else could a man do but keep clear? The marchers planned to assemble less than a mile away in Kennington Common, and on the very day of his son's wedding. He'd hired a couple of private duty men to be stationed outside the house for the day, just in case.

There was one more thing he wanted to say before Hobbs, who could be heard moving about in the adjoining bedroom, re-emerged. John was at an advanced age to be broaching the topic, but it had never arisen before.

"Huh! Anything you need to—ask—about the coming business?" The term "business" was as close to "conjugal relations" as his own reserve allowed.

John looked at him in such a way that he could not be certain whether the startle in his son's eyes was rooted in surprise or discomfiture.

"Ah—" John said at last, and released his father with a blink. There was nothing he wished to ask of him on this topic.

"Good. Well then."

Chapter Five

The Lamp of Life

London: 10 April 1848

The human cogs in the gears of Manufactory that had distressed John Ruskin were, on the day of his marriage, massing to protest the political machine profiting by their labours. One of the marchers—a young gentleman, and not a cog—would soon command the affection and esteem of the bridegroom, and play a decisive part in his life.

John Everett Millais pulled his velvet collar up against the drizzle as he made his way to Russell Square. He was eighteen years old, and this day, April 10th, had the markings of being one he might recall all his life. Ahead of him in the Square, under the awning of the tea kiosk—closed against the threat of violence—stood the man he sought. William Holman Hunt was twenty-one and had invited Millais to join him in walking with the Chartists as they marched to present their petition to Parliament. They greeted each other and set out down a deserted Southampton Row. Neither had carried an umbrella—what mattered wet and cold when men's fates hung in the balance—and instead grasped their brims as sudden gusts made attempts at their hats.

It was easy to see how seriously the burghers of London were taking the Chartists this Monday afternoon. Houses had their draperies drawn as if it were night. Most shops had failed to open and were securely shuttered. The normally bustling shopping streets of King Street and High Holborn were thus devoid of ladies on their errands, and a mere handful of cabs lingered kerbside. A nearly empty omnibus pulled by a team of greys passed them in the other direction, the driver's face blank as he scanned for potential passengers waiting at the corner ahead.

"I wish I had a revolver," said Millais, as the two progressed towards the Thames.

Hunt laughed. "I daresay it's lucky you don't! I won't answer for you blowing off those precious fingers of yours." In truth, Millais with his high colour and a bit of swagger in his walk looked as though he was seeking a fine lark. "Do the old folks know you're out here?" Hunt asked.

Millais shook his head rapidly. "Ha! Never. They think I'm up in the attic studio, painting. Even father wouldn't go to his club today, for fear of running into a rampaging horde."

They saw posters, dripping with wet, papered up on walls bearing the bold print heading "Chartist Demonstration!! Peace and Order is our Motto! Working Men of London. Monday April 10."

As they walked down Drury Lane to the Strand more people appeared, sometimes singly, but also in clumps of three or four. It was striking that they all moved, as they did, in the same direction—to the Thames. There were working men of every description —drovers, cabmen, brick-layers, joiners, dustmen, and many more whose exact work Millais couldn't guess, but whose respectable lower middle-class attire suggested as an endless number of clerks.

There were even a few men like Millais, young, well educated, and well dressed, but there was no way of telling if they were mere curiosity seekers or truly supportive of the aims of the marchers. They were surprised at the number of women they saw; not the typical prostitutes lingering on corners with their drooping feathered hats, drawn by the concentration of men, but working women. They might be tavern maids, or egg sellers, milliners or dress makers, all joining the march. Many bore black umbrellas and were cloaked against the rawness of the weather.

It was hard for the two friends to speak freely, surrounded as they were by the actual petitioners. Millais wished there was some emblem he could wear, a sign he could give that he was in sympathy with their goals and demands. He and Hunt had had long discussions about the Chartist's position, and both were solidly behind it. Hunt himself was the son of a warehouseman, and keenly and personally felt the correctness of Chartism. All men should be able to vote, irrespective of whether or not they owned property. Those votes should be cast in secret, without the coercion of watching landlords or employers. And if members of parliament received a salary as the Chartists wanted, then poorer men could serve; as it was, only the rich could stand for parliament because no salary was attached. And where was the justice in the big new manufacturing cities like Manchester, Liverpool, and Sheffield having no representation at all?

When they got to Somerset House Millais's jaw fell.

"Maybe there will be three hundred thousand people there!" he breathed to Hunt, as the extent of the crowds streaming across Waterloo Bridge was revealed.

The Chartist leader, Fergus O'Connor, had called for the working men of London to meet south of the Thames, in Kennington Common. After a rally there, he would present the gigantic petition with, he claimed, five million names on it to Parliament. But the group had been strictly ordered not to cross the river from Lambeth and approach Westminster itself. Any attempt to do so would be met by one hundred thousand police and soldiers who had been called on duty to protect the governmental seat.

Light, Descending

Revolution was roiling Paris; and Austria, the German states, Denmark, and Poland were in uprising. There were riots in Glasgow. Ireland was starving. An outpouring of this scale might end in bloodshed this very day, and the beginning of revolution here in Britain.

They crossed the Thames packed shoulder to shoulder, the rain picking up and the dull sky darkening overhead with each step. The crowd moved down Kennington Road. Six blocks away in a large square Georgian house, a rich sherry merchant who had stayed away from his office for the day emerged from his study. The hall clock chimed three and the merchant noted that his son up in Perth would be married in an hour. The merchant crossed to the front door and through the flanking sidelights saw the two policemen stationed outside under the dripping entranceway facing the empty street. One turned and saw him and raised his hand in a sort of salute.

On the Kennington Road Millais, despite his now-sopping clothing, felt a mounting heat and excitement as they neared the assembly point. The crowd stopped. Millais could see a ring of buildings beyond, but nothing but the expanse of his fellow marchers before him. A few cabs were drawn up nearby, their driving seats giving the men who jostled there a view, Millais imaged, of some sort of platform that he and Hunt could not see. The buzz of the crowd and the noise of the increasing wind made him uncertain if anyone were attempting to address them or not. They stepped back and disengaged themselves in an effort to find a vantage point. Two nearby men with a Daguerreotype apparatus fought to hold a protective oilskin above it.

The sky became dramatically darker, and was of a sudden rent by a brilliant, arcing fork of lightning. A breathless moment later brought its terrific explosion of thunder. At the retort the crowd erupted in a gasping wail. Women shrieked. The skies opened in a drenching rain that

61

pelted all with the fury of natural and unbridled violence. Millais and Hunt turned away with the rest of them and fled for any shelter they could find. There would be no revolution that day; English weather had seen to that.

Chapter Six

The Lamp of Life

Scotland: 10 April 1848

Mr. and Mrs. John Ruskin were alone in the coach for the first stage taking them to Blair Atholl for their wedding night. The rain had stopped and George Hobbs sat atop with the driver and their trunks as they headed north to the Highlands. They had been sent off in a shower of satin slippers after having tasted the fruited brides-cake, leaving the two score guests to sit down to dine and toast the new couple in their absence. Six-year-old Robert Gray had kissed his sister goodbye so affectionately, and shaken hands so gravely with the bridegroom, that it had seemed an additional benediction. The newlyweds had settled into the tufted seat cushions, and John slipped his arm around his bride's shoulders. He kept it there until it was uncomfortable for them both, and then withdrew it with a little cough.

The coach was soon free of suburban Perth and open country met them. The trees were coming into leaf, and the air was mild for early April. The couple's heads were turned, looking at the damp landscape out their respective windows. The bridegroom was more than content with the silence and the scenery passing by. John had been at the Gray's two weeks, and nearly every hour it had rung with children's laughter, tears, or shouts. He had had to share a room with Effie's brother George, and had been made aware of the preciousness of coal and candle-light. He had wanted to be out of the house, and remembered almost nothing of the ceremony, and now they were rocking steadily toward their first night together. John did not like to think of that just now, and to distract himself reached for his watch, only stopping when he realised it might seem rude to check the time. He sensed that at Denmark Hill his parents would have stood up from the table. His father might be reading aloud Don Quixote's adventures to his mother, and if he had been home he would listen and laugh too, and then head up to his large and familiar study to continue his thinking on early church architecture. That Chartist gathering was to have been today, and he hoped the neighbourhood had been spared any disturbance.

Effie brought her eyes from the window to her new husband. The fortnight past had been an immense strain on the entire household, and on John, too, she imagined. She knew he must have found Bowerswell uncomfortably cramped compared to Denmark Hill. And at times John had seemed less than happy with her. He had scolded her in writing, and again when he was there, for taking on too much care, for not hewing to her Balzac, for wearing herself out writing letters, even for playing her beloved piano too much.

> *Your best conduct would have been a return—as far as might be—to a school-girl's life—of early hours—regular exercise—childish recreation—and mental labour of a dull and unexciting character...Now—you know I mentioned French, Italian, and Botany as subjects—two of which it was necessary and the other expedient—that you should learn—and I thought that you would endeavour to occupy your mind—and—(forgive me the impertinence) to please me—by giving some time each day to these healthful and unexciting studies...*

Then the demands of producing a small wedding with the family in such straightened circumstances—her dressmaker charged her an unlooked-for £9 extra for her trousseau, which her father could ill afford to pay, and which caused Effie extraordinary distress to ask for—had tested even so strong a resolve as her own.

Light, Descending

John sniffled, and Effie spoke in response.

"Is your cold any better, my love?' she asked. She took his hand and sat back next him.

"I think so," he said. She had pulled off her glove to touch his bare hand, and her skin was warm.

She nestled by him. "I won't catch it; I never get colded," she proclaimed. She turned her face to him, and then lowered her eyes.

Her arm and side were pressed against his, and she was still holding his hand. He felt her as warm and solid and insistent, and he lowered his own eyes and tilted his head down and away.

John did not kiss her. He had never kissed her, except upon the brow, as he had before the Minister of Kinnoull who had officiated at the ceremony in her drawing room a few hours ago. After waiting a moment with lowered eyes Effie sat back, abashed at her expectation. John was, like her, tired; he had a head cold, and besides, he had warned her about public displays of affection. Alone as they were, a coach was a public conveyance.

I have great horror of showing such feelings to others—my manner to you shall be habitually quiet—respectful—attentive—but cold, and just, or nearly just, what it would be to any person whom I respected and regarded—

But she also remembered the letters that teazed her with his fantastical longings.

A letter from you has just come—ah, the sweet little mortar-coloured seal of wax, stamped with an E— one kiss—and then—No, I won't break it—I couldn't— I'll round it with my penknife to preserve it... When we are alone—You and I—together—Mais—c'est inconceivable—Oh my own Love—what shall I do—I shall not be able to speak a word—I shall be kneeling to you...Soon, soon you shall be mine, Deo Volante...God Willing!

Effie thought of the seal he didn't dare to break. "It was a lovely wedding, and grand to see Mama and Papa happy," she offered.

"Yes, a good end of it," he agreed.

"End?" Effie twisted to look at him more fully. "It's no end, my love—but a beginning. The beginning of you and me." His remark was not meant to be hurtful, she thought, but it was—dismissive, somehow. "Our whole lives begin now," she asserted, squeezing his hand.

He nodded silently. His old life had ended, and at times it had been a very pleasant one, couldn't she see?

They made a comfort stop at a stage hotel where the horses where changed. John handed her down from the coach and stayed outside as she made her way to find the conveniences. As Effie moved through the lobby she watched a young woman speak to a desk clerk. The woman held a little boy by the hand as he clung to her skirts with the other.

I am a married woman, the newly-wed Mrs. Ruskin thought of a sudden, and this thrilled her. She almost spoke it aloud—I am now a married woman!—and could not keep the smile from rising to her lips. And one day, soon, she would be just like the woman before her, with a child clinging to her skirt, possessing the confidence and quiet satisfaction that nothing but marriage and children could bestow. When Effie returned to the coach she feared she was grinning idiotically. To her relief John did not comment, and she had no need to explain her inexplicable excitement. But seeing the mother and her son put her in mind again of family and home, and the wedding just celebrated.

"Little Melville was as good as gold; he's such a happy baby," Effie added. Her newest sibling had indeed been quiet throughout the afternoon. "And so pretty."

She wasn't sure John was quite attending, he was looking out the window.

"Yes, if a blob of putty could be called 'pretty,'" he answered.

"Blob of putty? John, really my love—how could you—" she began, in laughing astonishment. "Melville is a beautiful child."

But babies were certainly ugly, he felt, thinking of the frog-like motion of their legs. "They're all so undefined—one never knows what end one has gotten hold of," he observed. "But I suppose Melville's a fine fellow, for a baby," he finished.

They rolled on in darkness towards Blair Atholl. It had been after five when they had left Bowerswell and they would not reach the inn until almost ten. John had secured the Best Room; being the Highlands Effie knew it would be modest enough. A small laugh escaped her lips, and John looked at her.

"Oh," she answered, "I am just recalling Mr. Ruskin explain that he asked always for the second best room at any inn when he was upon his business travels, for fear of having the finest room denied to one of his customers should they arrive after him—for as he told us, how would it look for the sherry merchant to be sleeping better than the squire he sold his wares to? And I'm happy tonight we shall have the Best Room."

"Father could have the Best Room anytime he chose, he asks for the second merely out of seemliness to his clientele," John answered. He could not imagine why this trifle had lodged in her memory, or why she had thought to mention it now, as if in ridicule.

"Oh yes, my love, I understand, I do," Effie said, aware that she appeared both ignorant of commercial decorum and to have made a jest of her new husband's father.

At the next stage the coach took on three more passengers, all men, and constrained by their presence the wedded pair barely spoke a word until they were discharged outside the door of the inn at Blair Atholl. They followed the innkeeper through the dimly lit and deserted reception room up a broad flight of stairs to their designated room. He unlocked the door, stepped inside, and quickly lit two lamps from the lantern he carried.

"Now a bit of supper for you both," he offered.

John looked at her, and she shook her head. "Nothing thank you; we've had a tiring day," he answered.

"Some biscuits and wine, certainly?" the innkeep countered. "'Tis your wedding night."

Effie could see from John's face that he had regretted mentioning this when he had written to secure the room.

John paused a moment. "Beef tea, please." It might serve to warm and steady him, and he had no appetite.

He looked again at Effie, but again she shook her head. "No, nothing for me, thank you," she said.

Beef tea, she thought—is he as ill as all that? But the innkeeper was showing them the appointments of the room. There were two chests of drawers, a large mirror, and a small table with two chairs between windows whose draperies were drawn. Everything was new and singularly ugly, and the innkeeper was proud of all of it. "Bath room just across your hall; we've no other guests of a Monday so you have it alone." They had their backs to the ornately carved bed as they bid the man goodnight. Effie could feel its presence behind her and was half afraid the man might say something about its size or comfort. She felt grateful that he ignored it, as they did.

George and the innkeeper's boy came bumping up the stair with the trunks, but at John's direction did no more than open them both for ease of access before retreating themselves.

The door closed behind him, and they stood looking at each other. This was the moment they had waited for over all these months. Effie had imagined the moment scores of times: John would open his arms and she would press herself to him.

He did not open his arms. After a moment he smiled at her, and then turned to his trunk.

What was she thinking—of course at any moment someone would come with the beef tea; he was thinking ahead and she was not.

She was too modest to unpack before him, and John too did no more than pull open a few drawers, removing nothing from his trunk. She hung her cloak on the door peg, and sat down at the table. A young girl brought up the beef tea in a covered pipkin; she was pretty and reminded Effie of her eldest little sister Sophie. John came to the table and sat and took a tentative sip.

She had never known him so silent and wished he would speak, say anything to help relieve her own anxiety and put her at ease. He smiled when he looked at her but made no move to embrace, or even approach, her. He was of course extremely devout, and she wondered if he was considering the sacred charge of the marriage act to come; but she longed for him to enact the passionate behaviour toward her which his letters had promised.

He was sipping the broth very slowly; its aroma rose from the pipkin each time he levered open the lid.

Seven or eight months ago John had had his spring and summer all planned out. He and his parents would be once again on their way to Switzerland, and after a few restorative weeks in the alpine foothills move on to France and its ancient cathedrals so he could continue writing about them. Instead he was in Scotland with a Scottish woman who was suddenly his bride. He had made his parents very unhappy in choosing her, although they had behaved handsomely in the end and given their consent. It was the first rupture he had had with them and one enormously painful to himself. The annual tour would now be a wedding trip, but revolutionists across Europe had stopped their going.

Effie was speaking to him. "I shall go and—" what? "change," "prepare herself"? She hardly knew how to put it. She stood and went to her trunk without finishing, found her new nightdress and matching slippers, and took them with her toilette bag to the door. She turned and smiled at him as she left the room.

She stayed as long as she could in the bathroom, fearful of knocking on their bedroom door before he had finished his own preparations. What to do with her travelling dress, stockings, and shoes? She would feel foolish carrying them into the bedroom; she wanted John to see her in her lovely nightdress unimpeded by anything so pedestrian as the dress she had journeyed in. The bath was theirs alone, she would leave everything else within.

Light, Descending

I shan't even see half of your wedding gown on the day we wed, he had written to her last month. *I shall be thinking of what I am receiving in you—and perhaps I shall be hardly able to look at you at all...then in the evening—when I can look at you as long as I please—or at least until I dare not look any longer for fear I should die of joy...*

There was a small mirror over the basin in which she could see herself, if she stepped back, from almost the waist up. The nightdress, she thought, was singularly lovely, prettier even than her silk wedding gown, and at that moment the extra £9 to the seamstress would have seemed a trifle well worth it if the thought of this additional outlay not given her a pang of regret on her father's behalf. But she shook this out of her head. The nightdress, of fine white linen, trimmed with Venetian lace, was cut so that it lay just upon the rim of her shoulders, framing the expanse of her white throat and bosom. She had never worn a garment which revealed so much of her flesh, and she was quite aware that beneath the slender drop of the fabric she was naked. Over this she slipped the matching wrapper, of a gossamer fineness. She loosened her hair, fearful to brush it, and pulled her little lace-bedecked slippers on her feet.

She stood outside the door of their room and gently knocked. "Come in," John answered. She stepped in and closed the door behind her. She felt radiantly happy and excited, and was almost trembling with fear as well. She had never looked as lovely as she did at this moment, and hoped the impress of her appearance would be sealed upon their minds and hearts.

John stood by the table. He too had changed. He was clad in leather slippers, stockings, and a long wool dressing gown of dark pattern, tightly sashed, under which the hem of his cambric nightshirt could be seen. His throat was wrapped with his blue stock; he looked muffled.

He gazed upon her. "You look charming," he said.

He was now alone with the young woman he had wed. He had written many things to Effie about this moment, and imagined many more than he had written to her, all of them as vague as they were passionate. The dangers the moment represented had dizzied him. In his fancy she had been a beautiful and seductive lure, and he utterly powerless against her, and this image had stirred his imagination. There was nothing dreadful enough to liken her to, he had written; and *gorgós*, dreadful, was the root of the bewitching and paralyzing Gorgon. Fear of Effie compounded her allure, and John had relished it. He had sent letters in which he had compared her to a snow field harbouring a deep cleft into which he might fall and not rise again, a cruel wrecker luring a ship to its destruction upon a rocky coast, or a forest thicket which would trap him with thorns. Imagining the hazards she embodied and writing them to her had so stimulated him that afterwards he had often taken recourse in pleasuring himself in shamed excitement. He wrote himself into flights of passion and could not help the action of his straying hands.

Now that she was before him no definite path of action emerged. His thoughts began to swirl in his brain. The excitement had drained out of him, leaving only the peril of her nearness and its consequences. He was fearful they would never get to Switzerland's mountains, which he felt he needed more than anything he could imagine; and he feared Effie would die in childbed as so many young wives did; and feared being left alone without her and with a baby as ugly as Melville; and feared the noise and confusion of a house full of children such as the Gray's; and remembered being back at Christ Church and young Lord Ward who he scarcely knew inviting him into his rooms and gleefully pulling open a drawer and waving his hand at an array of pictures of naked women in obscene poses, all lewdly beckoning with grinning faces. He heard Ward's laughter again, laughing him to scorn at his shock. Now here was Effie smiling at him, and waiting. He raised his arms and Effie ran to him and he embraced her.

The layers of his own clothing made it impossible for her to receive any sensation of his person, even through the filmy gauziness of her nightdress, but she felt the palm of his hand upon the skin at the nape of her neck as he held her. He placed his hands on her wrapper and gently pulled it back. She moved her face so that he might kiss her, but he lay his head on her bare shoulder. She waited for him to speak, utter some endearment, call her his own. She felt his breath upon her bosom and trembled.

He turned so that in lifting his head he shifted the nightdress where it rested upon her shoulder, and it slipped down below her elbow. As she dipped her shoulder to catch it the dress dropped from her narrow frame to past her hips. Nipples, waist, belly, the auburn triangle of hair between her legs, all was exposed.

They both reached out and grabbed for her errant nightdress, and as they bent their heads struck. He stepped back and she reclaimed her gown and her modesty, holding the dress up with her hands. Her cheek flamed in a flush of mortification. She realised that at any other time it could have—should have—been almost funny, striking heads like that, but a moment that should have been precious had been spoilt. Her forehead hurt where they had struck, and he placed his hand on his own brow. John looked steadfastly at the floor, his hand at his head, and Effie felt close to tears that he did not come and take her in his arms again.

John moved back and sat upon the edge of the bed, his face averted. He was profoundly embarrassed, and his sense of clumsiness was intensified by a feeling of being oppressed by Effie's anticipation. A long moment passed, and then he said, "We are both tired, and I think it best we—refrain tonight."

73

She nodded, afraid to speak, and went to the side of the bed and slipped in. From the corner of her eye she saw John untie his dressing gown, and heard his leather slippers hit the floor. He lowered the extinguisher on the bedside table lamp. She felt him settle in beside her, then his weight shift as he turned to her. He lifted himself on one elbow, and after kissing her brow, bid her good night. He felt perhaps his cold was getting worse after all.

In the morning they dressed privately. When she re-entered the bedroom John was sitting at the table taking his pulse, and at her question explained that his mother had daily taken the measure of his health in this manner, and he had promised he would continue the practice. They read the Bible aloud, and then had their breakfast in the inn's public room. They spent their first married day visiting a waterfall, supping with a local family who fed them trout and potatoes, and returning after a long afternoon to dine at the inn. They had been perfectly cheerful with each other, really the best of friends; and had laughed and jested upon the little white ponies they had rented. The day had been fine, the air clear, and the gorges vibrantly green.

Effie again dressed herself in her new nightdress, and again entered their bedroom in expectation. John was neither in bed nor standing, waiting for her entrance, but sitting at the table writing letters to his parents, a separate letter for each.

She got into bed and sat up as he wrote, watching him bent over his letters and hearing the scratch of his pen across the narrow sheets of paper. She had finished her own letter to her parents, full of news of the cataract they had ridden to and assuring them they were as happy as could be; and while she had done that John had been busy in his notebook, sketching out ideas for his book on medieval architecture. Now that it was bed-time he was occupied writing to his mother.

After a while she slipped out and retrieved the Balzac she had brought with her, but John did not lift his head from his task. Eventually she saw the small flare from his lamp as he melted a blot of sealing wax upon the envelopes. He rose and came to her side of the bed. She let Balzac fall upon her breast.

He pulled a chair close and sat down, as if she were an invalid and he an attending physician.

"Effie, my dearest, I know you'll understand and see the wisdom of what I am about to tell you. The fact is that as I hope we'll soon be starting for France, and then on to the Alps, I want you to be as fit as possible for the trip. I *need* you to be fit, as I have great need and desire—pressing desire—to make the most of every opportunity to measure and draw the buildings I hope to cover in my book."

She thought of her ability as a horse-woman, or of her scrambling with him up the gorge wall this morning to get a better view of the inside of the water-cave. "Few women are fitter than me," she said, and smiled, "think of our walk today. If my boots were heavier in the sole—"

He shook his head with a single but decided motion. "No, not what I mean. I don't doubt your ability now, it's your ability—or lack thereof—later."

"Later? When later? When we are in the Alpine foothills? Because of the high air, do you mean?"

He sighed at her. "No. The altitude is quickly adjusted to, for a healthy person. It's...in the event of your no longer being fit because...because you might be with child."

75

"Oh." Her voice was very small.

"I feel, feel quite strongly," he went on, "that we must guard against this probability—perhaps inevitability—and refrain from relations before, and for the duration of, our travels in France and Switzerland."

Tears pooled in her eyes. She did not even know what these "relations" were, just that she had expected John to have kissed her and folded her in his arms, that he would tell her how he adored her, worshipped her—all the things his letters had contained, which had made her heart beat so quickly and had made her feel breathless. Now she was being rebuffed.

Her own mother, having brought thirteen children into the world, was yet the soul of delicacy, and had never spoken to her about the actual relations between husband and wife, which she knew to be the closest in life. She knew a baby did not result from mere kissing, even though some of her Perth friends had told her of girls who had to wed after having been kissed. She knew, had somehow ascertained between novels and gossip that it was the sacramental *act* of marriage, an exchange of some sort, which took place in bed. She had bathed her little brothers and seen the differences in their bodies from her own, but just how the baby resulted was the mystery that was her husband's to teach.

And now her husband, John Ruskin, the celebrated young intellect, was telling her that whatever the mystery was, they—she—would not be initiated into it, for months. And he had never yet kissed her on her lips.

He smiled at her, and placed his hand over her own. "Dear Effie, let's save this experience for later, when the outcome will not threaten my work."

She returned his smile as well she could. Perhaps when they got to know each other better there would be the sense of rapture she had expected. She raised their hands and kissed the back of his.

"And this way your own health and beauty is preserved," he went on.

Preserved? Like one of his botanizing specimens? She wished he would stop.

The newlyweds' return to Denmark Hill after Scotland was met with a handsome reception. The entire staff lined up outside the door to greet them, with Mr. and Mrs. Ruskin at the head, and the gardener placed into the bride's hands a splendid bouquet of cineraria, orange blossoms, and heath, wrapped round in ornamental paper and tied with satin ribbon. When they dressed and came down to dinner Effie was amazed, and then delighted, to see a German band appear on the lawns outside the open dining room windows; John's father laughed in approval at her response. They played throughout the dinner hour. Afterwards she took up her old position at the drawing room piano to the acclaim of all three Ruskins. Their new home on Park Street was not yet ready for their occupancy, and the couple had been given the top floor of Denmark Hill as a suite of rooms. Upon retiring they went up the stairs together, but John paused at his study door. "I'd like to look over a few of my papers. You don't mind, my pet, do you?" he asked. Effie continued up the next flight alone.

The next day John and Mr. Ruskin took Effie to the private view at the Royal Academy, on a card sent specially from Turner himself. The elder Mrs. Ruskin never went out into society, even on such an honoured invitation; thus it was up to the younger to represent the distaff side of the family.

The crush of people and dresses made it hard to see many of the actual paintings, but as the majority of those invited were there not to view art, but each other, this limitation was of slight consequence. The brightest lights of British society, hailing both from its glittering capital and rich young manufacturing cities, milled about in a fashionable mob, as did all the great lions and hungry cubs of the art world. Young Mrs. Ruskin was an admired ornament circulating the rooms between her new husband and father-in-law. Dressed in a white silk dress with black mantilla she made a fine impression, and had to repress her smile as gentleman after gentleman came over to her father-in-law, begging to be introduced. There was a Mr. Blake of Portland Place, the Marquis of Lansdowne, Lord John Russell—all buzzing, and all, it appeared, because of her.

When they had returned home Mr. Ruskin came up to her alone in the little side parlour. "I'm glad to see your effect in society, my dear," he told her. "John would rather be in Switzerland, with his mountains—doesn't see the importance of it all. A few months ago he refused an invitation from Mr. Blake—one of the first men in London—you brought them together again. And a card inviting you for dinner from the Marchioness of Lansdowne is sure to follow." The old gentleman still looked slightly flushed from these triumphs and gave Effie cause for pride in knowing she was the cause.

"You're much better calculated for society than John is," he finished. "He is best in print."

The political unrest in France drew out over the months, and finally in July John determined he must begin his new work on architecture right here at home. London, he claimed, lacked the requisite subject matter, and he proposed a tour of certain medieval cathedrals around England. It did not surprise his new wife that he wanted his parents along, but that he simply announced they were going with them did.

The four of them, with George Hobbs and the elderly maid Anne in attendance, set out for Salisbury and its cathedral by rail in a warm summer's rain. They continued the journey by coach, and took lodgings in the town at the best inn. John had tried to make it clear this was to be a working trip for him. After the first morning spent inside the damp and poorly lit cathedral both the elder Ruskins were struggling to stifle their boredom. Their son saw this, yet they insisted on staying within sight. His bride found it amusing and rather exciting to see her husband in action, crossing the transept with a measuring line, or procuring a ladder from the sexton that he might raise himself to the level of a carving upon a crocket. It was easy to admire his concentration, and his moments of exhilaration at making a little discovery that proved a premise. She took pleasure in assisting, too; John wrangled two coaching lamps from the inn and she held one and George Hobbs the other when he needed light to sketch in dim recesses.

Then Mrs. Ruskin came down with a head-cold, which her son immediately caught.

"Don't sit by those towels, John, they're damp," warned Mrs. Ruskin when she saw him take a seat near his wash stand in their bedroom. "Let George take your clothes to the kitchen to be warmed."

"I don't like the sound of that cough," his father would judge, after hearing the slightest throat clearing from John. "I wish you would take care."

John continued to go to the cathedral each morning over his parents' protests, and each afternoon on his return the harangue grew. He had a stuffed nose and they wanted to

send for a doctor. Effie had before observed the Ruskins'
excessive caution over John's health, but had never seen
anything approaching this. He was cosseted and coshered up
like an infant. Finally he succumbed to their ceaseless
entreaties and stayed in bed one morning; the cold had gotten
worse and he saw no cause to tempt Fate. Mrs. Ruskin had a
predilection for potions, and she began dosing her son with
vile smelling salt-solutions, and ordering tea-papers for
application to his chest. Beef tea was sent up by the gallon.

"Really, it's nothing but the simplest of colds," Effie
made the mistake of saying at noon. "I haven't even caught
it."

Mrs. Ruskin turned to her, pop-eyed. "A simple cold? I
think a mother who's cared for her boy all his life knows
when he's in danger!"

Effie almost laughed, but if she had it would have been
rooted in scorn. Five of her little brothers and sisters had died
from scarlet fever. She knew danger. And she also knew a
simple cold.

"I've a great deal more history caring for him than you,
my child," ended Mrs. Ruskin, returning to the measuring of
her potion.

Effie received this declaration in silence, and ceded her
ground. "Well, if I'm truly not needed, I'll go out for a walk."
For the sake of propriety Mr. Ruskin did not like her walking
alone; at his insistence George or Anne must always
accompany her, trailing at a distance. And as Anne was busy
nursing John, George would go with her, though Effie
privately found it absurd to have a young man loitering
behind her as if she were a pick-up or suspected cut-purse.

The next morning Effie went in to read to John. He was
smiling. When she asked why he said, "Father thinks my cold
worsened due to some recent—connexion—with you, and

that's why he asked you to leave the bedroom until I'm better."

She laughed in spite of herself.

Chapter Seven

The Lamp of Life

London: August 1848

"Christ, of course, heads the list," dictated William Holman Hunt.

John Everett Millais turned where he was pacing his studio floor. "Yes, of course," he agreed. "Any list of Immortals would have to be headed by Christ himself."

At a studio table Dante Gabriel Rossetti sat, pen in hand, before a sheet of paper and wrote in large flourishing letters, Christ.

"And then next—" prompted Hunt.

"The author of Job, whoever that may be," said Millais. "Chaucer. And Shakespeare."

"Dante," said Rossetti, who was working on a new translation of the *Vita Nuova*.

"Yes, Gabriel—the original Dante," laughed Millais.

"Homer," said Hunt.

"A minute," answered Gabriel, scratching away with his pen. When he looked up he said, "Browning, don't you think—of modern men? Mrs. Browning, of course. And Tennyson, certainly." The other two nodded their assent.

"But it's not only the great writers we take as our exemplars," Hunt noted. "You write more than you paint, Gabriel, and we're all inspired by the likes of these. But our Immortals should embrace every worthy discipline, every worthy mind—"

"King Alfred," interjected Millais.

"Yes, Alfred," said Hunt nodding. "The perfect philosopher-king. And Jeanne d' Arc."

"Hogarth," said Gabriel. "Let's have an artist get his oar in." He had been working away over his paper and now Millais and Hunt neared him and spied the result. By each name Gabriel was drawing a small, expressive portrait of the nominated Immortal. Christ was shown in profile with faint nimbus, Dante with his characteristic cap and prominent nose, blank-eyed Homer clutching a lyre, the Maid of Orléans in her breastplate. Millais clapped him on the shoulder in appreciation.

"And for a name? To distinguish ourselves as really new men, doing new work—" began Millais.

"But it's not new," claimed Hunt. "That's just the point of our Immortals, isn't it? That painting and literature have lost their way."

"We can be 'Early Christians', decided Gabriel. "Like the Brotherhood of St. Luke in Rome, we strive to look back in our art to the work of the primitive Italians—art as pure devotion, illustrative of the greatest aspirations of the heart and soul. Strong colour, bold outlines, worthy subjects."

Hunt wasn't convinced. He'd seen more of the works of the aforementioned German and Austrian devotional painters, sometimes called The Nazarenes, than his two younger friends. "But the mere parroting of the early Italian monk-painters—it's the imitation we want to get away from—
—"

Millais chimed in. "Yes—the endless regurgitation of tired techniques and hackneyed themes and conventions; mistake and exaggeration and trick piled one on another, from Raphael on down—"

"To Sir 'Sloshua' Reynolds!" interjected Gabriel. "Mindless and sloppy canvases asking nothing, saying nothing, offering nothing. Mere slosh."

"But not "Early Christians," said Hunt, returning to the earlier point. "Too Papist."

Millais thought aloud. "We revere, we emulate, painters unspoiled by "artistic" affectation. Painters before Raphael."

"Pre-Raphaelite," affirmed Hunt.

"And what are we," asked Gabriel, "but a band, secret if need be, to spare us from the attacks of the critics? We're the Brotherhood of the Pre-Raphaelites."

"A Pre-Raphaelite Brotherhood," said Hunt.

"Put that down, Gabriel," said Millais. "The Pre-Raphaelite Brotherhood we are."

Before the newly minted Brothers parted that day, Hunt took two volumes from his satchel and pressed them into the hands of Millais. "I've just finished this," he said, indicating one of the volumes. "Reading it I had the uncanny impression that it was written expressly for me. You must read them, we all must. It's this chap Ruskin's *Modern Painters*, parts one and two. He says, 'Go to Nature in all singleness of heart.'"

Dante Gabriel Rossetti turned from the entrance hall window where he was watching for his friends. On this Sunday afternoon Casa Rossetti was vibrating with voices. The house on Charlotte Street, Portland Place was home to not only Rossetti's family, but a *rifugio* for revolutionary ideals. Gabriele Rossetti, the *pater familias*, Italian poet, librettist, patriot and exile of Abruzzi, was holding court in the crowded drawing room, his black cap flopping upon his head and battered snuff box balanced precariously upon his knee. The elder Rossetti's wife, daughter of a Polidori and an Englishwoman, was superintending the delivery of dinner to the sideboard. The younger Gabriel returned to the drawing room where his brother William Michael, a year his junior, and their two sisters, Maria and Christina, were attending to their father's wants and participating in the conversation. Seated around Gabriele Rossetti were three countrymen, gesticulating as they discussed Mazzini, Garibaldi, and Bomba in rapid-fire Italian, their voices rising and falling in condemnation or respect.

John Everett Millais and William Holman Hunt soon arrived and joined the circle. After paying their respects to Mrs. Rossetti and the delicately pretty Rossetti sisters, they excused themselves, and following Gabriel and Michael took their plates of macaroni up the stairs with them.

"Meet the newest member of the Pre-Raphaelite Brotherhood," announced Gabriel, as they seated themselves as best they could in his brother's small bedroom. He waved his hand at William.

The heads of Millais and Hunt turned in unison to look at William. He was not a painter, nor a writer; in fact he held an appointment at Inland Revenue. A tax collector as a member of the PRB? And was not their society a secret one? Why did Gabriel go ahead and invite his brother without consulting the other two original members?

"He'll write about *us*," Gabriel continued in anticipation of these doubts. "And he may paint, one day; he must have talent, like father, and me."

"I thought we were to work in secret; that the PRB would be a secret trust," said Millais. He was aware that William was looking on, discomfited, but the presumptions of Gabriel took him aback.

"I've asked Woolner too; he'll be along directly—and James Collinson." Gabriel was blithe and smiling.

Thomas Woolner was a sculptor, and former assistant to the portrait-medallion maker Alexander Munro, but Millais had never met him. Collinson was a meek, somnolent little chap, and a Roman Catholic; Millais knew him from the Royal Academy Schools.

"And I think we ought to ask Ford Madox Brown, as well," Gabriel concluded.

"Brown?" repeated Hunt. "Too old—he's twenty-seven! He'll be bound by academic strictures. If Brown's in, I'm out."

"Seven is the number of power, dear Hunt—a mystical number," Gabriel answered, not meeting the charge. "There must be seven Brothers in our Brotherhood."

"Oh for Heaven's sake—anyone but Brown," Hunt said. "Freddy Stephens, there's a chap. He'll make your blasted seven."

Millais had never heard of Stephens, and wondered if like William Michael Rossetti he neither painted nor wrote poetry. This was not what he and Hunt had originally conceived. Gabriel, once invited, had taken the bit in his merry teeth and had run away with the society. If Millais could have his druthers all the Brothers would be painters, and fine ones too—or at least with the hope of fineness. He had received, at age ten, the Gold Medal from the Royal Academy in their drawing competition—his friends called him their boy genius, from that and the fact that he was still younger than they—and everyone, including himself, believed he had a future as an important, if not great, painter. Young as he was he knew he carried the staff for the group. If he said No, the thing would fall apart before it ever began.

He looked again at William, sitting with an expression on his face between embarrassment and plaintiveness. He was just the same age as himself, nineteen.

"Yes, we'll ask Stephens, too," said Millais. He swept his hand before him. "The seven Brothers it is."

Chapter Eight

The Lamp of Life

Abbeville, 9 August 1848

Dearest Mama and Papa, and all the little bairns

We went on board the steamer at three and though it was a lovely day I went down stairs and, the Ladies Cabin being full, I went into the General Cabin and laid down all my length with a gentleman ditto at each end, and so on all round, with one or two on the floor; in about ten minutes all the Ladies were ill, and when two or three heavy lurches came in the middle of the Channel the whole assembly rose en masse from their reclining position dreadfully sick. I was very ill about eight times and Mr. Ruskin coming down once said it was like a scene of the plague or something. The Stewards however were very attentive and brought me some nice eau de cologne which revived me a little...At half past five we landed and were ushered into a custom house where our passports were looked at by some soldiers in green, and after that we took a fly and went to the Hotel des Bains, Boulogne, where John and Mr. Ruskin immediately broke into raptures at being in France and the inferiority of England, which amused me very much...They were unloading cannon from the ships in the harbour. They say this morning that the French have declared war with Austria and gone over the Alps but we have not seen a paper yet. John is out sketching a cathedral from a café opposite...He is quite in his element here and very happy...

Four months married, and the newlyweds had at last gotten abroad. The revolution in Paris had kept them away week after week. Now France was deemed safe again, and

they had set off. They were in fact a party of three, the two
male Ruskins and the younger's new wife. Old Mrs. Ruskin
stayed behind at Denmark Hill with neuralgia. But starting at
last seemed no little triumph to the travellers.

Paris still showed signs of the bloody street-fighting,
and remnants of burnt barricades lay piled at street corners as
they drove into the city. At the final coaching stop their
baggage was searched for weapons. Yet for Effie there was a
taste of expected Parisian gaiety in a few parties and
receptions they were asked to. Paris held little for John's
work, though, and on they went to Abbeville. There Mr.
Ruskin—brusque as always, though his eyes were filled with
tears—left them for his return to England. The young couple
were finally alone.

John had been at Abbeville before, with his parents. As
a youth he had drawn the old buildings, and had admired the
porch of the 13th century cathedral. He had been a child in his
knowledge and appreciation, and to again see Abbeville
cathedral after much reflection on the art and ends of
architecture was like confronting it anew. He brought Effie
early the first morning to the cathedral square, and in a state
of mounting excitement walked her around the complex of
mouldering yellow stone.

"It has," he stopped to tell her, "a luscious richness
about it all—so full, so fantastic, so exquisitely picturesque...I
see it now." He thrust his hands in his tailpockets and stood
with her so she might see it too, rocking forward on his toes
in the excitement of discovery. The native populace began
clattering over the cobblestones as they stood there looking.
They saw old women vanishing through the blackened
cathedral portal, fingers to foreheads in self-blessing; young
women setting up flower stalls against the peeling sanctuary
walls; cassocked priests moving in file from the chapter
house; heard cart drovers' warnings and bird sellers' calls and
the flapping of tavern awnings being rolled up for the day's

customers. They stood in the ever-filling square, Effie's hand shading her eyes against the sharply rising sun. He saw the cathedral as essential and overlapped in the lives of these Bretons as were the ancient pantiles to the integrity of the roof.

He knew then that his new book would not be Volume III of *Modern Painters*. He had always regarded architecture as an indivisible aspect of landscape. But now the subject demanded an independent study, and in a burst of insight he glimpsed the unifying structure under which to present his theory. They entered the cathedral, and as Effie wandered the aisles he sat on a rickety willow chair near the centre of the nave, notebook in lap, and dashed through sheet after sheet of paper jotting his opening propositions.

Architecture, he saw, was a distinctively *political* art— an art created by and for the *polis*, the people—and as thus was governed by *laws*. These laws—irrefragable, constant, and general—he termed Lamps.

The Lamp of Sacrifice dictated that architecture be created of the finest materials obtainable. If marble was at hand in abundance, marble should be used; but if beyond the budgetary means then Caen limestone, but from the best quarry; lacking that, let it be the best brick, preferring always the best examples of a lesser material than flawed stuffs from a costlier one, for what was architecture but the chance to present as Offering to God the handiwork of His greatest creation, man? The Lamp of Truth demanded the honesty of materials employed. No cheap wood painted like its better, no plaster masquerading as marble, no structural deceits in attempting to persuade the viewer that the building is constructed any way but what is obvious to the eye. When the imagination deceives, it becomes madness.

The Lamp of Power would deal with questions of massing and scale; the Lamp of Beauty, the recognition that the starting point of all that is visually pleasing spirals back to the organic beauties of Nature; the Lamp of Life, in which a healthy vitality of expression is demanded, and thus the satisfaction and happiness of the builders ensured; the Lamp of Memory, which insists that buildings be constructed to survive aeons of time, and convey the comforting solemnity of hills and sheltering mountains.

The Lamp of Obedience Ruskin saved for last. The wave of republicanism rampaging through Europe and threatening Britain terrified him with its potential for material and human destruction. Looking at history he thought Liberty a treacherous phantom. *Loyalty* instead was the noblest word in the catalogue of social virtues, loyalty to monarch and established social order. It followed that this Lamp called for an adherence to national schools of design expression, an architecture unique and responsive to the peoples of each individual nation.

Above all, he knew all true architecture must be, like all true art, a devotional act.

In the soaring nave of Abbeville, built to house Salome's handiwork, the severed head of the Baptist, animal energy surged through him as he jotted down the armature for his thoughts.

He felt the need as immediate, for the Abbeville around them was under siege not by revolutionaries but by a subtler foe—the restorers. Throughout the town workmen were busy, charged by Church and commune officials to re-work and re-carve the ancient facades. One afternoon he came close to fisticuffs in a confrontation with a workman chiselling 14th century stone cabling from the front of a building. He felt tongue-tied and ludicrous in his fury, unable to penetrate the man's Norman vernacular with his formal French.

All he could do, it seemed, was write. That night he wrote to his father at Denmark Hill a truth he had learnt about himself.

I seem born to conceive what I cannot execute, recommend what I cannot obtain, and mourn over what I cannot save.

It was Effie's first trip abroad. She loved France from the first, even ravaged as it was by the recent bloodshed, and was grateful to be seeing it now with only one Ruskin. She knew through a steady round of letters from Perth that her father's financial affairs were no better, and her brother George had still not found a position, yet she was happier here than at London. She took pleasure in drawing little sketches for John of architectural fragments he wanted record of, and was proud of her fluency in French. And although they stopped at a wigmaker's in Paris and bought her a length of human hair, once they were alone her own had at last ceased dropping out.

Yet her husband was always occupied, and seemingly uncomprehending that spending hour after hour in even the most beautiful of churches began to wear on his bride. If John had nothing for her to sketch, or no inscriptions for her to copy down, Effie worked at her knitting in any chair that afforded decent light, or excused herself with his blessing and took a purposeful walk to a garden or shops. After dinner at their hotel they spent evenings drinking coffee together in local cafés.

Tonight they sat surrounded by murmuring French couples, and John read aloud to her from a days-old copy of *The Times*. Back home a nation-wide "railway time" was being instituted. The exact time of day would henceforth be keyed via electric telegraph to receivers at rail stations across Britain. For the first time in history every town would keep its clocks accurate with the time decreed at Greenwich. It was all driven by the fact that there were now over 6,000 miles of rail track cleaving the country.

"Time itself has now been standardized," John said, folding the paper and tossing it down on the slatted chair. "Everything flattened into submission by the technologists and mechanists." It was one more blow at the root of rural character, another assault on the natural rhythm and demands of season, sun- and moon-light.

Effie was not sure what to say about Time. She well knew John's hatred of railways, he had been born before their advent and thought their noise and smoke barbaric. To her the railways were blissful conveniences. Casting about for a response she mentioned the Turner painting of a few years ago, of the locomotive speeding through the rain over Brunel's bridge at Maidenhead.

She saw the exasperation on his face; his lip curled in a certain way when she was being stupid.

"The beauty of that painting is not the steaming monster hurtling itself headlong down the track," he said, "it is in its colouration. The work is a commentary of the effects of rain upon an object travelling unnaturally fast, too rapidly for the eye to capture; a warning of sorts of life and experience rushing by us..." He sat looking at her, seated at his very elbow, and he felt alone. Turner's painting confirmed his views, not hers, on the modern distortion of Time; couldn't she see that?

A response seemed neither necessary nor appropriate. Yet Effie wished there was in fact a railway from England to France to save her from the discomfort of the Channel

93

crossing. She looked into her empty coffee cup in acquiescence.

To rest his eyes from his drawing labours Ruskin walked alone into the countryside. After the cool and lulling dimness of the cathedral interior the golden greens of ripened wheat and unploughed meadows invigorated his senses. The mingling odour of wild tarragon and mint rose from the heated Gallic soil as he crossed the dry and grassy fields. Bees lifted and fell from the flowers they forced. He was soon grateful for the broad brim of his straw hat, and took off his jacket and swung it over one shoulder. The sun dazzled high overhead in a sky of unvarnished blue.

It was a landscape without destination, save for a large boulder at the edge of a copse of tamarisk trees. Ruskin made for the rock, in an ambling and desultory fashion; it was, he thought at a distance, limestone; in the harsh light he could not be sure. At the root of the boulder lay several smaller rocks, tufted round with long bleached grass. As he neared, a looping coil of erubescent muscle and scale arced and fell amongst the rocks. He started, blinked, and stopped. Two red snakes lay entangled in their mating dance. The creatures had twined with a firmness that made it impossible to discern the grasped from the held, beginning or end. Identical in ruby colour and checked pattern the two snakes became one, lashing with a single purpose. Ruskin stood repulsed and transfixed. He called all snakes by one name, that given them in the original Garden. And Serpents were the genitive nexus of all mystery and abhorrence. The knowledge of Good and Evil! How Man had paid for knowledge. It was the first Bible story he recalled and the one that still had power to make him weep. And yet how great the delight in knowledge!

The mass of straining muscle slapped against the rock and fell back into the sandy dust. If he had had a stick in hand he might have thrashed at them, but he stood hands at sides, gaping, rendered as incapable of movement as if he had encountered the horror of the snake-headed Gorgon Medusa's gaze. At last the snakes separated in the tangled grasses to slide off soundlessly in opposite directions.

He felt weak in the knees and found himself laying back upon the hot and rounded curve of the limestone. He put his head back against the grained hardness and his hat rolled off into the grass. The sun beat down upon him and bee song filled his ears. His eyes closed, and purple images danced under his eyelids. He mastered his disgust enough to briefly speculate as to what physical sensation the serpents had experienced; if there had been pleasure or merely need. Recalling their writhing made his throat catch, and he could not calm himself. His breathing was noisy in the languid air. His hand rose to his throat to loosen his stock, and his fingers lingered to trace the line of his shirt buttons. They found the heavier edge of his waistcoat. The startle he had felt dropped from his chest to his loins. He was fingering the buttons of his trousers, the balls of his finger pads circling the bone disks. Heat and heaviness mounted beneath his touch. He knew the serpents could be near, or anywhere. Twined with a firmness that made it impossible to discern the grasped from the held, beginning or end. The serpent-headed woman who froze men in their tracks. The delight of knowledge. He was pulsing with desire, and his hands wrapped the root of his need. He did not want to, but he must. To gird himself he must hold himself. Limp snake to striking snake.

Denmark Hill

My dear Gray

The Society my Son and your Daughter are bound to move in, and the exclusiveness attached to it in relation to your son George might seem heartless but the facts are these. I happened to make my Son a Gentleman Commoner at Christ Church Oxford— partly to increase the comforts of a youth in delicate Health—partly to see during my own life how he would stand such an Ordeal—Partly from the vanity of showing I would give my Son the best quality of Education I could get for Money and lastly because the Dean of Christ Church said I ought to do so. He conducted himself well—he was resolute in moderation; he was at once introduced to the highest men by two young noblemen whom he had met on his Travels—he showed Talent and got the prize for English Verse. He was invited to the Duke of Leicester's and many places he refused to go to—but I was gratified to find him admitted to Tables of Ministers, Ambassadors and Bishops—but I was aware this arose from him having shown some knowledge in the fine Arts a subject chiefly interesting to the higher Classes—He is not a Tuft hunter and values people only for Intellect and worth and associates only with people who have tastes like his own. He detests crowds and London Seasons, but the Men whose Intellects he desires to come into contact with, are only to be found in distinguished Circles or Coteries and hence he will be found in high Society just so far as is necessary. I deem this long history due to George, that he may comprehend my hinting at a divided Society. It is not George alone, but Mrs. Ruskin and myself are equally excluded...

George Gray the elder folded the letter and slid in back into its envelope. There was no reason to subject Phemy's mother to its insult, and he merely summed up the import as best he could. He looked at his wife where she sat with her hand-work.

"Mr. Ruskin won't help our George find a position at London. Being in trade himself he's worked long and hard to assure his own son the privilege of being a gentleman. The fact that I, a professional man, must now stoop to place my son in business is nothing less than abhorrent to him."

The couple didn't return to England until October. While still in France Effie was crushed to learn that a beloved aunt at Perth had died in child-bed along with her newborn. Grieving for her young aunt gave her head-aches, and she was angered that John had learnt of the death first and, on his parents' advice, delayed two days in telling her. She had not been sleeping well; perhaps it was the late night coffee they drank, and he had withheld the information until he deemed her stronger.

As they travelled through France their sleeping ar-rangements varied. Some nights John slept in a sitting room so as not to disturb her when he wrote late into the night, but most times they chastely shared a bed as they had on the night of their wedding. Effie was at last tired of travel, but reluctant to return to the senior Ruskins. She wanted nothing more than to move into their own home in Grosvenor Square, which was nearly ready.

The Park Street house was tall and narrow, only two rooms per floor, and in one of the most fashionable parts of London. The young couple had had no say in its decoration, and the crimson wallpaper in the dining room, chosen by the bride's father-in-law, was not the happiest combination with her auburn hair. Still, Effie was delighted to have her own home in town; it felt a long way from suburban Denmark Hill, across the Thames in the south. And the couple's new brougham was quite the smartest in London—dark blue, and lined with fawn coloured damask, with a window of actual rounded glass in front. When the perfectly matched pair of bays pulled up to her door Effie felt again like the luckiest of brides. The separate house, their own carriage; it was yet another fresh start.

Lady Davy, their new neighbour, was immediately charmed, and took the young couple under her wing. Within days they were being invited to dinners, receptions, and balls given by the same nobs Effie had once read of in the Perth papers. She had to stifle her laughter at distinguished old men, ambassadors and Lords and Dukes and admirals, almost shouldering each other away to be in her company. To be brought into dinner on the arms of such gentlemen was a signal honour, and yet the recipient seemed to bestow an even greater one on her escort. Smart hostesses in Portland Place and Grosvenor Square were assailed with requests from dignitaries desirous of taking in or sitting at the left of the vivacious newcomer. The close observer would have noted that John Ruskin had his own circle about him at these affairs, to be sure. Wherever he appeared he was bound to attract serious-minded men and women eager to discuss the philosophical underpinnings of art, as well as equal numbers of those he considered time-wasting dilettantes. Society was a distraction, but he was aware that a segment of it envied him as Effie's husband, and admitted to himself that by her popularity he had been included in evenings at which he had been brought together with natural philosophers and connoisseurs whose acquaintanceship he valued.

The couple agreed to return to Denmark Hill over the Christmas holidays. When Effie awoke with a cold and a cough a few days after Christmas, she attributed it to sheer tiredness; since their return from France there had been party after party, even at Denmark Hill. To protect himself from contagion John had at his parent's urging moved down to his old bedroom, but one morning he knocked at the door of their shared one on the top floor of the house. She was sitting up in bed, and he again took a chair and sat by her bedside.

"I hope you are well enough to bear some news," he said. As Effie was not deemed well enough to receive her own letters, the Ruskins had learnt through those sent directly to them from the Grays of further sorrow in her family. John went on with his unfortunate duty without waiting for reply; he wished to get it out and over with. "I'm sorry to tell you your Aunt Lexy has died, being delivered of a son, who has survived. We had the news two days ago, but as you were in bed, I thought best to wait until you might feel stronger."

She did not in fact feel stronger; she felt only grief at this new blow. First her Aunt Jessie and now Lexy. She was already crying when he added, "This is, sadly, another example of the risks of babies."

What was to John a simple and cautionary fact—his cousin Mary Richardson, who had spent her adolescence with the Ruskins, had also recently died in childbed—was to Effie a thing extraordinarily hurtful and cruel to say.

"Risks?" she asked. "Will you make an object lesson of the loss of my aunts? It is what every woman risks—your own did—my own mother, who has been safely delivered of 13 children—babies are a part of life, of marriage. How can you..." The sobs which racked her frame were for her lost aunts, and for herself.

Later that day he returned, bringing her a moving letter of condolence which he was about to post to Lexy's young husband. Tears of gratitude sprang to her eyes in reading it. She was beginning to think she might never understand her husband.

The next two weeks were a misery to her. Her own mother was scheduled to visit in mid-January, and she yearned for her. Trapped as she was at Denmark Hill, Mrs. Ruskin insisted in taking over her "management," and Effie found herself subjected to the visits of physicians who prescribed an array of tinctures each more disgusting than the last. She coughed so long her ribs ached, and was forced to take laudanum pills to ease her way to sleep. They left her vaguely nauseated and drowsy all day. Mrs. Ruskin allowed her nothing to drink but spa water, whose sulphurous smell and oily taste revolted her, and beef tea, the family panacea. She was given so little to eat, even when she felt hungry, that her already slender limbs became stick-like. She was desperate to feel well enough to return to Park Street, and more desperate for the arrival of her own mother from Perth.

"I should think, Phemy, a little more allowance for a mother's feeling and anxiety for her son's health is in order," said Mr. Ruskin. She was standing with him in the room next to the bedroom at Park Street. John's mother had already fled the room, but the residue of her shrieking hung in the air. John was downstairs and she guessed Mrs. Ruskin had headed down directly to him. Her own mother was thankfully out of the house at the moment.

"It was understood when I engaged this house for you that it was unsuitable for overnight guests, unless they be willing to use the empty room. It is important to Mrs. Ruskin's peace of mind that she knows John's dressing room be warmed by a fire. By removing him to the attic he has been deprived of this comfort and she of her assurance that his health be safeguarded by basic precautions."

"I'm very sorry, Mr. Ruskin. I find it totally unacceptable that my mother, who has had a dreadful sea voyage from Perth, and is after all my mother, be expected to sleep amongst the servants in the attic. John is not being asked to sleep in the attic, merely dress there, but to assume my mother should is—an impossible notion."

She was shocked at her own boldness. Mr. Ruskin's stocky body jerked, and with his white hair mussed from having run his hand through it he looked shocked in the literal sense as well.

"Well—well!" he sputtered. "Huh!" But he turned and left just the same.

John Ruskin was puzzling out the underlying tenants of Obedience as it pertained to true architecture when he heard his wife's voice behind him.

"John, I am not feeling very strong yet, and I'm thinking that I should like to return to Perth with my mother for a rest." Effie stood on the threshold of her husband's small study on Park Street and delivered this news to his back.

He replaced his pen in his ink-pot, but did not turn to her. The friction escalating between his wife and his parents could not be confined to Denmark Hill; it invaded his rooms here, disturbing his efforts. Effie had revealed herself to be entirely too much of a presence around them all. Her liveliness had grown to be restlessness, and her quickness of opinion hardened into obduracy. It was galling to feel the rightness of his parents' original objections to her, although when he had admitted his growing reservations to them they had behaved beautifully in comforting him. He had not mentioned that the marriage had not been celebrated; it did not seem important compared to the larger issues of attitude and behaviour. John had chosen a girl extraordinarily unlike himself, simply because she seemed willing to have him. He had learnt that pining for a young woman and living with her were two very different states. Both were disruptive to his work but at least after procuring her hand he felt the surging return of work-energy. The distractions of actually having a wife were still to be solved. Effie kept herself busy during the day but at night when he finally came to bed he must be alone with her. Her very presence next to him felt a silent reproof.

His chair grated slightly as he pushed it back. He did not rise, but turned and spoke to her where she stood in his doorway. "I find that an excellent idea," he answered.

Effie and her mother set out by rail for Scotland a fortnight later. She was still enervated by illness and hungered for loving and familiar surroundings. At home in Perth she felt certain to regain her health and spirits. Recent European events were also hopeful; Louis Napoleon had been elected President of France, and at this stabilizing news Mr. Gray's railway shares at once became more valuable.

Several of the younger children were ill with whooping cough when they arrived at Bowerswell, and she was thrown into nursing them. Then the unthinkable happened, and seven year-old Robert, the darling of the family, died. She kissed his still hot-brow and recalled how he had kissed her at her wedding. And she got a letter from John telling her he had moved back to Denmark Hill.

Chapter Nine

The Lamp of Life

London: Spring 1849

"I'm going to try for the Academy show." Millais was cleaning his brushes over the porcelain basin when he turned his head and delivered the news to Gabriel. The latter, clad in loose dark blouse and brown over-smock, had just finished modelling for the large new work upon his friend's easel.

"You'll send in 'Isabella'? Benissimo! That's striking right at the heart! They'll have to take it, unless they're blinder than we think. It's by far the best thing you've yet done."

Even incomplete it was a riveting work, startlingly new and yet redolent of the early Italian masters. Millais had taken for his subject Keats' tragic poem *Isabella; Or the Pot of Basil.* In Keats' reworking of Boccaccio's story a young sister of a wealthy Florentine mercantile family falls in love with her brothers' clerk, Lorenzo. Her elder brothers aspire to an advantageous match for Isabella, and murder Lorenzo and bury his body in a shallow grave. After Lorenzo's ghost appears to her, she finds her beloved's body. To keep one part of him near her, she cuts off his head, which she plants in a large pot in which she grows basil. She lovingly tends the basil until her brothers, discovering her secret, steal the pot, upon which she herself dies. Millais had chosen to illustrate a key early moment in this romantically morbid work—that where Isabella and Lorenzo sit side by side at table under the conniving eyes of her brothers, and the unsuspecting presence of other members of her family.

His painting was peopled with the artist's friends and family, who generally posed one at a time so he could give them their due of time and attention. Gabriel had just sat for hours holding a small fluted Venetian glass to his lips. Gabriel's brother William had already sat for the ill-starred Lorenzo, Millais changing his hair from dark to blond to emphasize his vulnerability. Millais' own parents had sat for the two elderly people present, although he had aged them considerably, and so skilfully his mother laughed that it was like looking at herself twenty years hence.

The subject matter, taken from a poem from the revered Keats, was striking enough. But it was Millais' treatment that was arresting. He had grouped the twelve figures, four on one side, eight on the other, around a table projecting out at an angle to the viewer. A flattened and deranged perspective resulted, the composition further dramatized by the white-clad, out-thrusting leg of one of the brothers in the immediate foreground, straining forward to teaze the greyhound who has laid its head in Isabella's lap for solace. Millais had made the most of his models; the faces of each character in the drama were as highly individualised as in any Flemish painting.

If this were not enough the scene was rife with symbolism. The doomed Lorenzo bent towards Isabella as she accepts the half of a blood orange he offers her. A majolica charger before them on the table bore a scene, minute but decipherable to a careful viewer, of Judith beheading Holefernes. Knowing the fate to befall, even the red wine in the drained glass that Gabriel had held might be blood.

But it was the technique with which it was being painted that contributed the most telling particularity to the piece. Millais, taking a page out of the workbook of artists such as Turner, eschewed the practice of "dead colouring," the blocking in of the canvas in sections of grey, green, or brown to serve as under-base for the design to follow. Instead Millais ordered the whitest canvas he could find, and then coated it with gesso of the brightest white he could mix—

even heightening the effect of underlying brightness by painting onto this preparatory ground when it was still wet. Jewel-like colours of unabashed radiance was the result.

"You'll have good company, should the Academy take it," Gabriel went on. "Hunt's submitting his 'Rienzi,' too." Gabriel was busy these days sitting for the rest of the Brotherhood, posing too for the eponymous, vengeance-swearing hero in Hunt's painting. He had moved his studio from the rejected Ford Madox Brown's to share one with Hunt.

"And you?" Millais asked, wiping his hands as Gabriel slipped out of his costume. The small space was filled with the odour of mineral spirits and Millais flung open another window. "Your 'Mary Virgin' would make a perfect triad. What do you say?"

But Gabriel shook his head. He had no inclination to subject his first major oil work, depicting Christ's mother as a girl embroidering with her mother St. Anne, to the scrutiny of the Academy. Instead he was sending it to the less prestigious but jury-less and thus far more welcoming Free Exhibition. Like Millais, he had impressed family into modelling—his younger sister Christina for the tenderly demure Mary, their mother as St. Anne. Gabriel was essentially still learning to draw, and Madox Brown and Hunt had helped him along on it. Although crude in certain aspects Millais admired the picture very much, as did Hunt—Millais did not hold much stock in the opinions of the four newer members of the PRB. He was proud of the fact that Gabriel had added the initials PRB to his signature, which he himself intended to do upon finishing his 'Isabella.'

When the Free Exhibition opened in March, 'The Girlhood of Mary Virgin,' in a frame designed by Gabriel and inscribed with two sonnets he had written, attracted the attention of the Dowager Marchioness of Bath. She gave

Gabriel 80 guineas for it, and asked him to re-colour the Virgin's dress. The first painting signed by a member of the PRB had found a home.

. The entire Royal Academy was of course, packed. The private view was one of the most sought-after social events of each spring, and Millais and Hunt would ordinarily never have been there if their two paintings were not hanging within. They had seen them hung, days earlier, the galleries abuzz with workman on ladders covering the walls floor to ceiling with canvases, frame touching frame. Now they were back, in a flood of artists and patrons, aristocrats and rich manufacturers. And critics. The press was there in number, chatting with Academy officials, edging through the crowd attempting to get closer views, jotting down notes.

Millais' 'Isabella' had been favourably hung, just above "the line"—the natural line of viewing, and not "skied" up by the ceiling cornice. A few members of the Academy who liked and had faith in their work had seen to it that the paintings of Millais, Hunt, and Collinson be grouped together, "huddled for safety," as Millais quipped, and there they lay against the totally obscured damask-covered wall of the Middle Room.

The three young men tried to remain near their paintings, should they have the chance to explain anything, or be so fortunate to be asked by a prospective purchaser about its availability. But the crowd acted like a vortex whirling them slowly but inexorably away for introductions to so-and-so, or with the insistence that they come at once to see a certain painting in another room.

By the next day the papers told them all they needed to know. Hunt's 'Rienzi Vowing to Obtain Justice for the Death of his Young Brother' was praised for the sincerity with which it illustrated Bulwer Lytton's novel; and the novelist himself wrote to congratulate Hunt. Collinson's little picture 'Italian Image—Boys at a Roadside Ale- house' was generally ignored. But Millais' 'Isabella,' though attacked by the *Athenaeum* critic for the "want of rationality of its composition," was acknowledged by many as nothing less than a visual document which in one canvas proclaimed the coming of a new and noble school of art.

Effie stayed largely at Bowerswell, comforting, and being comforted by the rest of her family over little Robert's death. She tried to regain her own vitality. Her allowance of course continued, and John wrote her urging her to ask for more money should she have need. The fact that she would have to ask it of Mr. Ruskin made the likelihood of her availing herself of the offer remote. John, she realised, was utterly dependant financially upon his father. His father had subsidised the printing of his earliest books, and although *Modern Painters* was bought and read by some the most important thinkers in the nation, the print runs were so minuscule that no royalties ensued. This meant that she too was utterly dependent upon Mr. Ruskin, and meant as well that she would never ask for more than her original allowance of £25 per quarter.

In mid-April the three Ruskins left for the delayed trip to Switzerland. John was going on what was to be the crowning point of their honeymoon without her.

Light, Descending

The Channel crossing was stormy, but Ruskin preferred staying inside his brougham lashed to the deck of the steamer to huddling in the ship's crowded cabin with his parents and the servants George and Anne. It was terrifically cold for April, and sleet sheeted against the brougham windows. He had a desperate head-cold coming on, and the pitching of the ship made reading impossible. Snow had delayed their crossing for days, but the fact that once through France they finally could cross safely into Switzerland made any discomforts bearable to him.

They took the new train from Boulogne to Paris; his brougham and his parents' carriage loaded onto the flat trucks provided for the transport of private coaches. They would hire horses as they went along. He, like his father, hated surrendering the privacy of their own vehicles, but his mother was unexpectedly impressed with the comforts of the new train, and the tin containers of hot water they were given with which to warm their feet under their lap-robes.

His eagerness to return to the Alps made every border crossing of every Italian city-state a trial. Soldiers were everywhere; the king of Sardinia, Piedmont, and Savoy had declared war on Austria. An uprising in Brescia had been repressed by the Austrians with marked brutality. Venice drove the Austrian garrison out and proclaimed itself a Republic under Daniele Manin. Their passports were inspected innumerable times due to these unsettled conditions, and a certain number of petty bribes to petty officials were paid, to his disgust. Snow lay six feet deep in the mountain passes and his mother was terrified at each slippage of the carriages. At every inn, on every stage along the way, he continued on *The Seven Lamps of Architecture*, preparing his drawings and even etching the plates in washstand basins. If he was diligent he would have the manuscript ready to be published as a birthday gift for his father in May.

Ruskin had been three years away from his Alps, and he returned to them with a lover's fervour. His parents always tried to take the same routes they had in prior visits, see the exact views, to stop in the same rooms in the same inns. In his notebooks and diaries he would compare the rivers, the trees—great or scrub—, the flowers and grasses, the clouds crowning the summits or rolling in the valleys with his earlier observations of the place. It was not only factual data he sought, but a return of the feelings elicited by the scenery at first acquaintance. At fifteen he had stood here overcome with exhilaration, a revelatory awe that did not diminish, but enlarged, his sense of self. Great mountains had then bestowed upon him an inexplicable sense of joy, in them, and in himself. The verdant foothills of the Alps, the jagged frosted peaks, the deep and shrouded ravines and narrow rocky passes had instilled in him a keen sensation of rootedness, of safety, and of some kind of grand but unnameable invincibility. That feeling had leached away and he yearned to recover it.

"I am in Switzerland," he proclaimed while standing alone on a hill side. He repeated the phrase again and again until the boyhood evocation, his boy's soul, seemed his once again.

John wrote Effie regularly from France, and then from Switzerland. In their separation the act of writing renewed a sense of ardour and tenderness toward her. The idea of Effie, distant and waiting, charmed him. Holding the pen in his hand he could again summon the passionate excitement that had troubled his engagement. He began to feel himself a character in a novel by Walter Scott, a lover separated from his mistress through a long and complicated series of events external to them both. Such a man could be a hero—or could meet a hero's death.

> *Do you know, pet, it seems almost a dream to me that we have been married: I look forward to meeting you: and to your next bridal night, and to the time when I shall again draw your dress from your snowy shoulders: and lean my cheek upon them, as if you were still my betrothed only: and I had never held you in my arms. God bless you my dearest. Ever your devoted J Ruskin*

Effie wept at reading this. Was all that had been forfeited to be reclaimed? John wished a fresh start, to relive their bridal. She opened her heart to him in her response, describing her excitement, and then hurt at her seeming rejection, on their wedding night.

> *My darling Effie I have your precious letter here: with the account so long and kind—of all your trial at Blair Athol—indeed it must have been cruel my dearest: I think it will be much nicer next time, we shall neither of us be frightened.*

Two people can inhabit the same room at the same time in the same circumstances and come from it with vastly differing impressions. Shipwrecked men in a lifeboat labouring in running seas will discern doom, opportunity, and irony depending on their temperaments, self-regard, and expectation of an after-life. Effie's girlish apprehension of the physical transformation from maiden to wife had been a mixture of appropriate anxiety and excitement. Now her husband offered that he, too, had been frightened, and Effie clung to this admission as evidence of a sensitive nature without questioning what it was he feared.

Then, at last in Switzerland, at Jura, he wrote a letter that shocked her.

*Indeed we often and all think of you, and I often
hear my mother or Father saying— 'poor child—if she
could but have thrown herself openly upon us, and
trusted us, and felt that we desired only her happiness,
and would have made her ours, how happy she might
have been: and how happy she might have made us
all'...*

Had she been thus 'written off' by the elder Ruskins?
Was her chafing under Mrs. Ruskin's unbearable fussing, and
her removal to Perth for the sake of her own health, the root
and cause of some irreparable breech?

In Geneva he wrote he had bought her as a birthday gift
a bracelet of gold flowers at the best jeweller in town. And he
asked if it would be irksome to her to read Sismondi's 16
volume *Histoire des Républiques Italiennes au Moyen Âge*
and copy out for him every word that bore in the remotest
degree on the interests and history of Venice.

She went to Edinburgh to speak with a respected
professor of midwifery at the university there. After listening
to her symptoms he advised her to have children.

Chamonix 5 July 1849

My dear Mr. Gray

*Having heard the late correspondence between
you and my father I think it well that you should know
from myself my feelings respecting Effie's illness...I have
no fault to find with her...If she had not been seriously
ill I should have had fault to find with her: but the state
of her feelings I ascribe, now, simply to bodily
weakness; that is to say—and this is a serious and*

distressing admission—to a nervous disease affecting the brain...it showed itself then, as it did now, in tears and depression: being probably a more acute manifestation, in consequence of fatigue and excitement, of disease under which she had long been labouring. I have my own opinion as to its principal cause—but it does not bear on the matter at hand...

When she for the first time showed careless petulance towards my mother, I reproved her when we were alone...It disposed Effie to look with jealousy upon my mother's influence over me...No further unpleasantness however took place between her and my mother and we got abroad at last.

I had hoped this would put us all to rights; but whether I overfatigued her in seeing cathedrals—or whether we drank too much coffee at night—her illness continued to increase.

So she returned worse than she went and I am still in entire ignorance that there was anything particularly the matter with her.

The depression gained on her daily—and at last my mother, having done all she could to make her happy in vain, was, I suppose, partly piqued and partly like myself-disposed to try more serious reason with her. Finding her one day in tears when she ought to have been dressing for dinner, she gave her a scold—which had she not been ill she would have deserved. Poor Effie dressed and came down—looking very miserable. I had seen her look so too often to take notice of it—and besides thought my mother right. Unluckily Dr. Grant was with us—and seeing Effie looking ready to faint thought she must want his advice. Poor Effie like a good girl as she is—took—to please me—what Dr. Grant would have her—weakened herself more-sank under

the influenza—and frightened me at last very
sufficiently—and heaven only knows now when she will
forgive my mother...

If Effie had in sound mind been annoyed at the
contemptible trifles which have annoyed her: if she had
cast back from her the kindness and affection with
which my parents received her and refused to do her
duty to them under any circumstances whatever but
those of an illness bordering in many of its features on
incipient insanity, I should not now have written this
letter to you...Restiveness I am accustomed to regard as
unpromising character even in horses and asses...

Mr. Gray did not share John's letters to him with his
daughter. The claim that Effie was suffering from incipient
insanity struck him as too absurd for comment, although
privately it did make him question the judgement and motive
of the accuser. The comparison of Effie's temperament to that
of a horse or ass angered him. And what was meant when
Ruskin wrote "I have my own opinion as to its principal
cause—but it does not bear on the matter at hand"? If he had
an opinion as to the principal cause of Effie's distress, why
would he not share it? Gray could not fathom what was
actually wrong with the young marriage, and was grateful to
have his eldest once again under his own roof where her
comfort was assured. Between her mother's and her old
nurse's care, and the hearty and familiar dishes produced by
their cook, Effie had gained flesh and had stopped coughing.
She took long walks outdoors to improve her wind, and
frequent shower-baths, after which she rubbed her skin hard
with a Turkish towel. After checking her pulse and listening
to her descriptions of restlessness the family doctor
recommended horseback riding. Her father scoured the local
stables and procured for her use a dappled grey gelding.

John wrote Effie of astonishingly rigorous climbs with
his Alpine guide Couttet, scrambling over broken rock at high

altitude, and of the new mineral specimens he was able to chip from exposed boulders. He sought an easy way into a valley and slid down a perpendicular snow-filled ravine on his back from a height of 2000 feet. Hearing of these exertions Effie wondered if his worrisome parents, snug back in the inn, ever knew of their son's daily exploits. George Hobbs followed John almost everywhere, hauling his master's heavy Daguerreotype apparatus on his back. John was continually working on mapping the Alps, calculating the movements of its glaciers, and cataloguing its vegetation. After considerable labour George and he succeeded in taking the first ever light-picture of the Matterhorn.

> *I have your diary here, that you were keeping when we travelled together, and which when I called what you had written absurd, you let lapse—it was very foolish of me to think that then, and even more to say so—I will give you another book to write in when we come back, DV, and you will write in it steadily; but of this one I have taken possession—*

When she responded that she, and her parents, were sorry at their being parted his response was direct.

> *...the very simple truth that it was not I who had left you but you who had left me—...I wonder whether they think a husband is a kind of thing who is to be fastened to his wife's waist with her pincushion and to be taken about with her wherever she chooses to go. However my love, never mind what they say and think: I shall always be glad when you can go with me...I must follow my present pursuits with the same zeal that I have hitherto followed them or go into the church...*

She began riding every day, sometimes with friends ambling along lanes, other times alone into the countryside surrounding Bowerswell. As she grew certain of the gelding her confidence increased. Frolic was beautiful and eager to respond to the slightest touch of her heel or crop. She had good hands and with her right leg hooked in her side-saddle felt light and free upon his back. She would ride at a canter and thinking of her husband, occupied without her far away, urge him into a gallop.

Chapter Ten

The Lamp of Life

Venice: October 1849

The curved prow of their gondola slid directly into the doorway on the canal, with a red-sashed porter always waiting to help them out upon the marble steps of the Hotel Danieli. Their suite of rooms—all high-ceilinged pale gilt and crackled grey woodwork, with shell-pink silk upon the walls—was up one floor on the *piano nobile*, and in crossing the marble threshold one stepped into a world of ancient and noble Venetian taste. The suite would serve admirably. From John's dressing room he could see the golden-coloured brick of the campanile in the Piazza of St. Mark's.

After nine months apart they were again together, and to Effie's eyes, in the most romantic city in the world. At her insistence John had come up to Perth to collect her after his return from the Alps; there was no other way to quell the rumours about the disintegration of their new marriage. He had scolded her bitterly for this expectation, ridiculing her childishness in a letter so severely that she would have felt shamed if in searching her conscience she found herself guilty of the least bit of coquetry, or base desire to display a long-absent husband for her own, instead of for the marriage's sake.

He had at last acquiesced, despite his parents' objections that the autumnal cold of Scotland might do him harm. They made a brief round of appearances at dinners and receptions together, were seen chatting happily by the doyens of Perth society. John had wished to make a study trip to Venice, and when she suggested that instead of settling back at London they leave for Italy, even old Mr. Ruskin gave his blessing. As John intended to be perpetually busy document-ing the architecture and history of the fabled city, she must have a chaperone. Her friend Charlotte Ker from Perth was asked to join her as companion, and John must have George Hobbs along. John James Ruskin paid for all.

Their party travelled in two carriages to accommodate the four of them and their bags, and at last Effie glimpsed John's prized Alps. In Geneva they stopped at M. Bautte's, jewellers, so that she might see where her birthday gift had come from. She wore the gold floral bracelet John had presented her, and M. Bautte, flattered, himself waited upon them. All the necklaces, bracelets, and brooches were laid upon black velvet, and John paused before one. It was another bracelet, of green enamel work, and formed into the shape of a serpent. It was arresting, and the work exquisite. The head of the serpent was of opal, and it rested in a flower made of green enamel.

Without looking up from it he spoke to Effie. "You might exchange the one I gave you, for this," he offered. The quickening sinuousness of the serpent motif beckoned to him, and he took it in his hand. The bracelet of gold flowers was lifeless by comparison.

Effie was surprised. The reptilian subject would not have been her first choice, but John's enthusiasm was marked. He helped her place it on her wrist. "But opals—they're unlucky for anyone not born in October," she said.

"Superstition," he answered with a smile, and they left with the piece.

After the elegance of Geneva, nothing prepared the two young women for the wretchedness of the folk they encountered in rural Switzerland. In narrow valley villages where the sun did not make an appearance until almost noon, she and Charlotte were shocked to see armless and otherwise mis-formed children. Idiots abounded. Toothless women with goitres the size of small melons wrapped rosaries around their deformities. The gnarled and weather-beaten men wheeled drunken on dirt paths. Chamonix was better than most and Effie saw at once why its clean sobriety was favoured by the Ruskins.

They learnt cholera was raging in Venice in the aftermath of the siege and moved on to Milan via the Simplon, waiting for news of when the city might be safe. Milan was empty of all tourists and Austrian officers tipped their plumed cocked hats at them. The churches in which Austrian troops were now bivouacked and the food and fuel shortages suffered by the Milanese stirred Effie to sympathy with the Italian nationalists. The Austrian-run hotel at which they lodged produced fresh eggs, sweet butter, and cured meats for their meals, served by Milanese waiters whose eyes followed every dish with such undisguised hunger that she must stop herself from imagining the scene in the kitchen when their half-eaten plates were returned.

"I feel almost an Italian here, and hate their oppression," she said one afternoon when she and her husband had come in from the soldier-filled street and gained their rooms.

She knew John could argue any position, and he did so now, countering that as flawed as the Austrians were, only a strong authoritarian hand could guide so indolent, irrational, and wayward a people as the Italians. But then he paused, and said in a quieter voice that he had noted their suffering.

She smiled her challenge. "In France you were a great conservative, as you said everyone there is radical," Effie told him. "Around Austrians you are a radical, as they are all so conservative. You change your position as nimbly as a fish."

Light, Descending

"Like a fish I find it steadier going, swimming against the stream," he answered.

And in Venice the little party was aligned with the occupying Austrians from the first. John had despised the fact of the rail line which now meanly anchored Venice to the mainland. Much to his satisfaction the new rail terminus, built by the Austrians, had also been bombed by the Austrians during the siege. Their gondola landed them at a city deeply divided between the beaten *italianissimi* and the Italian *austriacanti*, those members of the Venetian nobility who had sided with the Austrians and acted as collaborators and informants. And there were, quite simply, almost no other English in the entire lagoon. They all had fled at the start of the five month Austrian bombardment and had not yet returned.

Once at the Hotel Danieli John left to go out and walk the city. The building which was the greatest in the world, the Doge's Palace, was almost next their hotel and unharmed by the recent action, though a row of Austrian cannon stood poised at it as threat. But they had heard fearful reports of destruction and he must revisit any number of *palazzi* and churches to assure himself.

So Effie and Charlotte set out alone and by foot, John Murray's guidebook to the sights in hand. Directly leaving the Danieli they heard a trumpet sound. Voices, indistinct but urgent, carried from the piazzetta in front of the Doge's Palace, and they followed a small number of dark-cloaked Venetians. On the Ponte Paglia, the "straw bridge" they must cross to reach the Piazza, they paused to gaze down the side canal at the small, roofed-over Bridge of Sighs leading to the old ducal prison. In the Piazza itself, nearly empty a few hours earlier, a curious scene was being enacted in front of the great basilica of St. Mark's. A large cauldron had been set in the centre of the pavement, in which a fire had been kindled. Austrian soldiers formed a semi-circle around it, as Venetians watched both nearby and from the sheltering shadows of the arcades. The soldiers passed wicker baskets of some sort of slips of paper down their line in almost ceremonial precision, and the final man emptied the contents of each basket into the cauldron, stirring it with a poker to ensure it burst into flame. The waving air above the cauldron was dark with ash, and each deposit elicited a cacophony of groans, shouts, and cheers from the crowd.

What is it, Effie asked a nearby gentleman who turned to them. She knew only a few words of Italian and Charlotte, none. He was much moved by the action of the fire and his distress marked his face. "*La moneta patriottica, signorina*"... he told her, and touching his hat, moved away. It was Manin's money, that printed by the short-lived republic. It was now worthless and its public burning an additional humiliation to the failed patriot cause. A few notes fluttered around them, driven by the heat of the blaze and the breeze sweeping though the piazza. She blinked against the particles of ash and bent and snatched at one that nearly hit her skirt. It was a two lire note. She stared at it as she grasped it between pale thumb and forefinger. Crisp and unfolded, the defunct note bore the slightest singeing along one blue edge. She looked helplessly at Charlotte for direction, and receiving none, tucked it away in her guidebook as memento.

Ruskin applied himself at once measuring and drawing at the Doge's Palace. Each of its hundreds of columns and capitals was unique, and he wished to draw every one. It was not whole buildings but the fragments of ancient architecture that most interested him, the stone window casings and doorways, arcaded passages, fonts and mosaics and wellheads. Much of this encrusted decoration had been carried off from the great and plundered cities of Byzantium to Venice during the Crusades, and been assembled and installed seemingly at random in the great edifices of Church and State. His goal was to record nothing less than the essential elements of each of the most important buildings of Venice, and to do so he had literally to scramble up and over roofs to reach chimney pots and spires. No alpine climbing proved as rigorous as his solo ascents up vertical walls and the ginger tracing of pathways across tiled spines or lead-spanned roof expanses to reach the delicate stone elements. Once gained he would rope himself to the object he sought—parapet or fretwork, pinnacle or frieze—and proceed to detail its contours in his sketchpad, annotating the drawing with careful measurements from his spooling pocket line. George Hobbs or Domenico, his recently engaged valet, waited below, ready with a whisk broom to brush off the soot and restore their master's stressed clothing to respectability. He knew the Venetians thought him mad, sometimes saw them gesticulating far below him, though with a few Austrian *zwanzigs* he could speedily buy the blessing of a sexton or caretaker to gain the access he needed. In addition to the drawings he was making, he had George carry his Daguerreotype apparatus, which they set up wherever he felt a useful image might be struck.

The act of drawing had always furthered his thinking, and it did so now. He saw within a few days of arrival that this new Venetian book would have to be far more than a study of prominent men and the buildings they erected. The Venice he walked was the ruin of the greatest mercantile force history had known, brought down by greed, hubris, and corrupted religious ideals. He recognised it as no less than a mirror, spotted and tarnished, but conveying glimmers of disquieting veracity. He knew it as a place that at its height was very like his own England today in its imperial pride.

Light, Descending

With letters of introduction from London the young Ruskins were soon inserted into Austrian society. A sense of, if not normalcy, then of accommodating routine was being restored, and with it parties, balls, and operas performed at La Fenice. The local hostesses found that *la signora* Ruskin spoke German well enough to make her a sought-after and amusing guest. Venetian noblewomen presented Effie to *marchesi*, and Russian princes in employ of the Austrians vied to dance with her. Her scholarly husband chaffed at being taken away from his work in the evenings; this was the time he sat at his little painted desk in the Danieli and consolidated his cascading pages of notes. When pressed into accompanying the ladies to a concert Ruskin would continue to write or take a book to read. One night at the opera, while Effie was rapt with the stage action, she had to stifle her laughter when she glanced at him to find him oblivious in their box, preparing a chapter on Chamfered Edges.

Soon Ruskin was urging his wife to accept invitations without him. He insisted he trusted her implicitly to protect her good name, and it would be a favour to him to be relieved of social obligations keeping him from his work. Miss Ker, he added, was a sensible and virtuous companion, and they each would have the best time of it by respecting the other's inclinations.

A succession of handsome and unfailingly polite Austrian officers presented themselves as escorts for the two young ladies. One, an artillery lieutenant, had designed and directed the awful balloon bombardment which had brought the city to its knees after the year-old siege. This talented young officer had made the acquaintance of the Ruskins at a party and respectfully requested permission to call upon them both. Although John Ruskin and his guest had only a few words of Italian in common—John spoke very little German, and Lt. Paulizza no English—the lieutenant was fascinated with the Englishman's work and the beauty of his drawings.

One afternoon the lieutenant proudly brought by his diagrams for the bombing of the same city his host was furiously documenting. John was utterly baffled, Effie quietly amused.

Freed from the omnipresent Ruskins, Effie hoped here, in Byron's magical watery setting, the intimacy she hoped for might now be attained. Dr. Simpson in Edinburgh had told her to have children, that this would help her health and cure her restlessness. But she had not been confident enough to tell him that her husband never did more than nuzzle her neck. Her mother had never asked and she could not bear to broach the topic with her. Indeed she felt ashamed to admit this; it seemed a reflection on the desirability of her person. Here in Venice they shared the same bed, and if John was pleased with his work or with her, he might hold her in his arms. But he kept his hands either upon her shoulders or at his own sides, and never would kiss her mouth. If she tried to press her body against his he pulled away. He held himself always back, and then bidding her goodnight, would turn away. She could not understand why, after laying next to her for some minutes, he sometimes got up and actually left the bed. For what purpose did he leave?

"John," she said one night as she was readying for bed, "I want—a child."

It had taken enormous strength to nerve herself, but she had said it. It was shortly after they had arrived in Venice and the delight of being there was full upon them both. Their bedroom was airy and the bed a fantasy of gilding and grinning cherubs.

He had just entered the bedroom and after pausing went to his side of the bed. She began to go to him but was checked by his look. She sat down instead near the foot of the bed.

123

"We have before discussed this," he said. They had been in Venice but a few days and his brain was teeming with ideas and impressions about the fabric of the city. The enormity of what he needed to discover to tell the truth about Venetian architecture—about the Venetian character— seemed staggering. Now this distraction.

"I don't want a discussion," she answered, confident in her claim and unwilling to beseech him. In fact he had posed argument after argument against it; demolishing her feeble attempts to persuade him. Even the need to persuade him shamed her. He had cited the necessity that she be a good travelling companion; the dangers to her of pregnancy and child-bearing; the sacrifice of her beauty. His argument varied and the result, never. She stood up and faced him. "I want to know what is—wrong."

Effie thought perhaps she knew. Impressed by his filial devotion she had written him during their engagement *You who are so kind to your parents will be a perfect husband to me.*

I find I am always happiest when I am most dutiful, he had responded.

Perhaps her in-laws' disapproval had acted as a curb to their son's ardour.

He was silent, and she went on. "Is it—for your parents? I know they did not wish you to wed me."

John's mouth began to twist. He looked as if she had uttered the worst blasphemy against God.

He was, in fact, not thinking of sacrilege, nor even of her opening demand for a baby. He heard only the accusation against his parents, and could not speak for himself. Her words moved his own concerns and reservations into the recesses of his consciousness. He saw his father's white head and thought of the old man's tireless toil, a toil underpinning and making possible his son's aspirations. If his father's monetary generosity had been sometimes grudging it had at least been constant, supporting both him and Effie on this trip and in their London lives. He was stung by a sense of impropriety that was unconcealed in his answer.

"How can you dare speak of them in this respect—as kind as they have been to you since girlhood—as if they were now obstacles to your personal felicity?"

Effie's response was swift. "I don't question their kindness, now or in the past." The table had been turned and she would fight to regain her ground and press her point. "Mr. and Mrs. Ruskin have been great friends to me, but not, I think, to our union." She stepped towards him. "And there has been no *union* for us. None."

She watched her husband's face, blue eyes wide but immobile. "You were, and still are, too much theirs, John. I know if they had to "lose you" to marriage, I would not have been their choice. That I was yours, just enough to get your way in the matter, has not been enough for you to truly defy or deny them."

But John had turned away in distaste and confusion. The passionate declarations he had written during their engagement, the fantastical and fevered longings he had suffered, were phantoms he could no longer recognize as having been inspired by the exacting and insistent woman standing before him. The once-delicious fears she had engendered in him, of losing himself in her, of being powerless before her, were the only remnants of his earlier captivation that remained.

He must say something, buy time and distance, and in order to obtain them risked sounding ridiculous.

125

"I shall make you my wife when you reach twenty-five," he said at last.

That was five years from now.

One afternoon when the rain had turned to sleet Ruskin took shelter from his outdoor labours in the Accademia. In the winter light the place was duskier than usual, but he had from prior visits intimate knowledge of the rooms and corridors and the paintings they held. The galleries were unheated and he warmed his freezing fingers above the candle he had bought from the drowsing *cicerone*. He found himself in the room with Carpaccio's St. Ursula series, and he visited each panel in turn. There was the golden-haired princess slumbering in her bed, starting out on her pilgrimage, meeting the pagan prince she was promised to, massed with her attendant 11,000 virgins, striding boldly to her virgin martyrdom. He went back to the painting of young Ursula asleep, asleep and waiting. Her face was inexpressibly tender, delicately mystical, receptive. He had never seen a woman look like that.

Effie kept intact her Scottish reserve and beliefs. She read her Bible in St. Mark's during Roman services, and refused all invitations for Sundays. Her letters home were filled with news of parties she had gone to, lace she had bought at a bargain, *principesse* who had complimented her taste in dress. To the world around them, to even Charlotte, she looked half of a happily married couple. Some afternoons John would accompany Charlotte and her to the Accademia

126

and explain the paintings to them. On one of these visits she wandered into the room which housed a set of pretty and old panels of a blonde girl in her bed, and what looked like the girl's martyrdom. She thought it the kind of thing John would like but when he saw her before it he walked away without describing it to her.

Sometimes he took them out in the lagoon in their gondola. Effie tried oaring it herself once, proud to master the balance required to turn the vessel, and John watched approvingly. But then he'd written of it to his father. Mr. Ruskin, who kept the Sabbath so strictly that he rarely wrote even a letter upon that day, was enough alarmed at such unladylike behaviour to do so.

And the Ruskins could be so ridiculous, Effie thought. In letters to them both Mr. Ruskin was grumbling about the expense of the vacant town house in Park Street—a place neither she nor John had ever asked for—complaining that they had spent less than six weeks there, and then it had sat empty all this time. It wasn't her fault her illness drove her home to Bowerswell, nor that John immediately decamped to Denmark Hill. She had to laugh at their sense of economy— Mrs. Ruskin paid fully £30 per annum to her cook, while boasting how cheaply she ran the household—while Mr. Ruskin begrudged every cent John pleaded for to buy precious manuscripts here, now offered for a pittance by desperate Venetians.

Far worse, she had made the mistake of mentioning in a letter to them that she had gone to the Protestant service there, at which John's mother had immediately leapt to the conclusion that *John* had attended Mass. Every moment he spent in Catholic countries made Mrs. Ruskin anxious, and the hours he stood lost in contemplating the framed Madonnas, Crucifixions, Depositions, Dormitions, and Lives of the Martyrs were, she feared, working on his brain. In England the tracts of the Puseyites and the Oxford Movement were swaying young people to Catholicism, and his mother knew that four of his friends from Christ Church College had abandoned the Anglican Church for that of Rome. A flurry of letters from them both was necessary to reassure her that John had not been corrupted. Effie would have laughed at his mother's lack of confidence in him if the entire small matter had not been made so absurdly serious to all.

   Venice had always drawn from Ruskin a confusing mixture of responses. Each subsequent return had deepened his knowledge of the battered yet dazzling creation risen from the mud flats of the Adriatic. It was a landscape wholly artificial, utterly man-made, anchored on piers of Istrian pine in fortified mud flats, a centuries-long cobbling together of precious stones and coloured *smalti* and looted treasure, elusive and shimmering and rotting all at once. No one but Turner could convey the visual effects of its aqueous setting: the shifting light upon the sparkling silver or oily virescent waters; the limitless expanse of luminosity—sea reflected in sky and sky in sea—crowning or mirroring the monuments along the Grand Canal. Northern Lombard and southern Arab culture had collided here, with the Gothic their architectural offspring.

   Now the more he looked the less he felt he knew. He spent days paging through ancient maps and cracked volumes in the vast and vastly contradictory resources of the Biblioteca Marciana, the library of St. Mark's. The history of La Serenissima, and thus of its buildings, was as twisted and convoluted as the progress of the serpentine canals. The story of Venice's miraculous buildings, the zenith of Gothic architecture, could not be teazed out through its innumerable state archives. It must be read in its stones.

"Signore Ruskin! Una lettera importante..."

He and George Hobbs were in the cemetery on
Murano, where he was drawing amongst the crumbling
marble of the graves. Now here was come a breathless
Domenico, by another gondola, across the lagoon after him.
He feared the worst at Denmark Hill until he saw the address
written in his father's hand, the "urgent" on the reverse
decidedly firm.

Turner was dead.

He was old; it was to be expected. His body had
betrayed him with the years, and so too had his mind. It was
to be expected. This brilliant Sun whose meridian had
illuminated landscape and seascape with its unmatched gift
was now returned to the eye of the Father whose message of
supernal loveliness only he could convey.

He sat down on a gravestone and wept.

Turner had painted these very walls surrounding him,
showing them violet in a long twilight. Cemetery wall, Doge's
Palace, Loire valley, Rhine cliff face, all had lost their great
witness.

When he had recovered himself he read the details of
his father's letter.

Turner had left every painting, every drawing, every
scrap of paper he had ever scribbled upon and which he still
owned, to the British people. It was to be preserved, kept
together, shown together, and made free for viewing. Tears of
astonished gratitude sprang to his eyes; he had to wipe them
again. He could have no more Turners fresh from the easel,
but they would all be saved, the entire contents of the

miserable little house on Queen Anne Street, the scores of oils, the thousands of watercolours, the tens of thousands of drawings.

Turner had left no painting to him, and it would have stung if he had not the great fact of the national bequest to recur to. His earthly Master had instead designated nineteen guineas be given him, for the purpose of buying a mourning ring to wear in remembrance.

With a gift such as that, his father reminded him, no one could ever say he had been paid to praise.

Disturbed Imagination. Ruskin was listing the vital characteristics of the builder of true Gothic design. A disturbed imagination fostered that sense of the grotesque that delighted in the fantastical and ludicrous, as well as sublime, images elemental to the Gothic temperament. The other essential elements were Savageness, or Rudeness; Love of Change; Love of Nature; Obstinacy; and Generosity.

Savageness was reflected in the fierce weather and rugged environs against which the northern builder, the inventor of the Gothic style, must shelter himself; and more importantly the honest and desirable imperfections inherent in work created by hand from original expression. Paired with savageness was a Love of Change, delighting in a multitudinous variety of form and ornament. Love of Nature engendered a loving observation of leaves, flowers, and vines, inspiring endless variations of these same to be worked upon the capitals of columns, and in other decoration. Obstinacy took the form of natural, active rigidity, as exhibited in the northern lightning-bolt depicted not as a curving arc but a forked angularity, and seen too in the strength of will and resoluteness of purpose—that natural obstinacy—of the Gothic peoples, the English, French, Danish, and German. Generosity endowed architecture with a lavish and costly ornamentation, an uncalculating bestowal of its labour, both in reflection of Nature's abundance and as a sign of sacrifice of materials and time.

He measured, sketched, and jotted notes all day as he explored the nature of Gothic. He climbed into the filthy and forgotten recesses of church alcoves and campaniles, and risked his life upon their roofs. His fingers froze drawing window jambs in January cold, and no matter how warm his stock, or how tightly wrapped, his throat was chilled in the bitter air. He returned to the hotel each afternoon with a portfolio crammed with information which he must then order when the impressions were still fresh. His stomach troubled him, a bitter taste lingering in his mouth; and his pulse was oftentimes fast, or irregular. Writing so much, drawing so much, had caused dark floating objects to appear to swim before his eyes; one looked terrifyingly like a serpent.

There was a feeling almost overpowering—an instinct perhaps—driving him with an inexpressible passion to embrace the city, to absorb it. It felt a physical drive like hunger or thirst. He wanted to draw all of St. Mark's, stone by stone, to feel it in his fingers. To eat it all up into his mind, touch by touch.

"Read me something," Effie asked John one day when lashing rain had driven him inside. He sat at his desk and had momentarily paused to rest his cupped hands against his eyes. "Something from what you're working on."

He rustled loose pages, found a folder with a slender notebook and opened it.

"Since the first dominion of men was asserted over the ocean, three thrones, of mark beyond all others, have been set upon its sands: the thrones of Tyre, Venice, and England..."

Chapter Eleven

The Lamp of Life

London: July 1850

"Her Majesty has asked that your painting be temporarily removed from the Academy exhibition so that she herself might examine it."

It was William Dyce who delivered this astonishing request to Millais. Dyce was older, a member of the Academy, but a great admirer of the Nazarenes. At this year's private view he had taken his friend Ruskin's arms and forcibly propelled him back to where Millais' painting hung, imploring him to take a second look.

Millais was speechless for a moment. It was awkward to be both the young hope of the Academy and by his newest works a rebel to its mores. His entry for the Royal Academy Summer Exhibition had from the first viewing engendered vitriolic censure. He had had the audacity—the blasphemous audacity, according to his harshest critics—to depict the Holy Family in a completely naturalistic manner. His untitled painting of Christ with his parents showed the working interior of St. Joseph's carpenter shop, down to the dirt under the saint's fingernails. The shop floor was littered with wood curls and the walls hung with ordinary and quite prosaic tools. St. Joseph and an assistant were seen planing a door, while in the centre of the canvas the boy Jesus, who has cut his palm with a nail, held his hand up for his kneeling mother to see. Another boy in furred loincloth, St. John, hastened with a basin of water.

No less a personage than Charles Dickens attacked the Christ-child as a "hideous, wry-necked, blubbering, red-haired boy in a night-gown" and the other commentators were little kinder. The questioning but generally admiring reception given his 'Isabella' was not to be repeated with this new effort. He had found a carpenter's shop in Oxford Street where he slept in a cot so he might detail the interior before the work of the day commenced. He bought sheeps' heads from the local butcher to assure the veracity of the flock, representative of Christianity, seen through the open doorway of the shop in his painting. His commitment to fidelity was so great that he pricked his own finger and squeezed out the blood onto the upraised palm of the boy posing as the Child so that he might capture the actual colour red.

Now the Queen wished to see it, free from the inconvenience on her royal person and the Academy viewing-public, of arranging a special view at the Academy's quarters in Trafalgar Square.

"I hope it will not have any bad effects upon her mind," he wrote to Hunt that evening.

When the royal personage stepped into the empty room where the summoned painting awaited her, she wasted no time in approaching. The President of the Royal Academy attended her, careful to keep his own eyes on the disputed work, and not search Her Majesty's for sign of approbation or censure. After glancing over the whole of the active canvas she settled before the kneeling figure of Mary embracing her little son, his wounded hand exposed to her gaze. The thirty-one year old Queen was already mother to seven children. Studying the painting, she noted the suffering and prescience that marked the holy virgin's face. It was exactly the face of motherhood, thought Victoria.

"Gabriel did it," Millais said. "He went and asked his brother, and Collinson, and Woolner, into our Brotherhood––*our* Brotherhood—without asking us; dodges hanging his pictures with ours at the Academy, yet put "PRB" first on his 'Mary Virgin', and now I know it was he who tipped off the papers about the name. It had to be."

Hunt and he had no evidence either way, but Gabriel certainly was the likeliest suspect. Someone had leaked what those three initials stood for—and the critics had gone mad after them for their presumption in "damning Raphael," the painter of the "great" 'Transfiguration'. Their "hieroglyphics" revealed, the *Illustrated London News* now accused them of "the reproduction of saints squeezed out perfectly flat."

"And no one even mentioned the 'PRB' painted on our work last year; it's as if they hadn't even seen it," Hunt said. The trajectory seemed to point from obscurity to notoriety and now back to obscurity.

Their experiment in publishing a journal of literature and art—their best chance for a public manifesto—had just failed. *The Germ* had seen only four numbers, with a print run, and sales, decreasing from extremely modest to non-existent. They had filled it with sonnets, reviews, and philosophical essays, supplied not only by the seven Brothers, but by guests. Ford Madox Brown wrote on painting, and Christina Rossetti contributed her poetry, as did Coventry Patmore and William Bell Scott. They had boxes of unsold copies. No one wanted their wisdom at a shilling a copy.

Millais had worked like a demon over the winter, with the result that three of his new canvases had been accepted for exhibition in the year's Royal Academy Summer

Exhibition. Hesitant to return to overtly religious themes he
had taken literature as his guide. 'Mariana' was accompanied
in the exhibition catalogue by a few lines from Tennyson's
poem. The painting featured a young woman in rich blue
medieval garb rising from her needlework in weariness, vainly
awaiting her lover. He had the satisfaction of entering it in
the show already sold to a dealer for £150.

His second painting was also sold by the time it was
hung on the Academy's walls. In the 'The Return of the
Dove to the Ark' two of the young daughters-in-law of Noah
are seen cradling the returning dove who has brought them
the olive branch.

It was the painting which came into the exhibition
unsold, and remained so for months afterwards, that changed
his life.

He took a Coventry Patmore poem, 'The Woodman's
Daughter' as his subject. His painting showed two children,
of five or six years of age. The squire's son, in brilliant red,
extends his arm with a handful of strawberries to little Maud,
the simply dressed woodman's daughter on his father's estate.
The woodman is at work hewing a tree behind the children,
oblivious to the act. Patmore's poem went on to tell of how,
growing up, the two fell in hopeless and forbidden love.
Maud bears their child, drowns it, and is driven mad by the
grief of her circumstances. Millais' painting, with the locked
stare of the children's eyes and Maud's cupped hands ready to
receive the proffered strawberries, presaged their sad future.

Hunt too turned to literature, painting 'Valentine
Rescuing Sylvia from Proteus' from Shakespeare's *Two
Gentlemen of Verona*.

The art critic of *The Times* was quick to respond.

> *We cannot censure as amply or as strongly as we
> desire that strange disorder of the mind or eyes which*

*continues to rage with unabated absurdity among a class
of juvenile artists who style themselves Pre-Raphaelite
Brethren. Their faith seems to consist in absolute
contempt for perspective and the known laws of light
and shade, an aversion to beauty in every shape,
seeking out every excess of sharpness and deformity...*

"Aversion to beauty?" repeated Millais. "Beauty, and
the Truth in beauty, is all I live for!"

But he threw up his hands. Patmore had been good
enough to contribute a poem for their failed effort *The Germ*.
He knew John Ruskin, whose *Modern Painters* volumes I and
II had so impressed the Brotherhood. Would Patmore say a
word to Ruskin on their behalf?

A week later he had the satisfaction of finding on the
back page of *The Times* Ruskin's long, considered, and not
entirely laudatory defence. And then a fortnight later another
letter from "the Author of *Modern Painters*" appeared.
Millais held it in his hands and read it slowly aloud to
himself, his voice nearly trembling with excitement. The
Times reviewer had been scornful, Ruskin wrote, and
unnecessarily severe. It is true he had not himself cared for
Mr. Millais' painting of Christ in the carpenter shop
exhibited last year, and he felt that one of the young wives in
the same artist's 'Return of the Dove' was marked by "dull
complacency." But, he went on

*These Pre-Raphaelites (I cannot compliment
them on common sense in choice of a* nom de guerre*)
do not desire nor pretend in any way to imitate antique
painting as such. They know very little of ancient
paintings who suppose the works of these young artists
to resemble them. As far as I can judge of their aim—
for, as I said, I do not know the men themselves—the
Pre-Raphaelites intend to surrender no advantage
which the knowledge or inventions of the present time*

137

can afford to their art. They intend to return to the early days in this one point only—that, as far as in them lies, they will draw either what they see, or what they suppose might have been the actual facts of the scene they desire to represent, irrespective of any rules of picture-making; and have chosen their unfortunate though not inaccurate name because all artists did this before Raphael's time, and after Raphael's time did not *this, but sought to paint fair pictures, rather than represent stern facts, of which the consequence has been that from Raphael's time to this day historical art has been in acknowledged decadence.*

And

...they may, as they gain experience, lay in our England the foundation of a school of art nobler than the world has seen for three hundred years.

Chapter Twelve

The Lamp of Life

Scotland: September 1853

Effie Ruskin and John Everett Millais had been walking in the swelling foothills of Ben Ledi for over two hours. They had left Brig o' Turk in the same drizzle which had opened nearly every day since their arrival, and as John Ruskin could not pose in the rain, and his wife did not mind walking in it, Millais proposed the two of them take a walk with the hope he could return to his portrait of her husband in the afternoon.

The party had left London on the summer solstice and arrived in the Highlands at the beginning of July. John Ruskin had needed a holiday, and Effie was longing for Scotland. It was natural Ruskin would invite his new protégé, so badly in need of rest himself, to come along. The Trossachs region was famed for the rugged beauty of its hills, lochs and streams, and their little group—Effie and John, Everett and his brother William Millais, and John's new servant, Crawley—had intended no more than a one day's stopping at tiny Brig o' Turk. But then Everett—Effie could not call him 'John' for confusion with her husband, so she and John both called him by his middle name—happened upon a setting ideal for the portrait old Mr. Ruskin was eager for him to paint of his son. Millais would have him stand upon an outcropping of rock before a whirling torrent of rushing water. The spot, a little further up the glen, was so singularly isolated and lovely, and yet with the convenience of a newly-opened hotel fast by, that the decision was made to stay. Everett had found the perfect setting for John's portrait, and it must be painted out of doors, with perfect fidelity to nature.

Although this was to be a rest for Millais, who had nearly exhausted himself in painting these past two years, his painstaking methods meant that his work was necessarily slow, and he wanted to start at once. He sent to Edinburgh for canvas; it arrived not white enough and he sent again. In the meantime he continued painting Effie Ruskin.

Since they had begun travelling in late June Everett had made scores of little studies of Effie, in sepia ink, or in pencil. Almost as soon as they had got into Scotland they made an excursion to the ruins of Doune Castle. John could not join them. He had twisted his ankle and remained behind at their inn, but Effie and Everett and William wandered amidst the broken walls and heath-filled hall. He sketched her standing, looking out of a glass-less window, and when he brought the sketch back that night John suggested that Everett consider a portrait of her.

The young painter had already begun one on the trip. It was an oil painting of Effie seated, looking down at the needlework she was working on, her hair adorned with purple foxglove flowers. He presented it to her husband and it was gratefully received. Ruskin wrote to his father to say it was worth at least £50.

But then, Everett told her, no one could capture her likeness as he felt he could. He knew Thomas Richmond had tried, as had George Watts, and even John. "You are made to look pensive to escape the difficulties of expression and colouration," Everett said. He saw something more, a truer way to depict the contrast of high cheekbone and narrow nose, the slight tilt of her eyes, the mobility of lips.

John had been surprised, and then quite flattered, when Millais had asked earlier if she might pose for him. Since John had taken up the Pre-Raphaelites and become their champion, Effie had seen Everett, but not often. She had been with John to make the first call on the Millais household following the letter of thanks which Everett and Holman Hunt had sent him. She met Mrs. Millais and the tall, blond and very lean John Everett.

"You don't recall it," he told her on their next meeting over dinner, "but we have before met. Long ago." He was smiling so she could not guess if he was teazing.

"At a party at Ewell Castle," he prompted. "You were a splendid lady of seventeen, and I but a callow youth of sixteen. You would not dance with me—alas."

She did indeed have no remembrance of him. But when earlier this year he had wanted to paint a Scottish subject for entry into the Royal Academy Summer Exhibition, he asked John if she might be allowed to sit for him. She was posed as the wife of a prisoner taken at the Battle of Culloden in 1746. Her injured soldier husband, wearing the tartan of Gordon, and with his arm in a sling, has just stepped forth from his gaol and has dropped his head upon her shoulder. She carries their little boy in one arm, while with the other holds out to the English gaoler the slip of paper she has brought securing her husband's freedom. Her expression is stoic, proud, but not insolent. Everett called it 'The Order of Release'.

It was not only accepted for the Academy show, it caused a sensation. The crowds were so thick that a protecting cordon was strung before it. Everyone knew she was the heroine of the painting; other than the fact that Everett had changed her auburn locks to dark, it was a perfect likeness. She forgot about the stiff neck she suffered standing for hours in her pose, the weight of the various child models she held, the fact that the man posing as the soldier husband turned out to be in truth a military deserter. It was an homage to the crushed Jacobite Rebellion, a reminder of England's injustices to her homeland, and she was proud of her role in the success of the painting.

This morning she and Everett had left Brig o' Turk walking in drizzle over the tracks hatching the foothills. The rain had thinned to mist and the sky fleetingly brightened upon glistening rock and dripping blue heaths. She wore her 'wide-awake'—a broad, flat-brimmed felt hat, against the perpetual wet. Everett had his blond curls tucked into his peak-billed hunting cap; with a tartan thrown over his shoulder he looked like a character in one of his own paintings. They came to a streamlet with a sandy bottom; despite the influx of new rain, the water ran clear.

"Would you like to drink?" he asked. She always walked with her little shallow tin cappie hanging from her waist, and she untied it now and handed it to him.

He knelt down upon the wet moss and dipped the cappie into the stream. Still on his knees before her he held out the cup. She took it from his fingers and he looked at her as she drank. She lowered it from her lips and to his extended hand. He did not dip it in the stream again, but put it to his own lips and drained it.

The next day Effie saw the sketch he had made of their walk. Everett drew continually and had made many amusing records of their holiday exploits. This drawing, in sepia ink, showed him kneeling before her. Both their hands touch the cappie, his in offering, hers in receiving. She studied it in silence. The eyes meeting, the hands touching the same proffered object recalled her of a sudden to his 'Isabella'.

In the corner was the monogram he used to sign his work, a large curving 'M' bisected by a descending 'J', with his middle initial E centred in the M. But on this one he had closed the terminals of the M so it looked like a heart, a heart enclosing the E that also began her own name.

Light, Descending

It rained interminably at Brig o' Turk. From almost the first day the fair weather they hoped for was denied them. The new hotel was comfortable but costly; with so few visitors in the area it must charge what it could for those who came. After a week they moved to the little schoolmaster's cottage. They were given a small sitting room with two minute closets at one end for bedrooms, furnished with a cot each and little else. Effie hung her clothing on a file of nails in hers, and Everett joked that in his little "snuffbox of a crib" he could open the window, close the door, and shave, all without getting out of bed. John slept on the broad sofa in an alcove of the sitting room.

If Millais thought the accommodation unusual he did not at first admit this to himself. As there was no actual bedroom in the cottage for the married couple, it was perhaps more decorous and practical for them all to live as brothers and sister, each to their own small beds. The walls were board thin and he could hear Effie moving inside her tiny room, just as he was certain she could hear him. Yet as the weeks became months he could not help but occasionally consider the import of these arrangements, though he strove to drive such thoughts, invasive and unworthy as he found them, from his mind. He did not allow himself to wonder that, five years into their marriage, the Ruskins had as yet no children.

"Rain again," said Everett one morning, calling through his closed door as he finished dressing. The rain, moderate overnight, was now a downpour outside his none too tight window; a little pool on the sill needed always to be mopped up.

"Another day's work on my index," responded John from the sitting room, without much regret. Once they had determined to stop in Brig o' Turk, he had had his father send up the materials needed to extract the huge index for *The Stones of Venice*. Always an early riser, he had been at work by lamplight.

"More battledore and shuttlecock," Effie answered.

Mornings were the happiest time of the day, the cheery calling out to each other as they all three dressed, the hearty breakfast by the schoolmaster's wife awaiting them, the expectation—usually dashed—that the day might be fine. To Effie Everett's presence was almost like that of her younger brother George; he made her laugh. They made up silly names for each other—he called her the Countess, and she dubbed him a Duke. His thinness made him refer to himself as "a specimen of a living paper-knife" and his unruly curls his "cockatoo crop." He was always clowning, always drawing, and alarmingly accident prone, with the endearing clumsiness of a young giraffe who hasn't yet mastered its legs. And he was good for John, she saw. John had "taken up" Everett. Once he began looking seriously at the work of the Brotherhood, it was clear that Millais possessed not only superior technical skill, but superior pictorial ability fuelled by a rare imagination. Millais was the genius of the group, and John would spare no effort to foster and guide such genius.

Everett began his painting of John by painting another of her, sitting on the rocks with her needlework, very near the place he would pose John. It was a small try-out of his ability to capture the intricate folds of the gneiss and the foam of the rapid waters. John even made his own watercolour of a large rock of gneiss, so Everett could see how best it might be painted. By the time the larger, whiter canvas arrived from Edinburgh, the rain had become persistent. When he was at last able to work, his progress was tediously, but they all knew, necessarily, slow. He had blocked in the shape that John would occupy, and spent his first day producing two inches of exquisite foliage near his head.

Whenever the rain ceased they would make haste to the site, Crawley carrying Everett's paint box, he his easel, and John the walking stick he was posed with. Everett's brother William, who remained lodged at the hotel, sometimes painted watercolours nearby, or fished for trout.

Any day that Everett could paint, Effie sat next him on the rocks, almost back to back, leaning against him to shelter the book in her hands from the wind. She felt her voice grow stronger with the effort of making sure artist and model could hear her. It was Dante's journey into Hell she read aloud.

"Ouf! Ah! Got you on that one!"

Effie and John and the Millais brothers were in the little school-room at the end of the cottage, battledore rackets in hands, whacking the feathered shuttlecock between them. The school room was little more than a converted barn, and the children only came for lessons in the morning. If it was pouring rain outside, as it was now, they could retire here to play and get some exercise.

Effie had a good eye and had played for years with her siblings, and could more than keep up her end of the game when one of the others flung the feathered shuttlecock her way. But when she tired and sat down to watch, the three men played with a phrenzy. Whether it was because of being cooped-up so much, or their natural competiveness coming out, or the fact they had a spectator in her, she couldn't guess. Today they lunged and leapt until they panted, cried out challenges, and charged red-faced about the sanded floor.

"Got you! Got you! You're mine!" shouted Everett, who had driven John around a table in pursuit of the flying shuttlecock. But John tipped it with his battledore before it touched the floor, and sent it flinging back to Everett.

"Mere presumption," answered John, pushing his hair out of his eyes with his free hand.

Everett dove and returned the shuttlecock with a slashing blow, his battledore sounding in the heavy air. With his long arms and legs he had a decided advantage over John or William when it came to reach. He sent it right back to John, and John returned it.

William stood holding his battledore, waiting for one of them to cast the shuttlecock to him. Neither of them did; they played as if they were alone. They staggered backwards or pivoted to the side, scrambling to reach and then return the object of their attention with a violence bordering on the vengeful.

Effie was no longer laughing and clapping, cheering them on. When John at last let the shuttlecock drop to the floor she was relieved to see Everett immediately resume his good nature.

He sprung forward and plucked the battered missile up to save John the effort of doing so, and thrust out his hand to receive his beaten opponent's congratulations.

John wrote his father nearly every day, with letters in return just as often. His father was concerned with the expanding length of the Highland holiday, and wanted John to get back to work on the next volume of *Modern Painters*. Mr. Ruskin had early signalled this as his son's defining masterwork and was impatient with the interruptions caused by John's architectural books, and now the lectures he was writing. As their stay in Brig o' Turk lengthened John needed to ask for more funds, which he hated doing. The Millais brothers paid for themselves of course, but even in so homely a place there were expenses to meet. He sent along a packet of drawings Millais had made of Effie, assuring his father that they were worth several pounds each.

Mr. Ruskin had sent up some bottles of Amontillado to supplant the harsh and undrinkable whisky which was the only spirit available to them. And the gentlemen complaining that the entire summer was passing without the eating of a single strawberry had caused Effie to write to Bowerswell to have a few delicacies sent them. William and Crawley both proved avid fishermen, and provided them almost daily with trout, and to that was added fresh peas, blackcurrant puddings, butter, and even champagne to augment their dinners.

After dinner she and the Millais brothers walked until dark along the stream course, telling stories and listening for nightbirds, while John retired to the sitting room to further his index or work on the architectural lectures he was to give in Edinburgh when they left here. Effie felt in no hurry to return to the hideously furnished house on Herne Hill—next door to John's boyhood home—where they were now obliged to live. The Park Street townhouse had been replaced by Mr. Ruskin with a dowdy suburban house decorated in so garish a manner that even John could not defend his father's taste. The lovely brougham was gone, and to get into town Effie had to ask use of the Ruskin's carriage, allowed her only once a week. Here, back in the verdant dells of her homeland, Effie put this out of her mind. She felt stronger and fitter than she had in many months. Despite the dismal weather she had not spent so much time out of doors since her girlhood. They even took their plates down to the rocks and ate their dinners by the swollen stream.

Light, Descending

If the perpetual rain limited painting time it fuelled other activities. For the sheer challenge of building something John and William rolled up their trouser legs and set to work deepening a channel through the stream. They cut saplings to use as pries and Effie laughed, disloyally perhaps, at the whiteness of her husband's bare legs and his determination at their task. She and Everett sat together upon the bank under a large umbrella, sketch books on knees, lifting their heads to check the construction efforts. Everett was giving her drawing lessons, and praised her growing ability with every new attempt at fern or flower. Knee deep in the water before them, pry in hand, John spoke of each type of stone they encountered, not just the geological history, but its allegorical significance. Much of it was fascinating but some of it seemed sheer nonsense. Overhearing John's continuous commentary with its digressions and contradictions made the two sketchers on the banks smile.

At night Effie and Everett sat in the little sitting room and quietly drew side by side while John worked on his lectures. She found a tiny child's bubble pipe one day and blew bubbles about the room in silent delight, breaking into laughter only when one landed on either of the surprised men. Spurred by John, Everett began drawing designs for new Gothic-inspired churches; columns crowned with heavily foliated vegetation, and huge arched windows in which embracing angels, all bearing Effie's face, held each other. When John was ready to quit his own work Everett read aloud. He had brought Tennyson's new "In Memoriam" with him, and read this poem of grieving with affecting feeling.

"I envy not in any moods—The captive void of noble rage—The linnet born within the cage—That never knew the summer woods...I hold it true, whate'er befall; I feel it, when I sorrow most; 'Tis better to have loved and lost—Than never to have loved at all..."

Effie was watching Everett's face as he read. His voice had dropped in pitch at this last line. Their eyes met for just a moment, and she lowered her head over her embroidery.

The rain made progress on John's portrait excruciatingly slow. Some days the midges were dreadful too, and Effie draped a veil over her wide-awake to protect herself. Everett took to tying a fabric sack over his head, with just cut-outs for eyes and nostrils, and then made fun of himself in a drawing showing himself so attired working at his sketchbook. He built a tent on the rocks, just large enough to shelter his easel and paint-box and himself from the wet. From it he could continue work on the trees, water, and rock-wall background of John's portrait. On a day when John was standing for it Everett asked the nature of the rocks on which he stood.

"I've always thought the undulations of the strata of gneiss to be a symbol of perpetual fear," John answered. "A sort of perpetual monument, if you will, to the infancy of the rock, folded in and upon itself while soft, through tremor and tremendous pressure."

Denmark Hill August 15th 1853

My dear John

I am not sure you have read the sermons I send I think you have not—glancing over it it seems to me even more admirable than it did when I heard it preached...Mr. Gray of Perth mentions that you have some purpose of giving a course of Lectures in

Edinburgh. I cannot reconcile myself to the thought of your bringing yourself personally before the world until you are somewhat older and stronger perhaps superstition may have something to do with it. I do not say to your father anything about it but I should be better satisfied if you continued to benefit the public by writing until you are turned forty two—pray do not let anything I write about this annoy or irritate you...I would rather be your Mother than the mother of the greatest Kings or Heros past or present—you know how all you say or do think or feel interests...My kind regards to Mr Millais I think of you always and pray for you always My love and best blessings to you both— how does Effie keep her health are your throat and eyes better ever My Dearest John

Your Affect Mother M Ruskin

Effie finished bandaging Everett's hand.

"I think you have had quite enough activity for the day, Mr. Millais," she said, but without reproach. His left thumb was badly mashed, and although he denied it she knew from the whiteness of his furrowed brow that he was in throbbing pain.

"Yes, my lady. That is likely the last time your humble servant attempts stepping stones for the Countess." They had all been down by the stream, and at one of its widest, shallowest points he had thought to take a page from John's book and build something. He was laying stepping stones so she might cross over dry-shod when one of the heavy rocks, slimy with growth, slipped and fell upon another. The left hand was crushed between them and he had screamed before he knew it.

"Thankfully it is not your painting-hand," John had remarked when they had all examined the damage.

Effie had walked with him back to the cottage, watching him wince as he held the hand before him, squeezing it at the wrist like a dying thing. Their landlady had brought her a basin and linen, and she had bathed his hand in warm water and gently bandaged each finger. All were abraded, but the thumb was truly injured.

"I'll lose the nail, for sure," he said, when she was done.

"Yes, you will," she said, "but it will grow back even stronger." She smiled at him, and the corners of his mouth turned up in return. She almost had to laugh, and keep herself from tousling his hair.

"You really have had quite the day," she said again. His nose was swollen, and a fresh cut lay across the bridge. In the morning while bathing in the deepest part of the stream he had struck his face against an underwater outcrop. He had been with William and they returned with both their handkerchiefs and Everett's shirt red with blood.

He looked down at the bandaged hand in his lap and shook his head. "I've felt seedy for a while," he admitted. "What with Hunt planning to leave for the Holy Land— I'll miss him awfully. And my friend Deverell, who can't sell a painting because the public hasn't any eyes, is ill; and now the rain..."

She sat down next him, perfectly quietly, and waited to see if he would go on.

"If you were not so delightful, I would not stay," he told her. When she moved to stand he put out his injured hand imploringly.

"No, please, I'm so sorry." She paused and he made light of it by a new beginning. "Countess—I beg your royal pardon." She sat down again.

"It's just that...all the rain, the delay, the slowness of the work..." He stopped and then found a train. "Hunt, who I love like William—perhaps more as he's such a good man, God forgive me—is truly heading to Syria, and I just don't think I can bear his going. And Walter Deverell—you met him once I think, at Gower Street—who supports his young brothers and sisters—there's something wrong, gravely wrong, with his kidneys, and I think he shall die. And he can't sell a painting, but I've written to Hunt and we ourselves will offer ninety guineas for one. And Hunt himself—blast him—forgive me—has sold just enough work, and now got a £20 prize from Liverpool Academy to boot, so he's off at last to the East to paint his religious subjects. He'll be gone years, and since he will be a runaway I'm begging him to let me join him next year. Three friends of mine have died since I've been here, my mother's letters tell me, and I'm having a hard time sleeping at night and I just—I just wish there was some sort of monastery I could go to."

Effie stood once more, and questioned him in a voice softer and graver than she had yet used with him. "Would that help—going away?"

It was at this point a rhetorical question, for Euphemia Chalmers Ruskin, née Gray, had known for several weeks that she was loved by John Everett Millais. He looked helplessly back at her.

"No, it wouldn't help," he answered, and left.

William had to leave to return to London, and Everett moved out of his little "crib" and back into the hotel. But after a few nights there he asked to return to the schoolmaster's cottage with Effie and John. Then he moved back to the hotel, and then returned yet again. His painting tent washed away in a torrent. The air grew sharply colder. Progress on the portrait was dismally slow, but he vowed to stay on and complete as much of it as he could; she and John must soon be leaving for Edinburgh. There was no way Millais could complete the figure of John, that would have to be done in his Gower Street studio, and despite the increasing chill he worked steadily on the trees and rocks surrounding his subject.

October 18 1853

My dear Mother

...I wish that the country agreed with Millais as well as it does with me, but I don't know how to manage him and he does not know how to manage himself. He paints until his limbs are numb, and his back has as many aches as joints in it. He won't take exercise in the regular way, but sometimes starts and takes races of seven or eight miles if he is in the humour: sometimes won't, or can't eat, any breakfast or dinner, sometimes eats enormously without seeming to enjoy anything. Sometimes he is all excitement, sometimes depressed, sick and faint as a woman, always restless and unhappy. I never saw such a miserable person on the whole...

"Awey-yegoo," Everett said as Effie set off with him for their evening walk. She laughed at his mimicking her Scot's burr; it was a habit to say "away you go" when she said goodbye to anyone.

The evenings were much shorter now, and they could not stay out long. Effie wore her brown jacket and he was wrapped in the tartan he wore against the cold. They walked in silence along the path, passing the place where he had painted her sitting on the rocks. The torrent was loud and they kept their silence until a little further on at the site where he had laboured so long on the unfinished portrait of John.

He glanced at the bare rocks. "This stay has meant so much to me—I hardly feel like the same man I was in June." They walked along the path until he spoke again. "With everything that's happened—the rain, my silly accidents, the snail's pace of my work—I'm grateful to you, and your husband, for asking me."

He had paused but she moved wordlessly ahead. He regained her side and she felt he was waiting for her to respond. If she did not speak now, perhaps she never would. She walked more quickly, again almost leaving him behind. He caught up once more and she feared he might begin to speak.

"He is not my husband," she said quickly before she could stop herself. They paused in the path and she turned to face him.

He looked at her blankly and gave his head the slightest of shakes. She had no idea what to say, but felt of a sudden emboldened by the question in his eyes, emboldened even by his bewilderment.

"He is *not* my husband," she repeated.

His eyes widened, his mouth worked wordlessly. "What then..." he began, but did not finish.

She must, must tell him, speak the truth she could not confide to her own mother.

"He has not made me his wife," is what she said.

"Not made you his wife...you mean that after all this time you—"

So great was his confusion that Millais could not complete the thought aloud. His walks with Effie, and her trust in him; Ruskin's oddness, and the sleeping arrangements. None of it made sense and all of it made sense.

"Yes," she said, wanting to spare him from saying it and her from hearing it. "I have never been, and am not now, his wife in truth."

She thought he might collapse; he seemed to sway. She knew her own body to be trembling, but had never felt so clear-headed and sharply aware.

There was a stone wall near them and he sunk down upon it. She stood before him and waited for him to speak.

He lifted both hands to his head and held them there. When he brought them away his face looked like that of child who had suffered a cruel hurt.

"He is monstrous," was what he said.

Seeing the tears spring in his eyes forced her own to well. She had made her declaration and he had received it. Now she feared to speak more. Her slightest gesture might result in ruin for them both, and she would not further implicate or influence him.

She moved well away from him, and when he raised his hands to her she thought her heart would break.

"What am I to do?" he asked. But Millais knew. He must go as soon as he could, go away from her so that she might not be harmed. He could not stay another day now, knowing the truth as he did.

At six o'clock on a late spring evening five months later, two gentlemen of the courts arrived at Denmark Hill and inquired after Mr. John Ruskin. He was in his study pulling books for a summer-long continental tour for which he and his parents were readying themselves. He had that day taken Effie to King's Cross and put her on a train bound for a visit to her family in Scotland. What he did not know was that Mr. and Mrs. Gray were already secretly in London, and at the very first stop out of King's Cross, at Hitchin, they had stepped on the train and found their waiting daughter.

The gentlemen were very polite and after identifying themselves and ascertaining that he was Mr. John Ruskin, served him with an order of annulment proceedings concerning his so-called marriage to Miss Euphemia Chalmers Gray, falsely known as Mrs. John Ruskin.

One of the gentlemen carried a packet which held a wedding ring, household keys, and account book, all carefully kept by their former possessor. This they presented to John James.

Chapter Thirteen

The Lamp of Life

London: April 1855

"Please to consider yourself a valuable object, something worth conserving."

Ruskin realised once it was out how awkward it must sound. "What I mean, Miss Siddal, is that if you were—let's say—a majestic tree in danger of being cut down to no good purpose, or a cathedral to have its best bits of ancient ornament all hammered down—as I have watched to my distress throughout France and Italy—I should take all reasonable—and possibly some quite unreasonable— precautions to stop such barbarism. To have you continue to labour in a bonnet shop when you should be painting is tantamount to these acts."

Miss Elizabeth Siddal sat almost motionless in her wooden chair in the little projecting gallery that hung out over the Thames. Gabriel Rossetti, that gypsy-romantic whose house on Chatham Place, hard by Blackfriars Bridge this was, sat there too, leaning forward in a lumpy chair covered over in some vaguely oriental stuff. He was smiling at his guest. Miss Siddal remained still, and unsmiling.

"What do you say, Gug?" asked Gabriel after some moments had passed. "Mr. Ruskin's offer is unusual, granted, but what man amongst us wouldn't be proud for such endorsement?"

Ruskin looked at the object of his unusual solicitation and waited for her response. From the first time he had visited Gabriel in his unhealthy and eccentric "crib" he had been taken by this young woman's work. She herself had been absent—he was uncertain where she actually lived, and frankly did not wish to know—but as soon as he saw the drawing upon the second easel he asked Gabriel about it. Gabriel could be slippery in his answers, and it took him a while to teaze out the story from different sources.

It was poor dead Walter Deverell who had first found her. He had want of models—all these young painters did, but most especially those working in the style of Pre-Raphaelitism; there was a rare and certain aspect they sought. Deverell had caught a glimpse of Miss Siddal in the millinery shop in Cranbourne Alley. Pale skin, masses of copper hair. And so slender as to be convincing as a maiden disguised as a page. He thought she would do, and perfectly, for the part of Viola in the scene from *Twelfth Night* he wanted to paint. She went on to sit for Hunt before Gabriel had claimed her.

It was Gabriel—who could scarcely draw himself—who began teaching her to draw; but that was, Ruskin thought upon consideration, one of the reasons her art was developing along such interesting lines. Both Gabriel and Miss Siddal were *original* in expression. Figures devoid of almost any modelling, a colouration either ghostly or garish, extreme flatness of plane in which the subject was presented. And what subjects! Gabriel of course went back and back again to Dante, she to the gristliest of old folk tales, and both of them to Shakespeare's bottomless font.

When he first saw her work Ruskin offered to buy up all her drawings from Gabriel on the spot. He had already engaged Gabriel to make him a series of paintings taken from Dante, and the thought of discovering and fostering a new and unique ability such as Miss Siddal's could only add relish to the association—Gabriel himself was so contrary that he rejected half of Ruskin's advice yet took all his money. Gabriel had hazarded to suggest the sum of £25 for the lot, but Ruskin would not accept them for less than £30. Gabriel asked him around to Chatham Place more frequently after that, and at last the drawings' creator was now before him.

"My proposition is simply this: that you leave off your labours trimming bonnets and turn whole-hearted and single-mindedly to your art. I will pay you an annual sum of £150, and ask in return that I be given first pick of all your output."

Gabriel clapped his palms upon his knees. A turn of Miss Siddal's head and a glance of her odd-coloured eyes silenced him before he spoke. It was her decision to make, Ruskin could see, and it made him all the more hopeful about her ability to maintain and express her distinct artistic perception.

He had a pretty clear idea of how Gabriel had described him to her earlier—as perhaps an undeniably queer chap; that his pamphlet about Pre-Raphaelitism had actually been all about Turner and a little about work; but that certain people listened to him nonetheless. And he had money in his pockets.

"I should rather sell my work on its merits, piece by piece," she said to him, "than accept your offer of annual support." Yet by the time Ruskin had left Chatham Place—needing to cover his nose and mouth against the foulness of the low-water-mark Thames—she had agreed.

As he drove home to Denmark Hill Miss Siddal occupied his thoughts. The passivity of her face suggested to his mind the stateliness of white marble monuments to long-dead Florentine princesses. But pale as her skin was it had the warmth, and apparent smoothness, of ivory.

There was something otherworldly about her, he realised, something close to unsubstantial. She was like a reflection of a golden mountain in a crystal lake, he thought.

Then he recalled a moment during their interview when she had parted her lips without speaking. He had met her image prisoned in a frame years before he had met the original—the singing, ecstatic Ophelia, floating down the flower-strewn river in her madness. His lost Millais had painted her.

Chapter Fourteen

The Lamp of Power & The Lamp of Beauty: 1858-1871

Turin: Summer 1858

The girl had flung herself down on a mound of warm sand, her brown arms thrown over her head, her long dark hair falling in loose tangles over face and shoulders. Her ragamuffin companions still ran and played along the river bank, and their sharp Italian cries rang in the hot afternoon air. She did not lift her head to their calls. Her faded black dress—little better than a rag—lay high upon her naked legs. The bodice of the dress was stretched tight over her ribs, showing breasts scarcely protrudent. Here and there about her arms and thighs sand was stuck in tawny patches.

She had the complete ease of a basking serpent, and Ruskin thought he had never seen anything more beautiful. He had come to Turin to gaze at formal splendour, but the beauty of a slum child stopped him in his tracks. One of the boys she had been playing with now approached and in dialect unintelligible cried out at her—an insult, he imagined, for she sprung up like a roused snake and shrieked back her answer. She was Alecto, and raced in angry justice after the taunting boy. He watched her until she was out of sight.

Ruskin had left the Alps, for the first time a little discontented with them, understanding at last his father's lack of sympathy with mountain ranges. To his surprise he found himself rather looking forward to visiting again the hoary capital of the Sardinian kingdom, of touring the palace--which as a youth with his parents he had chafed at wasting his time in—and walking in the laddered shade of the colonnaded piazzas. In Alpine basins he had been searching for specific views captured long ago by Turner, disappointed that the master—despite the warnings he recalled—had not recorded what was before him in ravine or mountain pass with complete fidelity; had in fact augmented or subtracted from the scene for sake of visual balance within four final gilded edges.

Most of all he came to Turin to behold again a painting by Paul Veronese. He had not written kindly in the past of 'The Presentation of the Queen of Sheba to Solomon', finding it guilty of luxury and idolatry. Now he was working, slowly and not very effectively, on the final volume of *Modern Painters* and wished to see it anew. Its imagery was troublesomely impressed on his mind and once before it he might understand why.

The massive Mannerist canvas was crowded with figures of courtiers, counsellors, slaves, camels and dogs, all looking, pointing, turning, or gesticulating. The backdrop of all this focused activity was a perfectly symmetrical classical archway opening to a cypress-dotted landscape. The young golden-haired hero sat at the extreme upper left corner of the piece, perched upon an impossibly high throne with an eagle and an imperturbable lion at his feet; the royal object of his royal gaze, splendid in her silks and pearls as large as quails-eggs, knelt in astonishment at his majesty in the far right.

The energy of her intent struck him; this was a Queen who *must* come to Solomon's court and see for herself, and having seen had no choice but to drop almost swooning into the arms of her waiting-women in acquiescence of his wisdom and prosperity so revealed. The glow of colour in the Queen's face, the amplitude of her gesture of surrender, the tender, almost juvenile profile of curly-haired Solomon, the black yet gleaming armour of an attendant knight, the richness of the ruched fabrics of the Queen's women, hung round with ropes of pearls all excited him beyond expectation. The Queen of

Sheba's tiny white dog, boldly confronting the viewer, delighted him.

He saw in it a triumphal procession of benediction pouring forth from Apollo-headed Solomon, King of Wisdom, down his chain of counsellors to the questing Queen and her train, enveloping all in his beneficent gaze. Every creature was beautiful to its type, King, Queen, warriors, priests, serving women, camels, birds, and dogs; all fulfilled perfectly their linked roles in a sumptuous economy forming under Solomon's gaze.

Ruskin was transported. Veronese he saw, was in all his worldliness no less than an archangel ordained by God with the gift of covering so many yards of canvas with magnificent figures in exquisite colouration. He was like Titian *noble* in his sensualism, and the frank animality of his conceptions led not to turpitude but spirituality. Veronese was boldly animal, like Homer and Shakespeare, or Tintoret, Titian, Turner— and confronted with their vigour they made 'holy' painters like Francia and Fra Angelico anaemic. Man, he saw, was perfected *animal*, and his happiness, health, and nobleness depended on the due power of every animal passion, as well as the cultivation of every spiritual tendency.

He would not run off to the Vaudois valleys but stay and copy such portions as were within his ken. He paid to have a scaffolding erected to lift him to the painting's level. He had not the slightest compunction in temporarily obscuring its view for others; he had seen the few seconds' attendance the English and American visitors afforded it and there were two other large Veroneses in the gallery they could also dismiss.

He dare not attempt the Queen of Sheba's own head; in its perfection of beauty it was beyond him, but he felt confident in copying a life size version of the head of the *chiaroscuro* ebony servant girl bearing gifts of two bejewelled

bird sculptures for their host. He then went on to a lovely
lady in waiting, her golden plaits a natural crown around her
head.

He had dined well the night before, and drunk a half-
pint of champagne prior to the *Opéra Comique*. The morning
he had left outside the gallery doors was fine, and being flung
open to that fineness through them came the strains of a
band playing in the campo. There on his scaffold, two feet
away from the triumph of Solomon's court, Ruskin was struck
with the gorgeousness of life.

Could it, he wondered, be possible that all this power
and beauty is adverse to the honour of the Maker of it? Has
God made faces beautiful and limbs strong–and created fiery
and fantastic energies—and created gold and pearls and
crystals and the sun that makes them gorgeous—only that all
these things may lead his creatures away from him? And is
this mighty Paul Veronese, in whose soul there is a strength
as of the snowy mountains—this man whose finger is as fire,
and whose eye is like the morning—is he, as he had once
thought, a servant of the devil? He would not believe it!

The following Sunday he sought out the Waldenstein
meeting house to hear service, the closest approximation to
the various evangelical congregations he might find at home.
It was a glorious, still, clear, Italian morning. He passed with
some reluctance out of it into the confines of a new church
built along the neo-Gothic lines he felt partially responsible
for and which in this instance he judged both vulgar and
unnecessarily large. It was a late morning service, conducted
in French to seventeen old women, rounded out by a few
decent looking French families and a handful of loutish
Turinois men, one of whom spat over the rows of empty
pews. The stranger from London sat behind them as a small
preacher in a squeaking voice expounded upon the
wickedness in every man's heart and assured them that all

those in Turin, in Italy, in the world, not within that chapel were damned.

He thought of his mother's intense fear of Roman Catholics, how every day he had spent alone in Florence or Venice she had prayed that he might not be ensnared by Popery. She might almost have him dead before Catholic.

He thought of Homer and Plato and Xenophon and all those good and wise thinkers who lived and died before the advent of Christ. He thought of the kindness of his "non-believing" friends—the American scholar Charles Eliot Norton who revered Christ as a great exemplar but held the *Reflections* of Marcus Aurelius in as high esteem; Robert and Elizabeth Barrett Browning with their modest but sincere religious philosophies; Thomas Carlyle's robust ethical but non-conforming mores—and could no longer accept that they were damned to eternal fiery torment. And he thought of the utter gorgeousness of Veronese's conception that he had spent all week aloft studying, and of the human carnality of the man from whose mind and hand this masterwork had issued.

He had raised his eyes to a window of the meeting house and the notion that all the tens of thousands of inhabitants of Turin at their various callings—in cathedral, church, café—were summarily damned struck him not only as impossible, but perversely absurd. He rose with the preacher in ringing mid-sentence and made his way out to the condemned city waiting in the light.

Ruskin had been called to Manchester the year before. The Art Treasures Exhibition had shown thousands of works of British and European art from Michael-Angelo to Millais, a vast survey of the development of art. It was thronged by viewers. There was also a programme of addresses by distinguished commentators.

He leapt at the invitation to participate. He enjoyed speaking, and surprised himself with his power of projecting his voice to the reaches of a crowded hall. Scorning the protection of the podium, he would walk to the very edge of the stage, hands thrust deep in his tailcoat pockets, rising up and down on his toes in rhythm to his ringing pronouncements. Hearing his audience laugh with recognition, or holding them silent in his thrall gave him a taste of the mastery actors enjoyed upon their stage.

He saw the haze of Manchester long before his train joined its own smut with that of the endlessly spewing smokestacks of the cotton mills. Manchester was the throbbing industrial centre of the nation, home of that school of thought that embodied *laissez-faire* economics. As proof of the excellence of those economics, the age expectancy of its residents was the lowest in Britain, 26 years.

As an intentional jab he had titled his address *The Political Economy of Art*. What was the 'value' of art? How should artists be recompensed? Who 'deserved' art? And perhaps most explosively, ought the state play any role in regard to art?

He told them it must. Art was a most definite form of wealth, and young painters should receive a decent income for their efforts, enough to eliminate the suffering endemic to the starting artist and ensure they might raise a family. As an enlightened state Britain had a moral responsibility to acquire and conserve the greatest works of art it could procure for the benefit of posterity, and responsibilities too, to prevent the destruction of art and architecture in Italy and France. To acquire and preserve it the nation should stand on the cliffs at

Dover and wave blank cheques in the eyes of the nations on the other side.

In impassioned language he decried the rampant waste resulting from modern taste—young married couples melting down handsome heirloom silver-services to have them re-cast in highly wrought, "fashionable" styles; the funeral industry with its demands for pomp and show, the outrageous and competitive tyranny of women's dress and its brutal exploitation of undernourished and overworked seamstresses—all must be seen as the selfishness and folly it is. In Art as in life, justice and prudence should prevail.

He delivered his lecture over two evenings to a largely middle class audience that received it with warm enthusiasm. *The Manchester Examiner and Times* termed it "arrant nonsense." The proponents of the famed economic theorists David Ricardo and John Stuart Mill scoffed at his words.

It was then he realised that economics was too important to be placed solely in the hands of those defined as 'economists'.

An opportunity to expand on his lectures presented itself. His publishers were planning a new periodical, and invited him to contribute. Thackeray was to be editor, and it was hoped Carlyle, Trollope, Mrs. Gaskell, Mrs. Browning, and Tennyson would also make an appearance in the pages of the new *Cornhill*.

He needed time and quiet to teaze out his essays, and wanted nothing so much as the sharp air of the high Alps. He settled in Chamonix and amongst gentians and wild roses went to work.

Once his main concern had been in instructing his readers how to look at art and architecture. But one could not stand before a landscape painting without considering the health of the water and soils it depicted, the lives and prospects of the field workers, the rightness or wrongness of the land usage, not even to the fate of the livestock.

He had earlier looked upon the artisan guilds of the Middle Ages and attributed their superior artistic output to the sense of self-determination and control each man enjoyed over his own portion of work. He had contrasted the fruits of their creative impetus with the cheap, showy, and shoddy produce wrought from the gross exploitation of mill and factory workers engaged in repetitive, dangerous and spirit-breaking labour. Now he stepped back to glimpse the economic foundations of modern life.

Wealth, he told his readers, is not the possession of a 'large stock of useful articles' as defined by John Stuart Mill; these articles must be of use to the owner. A horse, that most valuable of beasts, is useless if no one can ride; a sword if no one can strike, meat useless if no one can eat. Anything of real value must avail toward life.

Most astonishingly, Ruskin directly addressed the conscience of the consumer society made possible by mass production. In every object that is purchased, he insisted, the first consideration must be the condition of existence caused in the producers of that item; secondly, whether the sum paid is just to the producer, and lodged in his hands; and thirdly, to how much clear use, for food, knowledge, or joy, that this item can be put.

THERE IS NO WEALTH BUT LIFE.

He laboured over four introductory essays, paring his expository to convey his thought as concisely as possible, and returned to London never as satisfied with any bit of writing as he was with these. Thackeray ran them beginning in the August 1860 issue of *Cornhill Magazine.*

Reaction was swift and violent. *The Saturday Review* warned that "the world was not going to be preached to death by a mad governess," named the essays "eruptions of windy hysterics" and Ruskin himself "a paragon of blubbering." *The Manchester Examiner and Times* and the *Scotsman* were scarcely less rabid, and attacked Thackeray's judgement as editor. What was just as maddening were those reviews which dealt with the new directness of his literary style and not the substance of the essays.

The publishers of *Cornhill* deemed the papers too deeply tainted with socialistic heresy to suit subscribers, and ordered the fourth instalment to be the final. He was stunned. Not even his father, with his staunchly held capitalistic creed, had reacted as negatively as had the press; old Mr. Ruskin had even praised parts of the manuscripts for their elevated tone. Stingingly, he had the backing of none of his friends. The few that broached the topic commiserated about the harshness of the condemnations, but offered little support for the content of the essays. Thomas Carlyle alone was delighted with the papers, and unrestrained in his praise.

The sage and prophet of Chelsea wrote such an enthusiastic letter that Ruskin at once responded by asking if he might drop by number 5, Cheyne Row of an evening and pay his respects in person. "I have read your paper", Carlyle wrote, "with exhilaration, exultation, often with laughter, with *bravissimo*! Such a thing flung suddenly into half a million dull British heads on the same day, will do a great deal of good. I marvel in parts at the lynx-eyed sharpness of your logic, at the pincer-grip (red hot pincers) you take of certain bloated cheeks and blown up bellies..."

Ten years ago Carlyle had likened Ruskin to a bottle of beautiful soda water which incautiously drawn, might expel itself in the eyes of the unsuspecting and discomfited bearer. The younger man was mercurial, unanchored, and was squandering a fine intellect on endless musings on art rubbish which had profited—who? A dainty, dilettante soul, with a poet's temperament, thought Carlyle upon their first meeting;

and he, who had at age fourteen walked eighty miles to begin his own intellectual life at the University of Edinburgh, had read little since to undermine his first impressions. Now Ruskin was putting his shoulder to a heavier wheel, grinding the corn that might truly nourish men's souls, should they allow themselves to partake of it.

Carlyle was in the middle of his massive multi-volume history of Frederick the Great of Prussia, his right hand at this point so palsied that his niece must take down his words for him. Stop in his task he could not; were he blind, deaf, and dumb he should find some manner of recording the fruits of his labours.

His three volume history of *The French Revolution*, which had at last made his reputation, had been published a quarter century ago, after an exhausting gestation requiring two additional years to reconstruct the manuscript of the first volume. While in John Stuart Mill's keeping it had been burnt as waste paper by an unlettered house maid; what had there been to do but sit down and write it again? Grieving would have availed him not; nothing profited man but work. Close thy Byron, open thy Goethe, he had instructed the youth of the last generation. Eschew romantic self-absorption for a life dedicated to self-disciplined development of moral qualities.

Carlyle's satiric touchstone, his *Sartor Resartus*—the Tailor Re-tailored—had been variously attacked and ignored when it had been serialized years ago. Carlyle remembered receiving two—two!—letters of support for it, one from Emerson in America and another from an Irish priest. His semi-autobiographical, and to critics, hallucinatory ramblings about the nature of faith and reality, in the guise of a philosophy of clothing, so bewildered readers of *Fraser's Magazine* that many threatened cancelling their subscriptions.

Light, Descending

He knew the critics—blockheads who dared not unstopper their ears, who had once condemned his own works for their outrageous language, fantastic juxtapositions, and verbal wordplay—had been after Ruskin before, but never like this. Now, and unexpectedly, they were yoked together, and Carlyle exulted in finding himself in a minority of two.

Jane Carlyle greeted Ruskin when he arrived to renew their acquaintanceship. Her visitor bore an armful of lilies for her. As she took them she saw that their dark pollen had come off on Ruskin's hands. Their fragrance filled her head as she turned from him to find a vase. Unbidden she recalled the morning following her wedding thirty-five years ago. At dawn her new husband had ripped through the garden of their bridal home, tearing blossoms from plants, shredding them in rage and frustration in shamed fury at his failure in the marriage bed. Theirs had been a five year courtship, and it ended with Carlyle's hands stained with pollen from ravaged flowers. Nor were they ever to be truly man and wife. She had yearned for children and these, and much else, were to be denied her. It had been the great secret, and the great tragedy, of their lives.

After Turner died, Ruskin was asked continually when he would commence the definitive study of the man and his work. He had for years quietly assumed he would undertake such a task, but with the old man gone, Ruskin's scheme for the book collapsed like a skeleton deprived of ligaments and flesh. Some vital breath had gone out of him at the loss, a loss he felt more heavily every year. A great lamp of Art had been extinguished that might never be re-lit. At Turner's death more of nature and her mysteries were forgotten in that one long sob than could be learnt again by the eyes of a whole generation to come. Turner had seen everything, remembered everything, spiritualised everything in the visible world. Five volumes of *Modern Painters* had explicitly and implicitly argued Turner's enormity of vision and aptitude. There was nothing Ruskin could now add that a thoughtful viewer could not himself discover before one of Turner's best pictures. He felt with keen acuteness the futility of any kind of summing up, felt even the indecency of the attempt.

Yet he had never known where he stood in Turner's firmament, whether the old man thought him pest, champion, collector, or humbug. Of Ruskin's written work Turner had ever been silent. He had defended and extolled the master's pictures since he was seventeen years old, and Ruskin had no idea if—beyond his initial letter to him—Turner had ever read a single word of it. But one day on a visit to Denmark Hill Turner did something which gratified his host as much as any spoken encomium. Pausing before Ruskin's watercolour of the 'Falls of Schaffhausen' he pointed for a long moment at the churning white waters. Ruskin had *seen*, and faithfully recorded. The wordless commendation embodied in that single gesture of acknowledgement would suffice.

And Ruskin had no desire to plunge deeper into the biographical details of the man. This son of a Maiden Lane barber had come by his dejection of spirits honestly. His mother was carried off mad from the house when Turner was but five, to die, raving, in an asylum four years later. For decades he had attached snippets of his endless poem, the *Fallacies of Hope*, to his canvases. Blustering, secretive, and melancholic, the mounting bleakness of his inner vision was mirrored in the whirlwind, maelstrom, shipwreck, disaster, and ruin of his canvases, a turmoil redeemed by glaring sun that to Turner was God. It was the light that first caught one's eye, pulling one towards a Turner picture. And great light, Ruskin knew, always implies great shadow—somewhere.

Chapter Fifteen

The Lamp of Power & The Lamp of Beauty

London: Spring 1861

> *Dearest St Crumpet—You can't think how fusty the carriage was from Prato to Florence—but of course you can, you can think of EVERYTHING, including fusty carriages should you like, but Mama says you're too fine a gentleman to bother with such —but we are here now and tomorrow we go and see Mr Giotto's Campanile at the Duomo and I shall look at it with care just as you told me, and make Emily and Percy look too. And I am trying to draw what I see in the sketchbook you gave me and hold my pencil that way you showed me. And trying not to get scolded, I wanted to give my hat the blue one to a little dusty girl that was in the garden of the hotel but Bun—Miss Bunnett stopped me. She is Bun to me and so you are delicious Crumpet, but I think I should add the St for respect. I wish St Crumpet you were with me too. And that it were not so hot, it is too hot for Irish roses. Love—your Rosie-posie.*

Ruskin felt a sudden flush spring upon his cheek; his ears burned. "I am not alone," he said aloud. "I shall not *be* alone."

He read the letter again. She had never called him "Dearest" before, nor ended as she had— "Love—your Rosie-posie." *His* Rosie. His love. Rosie posie, Rosie fair, Rosie light and sweet as air. He thought of her oval face and more-slightly pointed chin; the tiny white-gold curls at the nape of the slender neck; eyes neither blue nor grey but some

un-named alloyage possessing the smokiness of dusk; the lips
perfect in profile but a little too full, almost petulant when
she turned to you—a glistening rosebud, offering itself. The
gravity of her gaze, like that, he imagined, of St. Ursula as a
child. The face he had first loved when she was ten and he,
nearing forty, had called at her mother's request to meet the
children and perhaps consent to give them a drawing lesson
or two.

For that first lesson at Denmark Hill he had sketch
books and new-sharpened pencils all prepared, and meant to
begin the initial lesson with the elementary rules of
perspective and the analysis of the essential qualities of
triangles. The company was so delightful that the pencils
remained untouched. After trooping the female LaTouches
up to his mother—confined by infirmity to her bedroom
suite, she gave the girls each a kiss for being able to identify
two obscure passages in *Exodus*—he had relished taking them
out into his gardens. The older Emily showed polite interest,
but Rose devoured all she saw. Her pink cheeks and dancing
eyes spurred him to drollery, and when they reached the pig-
pens he soberly introduced them to the grunting black-and-
white spotted denizens, insisting they were most intelligent
and spoke perfect Irish. Even Maria LaTouche burst out
laughing, but Rose laughed loudest and most charmingly of
all.

They traced their way back to the house, past the
kitchen gardens and flower beds to where golden-cheeked
peaches grew pleached against a red brick wall. The
September heat carried the fragrance of the ripe fruit to his
nose. There had been peaches too, long ago at Herne Hill,
but he had been forever forbidden to taste them lest he suffer
stomach-ache. Here in the gardens of a vaster house he
plucked the reddest peach before him and held out it to Rose.
Before her mother could stay her she had taken the fruit in
her teeth.

Light, Descending

Back in his study he had shown the trio the paintings. This was, after all, what they had truly come for, the eighty Turner oils and watercolours, and the sheaves of drawings by Prout and Hunt.

Emily had glanced over his cases of minerals and crystals before seating herself in a chair by the window. But Rose stood, sometimes on tiptoe, fast by his side as he spoke about the paintings with her mother. Mrs. LaTouche was silent for some time, and then turned to him with simple directness. The rustle of her dress released a faint and wholly agreeable fragrance from the Violetta di Parma toilette water she used.

"You who live with, and for Art"—he could hear the capital letter, yet it was not at all insincere—"will not easily believe that this hour will live before me, and my Rose, for many years to come." She inclined her head ever so slightly to John Brett's 'Val d'Aosta', showing herself in possession of a better eye than Ruskin had deemed probable.

When he took a few Turner drawings down from the patterned walls so he could point out the line work and shadowing, Rose leaned in over his arm and clung to it. He found himself addressing her more and more, and by the time tea was served Rose placed herself at his right, not at all shyly.

Before she and her mother and sister left he ran back upstairs and pulled a copy of his *King of the Golden River* from his shelves and gave it to her. It was, he told Rose LaTouche, a book he had written long ago for another little girl.

As his friendship with the family deepened, Maria LaTouche, mother of this remarkable creature, intrigued him. Mrs. LaTouche was more than what he had expected, in all ways: more pretty in her rather monumental way, more self-

175

assured, more knowledgeable about things that delighted him—she recognised and quickly named *Hylocomium splendens* amongst the mosses in his garden—than any absurdly rich Irish banker's wife had a right to be. John LaTouche was of Huguenot stock, and had prospered hugely in the Irish private banking system, but was no fast-riding hard-drinking squire. Ruskin almost wished he were.

From nearly their first meeting he had found LaTouche a fervent evangelical, free and easy only in the number of times he professed his gladness in his own salvation. LaTouche bore that happy certainty that all those who differed from his steadfast belief of Biblical inerrancy were destined for the eternal torments of Hell. Ruskin knew he was suspect on theological grounds in John LaTouche's eyes. More troubling was that LaTouche did not understand his fascination with his youngest child and feared his influence over her.

He recalled sitting shoulder to shoulder with Rose as he guided her drawing pencil, feeling her soft breath upon his hand as she bent over it. A gentle aroma of the lamb stew which had made her dinner clung about her. Her thin frame was almost elfin, the wrist slight and blue-veined. It had made him giddy to study her. He held his breath as his eye travelled along the curve of the tiny ear lobe; he inhaled sharply as it traced the delicate folds and crevices of her small pink ear.

"And do you like teaching me to draw?" she had asked. The girl's mother had several times told her how important was this sad man with his sandy whiskers. Being able to make him happy must be a difficult thing to do, Rose imagined. She cocked her head at him, smiling as she awaited his answer.

"There is nothing that gives me greater pleasure," he returned, with an exaggerated gravity that he hoped hid the truth of his answer.

"More than teaching Emily or Percy?" she demanded.

A lie was out of the question.

"Yes. More."

She looked down at her drawing pad. "Good. When I am naughty I feel I would rather break a thing than share it with them, and I don't like to share you." She turned her luminous face back to him and wagged her pencil his way.

Harming such a creature was impossible. She could no more be harmed than sunlight could be. One might shut out the sun or gouge out one's eyes but it would shine regardless.

Now Rose was thirteen, and in Italy, and he might never see her again. But knowing her—simply knowing she lived, and loved him, righted his ship. Hers was the steady hand on the keel, and Heaven—if there was such a place—knew he was ripped from his mooring these days. She was worthy of all adoration; she commanded it.

He could not work. Everything Ruskin put his hand to slipped from his grasp; his mind would spy an avenue of thought or pose a question worthy of investigation and within days or weeks find itself down a blind alley. He was given to enthusiasms and used to working on many projects at once, any of which he abandoned without regret when things more compelling crossed his path. But there had always been the steady drumbeat of his major efforts keeping time for him, setting the pace. After nearly twenty years of labour and twenty-five hundred pages *Modern Painters* was ended, all five volumes of it, the last painfully wrenched out of him just to please his father, who feared not living to see the completion of his son's *magnum opus*. He felt indeed he

hadn't actually finished it; he simply could not go on. For this
last volume he had thrown away half of his unruly text—
cutting out all the wisest parts as too good for this
generation—and most of the meticulous illustrations he had
made were spoiled in the engraving process and not used.
And now he was spent.

He had written in a phrenzy of white heat, and his
youth and young manhood had been consumed by the
creation of systems, the codification of art-theory, the teasing-
out of the laws—exact laws, he had ascertained—upon which
true aesthetic criticism must be based—nothing less than
discovering and then laying down rules for what was
beautiful. For naming Beauty itself. And what did he have to
show for it? Society matrons who wished to 'show him off' at
parties he despised.

He was still sick at heart—at stomach too, if he allowed
himself—at finding sketches whose indecent subject had
revolted him as he worked with the Turner Bequest. In his
will Turner had named him as an Executor with power over
his gift to the nation of a staggering 19,000 drawings. He had
laboured for months in the dank basement of the National
Gallery sorting and labelling these works, rescuing from
mildew those haphazardly stored by Turner—always careless
of his own work—or even worse those rotting under the
auspices of the Gallery itself.

He reckoned that as many as 10,000 drawings might be
considered for future exhibition, and all were in dire need of
being carefully pressed flat from the rudely rolled state
Turner had stashed them in, crammed in the dust and debris
of his Queen Anne Street lodgings. Many were falling to
pieces from worm or mouse holes, and he grieved as works he
had admired when newly drawn that now crumbled at his
touch. He hiked his shirt sleeves to the elbows to protect
them from filth, and his hands dirtied so quickly that he must
wash them every few minutes.

Light, Descending

He had never before been confronted with the totality of Turner's output and his head was splitting each evening when he ascended into the London darkness. Studies of mountain ranges, village scenes, ocean mist rising or city rain falling, trials with light, shading, technique, and paper types, reams of paper on which blotches of colour had been laid down to gauge the effects upon each other: in fine, thousands of experiments. Opening each new tin transport box occasioned exquisite discoveries. Every scribble, incomprehensible to others, held reams of meaning to Ruskin, and he alone could classify or categorize them. Every step of Turner's pilgrimage was preserved there in its naissance, from youthful sunny pastorals to his mature masterworks depicting plagues, deluges, and the futility of human effort; all scraps tracing the grievous metamorphosis of this Titan's urge towards catastrophe. It was as if the great old man still spoke to him, and with fevered assurance he traced the origins of scores of favourite works to many hundreds of preparatory fragments.

When his labours were nearing an end, he began finding them. Sorting through deposited loose sheets of landscape studies and pencil drawings of buildings, his eyes had been assaulted by the discovery of depictions of the intimate parts of a woman's anatomy. Detached from any larger figure study, sometimes floating as it were in space, he would be confronted by detailed studies of pudenda with fleshy folds springing with curling hair.

The first drawing he found was on the reverse of a detached sketch-book sheet bearing two small studies of sunlit water glistening over stream rocks. There on the verso of the masterful sketches was something he could not decipher. A cleft of mossy rock? No. He turned the paper, then stared.

"This—cannot be," he whispered into the stillness of the vast room. He had worked late into the evening in the damp and mould-ridden subterranean environment assigned

179

his task. His quiet words jolted him nearly as much as what he held in his hands.

He knew Turner frequented brothels and of course had lived with a succession of "house-keepers," widows all, who kept him spruce and did his laundry and cooking. The fact that these women had obviously exposed themselves in this way for him, that Turner—his Master—who painted Nature with God-given gifts unmatched by any man, had found delight in the very looking, let alone study, of this most intimate and frankly ugly aspect of female anatomy made him faint-headed. And delight was there; Ruskin when he could bear to look saw the attention Turner had lavished upon his subject. The results of these obscenities invoked a kind of gut-churning fear he had almost forgotten, and he was in a state of exhaustion when he deemed his work complete.

Now the loveliness of Rose LaTouche, with a mouth like her name-sake flower bud, expunged those images. When he felt sickened, fatigued, or near despair, he thought of her and took heart, as a weary pilgrim when considering the holy relic at journey's end. Within weeks of meeting her she was inhabiting his imagination, unwittingly offering in her childish way her pure beauty as a hand-hold to grasp at and save himself by.

But nothing roused him to real work. He felt at times almost prostrate with fatigue, plagued with giddiness or watering eyes. His physical exhaustion manifested itself in endless coughs and colds, to his own alarm and to the far greater alarm of his parents. His aged mother's worried chastisements were just as bad as her earlier nursing and hovering. His father's puzzled and reproachful demeanour smote his own heart; he could not be the son his father deserved. John James still read in draught form everything Ruskin wrote, every draught of every essay, every letter to a newspaper, and censored with a heavy hand. What had once been grateful and useful editorial advice had become more and more open dissension as his father grew increasingly dismayed at his emerging political and economic views.

His mother made of him an Idol and yet incessantly harped on the smallest domestic infractions. She despaired at his friendship with the great Carlyle, whom she feared was a freethinker, and his father, who had unwittingly thrown him together with immoral rakes at Oxford, complained that Ned Burne-Jones, the sweetest of his friends, was a bad influence. Together his parents made life at Denmark Hill almost unbearable. Yet he was without independent income, and bound in more ways than the merely monetary to stay on. For decades son and parents had lived and travelled together. Now that age and infirmity had made inroads upon them he was free to travel alone, grasping at any opportunity to bolt, and yet stricken with remorse by their distress at his leaving.

He had been aware for years of his inability to escape what he slowly realised was parental domination, a capitulation to his parents' desires and wishes. Here he was, forty-two years old, living with his elderly parents and their equally elderly servants in a pile of a house filled with massive mahogany furnishings. A house in which, at his mother's insistence, all his paintings must be screened from view, from enjoyment, every Sabbath to preserve the day's "sanctity." Living alone.

He wanted to flee London but the difficulty remained of leaving his parents at Denmark Hill. His own health was faltering; at night he coughed so that he worried of some recrudescence of his youthful problems with his lungs. He was seeing almost no friends. A devoted coterie of intellectually gifted women confidantes remained sympathetic to his sorrows, and he abhorred the thought of intruding even further in their own rich lives. The Brownings were away in Italy, and he realised that he couldn't possibly praise his London artist friends enough to keep them happy, so he was spending fewer evenings with them as well. Rossetti was up to such absurdities on his canvases—Madonnas so dark they looked like mulattos—that he had thrown up his hands over him. His wife Lizzie no longer would accept the allowance he had been paying to keep her working at her own easel; Ruskin's young painter friend Ned Burne-Jones had hinted that she might be in an interesting condition and so that was likely that. If he could ever entice her to paint again he would take many more pains with her than he had, but she—like every genius he had ever encountered—was almost as ungovernable as her husband.

He liked the sculptor Alexander Monroe, but he lived in a studio kept so damp with tubs of water and wet clay that every time he visited he caught cold. Even Ned, whom he truly loved, tired him. He couldn't look at Ned's ethereal paintings properly without working himself up to a state of Dantesque Visionariness, and that requirement was at this point beyond his limited reserves of health and energy.

His closest friend, Charles Eliot Norton, was back in Boston after having lived in London and the Continent for years, and Ruskin owed him a letter—he seemed to owe every blessed person on Earth a letter—and he ought to place a pen in his hand and write it. He had reopened Norton's translation of *Vita Nuova* last night and been comforted anew by his rendering of Dante. It was his fury over the American war which made it so difficult to write; he was appalled at the assumption of moral superiority by the North, and could not make Norton understand that right here in Britain supposedly 'free' white people suffered in such extreme want that would make black slaves with reasonable masters tremble to be released from their care. Equality was impossible in this life, this Ruskin knew with every fibre in his body, and the hideousness of the wars being fought in the name of it sickened him.

He could not write to Norton as he wished he might, yet it was from America that he had received the few shreds of comfort over his discovery at Turin. He had related his revelatory un-conversion, his 'Queen of Sheba crash' to his friend and had received letters of the tenderest counsel in return. Norton had, it seemed, started out nearly where he had ended up in his views of religion—revering Christ as a great teacher but valuing the ethics of Sophocles as highly, and—this was what was causing Ruskin's greatest struggle—having no expectation for life after death. These were to him painful pieces of new light, so much so that at times he longed for the old shades he had once inhabited. He felt freer, but much less happy; less innocent—for his whole-hearted belief in his mother's evangelical doctrines had been innocent—and less hopeful. The deception of his own spiritual superiority and a great deal of other foolishness had been forced upon him. Now that he saw himself a tiny leaf upon a tree he knew it as a less selfish view of his place in the world, but it felt a far less pleasant one.

Making his apologies to his parents Ruskin excused himself from Denmark Hill and went alone to France. He found his way to Boulogne, with its dusky red-sailed fishing fleet. The first boat he saw in the harbour was *La Rose Mysterieuse*. Wandering the coast he stopped and sketched what turned out to be the *Port d'Amour*. Rose was following him, even here.

> *Today I visited a field where the white wheat was growing high, full of promise,* he wrote her. *I stopped and pulled open a sheaf to satisfy my curious eye, but at once was sorry for spoiling it. Then across the way I saw a hedge of roses, which led me into reverie upon the symbolism, and destinies of Roses—but these thoughts could not be of the slightest interest to you, my Pet!...*

His spirits began to lift as he spent days walking the hard grey beaches. He spoke with the local fishermen often enough to be invited to join them mackerel-fishing; one even allowed him to take the helm of his sturdy lugger on an all-night netting expedition. The fisherfolk delighted him. Their honesty and natural elegance of manner worked as a tonic. The patter of wooden sabots ringing in the swept stone streets pleased his ear, and the village women in their chaste and flattering white coiffes seemed a throwback to a happier age. The faces of the old, seated in sling-chairs and quietly knitting under shade trees, exhibited that contented *vieille sagesse* seen in ancient prints. One fishing family bid him join them in their home, and Ruskin gladly forsook his inn for a snug room under their low eaves. They had two charming daughters, a little older than Rose, whose smiles brightened his mornings. He wrote to her of them and was sent a tartly jealous letter in reply, which gave him such sharp pleasure that he laughed aloud. He returned each night from his rambles with sand in his shoes and the bottoms of trouser-legs damp through and felt himself revived.

Then the summons arrived from Harristown—Rose's Irish home—and he made haste for London. The LaTouches had returned from Italy. Having lately entertained the young Prince of Wales at their residence outside of Dublin—the fact of which cast Mrs. Ruskin into an awe of agitation, and jolted his father with this direct proof of the exalted social circles in which Rose's parents travelled—they now, against all his expectations, invited him home to Ireland.

He arrived late after a day of hard travelling, fearful the children would be abed. Lights blazed along the gravelled drive as the coach drew up; the sharp square outlines of the windows on the ground floor were brilliantly lit in welcome. Harristown House was a blocky Georgian manor of pale grey limestone, the smoothness of which emphasised the uncompromising hardness of the place. He was shown into an immense drawing room hung with paintings from the last century and warmly welcomed by Mrs. LaTouche.

The children were in fact in their rooms, but after a few minutes they came bounding down the marble stair—Percy quite the young Irish squire despite his bare feet and grinning face, Emily demure in a gown and wrapper of butter yellow, and Rose, swathed in a tiny pink dressing gown which streamed out behind her as she ran to him. He was in the act of shaking hands with Percy when she came, and he made haste to free his hand so he could catch her up. Her slender arms were thrown about his neck. She kissed him full upon the lips. Nor did she pull away at once, but for a moment lay her softly rounded cheek against his side-whiskers. Maria LaTouche laughingly scolded, but as the children withdrew Ruskin found his own hand rising to touch his cheek, and knew when next his whiskers were scissored he would save the trimmings. He turned to come face to face with an unsmiling John LaTouche.

Maria LaTouche finished fastening her pearl ear-bobs and rose from her dressing table. Emily was practicing Schubert in the music room downstairs, and Mrs. LaTouche paused and attended appreciatively for a moment to the rising music. Mr. LaTouche was behind the closed door leading to his bedroom; the hour before dinner was one of private prayer for him. Percy was—wherever the boy was.

She moved to the window. The late summer sun dropping behind the row of beeches cast deep and reaching shadows across the mowed lawns, their green bleached to a striking yellow by the raking light. She turned her head and saw two figures walking side by side along the little copse of woods fringing the Liffey's banks. Rose in her white muslin gown was walking hand in hand with Mr. Ruskin. He was looking down at her, and speaking, she could see. Their guest had been with them for a week, and would be tonight asked to stay another.

Light, Descending

Thank God for Ruskin! she thought. This Summer had been more trying than most, with disquieting financial difficulties of her husband's at the bank, Rose's growing truculence, and the trials of entertaining the Prince of Wales and his military retinue. After that exertion the remains of the season at Harristown threatened to revert to mind-numbing regularity. She was starved—*starved* for intelligent and sympathetic company in her endless and stultifying rounds of calls, dinner parties, and county balls. With Ruskin near she felt a hope that her life at thirty-five had not climaxed; nor was to be given wholly over to the care of her children, which of late was all she had felt left to her. With Ruskin she could converse on the most important topics of the day; nay eternal topics too, and feel his interest in her intellect and ideas. She could discuss books with him, Shakespeare's dramas, the ethics of Scott's romances or Tennyson's poems; or listen enraptured while he spoke on the Ideal in Beauty. And he was delightfully playful as well, and touchingly told her he approved her pet-name 'Lacerta', after the lizard constellation, as an appropriate tribute to her serpent-like yet venom-less wisdom.

Despite his greatness he was altogether like no other man she had ever known. Walking with him through the grounds was an especial joy. Together they stooped and identified tiny, and by-others-unnoticed wild flowers through his folding magnifying glass, always in his pocket. She was no match for him, not in any wise, the magnitude of his mind was too expansive for her even to glimpse its full magnificence; but with him she felt vital and alive and recognised as a thinking being. He looked at her when she spoke.

She heard a dull sound and turned her head to the closed door of her husband's dressing room. He must be rising from his knees. Married at nineteen, she thought she had made a love match. A mutual attraction to their persons there had been, but she soon realised that there was little else. John LaTouche, ten years her senior, was given over to the fox hunt and the race course, and being made Master of the Kildare Fox Hounds at an early age earned him the sobriquet "the Master" which had followed him long after the conclusion of his hunt days. He had scant interest in the sort of books she liked, none in botany, and was indifferent to the Canova marbles gracing the house, souvenirs of his grandfather's more exalted tastes. He was not a brute—she had always been grateful for that; and he cared for the children as much as any father, she imagined; her own had died too young for her to remember. And by his extremes he was capable of surprising her.

She recalled awakening early one November morning, the first year of the Great Hunger, to a fearful racket of men and hounds out upon the South lawn. Through her frosted window she saw her husband in the dawn gloom, surrounded with Harristown's many gamesmen, mounted and turning to ride. But it was no hunt day, and her husband wore grouse-hunting garb. He returned at dusk as she sat writing invitations for an upcoming dinner party. He looked exhausted but exhilarated, and astonished her by his greeting.

"We took 67 deer, every one we could flush or drive within five miles."

She could not imagine such slaughter, nor the practical requirements for the dressing-out of so many beasts. The gamesmen would have to work far into the night.

"They'll be going out to the poor of the parish."

He emptied his game parks to relieve the suffering of those starving for want of potatoes.

Another time he provoked an outcry from local antiquarians by, without warning, pulling down the remains of the highly picturesque and quite ruined family castle, the stone to go as his donation to the building of a new village school. He shrugged off their protests in the name of Progress and a good cause, and she bit her lip to see the destruction of such a pretty place.

But his abiding passion had been for the fox hunt, which by its waste secretly disgusted her, the expense of maintaining the packs of high-bred hounds, the indiscriminate tearing-up of crop land by the riders, the loss of good horses to bad falls. When his twin brother dropped dead in the racing stands, John LaTouche took it as a clarion call. He resigned from the hunt, sold his hounds, and never rode in sport again.

At first she was delighted—why should she not be? After ten years of marriage, and with three young offspring, she felt they were beginning anew. But if he had once strayed from the straight and narrow by his dedication to race-course and fox hounds, she now witnessed an over-correction in her husband's path. He spent hours reading the latest tracts published by Dissenter ministers. He attended a gentlemen's Bible study group from which she was naturally excluded. He spent more time with the children, yes—but it was in expounding the new-found truths of Scripture. But she felt no real alarm until the morning he declined to accompany her to where they had always worshipped together, the charming Church of Ireland chapel by the family mausoleum. He would henceforth attend divine service at the local Baptist tabernacle. His quiet yet flat announcement pained her more than she hoped her face betrayed. Emily, Percy and Rose went with their mother and governess in the chaise to their Anglican service. They turned off the drive and she watched as he rode alone, erect and impassive in his seat, to his new destination in town. A rift—the depths of which was yet unknowable—had opened at her very feet, one she must calmly straddle.

Light, Descending

Ruskin troubled her, in his own way, but he never drained her, though any conversation with him was like a game of shuttlecock—her brain on tip-toe running in the attempt to return a worthy comment to his remark. It was his sorrow that troubled her, some deep and as yet to her unexpressed sorrow that crossed his soul. And she knew now, without doubt—for this he had confided in her—that he had lost his belief. She was frightened by his declaration—she ardently believed in God's love and presence in her decorous Anglican way—and yet strangely thrilled he had confided in her.

Three days into his visit Ruskin had walked alone with Maria LaTouche while the children were at their lessons. Their conversation had turned to the Rev. Charles Spurgeon, the Baptist preacher whose fiery London sermons both Ruskin and his father had occasionally enjoyed; they were like good theatre to him now. Ruskin knew from both LaTouche's own frequent citations of the preacher, and by his private conversation with Mrs. LaTouche, that John LaTouche was coming more and more under Spurgeon's influence.

"It's not the vulgarity of Spurgeon's Bible-thumping that disgusts me—his 'Turn or Burn' exhortations are no more than crude modernisations of certain of the Proverbs," he said as he strolled the gardens with Mrs. LaTouche. She was very pleasant to walk with, a pleasure that gave a fine, contrasting edge to his indictment of the portentous Baptist. The violet scent she wore mixed agreeably with the sweetness of the new-mown grass, and he paused for just an instant to consider the relative positions of violet and green on the colour wheel. "His arrogant *ignorance* is what I object to. Spurgeon ought to be shut up with some good books, or even better sent out into the fields where he might learn something of benefit." Ruskin lifted his hand to gesture at a few gardeners raking the gravel paths of the flower beds.

Maria LaTouche's ordinarily florid complexion had gone white. She remained mute, and he went on without prompting.

"It's all Faith, not Works, as the path to redemption—how far is that from Christ's own example? But Evangelicalism today is all rather greasy in the finger—with train oil I should say—with Spurgeon though I suppose it's olive—admixed with the slightest touch of castor." Ruskin would have laughed if he was not concerned about shocking her overmuch. But her silence seemed sympathetic and he went on.

"I do not single out Spurgeon," he told her. "All modern churches are nothing more than idolatry. The Roman Catholic idolizes his saints, the English High-Churchman his family pew, the Scotch Presbyterian idolizes his own obstinacy. Puritan—Brahmin—Turk—are all merely names for different madness. I think I see how one ought to live, now, but my own life is lost—gone by."

They had stopped walking. Maria LaTouche scarcely knew how to respond. He was being free in his speech with her, treating her as a trusted equal, but it was a gift she did not want. All she could make was an ardent plea. "You must, must promise, on all that you hold dear, that you will keep private these views of yours," she answered. She turned fully to him, and saw he registered her alarm.

"I fear for you," she went on, "and Rose will fear for you dreadfully—and her father—oh, I cannot be held to account for his reaction should he hear of your doubts."

Ruskin saw his folly. Why had he thought he could be truthful? It was all too easy to imagine LaTouche's response should this get back to him. But Rose? He yearned to tell her these things, in tempered language of course—yearned to keep her from hurtling headlong into the abyss of blind acceptance. It had taken him sorrowful years to arrive at these conclusions, yet sharing them now put his access to the life-quickening Rose in peril.

He did not answer as they continued walking, tracing the course of the Liffey from the grassy path along its bank.

He turned to her, and felt the smile playing around his lips. "I feel as Bunyan's Pilgrim, but older, so much older; and with the great religious Dark Tower before me to assault—or to find myself shut up in—by Giant Despair. And now you and Rosie order me out of pleasant Byepath Meadow."

She would not allow him to make light of it. Too much depended on it, and her voice took on a new and meticulous tone. "Mr. Ruskin, you must promise me that you will not tell Rose of this, nor publish anything of it where she or Mr. LaTouche might see it. For ten years. Promise me."

He looked across the narrow river before speaking. "I am never punished through my own faults and follies, only through the faults and follies of others."

"I beg your pardon?" she asked.

He swung his head back and met her eyes.

"I will promise," he said.

The Harristown estate ran to 11,000 acres—such a vast holding, and yet so many poor tenants paying rent, thought Ruskin—and in the fortnight spent there he and the children had covered a representative hundred or two. The afternoons were theirs. He took long and languorous walks through Harristown's parkland, sometimes with Maria LaTouche joining them, other times alone with the children. To this eager audience he pointed out the varieties of clouds dotting or filling the skies above them, and told them tales of each stone or wild herb they brought before him. There were boating picnics on the slow Liffey, drifting as he taught them about currents and aquatic plants. Emily and Rose were, to his pleasure, not a bit more afraid of wet or dirt than their brother, and the four of them attempted small dams and bridges over streamlets, rolling and positioning river-rock and returning to the great house soaked and with scratched hands but in the best of humours.

> *Today I stood for three hours altogether in the shallows of the Liffey with the younger LaTouches,* he wrote his father, *and though I picture the alarm on your face, can promise you that bodily I felt no ill effect whatsoever from this partial immersion, indeed, its waters are so sweet and warm that I found it far more salubrious than any full immersion within a London tabernacle.*

He wondered to himself if instead it was not the joyous vitality of Rose's small person which had kept him warm.

In the evenings he sat alone with Mr. and Mrs. LaTouche at their interminable dining table and attempted, generally without success, to engage his host in some sort of genuine conversation. Even witticisms failed; he found Mr. LaTouche almost entirely humourless. Mrs. LaTouche clamped herself down in her husband's presence and this stifling self-censure—he had seen it in intelligent women countless times—made him awkward with them both. He respected Maria LaTouche, and found hers to be a penetrating mind, but it was his friendship with the children that kept him on.

One morning he sat at his desk drawing a map of Mount Blanc. The peak's sharp aiguilles and ravines were, from years of accumulated observations and measurements, nearly as familiar to him as any boyhood landmark. As the lifting sun struck his window he became aware of children's calls ringing through the early air. He stood and pushed on the casement, and saw Rose and Emily and Percy out in the dew, playing croquet. Rose had heard the scraping of his window and stopped in her play and smiled. She swung her croquet mallet up at him, beckoning him to come down. She knew he insisted on working a few hours in the morning. Come down he would not. Nor, watching her from above, did he ever finish the map.

That evening the senior LaTouches absented themselves for a neighbour's dinner party they felt compelled to attend. Mrs. LaTouche had rather pressed Ruskin to go along, but he had relished the thought of an evening made gay by the children's company and begged off. The old butler served the four of them, with he and Emily sitting opposite and Rose and Percy *quatrefoil*. They called each other Lord and Lady and laughed over a delicious pudding with as much cream as they all wished. After dinner they retired to the music room where Emily played and he sang duets with Rose. Then Rose and Percy teamed to play him at chess—he let them win one, but was merciless at the second match—and when the children were called to bed he went up to his own room, unwilling to stay alone downstairs. "Divinest day of intense and cloudless Sun," he told his diary by lamp-light, "and Rosie a child at dawn and a Lady at dinner, and quiet & harmless joys as I've wanted for ever so long..."

The next morning, unable to work for happiness, he went out walking after breakfast. Behind the stables he passed a row of cottager's huts, their thatched roofs bristling and doors open to the warm air. He heard a girl's laughter, joined by that of an old woman's, and smiled to himself. Then Rose burst from the door of the closest cottage, still laughing, her little red cap jauntily askew on her golden head, a basket clutched in her hand. She pulled herself up short before him.

"I'm giving out tracts, there, do you want one?" Rose asked. Before he could answer she thrust a yellow pamphlet into his hands. She looked at him, smiling, thinking how bright his blue eyes were, and that his whiskers looked so soft she wanted to pet them. But she wanted him to read her tract first, and so she stood there in front of him, waiting.

"Let me examine the contents," he said, in his grown-up, not his playful voice, "before I commit myself."

He smoothed the paper and held it before him. It was one of Mr. LaTouche's distributions, with "Redemption Denied?" in bold heading.

But Rose had so many in her basket. "Oh, you must be redeemed, St. C—we all must be," she told him. She turned and ran into the next in the row of huts.

"Under whose orders?" he inquired of her disappearing blue cloak. She was out again in a moment with a toddling child at her heels, laughing and reaching for her basket. He watched her hand the child the basket and hold her steady with her other hand.

"Oh—Papa, gave them me, of course, but God will judge us all."

"Yours is a decided character, Rose," he told her.

She squinted at Ruskin in the bright sun and smiled up at him.

"You bear your name beautifully. You are, I would gauge, on your own roots, not grafted."

She shrugged her shoulders because she could not think of the right thing to say. She knew what "grafting" was from her mother's fruit trees, and knew you couldn't do it to a human.

Her very perfection had power to hurt him. He studied her, impressing on his brain the tilt of her chin, the delicacy of her thin shoulders. "You should never be grafted, but allowed to grow unspoilt by the hands of clumsy gardeners who attempt to prune or shape you. You would lose your natural coil, and that would be a tragedy."

Rose stood staring, still smiling, but nodding her head at him. The toddler grew restless, and she led her to the child's waiting mother in the doorway. Ruskin crammed the yellow paper into the recesses of his pocket and walked on.

Near the end of his stay Ruskin looked up the dining table to his hosts and cleared his throat.

"I should like to make a proposition to you, Mr. and Mrs. LaTouche." Both heads lifted from the fish consommé and two spoons were arrested in mid-air. "It concerns Rose."

LaTouche lowered his spoon; his wife's still hung suspended as she smiled at her guest. LaTouche made an indeterminate sound and looked back at Ruskin.

"She is as we all know, a bright child," Ruskin said, "and I wonder if you might consent to my getting her started in Greek."

LaTouche dropped his eyes to his cup and spooned up a mouthful of consommé. Greek. He had spent a woeful 18 months at Christ Church Oxford, wrestling with translations of Euripides and Demosthenes, at first rating only a *vix—*

with difficulty—and after much head-ache inducing labour progressing to a *satis*.

Ruskin did not look as if he were expecting an immediate reply, and in fact went on.

"My reasoning is simply this: knowing Greek, she will be able to read the Bible with complete understanding, untrammelled by the accretions of faulty translators. And in possession of that same skill—facility in Greek—the greatest riches of classic literature will be hers. Failing that, mastering even one Greek verb thoroughly will set her in correct habits of thought for evermore."

LaTouche thought again of Euripides. He glanced at his wife, who was leaning forward ever so slightly toward their guest, an infallible sign of her interest and approval.

Maria LaTouche knew enough Latin to bolster her interest in botany but had never been provided an opportunity for Greek. "Think of it, Mr. LaTouche, Rose reading the *Psalms* in Greek," she told him in her quiet, almost hushed voice. She seemed always about to convey a secret. LaTouche forgot Euripides and remembered his other offspring.

"Percy will be needing some Greek soon," he counter-offered.

Ruskin was ready. "Of course I mean to teach Percy and Emily as well, should they be interested." He could not imagine either one being so.

The next day after her Bible-reading with her father, Ruskin sat down with Rose in the nursery. She turned to him with an expectant smile, as if ready to receive a gift. Having no text to hand, he wrote out the Greek alphabet in elegant ink. He sounded the letters with her as he wrote, and she in pencil copied them as best she could while saying them aloud after him. His thoughts repeated themselves as he guided her hand. *If you will be a Christian, at least you shall know the truth of the Bible. And if you be Pagan, then the jewels in store for you with Homer and Socrates!* Bent together over her little school-table he initiated her into the beauties of the Greek script. It felt a sacred act, another bond between them. *The love of you is a religion to me.*

He promised to send her Milgrave's *Elementary Greek* when he returned to London, and in the meantime asked that she attempt the copying of the letters over again. He was astonished when she sought him out three hours later. She had mastered the entire alphabet.

When he left Harristown Rose fell ill.

Chapter Sixteen

The Lamp of Power & The Lamp of Beauty

My Dear Mr. Ruskin

Rose, you will be glad to learn, is making some advance. She seems quite her normal self (save for any outdoor exertion of any kind, of course) until about 5 o'clock each day, but then the change comes about her, and she gets so listless and restless and unable to occupy her thoughts, in fact claims when she can speak that even thinking hurts...

Almost as soon as he arrived home Rose had sent Ruskin her first scrap of writing in Greek, the salutation *Peace be to you.* He had it daily in his breast pocket. Then came her inexplicable physical collapse, now in its fourth week, reported through anxious yet chatty letters from Maria LaTouche. These, in attempting to quell Ruskin's fear, served to inflame it. The shortening days of autumn with their constant *memento mori* did nothing to shore up his frame of mind. He shut himself in his rooms in Denmark Hill or wandered about alone in the dripping garden, stopping long before the peach tree from which he had plucked ripened fruit to feed her.

His parents, recalling his own break-down at Oxford—would they never stop blaming themselves for it?—offered outspoken assessments that the study of Greek had proved too demanding for a girl of thirteen, which Ruskin vigorously refuted, barely able to stay civil. The Dublin doctors summoned by the LaTouches put an end to all "brain work" for Rose, and Ruskin counselled her by letter to attempt some simple hand crafts to help focus her thoughts. She was not allowed to write back—the exertion being thought too much for her—but his letters to her were encouraged, and he wrote her every day.

He wrote at first of subjects that he knew would interest and absorb her, the meaning of certain Greek verbs, or his insights into certain favourite passages of the Bible. But soon her mother was imploring him to keep to lighter topics, and he wrote all his way to Switzerland where he fled with his manservant, writing to Rose in detail of the wayside flowers in Alpine valleys, and sending her a trefoil sprig of oxalis, a folk symbol of the Trinity. For his effort he was rewarded by a short note in her own hand, enclosing a shamrock, that Irish symbol of the same, with the direction, "A Dieu, dearest St C, and my shamrock will tell you what you wish to know."

This then, the language of flowers, was to be a secret language between them, and Rose the greatest flower of them all.

By November Rose's painful head-aches began to stop, and she could more readily eat. As she gained strength she was permitted to walk downstairs, and to sit by her mother as she read aloud. Mrs. LaTouche was fearful of over-stimulation, and only by degrees were Rose's pet cats allowed, first one and then the second, into the drawing room. The girl responded gratefully to their soft tread in her lap, and would hold them, purring in her arms, for an hour altogether. Rose had asked almost from the start for her dog Bruno, and at last one day her father brought him in on a lead. She was sitting in the music room with her mother when she heard the unmistakable scratching of Bruno's nails on the parquet floor of the hall. The cats scattered.

"Bruno!" Rose cried, and reached her arms towards the open doorway. Her mother laid a gently restraining hand on her lap lest she forget herself and try to jump up.

"Here he is," answered her grinning father as they entered. Rose laughed aloud as the hound panted and strained at his chain, licked her face, and beat her legs with his bushy tail. She threw her arms around Bruno's shaggy pied coat, and when she looked up saw both her parents smiling at her. Bruno promptly lay down at her feet in adoration. She felt completely happy.

Maria LaTouche placed her arm around her daughter's thin shoulders. "There now," she said. "You have Bruno and everything. Are you feeling more yourself?"

When Rose was twenty-six and dying, she would look back on this first collapse and recall her mother asking her that. How funny that is, she recalled thinking; I cannot be anyone else. But she answered, "Yes, Mama, I do."

Her prayer-time proved a problem. Maria LaTouche held that during this crisis her daughter's prayers should be of the briefest and simplest. But Mr. LaTouche insisted on carrying in the large family Bible and reading aloud from it, stopping to discuss points of Scripture with Rose, questioning and correcting her. The girl's head hurt again at how angry her mother was with her father; she could see it in her mother's eyes, as she waited for the Bible lessons to be over.

Mrs. LaTouche read all the letters, arriving daily, from Ruskin to Rose, first to herself and then aloud to her daughter. Even when the girl was feeling stronger she was permitted to write back only once a week, regardless of her delight in a certain letter, or how much she wanted to say Hello to her St. Crumpet. In late November she was allowed walks outdoors, and in December she could ride her pony again.

Light, Descending

On a December morning when the air was soft Rose found a letter addressed to her from Ruskin in the silver salver by the door as she was heading out. There was one as well for her mother from him, so she didn't feel naughty in taking the one meant for her and reading it before she did. She opened it on the way to the stable where her pony Swallow was waiting, but when she rounded the corner saw her mother's mare being saddled too. She poked the letter in her habit pocket and buttoned it up, and though she knew her mother meant to join her, let Michaels help her onto Swallow and trotted off.

It was fine to have St. C there in her pocket, talking to her, so she thought, right through her waist—she felt him. And Swallow must have known he was there too, because the black pony was in such spirits to have that distinguished personage also upon his back that he danced and skittered under his doubled burden. Rose almost thought she along with St. C too might end up in the new-ploughed stubble, and that only made her laugh the more. Down the lane she could see her mother waving at her, and saw how quickly the long legs of her mother's hunter were closing the distance between them.

Mrs. LaTouche came up alongside, and Rose's pony quieted immediately. "Why, Rose, what is making you laugh so? I almost thought Swallow was going to toss you, for a moment." But she was smiling at her, not cross at all.

Ah, the pang of not being able to tell the secret of the hidden letter! Rose pressed her lips together hard, to keep from telling, and smiled back. If she were truthful the letter would be taken from her before she could finish it. "Nothing, Mama," she lied. "I'm only happy to be out." But she was no longer happy. She knew now she could never show the letter with its broken seal to Mama: how disappointed she would be. She could not bear disappointing either of her parents.

The next week she got another letter from Ruskin in which he scolded her for sending him her "best love" from the bottom of her mother's letter, saying that love could not be best or worst, just love. But that was her Mama's invention, the "best love," she wrote back, she never sent a bit of it, she didn't like sending messages on other people's letters, didn't he notice—she liked to say it herself, and besides he knew he already had her love, as much of it as he pleased. And that he should have the happiest Christmas there in Switzerland, and they were finally going to London now she was well.

He spent his Christmas day alone, shattering icicles in a ravine.

In his room in Lucerne the night after Christmas Ruskin paused in his diary entry to admire the brilliance of Venus through the small diapered-paned window over his desk. Despite his parent's entreaties that he return to Denmark Hill for the Christmas holidays he had—wilfully he knew, and at cost to himself in sorrow for their sorrow—extended his Swiss sojourn. The LaTouches had been in their Mayfair town house for two weeks now, and both Mrs. LaTouche in her frequent letters and Rose in her sporadic ones had expressed their desire to see him over Christmas.

He yearned to see Rose, to watch her come to him in her quick graceful steps, the heels of her little white shoes barely touching the floor. He yearned for the slender arms cast around his neck, and the shy sweet kiss that would follow. But he could not bear their parting. He might have an hour, an afternoon, with her and her mother or sister, and then the rest of life intruded, the carriage was called, the enchantment ended. Here in Lucerne, knowing she was growing steadily stronger, knowing she was now for the winter living at London just a few miles from his own home, he felt more ease than he could at Denmark Hill itself. He loved the thought of her.

He was trying desperately to work, to settle upon some task worthy of his efforts, and all his thoughts recurred to Rose. Carlyle was urging him on with his new political economy essay, and there was the geological study he also worked at, and the seemingly endless correspondence, hours of it each morning beyond the obligatory daily missive to his father.

He felt exactly that he was a youth of seventeen who had awakened to find himself a middle-aged man, with every desire of his youth intact but no capacity to accomplish them. As a youngster he had grieved that he had not yet the tools to spend his days immersed in metaphysical writing; in his forties he wished he could flirt, dance, and ride. *Wrong at both ends of life.* He wanted to see Rose, but she disturbed his work and thought.

Two days after he had sat at his window looking at Venus a letter from Rose arrived, the longest letter she had ever yet written him. It was dated 26 December. He began reading it standing in his room but sunk down upon his bed when she spoke of looking out her London window that night past the yellow glow of street gaslights to the immense and shining globe of Venus. She had been gazing West at Venus at the very hour he had. This was the perfect sympathy the child had with him—she seemed always to mirror, or even to anticipate him in act and emotion.

To her Venus was as the Christmas Star, bringing tidings of hope and joy to struggling humanity, and she hoped it would bring her St. Crumpet hope and joy too, because she knew he was not happy. She wrote at length about the Star as a sign of Peace, that inner peace which is the goal of all, and paraphrased passages from Isaiah, and wrote of Old Testament prophets, and of the love of Jesus. She said she had dreamed of him, and that she felt herself with him in his room there in Lucerne, and that she thought their rooms were not so very different. She went on for pages in serious childish fervour, and with such sweetness and concern for his well-being he felt faint by the time she reached her closing passage, in which his Posie-Rosie-Posie apologized for the blottiness of her pen.

He wished he had had some precious casket in which to store this letter, the Star Letter as he called it. It was not the call to faith he heeded—she was parroting her father there—but the utter tenderness to him he cherished.

In the morning when he wrote his father he wondered to him—Was Rose what you and her mother think—an entirely simple child? Or was she what he suspected, more subtle, more sweet and mysterious, than St. Catherine of Boulogne, that patron of artists and temptations?

He readied for his return to London. Rosie would be 14 beginning of January, and he had already chosen his gift for her, his 13th century manuscript from Liège, a Psalter and Book of Hours with an *Ave* to the Virgin naming her as a royal Rose. In it he inscribed:

Posie with St C's love 3rd January 1862

Lizzie dead. Please come at once. —William Rossetti

Ruskin sat in the jolting hansom repeating the words scrawled on the note which had reached him at Denmark Hill half hour ago. Lizzie dead. Last year Death took his dear

Elizabeth Barrett Browning, greatest of female poets, and now in this cruel winter had snatched the girl whom he had hoped would become Britain's greatest female painter.

The cab clattered over Blackfriars Bridge. The stench of the Thames, pungent even in February, forced his hand to his nose as he alighted at Chatham Place. Blast Rossetti for ever bringing that delicate girl here, with its charnel-house odours and rising damp.

He was not the first caller. The downstairs door was open and unattended and he climbed the narrow stair to their lodgings. Men's voices told him Madox Brown was there as well as William Rossetti. He did not hear the voice of Gabriel.

He must have looked stricken, for William Rossetti crossed the floor to him and clasped him in an embrace that was as much physical support as comfort. But he waved away the offered chair.

"When did it happen," was what he found himself saying in way of greeting.

"Early this morning." William's voice was raspy and he was hastily dressed, his hair barely combed. "Gabriel found her unresponsive when he returned last night, and brought a doctor at once. He and two other medical man worked hours trying to revive her, but her stupor only grew deeper. Just before dawn her pulse could be felt no more."

Ruskin shut his eyes for a moment.

William went on. "There was a nearly-empty bottle of laudanum by her side."

Lizzie always had difficulty sleeping, everyone knew she relied on the opiate to ease her way. The drug however demanded ever-increasing dosages to remain effective.

He could barely frame his next question. "Was it—"

William came to his aid. "It was not thought to have been, no. We hope they will rule death by misadventure."

Ruskin looked across the room to the closed bedroom door. "Why was he not here? Why was she alone, once again alone?"

"She was not alone, not all evening, at least," answered William. "She and Gabriel dined at a restaurant with Swinburne. Gabriel brought her back here and then went off to the Working Men's College to teach his drawing class. When he returned he could not rouse her."

Ruskin did not believe William's defence of his brother. He imagined Gabriel Rossetti rushing to the arms of one of his jades after dumping off his sickly wife. He had loved Rossetti, had championed both his poetry and his art, and hoped to bring the expression of his talents to a higher plane. For years he had forgiven his protégé's moral waywardness, his ignoring sound art-advice. He had given more out-of-pocket money to Rossetti than to any other artist, with no hope of such "loans" ever being repaid, and had not only repeatedly urged Rossetti to marry Lizzie and end her precarious social status, but had actually given him funds— twice—to do so. And once he finally married her his depictions of Lizzie took on a new radiance and truth; instead of exaggerating the few faults of her face and thinking them beauties, as he did with other sitters, he painted her just as she was, perfectly capturing her romantic and fragile nature.

"Where is he now," he asked, looking at the closed door. At last Madox Brown spoke. Ruskin had never liked his paintings, despite Rossetti's efforts to bring him round on his friend's talent.

"He's much too broken up to see you at present." Ruskin registered a minor note of triumph in his voice as

Brown denied him the opportunity to comfort Rossetti in person.

Ruskin turned back to William and raised his hands the slightest bit. "Let me see her," he said.

William nodded and turned to the closed door, and opened it without entering so that Ruskin might be alone with her.

He had of course never before seen the bedroom, but it was as he might expect from such a pair. Velvet curtains, rusty with age, were imperfectly drawn against the feeble morning light falling from the single latticed window. The walls lacked any paper but were covered over in great extravagant sketches in charcoal by both Lizzie and her husband. The old bed was carved of dark wood and the hangings upon them threadbare and faded. A striped rag rug and a newer floral one by Morris lay upon the worn boards of the floor. A cupboard with a few pieces of pottery and a clothes press completed the furnishings, save for a tiny and uneven table by the bed upon which a lamp burned. It was shabby with the profligacy of ill-spent love and talent and dreams unrealised.

Ruskin approached the bed. Lizzie lay on one edge of it. Whatever horrid exertions the doctors had resorted to in attempting to revive her, there were no signs left of it on her face or in the room. She looked more than ever like the 13th century Florentine lady Ruskin had first thought she embodied, a face and form that Dante would have loved.

She was dressed in a white night-dress and the pale coverlet was pulled up almost to her shoulders. Her thick red hair had been smoothed from its centre part and softly framed her oval face. Her complexion was always very pale, and it was no paler now. Her gentle lips looked soft and barely closed. Only her eyelids told Ruskin she was dead. In life they were almost translucent, as if the luminous agate-coloured eyes beneath could still be discerned with her eyes closed. This morning they were utterly opaque, windows shut against the new day.

He raised his eyes and saw in the corner the child's cradle he had not seen before. Last year Georgiana Burne-Jones had told him of coming to see Lizzie a few days after her baby had been born dead, and being stunned by finding the grieving mother huddled over the empty cradle by the coal fire. Her husband Ned was proceeding her on the stairs, and as they entered Lizzie had raised her head and called out, "Hush now, Ned! Don't wake her, she's finally asleep."

Every effort towards love was futile. He bent forward and pressed his lips against the cool forehead.

What, he asked himself, if Rose should die, and leave him adrift? He could not voice the question to himself without staggering above a pit of desolation waiting to swallow him whole. The LaTouches had been in London several months, and now were returning to Ireland. Ruskin had not seen them as much as he could have while they were in residence in Mayfair, in hopes of making their departure less crushing when it came. His body responded in sympathy. He could not sleep, his digestion was troubling, his teeth ached, his face hurt.

Still, on the morning of their leave-taking he presented himself at their door. A horse cart laden with trunks and crates was just pulling away, and the family barouche and a hansom stood waiting outside the house.

Light, Descending

The door opened as he mounted the steps, and the girls' governess Miss Bunnet appeared with a small handbag. Rose and Emily were just behind her.

"St. Crumpet," cried Rose as she spotted him. She ran to him thinking how strangely he looked at her; she didn't know if he was going to laugh or cry. "I knew you would come. Mama said you mightn't as you haven't been for ever so long, but I knew you wouldn't let me go!" She pulled herself out of his arms and they stepped aside to let Miss Bunnet go on to the carriage. He just looked at her, said nothing, just looked steadily at her, and so she threw her arms around him again just to change things.

Ruskin felt himself clutch at her shoulders, and the water coming into his eyes. Then Mrs. LaTouche, smiling in her veil and travelling dress, came out on the threshold and fetched them both inside for a proper good-bye.

At Denmark Hill that afternoon Ruskin's old friends Dr. and Mrs. John Simon came to tea. His mother was too crippled with joint pain to come down stairs, and he sat nearly silent at the table with them and his father, all his mind following the LaTouches on their way to the coast. When the Simons left he had to bear his father's criticism on his unsociable behaviour. In a day Rose would be back wandering the woods of Harristown picking anemones, or perhaps even plucking crayfish from the Liffey as he had taught her. If his physical heart had been wrenched from his breast he could not have felt more hollow.

As the days passed he decided to draw her. As skilful as he was as a draughtsman, as accurately as he could render architectural perspective or the sinuous curves of a convolvulus, he felt he had little gift for drawing any living being. How much less could he hope to capture Rosie's beauty. He thought of the gold of her hair. If one were to attempt painting it he should turn to Perugino and use real gold threads to catch the effect of sunshine upon it. Still, he would try. He needed no sitter; her image was graven upon his heart. *Flos florum Rosa*—Rose, the flower of flowers.

In May, completely unexpectedly, came a startling invitation from Maria LaTouche. She offered him the use of a little cottage on the Harristown property, henceforth to be completely at his disposal. Ruskin remembered it well: it was just beyond the gates of the park, and had a garden, and fields, and was as well within sight of the Liffey. Rose, she had written, would walk by it each morning on her way to the village school she was now beginning to attend.

He was wild with delight. At the same time, thinking of actually living at Harristown in such close proximity to Rose seemed utterly fantastic. How could he hope to work there? How in fact could he leave his failing parents, his eighty-one year old father suffering now from the painful spasms of gravel, his mother unable to walk? But he wrote his letter of acceptance and proceeded with plans to take Georgiana and Ned Burne-Jones, too poor to travel on their own, to France and Italy.

He was in Paris when Mrs. LaTouche's letter retracting her offer reached him. After consideration she and Mr. LaTouche had decided that their parochial Irish neighbours might misunderstand such an arrangement, & etc. He fired off a letter to Rosie, angry she had not fought harder for the scheme.

He was not to see her for more than three years.

Everywhere Ruskin looked he found destruction, war, or idiocy. Continental travel afforded a temporary respite until he happened upon the ongoing assaults of brutal restorers attacking cherished 14th and 15th century buildings, or found valleys and villages he had loved as a boy choked up with shoddy new construction and suburban sprawl. The Swiss lakes were no longer as clearly pristine as he had found them in boyhood, when he had filled his travel diaries with descriptions of their colours. Even Venice, which to the untrained eye seemed to have escaped the 19th century, filled him with despair, the accursed steam-powered passenger boats—*i vaporetti*—exhaling soot while depriving gondoliers of their honest living.

The entire world was unravelling. America was ripped asunder, North from South, with war resulting in appalling carnage. The French were fighting the Austrians, and Poland and Russia seemed teetering upon the brink. Prince Albert, but forty-two, was suddenly dead from typhoid fever, plunging Queen and country into mourning. And mechanization was running amok. The double-hulled steam leviathan *Great Eastern*—that final fruit of the prematurely dead megalomaniac engineer Brunel—five times larger than any ship ever built, was now plying the Atlantic, belching coal smoke from the labours of 200 stokers working day and night. Ships were dropping telegraph cable from gigantic reels into deep and formerly silent ocean waters and linking Britain and America. No place was safe from the intrusion of modern engineering, and the thought made Ruskin shudder.

For the first time he felt unable to keep up with scientific innovation and thought. Chemistry was advancing so quickly that seven new elements had been detected—all, he thought wryly, ending in "ium"—and all manner of specialist laboratory equipment developed for ever-narrower purposes. The broad spectrum of his natural philosophy interests in geology, meteorology, and botany demanded an ever-deepening commitment to adopt new systems and methods. He simply could not withstand the onslaught of novel information, discoveries, and techniques.

He liked Darwin personally but despised the man's reductionist theory applied to mankind. And Industry itself was pushing the hand of the theorists. The new railway cuttings scoring Britain revealed dramatic layers of sediment which had to have taken aeons to deposit. Deeper mines brought heretofore never-seen fossils to the surface. The earth was far older than the Old Testament reckoning of six-thousand years; the tangible scientific evidence was there for all who cared to see. With a bitter humour he realised that at least he was now spared the crisis of belief that swept the Christian world as it tried frantically to recalibrate Biblical inerrancy with scientific fact.

The full use of his talents and powers was what he required, yet in his fractured state he grasped at anything that might absorb his attention temporarily. Rising at four, he lost himself in the work at hand. He spent silent hours meticulously drawing a hummingbird's feather in microscopic detail. He arranged and rearranged his vast collections of minerals and crystals, experimenting with original systems of classification. He composed music inspired by the Epicurean fatalism of the newly-published *Rubáiyát of Omar Khayyam,* finding solace in its imagery of fragrant roses and admonitions to seek the earthly joys that had so far escaped him. He would answer correspondence, write in his diary, walk or drive for hours, visit a picture gallery, sit in a darkened box in a music hall where some well-trained singer might win his admiration. He filled his days with ceaseless activity.

His friend Norton had asked Ruskin to name the things that made him what he was, and he, not at all in jest, wrote back

Light, Descending

What?—an entirely puzzled, helpless and disgusted old gentleman. Good nature and great vanity have done all of me that was worth doing. I've had my heart broken—ages ago, when I was a boy—then mended—cracked—beaten in, kicked about old corridors, and finally I think, fairly flattened out. I've picked up what education I've got in an irregular way— and it's very little. I've written a few second rate books which nobody minds; —I can't draw—I can't play nor sing—I can't ride, I talk worse and worse,—I can't digest. And I can't help it. There,—Goodbye.

He couldn't explain himself, and he couldn't explain to his father his abrupt giving away of no less than 77 Turner watercolours and drawings, all bought by the old man's generosity for his son's delight and now stripped from the walls of Denmark Hill and laying in boxes at Oxford and Cambridge. Ruskin said he did not wish to actually possess them, only to know that they were safe, and where he could see them; just as he wished for the safety of Chartres Cathedral. John James could not understand his son's linking a gigantic, mediaeval, and more or less public edifice with Turner's fragile works on paper, with which his son had an intimate and longstanding relationship. Every Turner sketch of Venice was sent away.

Nor could Ruskin explain why that same spring he broke down in the middle of a lecture on Tree Twigs at the Royal Institution. The evening had begun well. His notes, while perfectly ordered, served as departure points for his address, mere touchstones to refer to: *Every leaf a tree— harmony of disparate parts—deceits of the eye in registering distant trees—Turner's superiority in the painting of foliage- -green contains every shade needed to convey all parts of non-flowering vegetation in all light—Turner's treatment of shaded grass, sunlit grass, branch shadows on grass—*

Light, Descending

He saw then in his mind's eye some novel and exciting connexions between the economic distresses of Welsh miners and the deforestation and profaning of Athenian sacred groves. His voice seemed to grow louder; the hall had not the good resonance of some venues. He was aware he was waving his hands, and perhaps he was shouting. Then it was quiet and he heard only the pumping of his own blood in his eardrums. A disturbance at the side door drew his eye; a man, tall and thin, was entering, removing his hat as did so. His hair was a tangle of yellow curls, and his mouth set in a familiar quizzical smile. The speaker could only stand there, hand in air, and watch. It was his own lost Millais, self-exiled for years beyond the realm of his influence. With him was...a lady. Effie's tart pink bonnet had trailing pink ties edged with lace. Ruskin watched them sway under her pointed chin as the couple moved in and claimed seats from the file of empty ones in the very first row. When she was settled she looked up at him: What a tight smile on her face!

He stood at the wooden podium before five hundred listeners, but he had forgot they were there. He was silent a long time, and they were staring back at him. He searched the faces before him. A craggy old man with a white beard sat like a beacon, staring at him with burning eyes. If Carlyle had not been there in the audience he did not think he could have mastered himself to completion. The dreadful apparitions in the first row vanished as he lowered his head to accept the applause of his listeners; raising his eyes he saw the flash of pink skirt shut out by the closing side door.

He was still stung by the public's rejection of his *Cornhill* papers, but could not turn from his conviction that these were his most vital utterances to date. He had them published in book form bearing a title taken from the Gospel of Matthew, *Onto this Last*. No one bought it.

No one understood his frustration at having the few certainties he clung to being ignored. He felt, as he had once written to Mrs. Browning, exactly like an old woman locked up with a score of wicked children who never let her alone to do her knitting.

As soon as I've got a house of my own I'll ask you to send me something American—a slave perhaps. I've a great notion of a black boy in a green jacket and purple cap—in Paul Veronese's manner...

Charles Eliot Norton lowered the letter from Ruskin and looked out over the snow-carpeted garden of his home in Cambridge, Massachusetts. Norton loved Ruskin, and knew he was loved by the man, which made the constant prick of the spur that Ruskin lately employed all the more painful. Nor was this the only extravagance in the letter. Norton had written to announce that despite all expectation to the contrary he had been blessed with finding love with a like-minded woman, and to tell Ruskin of his forthcoming wedding. For if Norton had Yankee breeding, high intelligence, and limitless work capacity as scholar and magazine editor to recommend him, he was, despite being several years his correspondent's junior, also of uncertain health, slight, stooped, and already balding. Winning the love of an intelligent, kind, and sagacious woman was a triumph he had not allowed himself to consider possible, and yet now Susan would wed him in a few short months.

And his dear friend Ruskin wrote back, frankly and without a trace of shame, that he was jealous of Susan and wanted Susan to be jealous of *him*.

I don't think I shall like her, he admitted, *especially if your having a wife makes you write less to me, even though I don't write you as much as I once did since we differ so much about your horrid war.* Norton sighed at this conflation. Before the advent of the war to preserve the Union Ruskin had teazed that he would never deign to visit America, for he could not countenance stepping foot in any country so miserable as to possess no castles. That humorous pretext had hardened into an almost violent prejudice against the American democratic ideal. Norton read on in the letter, more rambling and digressive than most. Ruskin reminded Norton that he was writing him on the shortest day, the solstice, with Christmas nearly there, and told him piquantly and defiantly that he'd become a Pagan, and was now searching for Diana in the glades, and Mercury in the clouds, but he wouldn't make sacrifice to either of them if it meant killing an animal. Norton folded the narrow papers; he would answer tomorrow when he could re-summon his natural enthusiasm.

Alone in his rented villa in the sheltering declivity of Mornex, Ruskin thought of buying a hilltop above Bonneville, where he might build a home of his own and escape every pressure. It would give him a chance to design a dwelling of unique character, and to experiment with a plan for damming glacier run-off to give him water and improve agriculture for the peasants. The commune authorities were sceptical and the old farmers whose parcels he hoped to assemble amused.

Then in March, still at Mornex, he received a letter from Rose that staggered him. He had long confided his religious misgivings to Mrs. LaTouche, and felt his confidences safe with her. Now she had shown portions of a recent letter to her daughter.

Rose scolded, "How could one love you, if you were a Pagan?" and went on in fearful agitation over the fate of his soul. For the first time he felt exasperation at the precociousness of a fourteen year old lecturing him. For decades he had wrestled to discern spiritual truth, and she was sputtering pieties from her father's evangelical tracts at him.

Rose LaTouche could not understand her parent's unhappiness, and her parents could not understand each other. That her mother should be so distressed with her father, and her father so sorrowful over her mother, was something that hurt the girl's head attempting to puzzle out. The facts were that John LaTouche had gone to London and been baptised by Charles Spurgeon at his Baptist Tabernacle, an unnecessary and provocative act in the eyes of Maria LaTouche, for her husband had, as all the family, received that sacrament as a child.

"And that is where we were wronged as children," was her husband's retort. "Only thinking adults can receive valid baptism, freely understood, freely accepted. Infant baptism is but another of the great errors of Popery—another yoke of Rome—which we must free ourselves from. No infant can judge for himself."

"But loving parents can," answered Maria LaTouche. They had argued this point all week, and she was exhausted by it. Now, as they faced each other in the centre of her bedroom she struggled to keep her voice down. "Our own parents had us baptised as infants. What were we but loving parents when *we* took our three to the font?"

"Ignorant, misguided wretches!"

His face was red and she could barely stand to look at him.

"I'll not have you say that our considered, reverent observance of our faith's sacrament was made out of ignorance! Next you'll be saying you wed me out of ignorance—there will be no end of your back-tracking and fault-finding!" In her anger she was close to tears and wished she had not said this last. He seemed not to have heard it, or if he had, deemed it unworthy of comment.

It was just before the dinner hour when these voices were raised. Rose had changed her pinafore and was starting down the broad stairs when she heard them. Her hand had stiffened upon the polished banister, and yet she had let it go and found herself standing just outside her mother's closed bedroom door.

"Percy I have likely lost," she heard her father go on, "due to my own inability to awaken to the truth in time. But Emily and Rose—especially Rose, marked by God to be His Holy Prize—how can I stand by and consign her to eternal Hell-fire?"

Her mother's voice was piercing. "Hell-fire! How dare you presume to judge our daughter—judge Percy or Emily—three good children—"

Rose could listen no more. She burst in with a shriek, and ran, sobbing, to her mother. The girl twisted her fists in her mother's skirts as tiny children do, struggling to bury into the silken folds. Maria LaTouche had her arms around her in a moment, but Rose lifted her head and broke and ran to her father. He stooped to lift her up but she fell at his feet, shaking and sobbing.

"Now, now, my Rose," he said, as he knelt and took her in his arms. "Don't cry. I have a surprise for you. Reverend Spurgeon is coming here, to Harristown. Coming all the way from London, to meet His Holy Prize."

Light, Descending

A truce was called in the household until Rev. Spurgeon arrived. The following week he swooped down upon Harristown to receive a dignitary's welcome. Within his first two days he was driven through a quarter of Harristown's parkland, with stops at tenants' farms so he might view living conditions. John LaTouche took him round to the school he helped fund, and Mrs. LaTouche gave a sumptuously tasteful dinner in which he met the local gentry. Spurgeon was a portly, vigorous man just entering middle age, and enjoyed a fine meal. He and LaTouche talked late into the evenings about the latter's charitable efforts and aspirations, and the host was not found wanting by his guest. LaTouche cared about fallen women, about education for poor children, about care of the widowed and ill. And he was an immensely rich banker, able to act upon his precepts. If ever there was a modern Croesus sent to extend Christ's message here on earth, it was John LaTouche, thought Charles Spurgeon.

Their honoured visitor had the most luxuriant curling brown whiskers Rose had ever seen. She was always being told to stand up straight and Rev. Spurgeon certainly did; he kept his head directly above his spine and moved his neck slowly, as if to show his beard to best advantage. She was certain he must use a curling iron on it as her mother did her fringe-hair at her forehead. On the second morning of his visit Rose, down in the garden, saw Rev. Spurgeon at his open window, still wearing his night-shirt and doing his setting-up exercises for the day. She was surprised he did not wear his curled whiskers in a net overnight, as her Mama did her fringe-hair.

He smiled a great deal, and was given to lowering himself to the children's level when he spoke to them. Rose liked that he had as many different voices as an actor at the Pantomime. He used a sort of everyday one when he was speaking to her parents about Harristown and its countryside, another richer, slower voice when he presided at grace at the big dining table, a third, more high-pitched jolly one when he spoke to her and her siblings, and so on. Rev. Spurgeon's kindest, quietest voice he reserved for when her father brought her alone before him.

The preacher had already examined the children to his satisfaction over their Scripture, and Rose knew it was a special honour for her to attend him alone with just her father.

"Now, my dear, your father tells me what I can see myself: That you are an exceptional child, both quick, and good. But that also you are troubled in heart."

She was seated with Spurgeon on a stiff little sofa in her father's study, with her father sitting opposite in a wing chair. Their guest was much younger than her father; no gray yet streaked the preacher's chestnut hair, yet her father treated him with more attention and respect than he had the Crown Prince when he had visited. She did not want to say the wrong thing in front of either of them.

"I want to be good," Rose began. "I want to love God, and Mama and Papa and Percy and Emily, and the world and the poor—and I want everyone to love God too. I want everyone to be happy, and I want to make them happy."

"And you do, I am certain; being good is a true path to happiness; your own and other's."

"If I pray enough will I be happy, and make others happy too?"

"Prayer is a true path to serenity, and there can be little happiness without serenity."

"I have a friend, St. Crumpet—Mr. Ruskin, that I want to be happy, too."

John LaTouche shifted in his chair, and Spurgeon glanced at him, but his host remained silent.

"You take quite a bit upon that little head, Rose," Spurgeon told her. "Mr. Ruskin is a man of many and complex parts." Rose cocked her head and he went on. "You are not responsible for his happiness, nor goodness, only your own." Spurgeon looked up at the girl's father for an instant. "And I would warn you that we must be careful of those we think our friends. Sometimes friends can lead us astray."

Rose was still, looking raptly at the preacher. He looked back at her with perfect and practised steadiness.

She felt there was something wonderful in the way he looked at her, the same way he looked at adults, giving her all his attention. She felt him take one of her hands in his own.

"But we always have a choice, Rose. Let your father, and your heavenly Father, be your guide. Your earthly father can help you make that choice, and your heavenly father will reward you. It is Heaven or Hell. God or fiends."

Rose let go of the preacher's gaze and hung her head. "Oh, I am a naughty one! And when I am naughty I make everyone so unhappy. And I must make God sad too. How wicked of me! When I am good I make Mama and Papa glad. I want to make everyone happy. I want to be perfect. I will be perfect!" Rose had jumped up upon her feet at this last, no longer able to sit still.

Spurgeon could not help but let out a gentle laugh. Rose looked at him as if she might burst in tears. He too stood, and placing his hands upon her shoulders, deepened his voice.

"I lay hold of you for Christ," he told her. Rose opened her mouth as if to gasp; her father reached towards her lest she swoon. But she straightened at once, and reached up with

221

her small hands and drew the preacher's hands to her lips and kissed them.

Spurgeon had tears in his eyes at his next words. "You are indeed a Holy Prize. I claim you for Christ."

Ruskin surrendered his hopes for his Alpine paradise. His father found the scheme absurd and told him so in every letter. None of his friends encouraged or approved, and the practical obstacles to its purchase, construction and maintenance began to seem so daunting he capitulated. And where after all, would he get the money? He could hardly ask his infirm father, grieving over his absence, to give him funds to build a house away from him.

After Rev. Spurgeon left Harristown, Rose began pressing to take communion at Sunday service. She dare not ask for a second baptism——and in another tradition, as her father had done——but wished fervently and repeatedly to profess her spiritual worthiness by receiving communion. Maria LaTouche was adamant that Rose must wait until her Confirmation; that was the accepted order. A difficult period ensued in which John LaTouche repeatedly took Rose for chats with Rev. Hare, the local vicar, who knew the girl's seriousness of mind and was inclined to grant her request. Finding herself outnumbered but not yet outmanoeuvred, Maria LaTouche responded by penning, and insisting the girl read, a quantity of religious pamphlets reinforcing the wisdom of adhering to the Anglican Church's ordained schedule. Her father countered by urging Rose to fast and pray, two acts of which his youngest had more than usual experience for her age. He finally took her to again see Rev. Hare, and the exhausted Rose cried out her difficulties so movingly that he walked her home with the assurance that she should receive the memorial of Christ's death at the service next morning. For, as she had herself persuaded him, being heavy-laden and penitent, it was meant for her.

Rose went to bed light of heart for the first time in many weeks; even the knowledge that her mother was at that hour locked in a heated debate about her with her father could not quell her giddy happiness. The morning was so darkened by rain that Mrs. LaTouche called it an omen, and Rose felt a pang seeing her mother's red-rimmed eyes when she went up to hug her goodbye. But she went off with her father and governess and was received of her first Communion that day.

Her father expected her to return from this service in a state of elation, and was not the least alarmed by his daughter's extreme light-heartedness. She seemed to have given gravity itself the slip, and by the end of the day no one would have been much surprised if Rose had been observed treading upon the ceilings. Only her mother was concerned. On Monday Rose awoke with a head that ached so badly she cried out that it would burst. She could not bear the slightest sound, and the merest crack of light was agony to her. Everything, she told her mother, hurt her, and thinking hurt worst of all. She wanted no one in her room but her mother, and Mrs. LaTouche, cursing both herself and her husband for the mental exertion and spiritual anguish Rose had been subjected to, stayed with her day and night. Weeks of invalidism followed. Rose claimed she could not eat—food hurt her, she insisted. The physicians her worried parents imported tried tempting her with delicacies and threatening her with noxious solutions. They failed equally with both. Rose, all but mute, was not listening to them. She grew very thin but was never afraid. She knew if she were left alone He would guide her.

When Rose could speak again she would whisper to her mother things she knew would happen to her during that day to come. When things happened as she predicted her mother began to ask the doctors to leave her alone. Still, they forced her to take things she didn't want and knew were bad for her. At last they asked her why she was so firm, how she knew what was good for her and what bad. Although it was very strange and very hard to say Rose had to tell them that God was telling her what to do.

Chapter Seventeen

The Lamp of Power & The Lamp of Beauty

Ruskin received Maria LaTouche's report of her daughter's collapse as he was working building a dry wall along one edge of his rented villa's vegetable garden. The day was unseasonably warm, and under a brilliant Alpine sky he had removed his jacket and worked in shirt-sleeves and old straw hat. He had impressed his servant Crawley and the resident gardener for his task, and procured the services of a local farmer's donkey that was single-minded in its attempts to decimate the remains of the chard rows when not occupied hauling new stone in the baskets slung across its back. When it was time for lunch Ruskin bathed his face and arms and resumed his jacket. He sat at the table on the flagged terrace and opened the newly arrived post. An hour later, his lunch untouched, he wrote in his despair a note to his father both announcement and plea: I think she's dying.

She did not die, Maria LaTouche wrote him. Felled by unexplainable listlessness and debility, Rose was in bed for weeks, weeks spent in silence as she seemed to grope for an ability to speak. Once she could whisper she warned her mother she would become for a time in body almost as helpless as a baby, but that she would recover. It was, she knew, her mind which would recover last of all.

Jane Carlyle had written him asking when he would return to London. It was November, she reminded him, were not his Alpine valleys growing cold? More importantly, people there missed him.

No, I can't come home yet, he told her. *There's a difference I assure you—not small—between dead leaves in London Fog—and living rocks—and water—and clouds...No– I can't come home yet...Yes, it is quite true that I not only don't know that people care for me, but never can believe it somehow. I know I shouldn't care for myself if I were anybody else.*

He returned from the continent to Denmark Hill in the late autumn to find that in his own discontent, life with his parents was even less bearable. He grasped at any distraction from his preoccupation with Rose's survival. When she was well enough to write, her letters were despairingly short and irritatingly laden with pietistic maxims. From mutual friends of the LaTouche's he was sometimes sent scraps of poetry she had written in adolescent wonder about bird's nests or the beauty of the dawn. In mid-November he escaped to Winnington Hall in Cheshire, the progressive girls' school— the girls were taught to play cricket, and urged to develop their own unique personalities and intellects—where the directress Miss Bell had in recent years kept a room for him. He had spent happy evenings there when happiness was hard to come by. The girls were sweet-voiced and sang for him in choir, their music drifting through the open windows while he walked under the quiet trees. Being surrounded by Winnington's "birds" eager to go on nature walks with him gave him comfort, even though Miss Bell once again apologetically approached him for funds to keep the school afloat.

His latest loan of £300 was never meant to be repaid, and he had in fact entered it in his ledger book under "Charity". He had by this point given considerable sums to assure the school's continuance, and of itself it meant nothing to him save that it was all his father's money, and he must ask his father for it beyond his yearly allowance. His earnings from his own writings were so slight that nearly everything he possessed materially—mineral specimens, rare books and manuscripts, and most of all his collection of paintings and drawings—had been in fact purchased by his father.

Meditating on this one morning at Winnington, he began to collect his scattered thoughts about the two people he revered more than all others. He was rent by competing emotions: sorrowful to be forever chafing under his parent's loving yet unwarranted concern; grateful for his father's grudging generosity—the sums he had to ask for to help those causes and friends he found so worthy of aid—and resentful when it failed: those Turner paintings his father, through bull-headedness, refused him fresh from the easel, and so were never to be his. He lived in a state of fury that he was regularly being driven out of their shared home by his mother's eccentricities and his father's domineering caution. They were, he thought, so good, so well meaning towards their only child; and had raised him so wrong-headedly.

He realised now he had been baulked by them at every turn. His morning letter to his father began in an intentionally contentious manner, denying that his friendship with Thomas Carlyle had ever affected his revised thoughts about religion, and then went on to fever pitch in personal accusation.

Men ought to be severely disciplined and exercised in the sternest way in daily life, he told him; *they should learn to lie on stone beds and eat black soup, but they should never have their hearts broken— a noble heart once broken never mends—the best you*

*can do is rivet it with iron and plaster the cracks over—
the blood never flows rightly again. The two terrific
mistakes which Mama and you involuntarily fell into
were the exact reverse in both ways—you fed me
effeminately and luxuriously to that extent that I
actually now could not travel in rough countries
without taking a cook with me! —but you thwarted me
in all the earnest fire and passion of life.*

About Turner, he went on, freely mourning the
lost paintings, *you never knew how much you thwarted
me—for I thought it was my duty to be thwarted—it
was the religion that led me all wrong there; if I had had
courage and knowledge enough to insist on having my
own way resolutely, you would now have had me in
happy health, loving you twice as much, and with power
of self-denial; now, my power of duty has been
exhausted in vain, and I am forced by life's sake to
indulge myself in all sorts of selfish ways, just when a
man ought to be knit for the duties of middle life by the
good success of his youthful life...*

He had said it. The reading of it would sting, and
nothing about the old people at Denmark Hill would change.

In late February Ruskin arrived home at Denmark Hill
in the early hours following a dinner party which had
devolved into long conversations on Life and Art. Seeing the
lamp still burning in his father's study he went in to say
goodnight, but was detained by the old man's insistence that
he listen to two lengthy and intricate business letters which
he had just completed. Having long experience in practical
lying he was successful in feigning enough interest not to
yawn until his father began the reading of the second letter,

at which point his father rose and bid him goodnight. In the morning John James came down so much not himself that his son insisted on bringing his own work—which for that morning was the drawing of a coin depicting the water nymph Arethusa—from his upstairs study so he could sit by his father, should he need anything. When Ruskin went back upstairs an hour later to fetch a softer pencil he heard his father following him up, and then the latch fall on his father's bedroom door. He was never to leave the room alive.

After some hours a ladder was brought to lay against the brick wall beneath his father's bedroom, and it was white-haired Anne Strachan, his old childhood nurse, who pushed to the foot of it and insisted climbing to the window. John James was collected off the floor and put to bed. Ruskin was holding his father in his arms when he died four days later. Here was a man who would have sacrificed his life for his son, he thought, and yet forced his son to sacrifice his life to him, and in vain.

John James Ruskin had never trusted his son with money and complained bitterly about the petty misuse of it. To his wife he left Denmark Hill itself and £37,000. To his son he left the unrestricted residue of his estate: £120,000 in cash, and all of the paintings.

Rose had gone to a party at a neighbouring manor, and upon arriving was told a missing friend was ill. The only natural thing she could do, she wrote Ruskin, was to fall down upon her knees there on the carpet, and cry aloud a blessing in the absent girl's name. She pulled a hall chair from the wall and using it as a *prie-dieu* clasped her hands and prayed most earnestly for the girl's recovery. Her young friends and their parents stood watching in surprised silence until they one by one joined her upon the floor. And look, she added, these are for you—and a wild pansy and a mignonette blossom fell into his hand. Folding up the cream-coloured sheet he was touched not by her piety, but by her love.

He had a box made of rose-wood in which he kept all her letters, save for the most precious to him, which he pressed between sheets of gold and wore next his heart.

Although his mother considered him now head of the household it did not stop her, when distinguished guests arrived for dinner or tea, from telling her son before them that he was talking like a fool. If young people visited and Ruskin wished to take them to the theatre, he must still ask her permission to do so, which she on more than one occasion withheld. When his young Scots cousin on his father's side, Joan Agnew, visited Denmark Hill following John James' death, he was grateful for the buffer. His mother was drawn to the even-tempered seventeen year-old, and to both their satisfaction Joan was asked to stay on.

In early December Mrs. LaTouche wrote that the family was coming to London. She reminded Ruskin that Rose's eighteenth birthday was in January, as if that date could be forgotten; and shared that plans were being made for

presentation to the Queen. She added that Rose was
particularly looking forward to seeing him.

Ruskin asked the female LaTouches to come to
Denmark Hill for tea as soon as they were settled. He did not
know what to expect of her, but he wanted to see Rose there,
in his own setting, before he saw her anywhere else, to place
her foremost amongst the beauties of natural and manmade
art that surrounded his days. He forced himself to wait
upstairs in his study as their barouche drove up, and he
watched from the window as Rose and Emily and Mrs.
LaTouche were helped down. Rose had grown tall, taller even
than her older sister, and was very slender. They had scarcely
made it to the opened door when he arrived at the bottom of
the hall stair and stood awaiting her.

Rose moved past the maid and gave Joan a quick
embrace. It had been three years since she had seen the
house, and it struck her as strange that it looked different—
smaller somehow—now she was grown. There was her St. C
on the step of the curving stair, and with the flurry of her
sister and mother and Joan behind her she stood staring at
him. Rose felt a second strange feeling, stranger even than
the great house's relative diminution. She looked at John
Ruskin and said to herself, He is a man.

She saw that he was almost as old as her father, and
that his sandy hair was silver at his ears, and that his smiling
mouth was crooked from the dog bite he had received as a
boy. He was not the huge limitless looming figure whose life
she could not even imagine. She saw that he was a man, who
loved her, and if she was not quite a woman yet she was close
and she loved him back.

Because of this love Rose could not run into his arms
and kiss him as she had always done. But as she smiled at him
his hand lifted in a small gesture, a move towards her, and
she came to him. Her mother was already crossing the floor to

him, and Emily was laughing about something with Joan, and St. C could not so much as touch her hand before her mother blocked her way by taking his hand in her own.

Ruskin stood looking over Maria LaTouche's shoulder at her youngest child. As their eyes locked he felt their hearts enfold, and he was aware that no coming moment would surpass this one. Her face was so radiant he could die then, looking at it.

They all had tea in the drawing room, the four females surrounding him so pleasantly, laughing and talking together. Then he walked them about the house, revisiting the larger paintings. Last of all they went up to his study. He had hoped they would come up, to have Rose there once again in the centre of all that was most meaningful in his work.

She stopped in the centre of the room and looked about her, and he stood at her side as her eyes travelled over the walls covered with books, the cases of geological specimens, the shelves of labelled seashells, the pressed ferns mounted on blue paper, the microscope on the table with its paste-board box of glass slides. One wall was devoted to his favourite watercolours.

"Ah! The Turners. They are lovelier than I even imagined, in all my happy remembering! And this one," she went on, "is the one you spoke so long to us about, the first time we saw it." She had just touched her fingertips to the frame of Turner's view of Gosport, the waters of Portsmouth harbour alive with boats.

"It is the last of his watercolours I would part with," he said. More so since you have blessed it with your touch, he thought. It was almost too much, having her there with his Turners, minerals, shells, and books; she was both too rich and splendid and too simple and pure for the setting.

They retraced the path of that long-ago first visit, and went out into his gardens. Rose had not the slightest compunction in removing her bonnet in the mild air. Her hair was still the tint of pure gold thread. The sight of her bare-headed in the winter sunshine, walking between his laurels and primrose bank filled him with exquisite joy. She was life-giving Proserpine, returned. The south London garden was Paradise; he expected and needed no other.

On the evening of her birthday Ruskin and Joan were invited to the LaTouche's house in Mayfair. When the moment came to take the ladies in for dinner it was Ruskin who stepped forward to take Rose's arm. She had already passed over from her father's protection to his own, he felt; was given over to him. Very soon now he would ask for her hand in marriage.

The man to whom Ruskin would present his suit was more than ordinarily silent during his daughter's birthday dinner. Even Mrs. LaTouche, a woman who took pride as a hostess, was less interlocutory than usual during that festive hour. Her skills at prompting conversation and drawing out her guests were not required. Her son Percy was seated across from Joan and was animated, and even boisterous, in entertaining the young Scotswoman. Rose was sitting next Ruskin at the end of the table, too far for her mother to hear their conversation. Rose was delicately flushed and her head almost always inclined close to her guest's ear. They may have been dining alone, their absorption in each other was so complete. Maria LaTouche hoped to catch Joan's attention about this, and tried raising her eyebrows to question her puzzlement, but Percy had so monopolized the young woman that she too was oblivious. John LaTouche sat impassively at the table's head, chewing thoughtfully and staring down at his plate with knitted brow. The pairing up at the table was marked; and Mrs. LaTouche, glancing at the two captivated couples, was left paired with a man as unresponsive as a figurehead.

At the conclusion of the meal Rose placed her hand on Ruskin's arm as they passed into the drawing room. Mr. and Mrs. LaTouche led the little procession, and it was only once seated over cordials that Mr. LaTouche began perhaps to make a closer observation of his male guest. Ruskin rose, and smiling all the time at the birthday celebrant, took a paper from his breast-pocket and read aloud a poem he had written in her honour, one in which he compared her to a holy Queen.

But he was resigned not to ask her yet, nor here in a hurried moment in her father's house in Mayfair. At the beginning of February Joan invited Rose to spend the day at Denmark Hill. There on Candlemas Day, the Feast-day of the Purification of the Virgin—the anniversary, too, of his own parents' wedding—he led Rose into the garden once more. They walked again the gravelled path by the primrose bank, but the day was dull and there was no sun to glint over the wall at them. He directed her gaze to a vivid patch of moss by the stone stair, and she bent and plucked a tiny white star-flower thrusting from the mat of green. She held it to him, and in taking it he lifted her palm to his face, and pressed it with his lips.

"I cannot answer yet," she said, before he had spoken a word. "I cannot tell you Yes or No."

"My darling—my sweet and wild Rose," he said, still holding her hand.

She lowered her eyes but did not pull her hand from him. She wished she could keep him as happy as he was at this moment, but could not. "Will you, could you, wait three years for my answer?"

It was as a blow struck between his shoulder blades; his breath left him.

"Do you know how old I shall be in three years?" he finally asked.

"I do, of course." The lightness of her tone suggested that she had asked him to wait three months, not years; and that even if it had been three decades the outcome would be a happy one. "You shall be fifty, and I twenty-one, and fully of age to marry or no."

"With or without your parent's consent?"

Rose wished he had not said this, and she found herself shaking her head. "With all my heart I hope it is with."

"And, may I speak to them now about us? Have I leave?"

Now the warm hand was withdrawn.

"My dear St. Crumpet, they won't I fear be pleased. Mama I think is angry now and will only be angrier. She felt––I don't know—surprised to find you liked me so well...She thought from all your letters and visits, and all the nice talks you two had had, that you were, well, *her* friend...And Papa––Papa I think will be very cross with you; after my birthday dinner he had a talk with me, naming no names, but telling me he should never like to see a daughter of his wed to an— old man like him. I tried to make him laugh by telling him he wasn't old—but I knew what he meant to warn me about."

The path was clear before him, as clear as if she held a lantern in her hand and she his only goal.

"Then I shall go to them and tell them exactly what I tell you now: you have my utter obedience to your slightest wish, forever; that I will never in these three years of waiting stand between you and any other suitor you might entertain;

and that my love for you is absolute, final, and has been tested by years. And that I shall die loving you."

When she left he went silently to his room. He opened his diary and wrote 1097—counting down the number of days to her 21st birthday when he might know her answer. Then he realised he did not have the star-flower she had offered him. He returned to the garden and searched until dark in vain to recover it.

Mrs. LaTouche was so very much occupied that it was some days before she could see him. He wished to speak to her first, and privately, banking on the past sympathy between them. He was surprised then when he arrived in Mayfair for their interview not to be ushered up to her small fern-and-orchid-filled conservatory where they had enjoyed prior *tête-á-têtes*. Instead he was shown to Mr. LaTouche's library on the ground floor.

She was not there to greet him. The room was empty, and the smallest imaginable fire burned in the grate; it looked like a single coal. He stood in the centre of the room, casting his eyes from the oxblood leather-topped desk with its impossible ink stand to the bronze ceiling lamp suspended by swags of dark coppery chain. Matched sets of leather bound, gilt-stamped *octavo* and *quarto* volumes surrounded him, books he knew had been purchased for this house when it was built, and suspected had never been touched since save by the maid's ostrich feather-duster.

Maria LaTouche entered, in a steel-grey dress and jet jewellery. Her familiar scent of Parma violets was missing, and Ruskin recognized—as if his anxiety had heightened his olfactory nerve—that it was the first time he had been in her presence without that gentle fragrance surrounding her.

"Mr. Ruskin, forgive my delay. Emily's wedding, Rose's presentation plans—" She offered her hand readily enough, but the smile faded at once. "Please sit down," she said, although she did not. He remained standing as she began.

"I know why you have come to see me—and no, I am not pleased about your startling proposal."

He began to protest having made any mystery of his devotion, but she went on.

"I don't think you have any idea of Rose's real condition. Despite her apparent high spirits here in London she is neither physically nor mentally fit to entertain the idea of marriage to anyone."

She folded her hands and sat down, and he took a chair opposite her.

"Mrs. LaTouche, Rose to me is the most precious member of Creation, but I respectfully—most respectfully—contest your idea that she is in any way unfit—"

"I don't think you understand me, Mr. Ruskin, and so I forgive you for supposing a mother's judgement inferior to your own. Rose is young for her age and still recovering from her illness—which might re-occur at any time should she be over-excited."

She let this last term hang in the air, almost as an impropriety.

"You are, moreover a man of shipwrecked faith, and have already made Rose suffer particularly, and acutely, for you."

"If she has suffered it was from her own—"

But Mrs. LaTouche was on her feet.

"And there is the age discrepancy. Of course some girls marry much older men, but Mr. LaTouche and I do not favour such unions."

She hesitated. "And in this case—in this case, are you not in effect forfeiting the role of a *beloved uncle* in an attempt to become a suitor?"

The indecency of those words, of the thought behind them, queered him from any attempt of declaring his true and pure love.

"I have told Rose she is utterly free to accept other suitors," he said, "but I will be guided by her actions alone."

"Rose is still a fragile child who must be guarded and guided by her parents' love," returned Mrs. LaTouche.

The interview was at its close. Her shoulders seemed to soften at last.

"We have been friends," she ended, "and allies too; but I cannot be allied against Mr. LaTouche."

Before the family left for Harristown in April he had had a scant handful of occasions for seeing Rose, but never for one moment alone. There were few points of intersection between their respective social circles. He could not introduce her or any of the LaTouches to the coterie of his artist friends, despite the charm, intelligence, and conviviality often found there. Almost as an act of benediction he brought Rose to meet the irascible Carlyle, but could not countenance inflicting a pious and wealthy banker like John LaTouche upon the fiercely anti-materialist sage. He bought tickets for Mendelssohn's *Elijah*, knowing that Rose would enjoy it, but as the lights dimmed and the chorus started he and his cousin Joan sat in their box with three empty chairs. In the interval a boy brought a message saying Rose was sick with head-ache and begged their pardon for herself and sister and mother. He recalled nothing of the triumphal second act.

I want *leave* to love, he thought, sitting in the darkened theatre; and the sense that the fair creature whom I do love is *made happy* by being loved. I do not even care that Rosie should love me, just that she be happy in being loved... He was struck by the imbalance of condition this implied, and by his own helplessness in awaiting her twenty-first birthday. Ahead of him lay nearly 1100 days of uncertainty before he might learn if Rose was to be his. He found himself remembering golden-haired St. Ursula, martyred with her attendant 1100 virgins. Ursula began appearing in his dreams, not once but repeatedly, from which he awakened with eyes wet with tears. As the dreams deepened and developed he heard the angel who visited her insist that the pagan prince who sought her hand not only convert, but wait three years for her. It seemed a sentence for them all. Ursula would not live to wed her pagan prince, but die a virgin.

The day before the LaTouches departed for Ireland, Maria LaTouche sent him a note with express instructions forbidding—*forbidding* him—to write to Rose. The child had been rash enough to make a three year compact until she gave her answer, and he must be content with that. Lacerta had found her venom after all.

How much more puzzling then to find a letter coming for Joan, inviting her to Harristown for a visit of several weeks' duration. By September she was engaged to Percy LaTouche.

Light, Descending

Rose had promised to find a way to send him a letter for Christmas. She was allowed to write to Joan, and Joan in turn would convey such a missive to him. When the day passed without a note he cursed her cruelty. Why deny him even a sprig of holly, or a few rose leaves, for her message? He spent much of the day wandering heedlessly through the neighbourhood, and when no letter arrived on Boxing Day felt he could understand the worst acts that men could do.

Percy LaTouche made several trips to visit Joan at Denmark Hill, never carrying a letter from his sister. Through friends he heard occasional word of Rose. One red-letter day she wrote him herself, enclosing some verse from her own hand, and the news of Emily's baby. Responding was torturously difficult. He, so free in words, agonised over his letter, attempting to strike the correct note of nostalgic playfulness and lover's ardency. Nothing came in return.

On her birthday in January he marked off as complete a year's waiting for her answer. Then came the news that Rose was in a nursing home in Ireland, and had even once to be restrained in her bed. He hung between hope and despair on every word that reached him about her condition. Mrs. LaTouche sometimes wrote Joan, and it was through her letters he learnt of Rose's gradual recovery.

In late Spring Joan was again at Harristown, happy to be so near Percy. It was only Ruskin's inviting her to join a hastily arranged trip to Switzerland with his confidante Lady Pauline Trevelyan and her naturalist husband Sir Walter that brought her back. Lady Pauline was unwell with a stomach ailment which had been growing steadily worse, and the high air might be found salutary. And he hoped he might lose himself in undertaking a study of alpine mosses.

"How did she speak of me?" he asked Joan when she arrived back at Denmark Hill. She had been home for several hours, and Ruskin could contain himself no longer.

Joan had been uneasily expecting this question. Her anxious cousin seemed to be staring holes right through her, and she didn't like the look of his colour. "She said nothing of you, Coz," she finally told him. "When I arrived she let me know her parents had forbidden the mention of your name. She even wrote it in a note to me, so as not to disobey them."

Her unaffected Scot's accent, never neutralized through social aspiration, fell the blunter on Ruskin's eager ear. He was unable to answer, and unable even to turn from her to conceal his pain. Joan put her hand on his arm in silent consolation.

Before they set out for Switzerland he sent a bouquet of flowers to Cheyne Row to cheer ailing Jane Carlyle. Instead of a thank you acknowledging receipt the boy carried back a terse note from a physician saying she had died that afternoon after running after a carriage which had slightly injured her pet dog. An added cruelty was that the dog had been a gift to Jane from Lady Pauline. Carlyle was away in Edinburgh receiving honours and beyond the reach of any comfort he might give.

He could not bring himself to dampen the spirits of his little party. Despite their inquiries he did not reveal the additional grief he was harbouring until they reached Paris and read about the death themselves.

In Paris Lady Pauline became too ill to leave her bed. After some days they moved her with difficulty to Neuchâtel, where she died with Sir Walter and him at her side. Loss after loss.

In the alpine heights Ruskin dreamt of a small green snake he found lacing through tall grass. Rose was at his side, and in his dream he had no fear of the creature, and allowed it to entwine about his fingers. He made her feel its scales, and she did so, laughing; then she placed it back in his hands so he would feel them. It was then the snake transformed into a fearful, fat thing, a monstrous thick serpent which sucked onto his hand like a leech, and which he could not shake off. He awoke trembling, trembling with dread and excitement.

In August Joan returned to Harristown for Percy's 21st birthday celebration. The careless manner which had charmed her on first acquaintance had taken a more decided course. She was frightened to see him riotous with drink at his birthday dinner, and by mutual consent the engagement was quietly terminated.

Joan was heart-sick at her forfeit, and Ruskin felt unable to comfort one so tender who had, like him, been harmed by the LaTouches. And he had lost an important conduit for news of Rose. He wrote again to the senior LaTouches, begging that he might he allowed to correspond freely.

It was not in the best interest of their daughter's health, came the reply. He re-doubled his pleas to any mutual friend he could conjure to intercede for him. The year passed, and in his diary each dawn he wrote the number of days remaining until he should learn his fate.

An entire hemisphere of his life was in suspension, and with it his efforts at work, drawing, and sustained thought blasted. How galling for a man whose personal motto was 'To-day'—who awakened each day before dawn to labour against that coming dark when no man could work. It was his work that had driven him, given him meaning and pleasure, and a girl with a heart of flint had robbed his hours of his essential desideratum.

Then a letter came.

Dear St. C—I want you to know I am Yours, and nothing can come between Us.

It was the complete contents, one line. She had gotten it to a friend who had sent it on to Denmark Hill. To mark the day in his diary he placed beside the number 245, *Peace*.

He travelled to Dublin to deliver a lecture, his heart racing as he drew so close to Harristown. His subject—*The Mystery of Life and its Arts*—would hold appeal for the LaTouches. Might they themselves be amongst the sold-out house? There was much in it meant for their ears: an appreciation of those who fed and clothed the needy; the necessity for the artist to hold before him an ideal ever exceeding his grasp; and in stunning contrast to his earliest writings in *Modern Painters*, a rejection of certainty. He would speak of the impossibility of plumbing the depths of the 'mysteries' of life and art. One of the greatest mysteries, he would tell them, was the corruption of religion, particularly when it wasted the vital powers of earnest young women in fruitless agony over the Bible.

On the morning of the lecture a letter was brought to him: *Dear St. C, I am forbidden by my father and mother to write you.* She enclosed two petals from a rose.

Rose, it turned out, was there in Dublin. She was in a nursing home. Through the simple bribery of a staff member he arranged to meet her on its wooded grounds. A female attendant led her to him as he waited near a leafless copse of trees. The woman nodded at him and left to take her position a few yards off.

Rose was gaunt. The warm and liquid eyes looked dry and glittery, and the pallor of her cheeks was such that even the East wind did not colour them. She seemed both enfeebled and agitated, and would not permit him to so much as take her hand.

"I have been shown a letter," she began. "It was from your wife."

His wife. He was too staggered to respond.

"She that was your wife, I ought to say. Mama wrote her, and she wrote back the awfullest things about your— marriage. She said you are incapable of truly loving a woman, and ought not to spoil another one's best years as you did hers. And Mama wrote to our lawyer, and he said he guessed Mrs. Millais was right, that if you should wed again and have a child, her marriage now would be invalid, and their children not in law." Tears were rolling from her eyes, and her lower lip was quivering.

"We can't ever, ever, ever wed. And she said you were— —unnatural—and most impure in your actions to her..." Her tears stopped her speech, but when Ruskin again attempted to touch her she stepped back like a frightened doe.

His mind was racing, and he felt out of breath. He could not answer.

She wiped her face with her handkerchief and drew breath. "I wish you to be Lover and Friend to me always—and no more. That is what you must have wanted with your wife, and that much I can grant, with all my heart."

Now he had an answer. "It was *not* what I wanted, at least not at first, and it is not what I wish from you now. I come to you in utter purity of heart, as one who has loved you faithfully for ten years, as one who awaits upon your word as a sacred vow."

"You have no need to wait."

He could not bear this injustice. "I don't accept that. You promised me to wait three years to make your answer, and those years have not yet passed. And even after that day when you can refuse me, you cannot refuse my love and my sorrow; it will always be yours."

"Then we will trust in God."

What would it mean, he asked himself in watching her tear-stained face, if he could go down upon his knees on this cold Irish earth and tell her in complete truth that in the long months of separation he had once again found Faith? That all the prim little homilies and exhortations to belief she had peppered her old letters with had acted upon him, and he was now redeemed through grace of her love and concern for him? If he could claim this as truth, would it expunge the foulness of the machinations of her mother, or the evil served him now by a vengeful but utterly forgotten wife?

How Rose had made him suffer in the past—how her mother now crucified him with her actions. He had been silent in pain, he had laboured and wept, he had borne every insult. How cruelly he had been injured, and yet she remained the innocent! It was she who had been perverted, through the wrongness of her religion, to see evil in him.

Could he in one gesture, one proclamation, cut through her fear and win her wholly?

He wished to smite his head with his own furious hand, and force himself upon the ground at her feet. But he could not lie, and claim a return to his former narrow and naive faith.

His torment must have shown on his face, for she said, "There is nothing but this frail 'cannot' to separate our life and love."

He was not aware of his own tears until she lifted her hand and brushed one away. "What do you mean?" he cried in an agony of hope.

"Fare-well, dear friend," she answered, and turned away.

He went to Chamonix and tried to take comfort in his Alps. Even they were not immutable, the Glace du Mer was shrinking, and new and ugly towns springing up. He stared at barren mountain peaks and envied their insensibility. If he believed in a personal way in a heavenly Father—which he no longer could—he would have demanded: Why have you teazed me in this way? If there were no toys in the cupboard, I would have been satisfied—but the one I can't have?

Awaking from fitful sleep, he could not understand why his dreams were not nobler. He dreamt of floating under the bronze horses of St Mark's. He dreamt of his father; of dark waters rushing by him; of standing in empty and crumbling cathedrals. He dreamt of snakes in all their many guises, not knowing if they were the death-dealing serpent in the Garden, the wisdom-bringing python of the Pythia, or the twined pair upholding the caduceus of the healer. Most hideous were dreams of the Gorgon, every hair a springing snake, sneering at him as he stood transfixed and powerless.

And he dreamt of Rose as a young girl, attempting to sell him a set of keys that were snatched from them both, and crushed.

He stopped numbering the days in his diary.

He went to Abbeville, and lost himself each day in drawing the spalling beauties of Northern Gothic churches. He saw an antelope which reminded him of Rose. One night in his room he was frightened to see the wallpaper resolve itself into leering faces.

January 3rd 1869 was Rose's twenty-first birthday. No message came.

He was working on a book drawn from a linked series of essays as an expression of his new cosmos. He employed the goddess Athena, and the gods Apollo and Hermes in an attempt to unite the worlds of nature, society, and self. He wrote of the birth of Hermes almost as the birth of Christ, and used Hebrew figures as well as the inventions of Dante and Shakespeare to point a path to the key of all mythologies: all true visions by noble persons reverberated in every other;

lent new depth, shading and perspective to the grandest conceptions of the spirit and imagination, as the seed contains the flower.

But *The Queen of the Air* contained the specific as well as the grand, and he examined closely two strains of myths—that of the Dove, and that of the Serpent.

The strain of writing it was too great; he must retreat to Switzerland or risk collapse. Norton was now living in London. Ruskin asked his friend to see it through the presses, and fled.

Poring over the manuscript, Norton felt passages pierce his heart like arrows. Bereft from the death of his wife, he himself stayed alive only for his young children's sake. Faced now with the legal aspects of seeing Ruskin's book through to publication, Norton inquired if he had made a will. Not yet, Ruskin wrote back, but all my work's posthumous now.

In her bedroom at Harristown Rose LaTouche read her slender copy of *The Queen of the Air*, marking the margins with pencilled comments as she did so. Almost as soon as she began reading she realised it had been written for her, and began to be fearful as she turned the pages. Their love was impossible, why could he not leave her alone? She wanted to feel close to him yet, even though they could never wed—why did he drive her away with his words? She looked down at the slender volume, afraid to go on, unable to stop.

The author was decrying those who would not attend to the wisdom of a pre-Christian age and dismissed the sincerity of those who, through their accident of birth, had no other gods to worship but Pagan. How cruel and unpardonable it was for such readers to claim, 'There is no God but for me.' Later she found a passage in which he derided the "insane religion, degraded art, merciless toil" of the modern age; "the race itself still half-serpent...a lacertine breed of bitterness."

By it she could only write, "Poor green lizards! They are not bitter; why not say serpentine?" She knew he meant Lacerta, her mother's pet-name; and he went on in ways that horrified her about creeping serpents; dark oriental mysteries concerning snakes; of poisoned life lashing through grasses. She could not understand it, she wrote; and it all was so terribly heathenish.

At the end of the first week of January 1870 Ruskin walked up the steps of the Royal Academy at twelve o'clock. Entering the first gallery he saw a woman, alone. It was Rose.

She turned from the canvas she was standing before and caught sight of him. She started and fled. He would not let her escape. Catching her up in the next gallery of green landscapes he held out his hand. Her eyes were wild with fear and her small nostrils flared. Wordlessly he drew from his breast the silk wallet he carried each day. Within were two thin sheets of beaten gold which enclosed her most treasured letters to him.

"Here are my most precious belongings—they are yours. Take them."

Her eyes did not leave his face, did not register the offered wallet.

"No."

If she would not have them back—? "No?" he asked, barely able to frame the word.

"No," she breathed.

Yet her thin frame was so rigid that there was nothing of hope in it. He slid the wallet back next to his heart and left.

He wrote no diary entry for January 7th, only marking the worst day of his life with a cross.

The next month she wrote him.

> *I will trust you, she said, I do love you. I have loved you, though the shadows that have come between us could not but make me fear you and turn from you. I love you, & shall love you always, always—& you can make this mean what you will. I have doubted your love, I have wished not to love you. I have thought you unworthy, yet—as surely as I believe God loves you, as surely as my trust is in His Love, I love you—still, and always. Do not doubt this anymore. I believe God meant us to love each other, yet Life—and it seems God's will—has divided us...I am forbidden to write to you, and I cannot continue to do so—And now—may I say God bless you?*

In Siena Ruskin greeted Charles Eliot Norton as he always had, with both hands outstretched and pulling him close. Norton, holding Ruskin at arms' length, was struck by his friend's otherworldliness. Ruskin was not of this sphere, Norton thought, but a 12th century angel who had somehow lost its wings and been waylaid on this Earth, to his sorrow.

Ruskin took his friend's arm. They walked through the same arches Dante had passed, and wandered the hills above town where sudden fireflies flitted and shone like flying candles against the golden twilight. They spoke of the paintings of Mantegna, of Raphael, Luini, and Lippi; they watched in silence as the colours of the striped facades beneath them paled into blue dusk. Even Norton, at Ruskin's elbow, grew indistinct. Everything began to meld and mingle before him. Everything—the faded crumbling stone, the hidden birds calling in the dark cypresses, the rising scent of wild thyme bruising beneath their feet, the fearful glitter of the fireflies about their heads—seemed to merge. It was intoxicating to eyes, ears, and nose; it made Ruskin dizzy. How things bind and blend themselves together!

Chapter Eighteen

The Lamp of Power & The Lamp of Beauty

London: 1865

If Ruskin could not focus his mind to work he could still work through others.

Miss Octavia Hill sat at tea with him in the front parlour. It was not a room which gave Ruskin special delight. His father had long ago selected the red flocked paper covering the walls, and the ungiving, almost-purple chairs upon which they sat. But the room had large windows opening to the cedar of Lebanon outside, and the table before them was set with his favourite blue and pink Staffordshire china service. On the work table they had just turned from lay a few pages cut from one of Ruskin's medieval missals. Miss Hill had copied their delicate paintings and these had appeared in Volume V of *Modern Painters*.

"One feels so strongly the call to be of service, the dire need of so many," she said. Miss Hill was not yet thirty and had known Ruskin for nearly fifteen years. She had been an early and enthusiastic reader of his books on art and architecture, and, unlike many of his initial readers, had responded warmly to their embedded social message. She also possessed enough artistic skill so that when they met he had been happy to train her in copying medieval miniatures to illustrate his writings; he employed a number of able young persons in this way. She had received a regular allowance to paint for him, and he helped her found a small school for girls so that she might be more fully employed.

"Think of the shameful instance of that woman dying in that unventilated basement hovel—the rent she paid to her drunken land-lord—the hordes of children playing in and around open sewers throughout London—children raised in savagery, with no hope or prospect of living to adulthood in such filth."

Ruskin sat back and smiled at her. "I believe, my dear Octavia, that you have a solution to propose to me?"

Miss Hill did not flush, and did not even pause. "I do indeed, and would not risk the telling of it to anyone but you." She replaced the china cup in its scalloped-edge saucer. She was not a demonstrative speaker, but being quietly forceful none the less needed both small hands free.

"I have found three houses off the Marylebone High Street, on Paradise Place. They would require considerable work to make them habitable to a decent standard, but I believe the owner could be assured of a 5% annual return on his investment, for I should only rent to poor working women of the highest character."

There, it was out, and before him. Here—and on the ill-named Paradise Place—was Ruskin's chance to experiment with his ideas on ethical political economy, and here too was an energetic, strong-minded, trustworthy discipline of his social doctrine to execute it.

"How much is the lease-hold?" was how he answered.

"£1,500, and it would be a dead loss; and then there will be the expenses to clean and modernize the lodgings." Miss Hill was meticulous in her copying and equally so in her planning.

His father's old friends had attempted to advise him on the wise disposition of his sudden wealth. Ignoring them

Ruskin had promptly lost a good deal of money in buying up mortgages which turned out to be faulty.

"It is important that the venture not come to a smash," he said.

"The initial investment is—well, I suppose lost; but I believe I can promise the owner a firm 5% return per annum on rents from the women." She looked at him brightly, eagerly, until she became aware she had held her gaze a moment too long for seemliness. She glanced down and smoothed her skirt with her hands, then shifted her brown eyes away to the damask draperies.

Ruskin already owned property in working-class Marylebone. He had been left with the problem of how to accommodate the elderly servants his parents had accumulated over the years. *The Daily Telegraph* had claimed it was now impossible to find good servants, and Ruskin answered this charge in a number of letters pointing out the necessity of first being worthy of being served. His direct action was to buy up a few suitable properties in Marylebone and so provide homes for the superannuated members of Denmark Hill's staff.

A five per cent return was what he had written was a just and proper rate of return on such investments; anything beyond was criminal, predatory.

He had already made up his mind, but sat there silently, with his eyes upon Octavia Hill. Her person was tidy, with a level of comeliness common to good health and natural vitality. She was highly intelligent. Her social aims and values were his own. She was devoted to him.

Why then, he asked himself as he looked at her, did he feel nothing, no stirring of emotion or even affection beyond what he might bestow upon any industrious do-gooding maiden lady of his acquaintance? She, or any number of other

young ladies he associated with, could be a perfect help-meet
for him. He had only to move his chair closer to hers, and
take one of those capable small hands in his own. Soon she
would no doubt be the one to take *him* in hand, to worry and
fret over him, make of his comfort a project that like all else
she undertook she would make a success of. This bustling
little woman before him had a heart filled with warmth,
ready, perhaps yearning, to love: Why could he not accept it?
He was acutely aware of a limiting factor more important
than Miss Hill's creditable appearance, aspirations, or
emotional capabilities, a limitation or absence in her very
fibre that precluded any romantic imaginings. Miss Hill
lacked poetry.

He asked no further question, and returned to the
venture on Paradise Place. "Then let it be so. I will tell my
attorneys to attend to it tomorrow."

Carlyle had been like water flowing under a glacier to
him, unseen but there, helping to advance the massive ice
sheet to its goal. His was a light in which he saw himself
differently. He stopped appending "by the author of *Modern
Painters*" to his published works. And now that his own
father was dead, he began calling the old man Papa.

Over the last few years Carlyle had become as well his
closest friend, even displacing Norton in his trust. Norton,
clinging to his doomed American ideals of democracy and
equality, could not enter into sympathy with much of
Ruskin's political thinking. When Carlyle completed his six
volume study of Frederick the Great the old man confessed
that he felt actual despair at the thirteen year burden of its
writing having been lifted. He recognised in Carlyle the

slough of stupefaction he himself had laboured under when *Modern Painters* was concluded.

There was only one topic he could not speak to Carlyle freely about, one pain he could not seek comfort for without risking impatience or misapprehension. He could not hazard speaking about his Rose.

Sitting up one night at Cheyne Row, Ruskin rehearsed his physical symptoms and told Carlyle he thought he was dying. The old sage drew from his pipe and finding it cold, rapped its contents out against the fire-breast. "Moulting is the better term, my boy. Keep writing."

In London Ruskin went to a lecture on Shakespeare and was left wondering how truthful was the speaker's suppositions of the bard's intent. Walking from the lecture hall he was struck that perhaps he himself had read too much into the work of Turner.

Turner's art was the first light Ruskin had ever grasped toward, the fountainhead of illimitable truth and splendour at which he had endlessly replenished himself. Every following passion was rooted in the wake, and watered in the shallows of that grand discovery. And what harvest had this adoration reaped? He had made of Turner's genius an elaborate scaffolding encompassing a world of his own devising, one of complex and even conflicting artistic and moral principles and precepts, which, coincidentally, the artist himself had had no interest in. The scaffolding which bore Ruskin aloft to such heights of wonder lacked a steadying foundation, and was never high enough or long enough to enclose the limitless world it had been erected to surround. Every attraction and attachment he had formed, whether to the human heart or to human creativity, had ended in frustration. How the power of his intellect, the passion of his longing, heart-ache, rejection, confusion, and misapprehension, had been squandered by those he had most yearned to bless! How he had squandered himself! Everything and everyone he believed in betrayed him in the end.

If he thought he could see Rose he would go to Ireland and lay down at her gate— beg her father to take him as a common herdsmen—anything to place himself near her. He was so sick for the sight of her he would risk being dragged away from their very door.

Forbidden Ruskin's letters, there was yet a way to speak to Rose, and that was through his published writings. *Sesame and Lilies* discussed the social inequities which troubled him, and dealt too with the proper education and responsibilities of the young. But it was his focus on the upbringing of girls that marked the book. He examined the characters and actions of Shakespeare's heroines, calling the catastrophe of every play the fault of a man, and the redemption, if redemption were to be found, brought about by the wisdom and virtue of a woman. He urged that adolescent girls be kept away from modern magazines and novels, but set loose in old libraries to find their way amongst their treasures. He spoke of the essential Queenliness of womanhood, and the necessity for queenly action amongst women. He urged them not to be cruel. It was meant as a letter to one girl.

Light, Descending

Its commercial success surprised him. The numbers of intellectuals and artists who had waded through the five volumes of *Modern Painters*, or the economists and social reformers who had reviled or endorsed *Unto this Last* was minute compared to those dutiful mothers and doting aunts who now swept into their local book sellers to place *Sesame and Lilies* into the hands of their female charges.

His mother had for years insisted the family move out of the house each spring that Denmark Hill might be thoroughly cleaned. He now took advantage of this annual inconvenience by pulling from his walls fifty paintings, forty of them Turners. The jewel of the collection was Turner's 'Slavers Throwing Overboard the Dead and Dying' which his father had presented to him as token of the achievement embodied in the first volume of *Modern Painters*. He had it and the other Turners unceremoniously crated up, along with paintings by Copley Fielding and a few others he had collected over the years. As the packers hammered down the lid over John Brett's 'Val d'Aosta', he could not but recall Maria LaTouche's rapturous response to seeing it upon her first visit with Rose to Denmark Hill.

He was heedless of their disposition. They might end up in Paris, or Moscow, or Boston; he cared not. He sent them all off to Christie's, and wrote the auction catalogue descriptions himself. He reaped the better part of 6,000 guineas for this expurgation.

Light, Descending

At the end of each decade he re-read Thomas Carlyle's complete works, making notes of new impressions and changes in his understanding. He began this time with *Sartor Resartus*—and wrote his Papa that he had nearly all his clothes to make fresh—but more shroud-shape than any other.

In August at breakfast on his terrace in Lugano, Ruskin opened a telegram brought to him by a panting boy. In recognition of his contribution to art criticism his alma mater had elected him Slade Professor of Art at Oxford, and thus the University's first professor of art. In his new capacity he would prepare and deliver a series of lectures upon art-subjects, intended for undergraduates of that institution but open also to the public at large.

His first thought was the amount of pleasure news of his appointment would have given his dead father. His second was that it might yet give pleasure to a certain someone who had dealt him his greatest pain.

In the Hilary Term of 1870—the day of his birthday, 8 February—he stood in the Sheldonian Theatre where thirty-one years ago he had read aloud his school-boy poetry that had won him the Newdigate Prize. He was to have made his Inaugural Address in the theatre of the new Oxford Museum, but the size of the waiting crowd dictated the impromptu switch to the larger Sheldonian. He had not imagined he should stand there again.

He found lecturing as freeing to the imagination as ever, and devised dramatic ways of capturing his audience's attention—laying glass over a Turner water-colour and drawing directly upon it to illustrate the master's perspective techniques; summoning scouts to rapidly enter holding aloft a sequence of bold line drawings on the development of ecclesiastical architecture, appearing with arms laden with blossoming tree branches for a talk on colour harmony.

During term Ruskin took up lodgings near Oxford. Out walking a country lane he struck up a conversation with an amiable old man, and asking him if he could send him one of his books as a token, was told that he had never learnt to read. For response he took him in his arms and kissed him.

Chapter Nineteen

The Lamp of Power & The Lamp of Beauty

June: 1871

The wedding breakfast was winding to its close, and the dancing was soon to begin. The bride had signed the church register "Joan Agnew" and had been Mrs. Arthur Severn for three hours. Now she was in her bedroom pinning on her travelling hat. Joan smiled at herself in the glass. What a lovely morning she had had! Her dear Coz had given her and Arthur the most heartfelt of toasts at the table. Coz looked dapper in a new grey suit with a rose in the button-hole, and a bright blue stock about his throat. How dear he was—as dear as her own dead father—and more generous than she would have ever hoped.

Ruskin had made Arthur Severn wait three years for his cousin Joan, years in which the aspiring watercolourist was forbidden to write to her. Severn had duly reappeared and Ruskin, granting what he had not been himself given, rewarded his faithfulness with the young woman's hand. As a wedding present Ruskin conveyed to Joan the lease on his London childhood home, with his sole request that she save Herne Hill's third floor—his old nursery—for his own use. Margaret Ruskin had taken a shine to Joan's new husband, and had given Arthur a sum of money, to be spent only on furniture, and that mahogany. After the engagement was formalized the suitor had been allowed upstairs of an evening to Aunt Margaret's rooms for a chat, and come down many times with a "tip" of a guinea or two which the old lady drew from the netted purse under her pillow. If young Arthur Severn had not felt it unusual to accept a gratuity from his future kin, Joan's own experience as poor relation in an

261

eccentric household did not equip her to sense the impropriety of either offer or acceptance.

Now Joan Agnew Severn was heading off on her wedding trip. Ruskin had arranged that as well. She and Arthur were to spend their first married week not in the anonymous privacy of a hotel or rented cottage, but in Yorkshire under the consecrating roof of a country vicar who had communicated to Ruskin his interest in the paintings of Turner. When Joan had suggested that she and Arthur were anticipating a six weeks' honeymoon tour, Ruskin paled. Her cousin made her promise that upon their return she would go on living with him and his mother at Denmark Hill.

Five days after her wedding, Joan, in Yorkshire, opened a letter from Denmark Hill. She had written two letters home this first week, one to her aunt and one to her cousin himself. It was not enough.

O Doanie, Ruskin wrote, using one of his pet names for her, *Me was fitened dedful for no ettie—no ettie—no ettie—Sat-day—Sun-day—Mon-day—Two's-day—so fitened...Today—no ettie again—me so misby–misby–misby...Oh me miss oo—more than tongue can tell...*

They'd used baby-talk between them for years; her cousin enjoyed it, and she indulged him. But reading this, she turned to her new husband and murmured, "John is not well."

Heedless of the new couple's honeymoon privacy Ruskin wrote a second letter and told them he would join them—that they should meet him half way at the spa town Matlock in Derbyshire. He arrived in the first few days of a July that may as well have been November. The skies were cold and dark, and waiting for Joan and Arthur to arrive Ruskin wondered if these were the sorts of winds that had once brought the plague.

Light, Descending

He left the hotel early to sketch; there was a bank of wild roses he had seen. The morning sky seemed devoid of actual light and he could not get in the right position to the spray of thorn and bud he wanted. His paper blew and creased in the dry wind and his pencil point kept breaking off under the pressure of his hand.

He returned to the hotel and wanted no lunch. In his room he lay upon his bed perspiring. Water came into his mouth and great waves of bile forced their way out. Then Joan was there, and Arthur too. After a long time Henry Acland came and they spoke of their days together at Oxford. He was very hot and Acland held his hands and forced open his lips. He could not stop shivering.

When he opened his eyes there was a bowl of goldfish Joanie had brought him, goldfish and a bowl of purple grapes. He looked at them for days. Joanie sang Scottish songs to him.

When he could speak again he recalled from his boyhood a place in the Lakes where he and his father and mother had all been happy.

If only he could lie down in Coniston Water, he felt he should get better.

Chapter Twenty

The Lamp of Truth: 1877-1878

London: Summer 1877

Ruskin determined to view the paintings at the Grosvenor Gallery alone. The faintness and bouts of dizziness were less frequent, and if he were mindful and above all avoided chatter and disruption, the viewing might allow him to add a few words about the gallery's maiden exhibition to the issue of *Fors* he had nearly completed. He must go alone, and view the imagined extravagances and, he suspected, vulgarities of this new gallery without the yammering distraction of a companion. It was enough he would dine afterwards with Ned and Georgiana Burne-Jones; their undemanding company soothed and comforted him.

He finished his *toilette* in the top floor of the old Herne Hill house—"my old nursery-room, feeling like my true home" he had told his diary—by wrapping his habitual blue stock about his throat before pulling on a light coat appropriate to the June weather. The stock was silk, of corn-flower blue: a colour to be found in the miniatures gracing a medieval missal. It suited him, and his eyes, still blue and bright, brighter perhaps than loving friends should like to see. It was old-fashioned, that wearing of a stock, but he would no more surrender it than go out in public in his dressing gown. He caught a glimpse of himself in the looking glass by the door of his aerie and for the briefest of moments shuddered. He *had* gone out into the streets in his dressing gown, not here in London, but months ago in Verona, gone out of his rented rooms into the *campo* wearing his dressing gown of Turkey-red damask, and became aware of this lapse only by the admiring glances and *La Giaconda* half-smiles of the Veronese he passed. And he had written about this episode—

264

why not?—in the following issue of *Fors*. Odd, how the attention wandered!

He kissed the sleeping image of St. Ursula and left.

The Grosvenor Gallery on New Bond Street had opened in May. The product of Sir and Lady Coutts Lindsay's cultural aspirations (and Lady Mary's considerable fortune) was yet another alternative to the strictures of the selection committee over at the Royal Academy. It was purpose-built, and at great expense, as an art gallery, contained the suspect innovation of a restaurant, and had been hailed by several reviewers for its "Venetian atmosphere." As Ruskin approached the massive mahogany doors he wondered how Sir Coutts' decorators had conjured Venice.

Venice! Ruskin was lately returned from nine months wandering that hoary ruin, from glimmering September through the dank and frosty depths of winter and out again to the brilliance of May. He knew *La Serenissima* for the fickle and painted mistress she was—the allure of glittering mosaic and glinting water distracting the eye from the crumbling of rotten stone, the silent leaching of lime from ancient *palazzi* stripped naked of their marble by mercenary Austrians or the rapacity of Venetians themselves, the faded indecency of the hollow-eyed empty warehouses, once splendid with the world's mercantile treasures.

Thank God back in the '40's and '50's he had been there to document what he could. He had made notebook after notebook of measured drawings, delicate sketches of marble and limestone tracery, whole aspects of buildings before they fell to the brutal hands of the "restorers" and were spoilt forever! And what was left carted away, booty taken from this greatest repository of booty—doorways and archivolts prised out, window jambs, porphyry roundels, well heads, downspouts, even chimney pots wrenched off, crated up and shipped away for the delectation of American oil

magnates and Liverpool button manufacturers. This very
Grosvenor Gallery doorway had been ripped from the main
portal of Santa Lucia in Venice! And hideous it was, too, the
work of Andrea Palladio, that standard bearer of the
Rinascimento—the end of all honesty in architecture and
painting, the beginning of "Classical" conceit and corruption
made manifest in stone and tempera.

But the paintings of Venice! In Doge's Palace and
locked chapels in forgotten side canals they remained, in their
majesty and quiet dignity—the Bellinis, the Tintorets, the
intimate Annunciations and Visitations and Nativities and
poignant palm-bearing martyrs. And above them all,
Carpaccio, in the Accademia, with his cycle of the life and
death of the little bear, Ursula, Celtic princess trothed to a
pagan British king, choosing God and death.

Venice. His fingers brushed the raised carving of the
entry door, and he recalled his Christmastide in Venice,
tourists fled, few shops and restaurants open, even the
beggars gone. Where? He'd walk each night as was his wont,
fog rising from still canals, the dark water smoking and
invisible beneath it, unlit *calles* forcing him to grope the
peeling stone building fronts with his hands to make his way
from *campo* to *campo*, the stone powdering under his
fingertips. Walk back to his rented rooms in the Calcina, back
to the gimcrack gilded furniture and the sputtering coal fire
and his copy of St. Ursula, sleeping. Waiting for him.

Too much, too long had he studied that Carpaccio,
crossing the palm of the *superintendente* of the Accademia to
take it from the wall and set it up in an unused side room
where it was his alone. The young princess-saint asleep in her
high-canopied bed, receiving from the brilliant angel in her
doorway the dream of the quest which would lead her to
martyrdom. How he laboured over his copy, morning after
morning with pencil and water-colour wash and over-glaze.
His hand had trembled each time his brush touched her face.

She was so like—so like—another, who now slept, and eternally. He had spent too long on it, and too long in that city of glorious decay. His wits had strayed.

Today he had walked part of the way, a mistake. It was no longer possible to breathe deeply in London without the stink of sulphur burning one's nostrils and stinging one's lungs. A mephitic stench clung to his garments. Even his home at Coniston Water in the Lakes was fallen prey. Fewer and fewer clear days graced Brantwood; it too was being swallowed up by the miasma of locomotive smoke and the ghastly belchings of factory fires. Filth and more filth, all to line the pockets of industrialists and the madness of consumers clamouring for ever cheaper and more degraded goods. England was as good as gone, and at this rate, could any part of Europe escape? Could even the Alps survive?

Now he was inside, blinking against the sky-lit harshness of the main gallery room beyond. A mildly astringent odour of freshly brushed shellac wafted to his nose. He picked up his programme and scanned the list of exhibitors: Burne-Jones of course; Watts; Poynter; Alma-Tadema; Moore; that clever girl Maria Stillman (she could show some of these men a thing or two about colour and subject!); Sir Coutts and Lady Mary Lindsay (that was rich—showing their own work in their own gallery); Whistler; the Frenchman Tissot; Millais…

Millais. There was genius! Natural, God-granted greatness, cast aside, lost and mired and squandered now in cranking out chocolate-box prettiness. Millais, a young David, his harp a paint-brush, fountainhead of the little band of truth-seekers who called themselves the Pre-Raphaelite Brotherhood, who Ruskin had taken up as a younger brother—and then who had fallen in love with Ruskin's wife! He blinked again. That was twenty years past. More.

It was Saturday afternoon, late, an unfashionable time to be out, and there were blessedly few viewers in the main gallery. But the absence of attendees meant that the full force of the decoration of the place hit him without the mitigation of human figures in the foreground. All was of a matter of course, achingly new; the aniline dyes from the surplus of upholstery stung his eyes. The walls were covered in patterned crimson, the floors with Persia carpets. Tables and benches in white alabaster, looking for all the world as if your hand would freeze if you touched them, stood next to couches of dark green velvet. There was gaslight blazing overhead, and glass globes fashioned in rainbow colours, and looming vases of flowers and Minton china and painted silver stars and moons upon the ceiling coving.

He caught himself swaying under this assault, and sat down, perching on the edge of a velvet couch. From one of the entryways to the smaller galleries emerged the leonine figure of Sir Coutts, handsome as an actor. The baronet scanned the gallery and with a start of recognition caught sight of Oxford's Slade Professor of Art. One paragraph, nay one epigram, from the Master's pen could assure the success of his venture. The standard press had so far been kind, but should Ruskin endorse it—!

Smiling, Sir Coutts began to stride forward to meet the eminent personage, but was checked in his progress with a single yet severe shake from Ruskin's head. He was here as Art Critic, and must not be fawned upon or distracted. Sir Coutts retreated, with a word to one of the uniformed attendants to be attentive to any needs or requests of Mr. Ruskin's. Ruskin rose and addressed himself to the task at hand.

Yes, he would write about this exhibition in this month's *Fors*. A representative slice of modern art-commerce lay around him. Here was a fit battleground on which to examine and joust with the pressing matter of honest value for work honestly done. Words began forming in his head, not rushing nor tumbling but an orderly march to conscious utterance. He had the unerring ability—an absolute ability— to ascertain from the opening word the conclusion of every sentence, regardless of length, subsidiary clauses, digressions– –and drive towards it with utmost confidence. Not an *ability* he of a sudden realised, for that implied the acquisition of a skill—it was instinct with him.

An hour passed.

It was not all new work shown at the Grosvenor; some had been displayed in other galleries or in their artist's studios or the drawing rooms of fashionable London and Manchester and Birmingham. But there was enough fresh work, and fresh artists, and artists known to be "the coming thing" to offer variety, and enough really well-known men, like Watts and Millais, to pull a cross section of the art- viewing world through the looted doorway. It did not all exert the same demands on him; sight and time were too precious to be thrown away on amateur production or wrong- headedness. He studied his programme and planned the visit to leave the best for last, as a treat, and made his steady way through the rooms, stopping when warranted.

He was aware of a little murmur as he was recognised by the few viewers, some polite coughing and subtle gesturing behind him, and an almost imperceptible parting of onlookers making way before him. Some of them knew him by sight, or from photographic prints, and perchance some had attended on his words at lectures he had delivered.

They'd stored up their treasure in him by his early works, many of which he now thought useless, and worse, damaging to their readers; and it galled him that those juvenile efforts, his language over-shot and over-laid with gilding, or rabid with Protestantism, were read more frequently than those that would do them, and society, real good. He allowed himself a short sharp glance back at his fellow gallery excursionists, overdressed and self important, yet with vague and timid eyes. As a group they failed miserably in comparison to the nobility of character evinced in the average Venetian portrait of the 15th century. No wonder there were no good portraits these days; there were no faces worth painting. Yet to their credit this afternoon's art viewers left him blessedly unmolested, for which he was grateful to be uninterrupted in his course of effort.

Near the end of his circuit he quickened his pace. His eyes felt tired and one was watering a little. In the past he had admired the realism of the veins in the Carrara marble depicted by Alma-Tadema's evocations of the ancient world. Today he passed by some "Roman" scenes of the Dutchman's, inhabited by sloe-eyed, milky-fleshed young women clad in film of gossamer, wanton and vacuous at once.

That Tissot—he had an eye, and a hand too, but was soul-starved for want of worthy subjects. Airless, trivialized studies of vulgar "smart" society, young women with an awful macadamized look of hardness; the men cachectic "swells" who might be guilty of Uranism.

What a relief to escape to the room dedicated to darling Ned's work! This invitation to exhibit had been important to Ned; since his nude 'Phyllis and Demophöon' had been removed in an uproar from the Old Water Colour Society exhibition seven years ago he had scarcely been able to show anywhere. Now he was given a single gallery room to himself, save for a few pieces by that odd American-French chap Whistler.

The crowd was thicker here, more viewers in fact than in any other room, which irked him for his own sake but made him happy for his friend.

The centre piece of Burne-Jones' work was the six-panel 'Days of Creation', each panel presenting a life-size angel bearing a luminous globe in which was depicted the work of God's hand for that day. He felt the tension draining from his body as he stood before Ned's angels, placidly presenting the handiwork of the Creator. *Fiat lux.* Their round eyes and finely drawn lips belonged to neither man nor woman, rollicking *putti* nor sword-bearing archangel; and their manifest and yet neutral beauty made gazing upon them an almost salvific activity in itself. Surely these were what cherubim, if they possessed any corporality whatsoever, would resemble, an unknown and impossible mixed sex, lacking all carnality but combining the physical perfection of an idealized youth and maiden.

He was wearied now, and nearly sleepy. He had not slept well in months. But there was more of Ned to see, the Merlin. 'The Beguiling of Merlin', Ned called it, with the old and unwise sorcerer sinking to the earth amongst a fall of blossoms under the charms of the unscrupulous enchantress Nimuë. Both figures were swathed in dusky draperies, and Nimuë bore the strikingly beautiful face and form of Maria Zambuco, the woman with whom Ned had made such a fool of himself. The eyes of victim and prey were locked, Merlin's long-fingered hands powerless to rise against the female to whom he had lost his heart. How terrible was love! Ruskin looked at his haggard face, the dark-rimmed eyes suffering under the pitiless gaze of the temptress he had succumbed to. Merlin, the great adept of Arthur's court. Stricken, stricken.

Ruskin roused himself and turned to view the end wall. A group of Whistlers hung there, but he had turned directly in line with one. It was marked by Whistler's signature, the wings of a butterfly or moth, painted on the rippling wood of the frame. The canvas within was dark, of an indistinct blackish green. A golden sprinkling of dots and smears, bright as phosphorescence, ran down one side and dropped into a void of blackness. They were specks of fire falling through an impenetrable murk, like sparks of destruction glittering in an unholy night, thought Ruskin. Hell-fire. There was a foulness to the work, something innately unwholesome, like the worst of the plague winds darkening the skies of modern Britain. Ruskin felt held in place by the very sense of revulsion that urged him to look away. He pulled out his programme. 'James McNeill Whistler. Nocturne in Black and Gold'. Ruskin exhaled sharply, and a Mayfair matron with her son up from Cambridge caught the great man's single ejaculatory verdict: "Coxcomb," he uttered, and turned on his heel and left.

Whistler lay sprawled in a lounge chair in the dim smoking room of the Arts Club. His dark, curly-haired head lay cushioned on a pile of shapeless crewel-worked pillows, and—heedless of the upholstery—his polished boots on the arm of the next chair. With his narrow silver-crowned walking stick he idly beat the top of the low table before him, nearly upsetting a shallow copper ash-tray. If the walking stick had been a sabre Whistler's resemblance to a bored dragoon in mufti would have been complete.

The smoking room was called the "Dugout" by its frequenters for its small size and knotty wood panelling, but was empty and smokeless today. It was nearly six p.m., Whistler had had no lunch, and with yet another dunning bill in his pocket reminding him of his overdue account here, he felt little inclination to rise and seek out tea. In an upstairs room he had just lost £15 at cards to an art dealer named Wilmer, whom he had been attempting to entice into making good on a prior expression of interest in stopping by Whistler's studio to view some works in progress.

Light, Descending

George Boughton rounded the corner into the Dugout, clutching a folded-open magazine, which he thrust into Whistler's hand. It was the new number of the *Architect*, and Whistler scanned the piece "Mr. Ruskin on the Grosvenor Gallery." Whistler's own name leapt out at him, and he read:

> *For Mr. Whistler's own sake, no less than for the protection of the purchaser, Sir Coutts Lindsey ought not to have admitted works into the gallery in which the ill-educated conceit of the artist so nearly approaches the aspect of wilful imposture. I have seen, and heard, much of Cockney impudence before now; but never expected to hear a coxcomb ask two hundred guineas for flinging a pot of paint in the public's face.*

A long moment passed, far longer than required to read two sentences. Whistler raised his eyes to see Boughton, almost pop-eyed, staring at him, waiting for his reaction. Whistler quietly handed the folded magazine back.

"His style of criticism is debased."

Then Whistler began to laugh. Boughton stood by, eyeing his friend. Whistler was pugnacious and relished comment on his work, and typically the harsher the comment the better he enjoyed it, for it cleared the path for him to expound his own theories on art.

"Hand me a gasper, George, and read it once more," Whistler said, and Boughton dutifully opened his enamelled cigarette case and laid it on the table before them. Boughton rolled them extremely thin, and for his efforts had won a place as Whistler's favoured tobacco benefactor. Boughton was provincial, American, a complete hack as an artist, even tempered and steady. He regarded Whistler as a genius, and besides keeping his friend in cigarettes, lent him canvas and oils without expecting repayment.

Boughton read the excerpt again as Whistler sucked the life from his cigarette.

"And that's it, there's no more of this, that's all he said of me?" asked Whistler. He turned his head and looked towards the library room. "Do we take that blasted *Fors?* Anyone here read it?"

Whistler rose and both men went from room to room in the club. *Fors Clavigera* was not a publication the Arts Club subscribed to, but old Meriwether had by chance brought his own copy from home to peruse in the quiescence of his club and they lifted it from him and carried it back to the Dugout. Albert Moore and Joseph Boehm came with them, intrigued by the search and clewed in by Boughton's digest. Moore had exhibited his paintings at the Grosvenor as well, and Boehm was a sculptor and friend of many year's standing, currently adding some decorative embellishments to the exterior of Whistler's new London home to satisfy the requirements of the Metropolitan Board of Works who had found the plain white façade too severe.

The little party gathered around the lounge chair Whistler had reinhabited. Boughton dropped the offending journal on the small table between them. It was a modest production, eighteen or twenty pages, closely printed on pale yellow paper. "Letters to the Workmen and Labourers of Great Britain" was the subtitle, "by John Ruskin, LL.D Letter the Seventy-ninth July 2nd 1877".

Whistler conned the plain cover with a quick glance. "Workmen and labourers," he snorted. "Ha!" The scavenger hunt about the club's rooms had restored his spirits, and he seemed almost sanguine. "He means 'Antediluvian dreamers snug in their Oxford and Cambridge redoubts.'"

Boehm looked down at the light yellow cover. "For the workmen of Britain? What honest labourer can throw his chink around like that?"

"Yes, ten pence an issue! It's not much value for money," agreed Boughton, weighing the slight publication in his hand.

After his cursory glance at the cover Whistler leaned back in his chair and crossed his legs. Boughton rifled through the pages, picking out key themes, scanning paragraphs. It was a wildly discursive colloquy, and Boughton had an image of Ruskin as a heedless boy running on a beach, snatching up one shell or shiny pebble after the next, only to cast the first down and reach for another.

"Here, here it is, the Grosvenor bit," said Boughton. "…Sir Coutts Lindsey is at present an amateur both in art and shopkeeping. He must take up either one or the other business, if he would prosper in either. If he intends to manage the Grosvenor Gallery rightly, he must not put his own works in it until he can answer for their quality; if he means to be a painter, he must not at present superintend the erection of public buildings, or amuse himself with their decoration by china and upholstery…"

There was a hoot of laughter from Whistler, and snickers from the other men.

Boughton went on scanning and reading. "Ah…puffing on about Burne-Jones…his 'is simply the only art-work at present produced in England which will be received as "classic"…the best that has been or could be…I *know* that these will be immortal…'—Oh, here's a scold coming—'the mannerisms and errors of his pictures, whatever may be their extent, are never affected or indolent. The work is natural to the painter, however strange to us…Scarcely so much can be said for any other pictures of the modern schools: their eccentricities are always in some degree forced; and their imperfections gratuitously, if not impertinently, indulged.'"

Boughton took a breath and slowed down, and read again the damning two sentences. Then abruptly as the attack began, it was over. Boughton read a few more bits aloud. Ruskin went on to Tissot's paintings, citing their dexterity but chiding him for producing "mere coloured photographs of vulgar society" and Millais, in which he lamented how much greater his achievement would have been if he "had remained faithful to the principles of his school when he first led its onset…you will never know what you have lost in him…"

The concluding passage was a maudlin tale of a race horse, a Derby contender, grown ill upon being separated from his stable-mate kitten, and the resumption of his appetite and fulfilment of his owner's racing dreams when his feline castellan was returned to him. It was bathos of the sort a desiccated unmarried aunt would tell a fretful child to assure him of eventual happy endings. Coming on the heels of the vituperative attack on Whistler made it seem even more absurd.

"He is cracked," said Whistler, unfolding his legs.

"Yes," agreed Boughton, but in a very different tone. "The great Ruskin is cracked." The once-inerrant had erred, grievously in this case, but Whistler (as usual, it seemed to Boughton) did not appear to grasp the significance of the situation—the Master's utterance as it pertained to him.

Moore clucked his tongue. "And this was the man who as a boy proclaimed the genius of Turner when everyone else accused the man's seascapes of looking like soap-suds!" He shook his head and rapped out the contents of his meerschaum into the ash-tray.

Boehm's response was more measured. "His is the greatest voice in art criticism, not only here, but the world," he said. But he too shook his head. "It is some gibe."

"He's hopeless," answered Whistler. "The enemy of art today is convention, and Ruskin's blathering only confirms the narrowness of his conceptions. He knows nothing. Once again the cause of us doers and workers is at stake against the mere writers and praters. Mine is modern painting. It doesn't 'mean anything' nor does it intend to entertain or scold the viewer in relating a story. I seek to convey an atmosphere, nothing more."

They had all heard this before. Boughton still stood, now with pursed lips, above his friend, and looked down at Whistler's grin. "I believe this to be actionable."

Whistler blinked. His single lock of white hair stood out from his dark curls like a tongue of Pentecostal fire.

"I'm a painter and no solicitor, you'll have to obtain a professional consultation—ask Rose or any other good man—but this"—here Boughton waved the offending number of *Fors*— "coming from such a one as Ruskin, this might be libel."

"Libel?"

"Yes, and if it hinders your sales or in any way injures your reputation, it might be actionable."

"With a settlement?"

"Yes, should you win; a settlement, damages, court costs, everything."

Whistler's eyes, which had been glued to Boughton's face during this startling allegation, now dropped to the floral tracery of the maroon carpet. He hadn't sold a major painting in two years, and was far from having the resources to embark

277

upon the Venetian trip which he hoped would result in a series of always-lucrative etchings. His greatest client and patron, Frederick Leyland, was now sending *him* bills for materials and incurred expenses in the unauthorised (so said Leyland) decoration of his fantastic Peacock Room. Leyland, once so warm a friend, was so enraged he had threatened to publicly horsewhip Whistler should they meet. The building of Whistler's new home and studio in Chelsea, which he had rashly pursued despite his financial difficulties, was straining him even further. And he feared that Maud Franklin, his long time model and mistress, was again with child.

His friend spoke again. "But it all hinges on whether or not it's actionable."

Whistler rose and lit a second cigarette. "Well, that I shall try to find out," he answered, and left.

Away in America, less than a mile from Harvard Yard, Charles Eliot Norton took his seat in a green wicker chair on the deep piazza of his ancestral home, Shady Hill. He placed on the glass top of a wicker table the morning's post, sorting through art-journals, a paper on linguistic studies, book sales circulars, and a slender packet from London. Within this last was the July number of *Fors Clavigera*, which Ruskin's publishing agent shipped Norton punctually each month.

Norton knew the letters of *Fors* were titularly intended for the 'companions' of The Guild of St. George, recently created by Ruskin to test his ideas of a return to a hand-labour based agrarian society of artisans and farmers, living a simple yet ennobling life circumscribed by mediaeval precepts, obedience to God, and to their Master, Ruskin himself. The reality was that the 'companions' were few, and the actual subscribers tended to absorb the contents of *Fors* seated in plush chairs in well-furnished library and drawing rooms rather than at deal tables in country cottages.

Norton settled into his chair with a pot of strong tea before him and began to read. The issue opened with Ruskin's examination of the relationship of labour to recompense, and the seemingly ever-increasing demands placed on men in industrial society. "What are all our machines for, then?" he posed. "Can we do in ten minutes, without a man or a horse, what a Greek could not have done in a year, with all the King's horses and all the King's men? ––And is this the result of all this magnificent mechanism, only that we have far less leisure?"

A long and scathing review of the current exhibition hung at the Royal Academy came next. This was followed by a lengthy passage about the ugliness of the contents of the citizenry's houses, and the deleterious effects upon the impressionable minds of their children. Pedagogy being Norton's special genius he read slowly and carefully. To counteract the vulgar ugliness of modern life children ought to be exposed in school to great art, and made to pay attention to Nature's own mysterious beauties. The physical plant of learning was not to be overlooked: "In these large airy rooms let us place a few beautiful casts, a few drawings, a few vases or pretty screens…Then, whatever you can afford to spend on education in art, give to good masters, and leave them to do the best they can for you; and what you can afford to spend for the splendour of your city, buy grass, flowers, sea, and sky with. No art of man is possible without these primal treasures of the Art of God."

After the bullying and the ranting, a passage of almost ethereal beauty and sensibility.

Norton had now reached nearly the end of the issue, and came to the review of the Grosvenor Gallery show. His tea was grown cold, and when he raised his eyes again the afternoon sun had abandoned the lawn before him. Norton himself wrote much art criticism and many reviews, and his own pen could be biting, even caustic; but here Ruskin's dripped pure venom. He felt old and tired and almost inexpressibly sad, yet the one word which formed in his head made its quiet way to his lips: "madness."

Chapter Twenty-one

The Lamp of Truth

Lancashire: Friday 22 February 1878 Midnight

Ruskin had been so absorbed in his diary that the fire had died in the grate. He knew his hands were cold but did not mind them. His lamp was out of oil and when it sputtered he did not refill it but rummaged quickly through his desk drawers to find the stub of a candle to light his work. The pinpoint brilliance of the unshaded flame made him squint, and he looked away from his diary entries. His gaze fell upon his father's gold watch on the blotter before him. At an oblique angle to the face he could not read the time to see which numerals the sweeping hands approached, held, and overtook.

For weeks Ruskin had foundered in a stony and cold state of mind, his thoughts muddy and poisoned. He felt seized from without, and no effort of his own could make it quit hold of him. An absolute coldness and obtuseness of thought alternated with hours of dreamy scatterment and bewilderment, hours in which he looked internally for something precious he had lost and could not quite name. Today had been Good Friday. The bleak commemoration of the earthly Christ's death and descent into Hell had shadowed every hour of Ruskin's day. Now, past midnight at his desk in his frigid bedroom, he began to play a new and favourite game, one which like many of his pleasures promised danger.

He sat surrounded by beloved books, and in the divination of Sortes balanced each on its spine and let it fall open. With eyes closed he ran his finger down the page, stopping when inspired, and read the passage his finger marked for significance. He began with the Bible, then had opened one book and then another, seeking patterns and correspondences in the texts. It all gave him such joy.

When he finished looking at the books he turned his narrowed eyes to the guttering candle. He recalled writing a letter that morning, full of rapturous happiness at the news it bore, but now was unable to remember what the news was, or to whom addressed. Tintoret's words came again into his head and mouth, and he said them aloud in the near darkness. *E faticoso lo studio della pittura, a sempre si fa il mare maggiore:* The study of painting is laborious, and the sea always gets larger. The sea was endless before Ruskin.

Flaring candle light struck the gold case of his father's watch, and forced his eye to it. The dazzle and sparkle frightened and then enraged him. He picked up his pen and re-dipped it to return to his diary as distraction. There was too much in the pen, nine million words had issued from its split lip, with many more aching to spill forth; the world could not contain them all. He put the pen down again. He focussed on the white face of the watch, crowded with numerals chasing each other around the dial. The tick was infernally loud, and the longer Ruskin looked at the piece the louder it grew. It filled his brain. He slammed the palm of his open hand into the candle flame, mashing it into a hot pulp. He stood up, suddenly, upsetting the chair. Now he knew: Time would be meaningless in the eternity of Hell Fire. The Devil was coming for him. Tonight, and in this room, Beelzebub would present himself and try to claim him. Like an Old Testament hero Ruskin knew, too, what he must do to prepare. He must throw off his clothing and greet his tormenter in the same state in which he had entered this world, naked. Naked, but not helpless, for Ruskin would be called upon to grapple with and overpower his foe. It would be mortal combat, not for the deathless Evil One, but for Ruskin if he lost.

He began to tear at his clothing, pulling so hard on his stock that he nearly choked himself, then found the loose end and yanked it from his neck. Buttons flew across the room and pinged to the floor as with both hands he wrenched off his waistcoat. Shoes, stockings, trousers, underdrawers all came off and were thrown to the floorboards. The cold was intense and he knew it was a weapon he could use against his foe. Inspired, he flung open the window casement to the winter night. He saw this as an invitation to the Devil, and he laughed. Let him fly through the window into his room and join him! Ruskin moved from the open window and swung his arms through the frigid air. He began pacing, marching up and down across the floor, swinging his arms in military rhythm. He would use his arms and fists in battle, and if that failed he would challenge the Devil to a contest of words! But can the Devil speak truth? he asked, a Banquo consulting with the witches in Macbeth: And oftentimes, to win us to our harm, the instruments of darkness tell us truths, win us with honest trifles, to betray us!

He noticed he was not alone in the room. Ophelia was there—an Ophelia with copper hair—singing her lament of lost maidenhood, and Desdemona, made wonton and the night with her, and the naked sleeping Imogen, with vile lusting Iachimo standing over her. He lunged at Iachimo, driving him from the innocent Imogen, and then all three women merged into one, a Visitation. The face was soft and beautiful, and the hair was every colour, but then the face hardened and the hair thickened into writhing serpents circling her head. He threw his arm up over his eyes to stop her paralysing stare. He was St. George, slayer of dragons, imbued with strength to kill his sister Gorgon, their names rooted in *gorgós*, 'dreadful', dreadful mother to both George and Gorgon. He rushed at her and fell into the desk and she was gone.

He was tangled in a net and could not free himself. Rose came, just a child of ten years, and tried over and again to untangle him, until she blamed him for getting wilfully entangled, and left him despairingly. He was shot 20 times over, and forced to be attendant on a desperate artillery man who fired batteries of ball and grape into opera-houses and shot whole audiences dead at a discharge. But he must not be distracted. The Devil was coming to claim him and he must march and swing his arms until he arrived. The wind blew and ruffled the loose papers on his work table and one by one the sheets were licked up and flew around his room, his introduction to the Turner exhibition, Turner who was in Heaven, with Rose. Turner and Rose, it was ever Turner and Rose.

He marched for hours and miles and when he was going to fall he thought the sky was lightening and he had deterred the Devil from his call. Then from his mirror something cat-like, black, leapt out at him. Here! Here he is now! He caught it up in his arms and flung it against the floor. He heard the dull thud but the fiend had vanished—he waited—nothing more! He had triumphed, and fell down in ecstasy and anguish.

Ruskin's manservant, Peter Baxter, rapped on his master's door punctually at seven with his morning coffee. The passage was cold and almost completely dark, and the candle on the tray flickered in an unusual draught. Mr. Ruskin got involved with his morning letter-writing and sometimes didn't respond at the first knock. "Mr. Ruskin,"

called Baxter, rapping again. His knuckles were cold enough that the slight action hurt.

He shifted the tray to one arm and pressed his ear to the door. He could hear something, though no crack of lamplight shone at the bottom of the door. Was Mr. Ruskin reading aloud within? Yesterday had been Good Friday, perhaps he was in prayer.

Baxter repeated his call. He heard, in return, a low wailing groan. "Mr. Ruskin, sir?" repeated Baxter, and pushed open the door. The candle blew out at once in the wind gusting in through the open window, but the daylight had advanced enough for him to discover his master. John Ruskin lay, utterly unclothed, across his still-made bed, while snow blew in from the unlatched window. His blue eyes were startlingly open and his mouth was slack, and from it came a kind of ghoulish singsong.

Baxter dropped the tray on his master's bedside table, hooked the window closed, and pulled a blanket off the end of the bed with which he covered Ruskin. Then he turned and ran for Mrs. Severn with all the energy of his twenty-two year old legs.

Two hours later Joan Severn wrote out a telegram message for Peter Baxter to carry across into Coniston village. She would let herself cry after he had left and she was alone for a moment. She had done all she could for her cousin John; with Baxter's help he had been dressed and laid under a quantity of coverlets. The room had been warmed and in the few moments when he was not thrashing she had even tried to squeeze a few drops of brandy between his now-clenched teeth. The side of her face was aching from where he had struck her at the jaw-line, and Baxter had been bitten twice. Yet her cousin had no fever, his skin was still cool from exposure, and his teeth showed no sign of chattering. It was a form of physical delirium that started and abruptly ceased, yet the unfocussed vocalizations were almost constant.

Down in London Sir John Simon had received Joan's telegram at his offices just before eleven o'clock. Simon had been Ruskin's physician for more than twenty years, and after dispatching a message to his wife at home asking that a bag be made up for him arranged his affairs as best he could to permit his hasty departure to Brantwood in the Lake district. It was now almost twelve hours later, and Sir John stood, fingers grasping the emergency stop cord, in the dim vestibule of a railway carriage as the locomotive pulling it slowed, without stopping, to pass through Coniston station. He rolled the ribbed surface of the cord between his finger pads and waited as the station came into view, a lone lantern hanging from the sign standard. He had left London too late for a train which made a scheduled stop, but Simon timed his arrival well. A quick jerk downward and the deed was done. As the suddenly arrested train squealed to a halt Simon handed his card to the confounded conductor and stepped down at Coniston.

Ruskin's carriage stood in the dark of the station yard to meet him. Simon was already fatigued and assumed he had a sleepless night before him. The drive along the tip of the lake to Brantwood took the better part of an hour, but all the front room lamps were lit when he stepped down before the door. Up above, by the tower room he knew to be Ruskin's, a lamp burned. The front door opened, framing Joan on the threshold, waiting for him.

She must be, Simon thought, just past thirty now; a healthy, plain-faced, sweet-tempered Scotswoman with the patience and resourcefulness of her tribe. Tidy foot and hand, and an attractively mature figure. Three little ones under the age of five, and the whole household to run.

As soon as he removed his coat and turned to her he saw the mumps-size swelling on her jaw and attendant discolouration. "Did he do this?" he asked.

She nodded her head, ashamed at the look of her, ashamed for her cousin.

"Right," murmured Simon. "Well then, let's see him."

Joan took a lamp in hand and Simon reclaimed his grip on his medical bag and followed her up the darkened stair and along the passage to Ruskin's room. The door was closed for warmth and when Joan opened it Simon saw a youth sitting on a stool at the foot of the bed. He rose at once, and Joan said, "Peter, Sir John is here. You may go now."

The boy glanced down at the still figure in the bed and Simon read his reluctance to leave. "No, let him stay, at least for a while," he said. Ruskin had always inspired devotion in his servants; with his confused social philosophies alternating between extreme Toryism and communism Simon couldn't fathom how servants puzzled him out.

"Hold the lamp for me, Peter—what?" instructed Simon.

"Baxter, sir," he answered, taking up the lamp and moving in over Ruskin's head with it. Ruskin's face was white, his lips colourless. Simon reached under the blankets for Ruskin's wrist, but as soon as the lamp light fell on Ruskin's face the inert patient came to animated life, twisting sharply away from Simon's grasp and kicking out with unexpected force with his blanketed legs. A piercing shriek accompanied these actions. Simon turned to the recoiling Joan.

"Joan, go to bed," he ordered. "Baxter and I will suffice."

During the night Simon administered morphia in combination with chloral that his patient might sleep, but as he awoke Ruskin resumed a state of such agitation that soon chloral needed to be administered continually. Two days into Simon's visit Ruskin became almost completely unresponsive, and later that night Simon thought he had lost him, so depressed was pulse and breathing. But the physician had not upended his life and responsibilities to lose his patient as quickly as this. To increase vital action stimulants were urgently required. With Baxter aiding him Simon force-fed brandy and water as antagonists, along with copious amounts of tepid coffee and milk, and Ruskin lived.

Simon did not discover the diary until it became apparent that the episode would be prolonged and outside assistance was imperative. A complement of male nurses were sent for. Prior to their arrival he and Joan had swept through Ruskin's bedroom, gathering small treasures to be kept in Joan's safe-keeping. She gathered up John James Ruskin's watch, a golden chain, Sir Walter Scott's silver pen—a few precious and pocketable items, and carried them off to her own rooms. Certain things were already kept locked by Ruskin in his desk, and she took as well the key. Simon then approached Ruskin's desk, covered with opened books. There was his ancient box Bible with the frayed red velvet cover, open to II Timothy. Atop the translucent page was a closed copy of Smith's *Dictionary of the Bible*, placed as if to mark the passage below. Simon allowed his eye to travel down the narrow columns. "For men will be lovers of self, lovers of money, proud, arrogant, abusive, disobedient to their parents, ungrateful, unholy, inhuman, implacable, slanderers, profligates, fierce, haters of good..." he scanned. Three other books he did not recognize, and closed them to see their titles. One was Ruskin's neighbour Miss Susie Beever's commentary, *Remarkable Passages in Shakespeare*. Another was a treatise by one Thomas Brassey, *On Work and Wages*. The third was Ruskin's diary.

Light, Descending

Simon was not the kind of man to read another's diary, and if Ruskin had been incapacitated by a mere physical ailment the doing so would be unthinkable. But now, regarding the narrow, long, buckram volume before him, he wondered if he might find some valuable clew to the cause of Ruskin's distressed mind.

The diary was open as Ruskin had left it. Behind it, laying in a holder, was a steel pen, dried ink on its nib. Ruskin, always so meticulous, had not used his pen-wiper after his last entry.

Simon was decisive by nature, and he knew he must look and read or close the book and lock it away. He lifted the book in his hands and read.

> *Finished, and my letter from 'Piero' my Venetian gondolier put in here, and all. I am going to lock up with the Horses of St Marks. ¼ to one by my Father's watch—22nd February 1878—*

> *I couldn't find the key and then remembered I had not thanked the dear Greek Princess—nor Athena of the Dew—and Athena κεραμτς*

This was the final entry. "Athena 'of the Earth'," Simon repeated to himself. These goddesses were from Ruskin's *The Queen of the Air*, he thought. He backed up to the beginning of the entry for 22nd February and scanned.

> *—Too much to write. —I don't think I shall forget—the chief message to myself as a painter, coming after a Sculptor...*

> *Good Friday. Recollected all about message from Rosie to me as I was drawing on the scaffolding in St Georges Chapel—My saying I would serve her to the death—...*

—Can the Devil speak truth (confer letter to Francie about her little feet)...

If that thou beest a Devil &c. connected with, (Made wanton—&c. the night with her.) Tintoret— (sempre si f ail mare maggiore) I did'nt know where to go on—but don't think I should stop. —And Andrea Gritti-then? Quite unholy is he, you stupid? ...And the Blind Guide that had celestial light? Yes—and you barefoot Scotch lassies—Diddie and all of you dears—if only you would go barefoot a bit, in the streets So pretty—so pretty. Naked foot, that shines like snow— and falls on earth—or gold—as mute.

Simon closed the slender volume and carried it away to his room.

Ruskin was never left alone. The male nurses imported for the occasion had stocky bodies fitted for pugilists; and one of them, Jackson, had the stance and deformed ear of an actual prize-fighter. In addition to these trained hands, Baxter, and Joan when Simon permitted, attended the patient when Simon was not in the room. Sitting up with him in the watches of a night in which Ruskin slept, Simon listened to the shallow breaths drawn and the slight rise and fall of the blankets covering him. He reached to check the pulse, and then was startled by Ruskin's hand curling around his own. Ruskin's hand clasped his own, the pale skin dry but the fingertips soft, and Simon held his friend's hand as his own eyes dimmed.

Such moments of peace were fleeting. Simon could not predict which phenomena might spur his patient to wild delirium. He had a horror of any dazzle. Care had to be taken to prevent Ruskin from seeing any sparks from the coal-fire, or glint of fire-light reflected in the polished mahogany of his bedstead; the sight of any gleaming, twinkling light reduced him to wild screaming.

In an attempt to restore equilibrium Simon had pondered fomentations of various kinds. He had read of American physicians experimenting with a fall of cold water upon the head of an insane person, but, having no access to a douche to provide the necessary water drop, had resorted to applications of cold water to the head and feet. He considered, then discarded, the plan of employing a rubifacient as a counter-irritant; he could not see himself subjecting so weakened a patient to mustard-plasters or blistering ammonia liniments.

At this point Ruskin had periods when chloral was not needed continually, but though the bouts of violence had abated the mania had not. He spent hours repeating a single word or phrase. One day it had been "Everything white! Everything black!"; another, endlessly and mournfully, "Rosie-Posie," one of Ruskin's myriad pet names for his late beloved. There was also a ceaseless, rhythmic clapping of the hands. Today this had been accompanied by inchoate shouting so extreme that daytime chloral was administered as a calmative.

Materia medica is finite, thought Simon as he stirred and measured out the mixture; the depths of the abyss into which Ruskin had plunged infinite.

Joan moved to the window and pulled back the curtains, coaxing from the mid-March afternoon as much light as the sodden landscape would allow. With the house teeming with nurses the study was the only room in Brantwood in which she might sit down for an hour in relative quiet with her departing guest. And as it was *his* room, filled with his geological specimens, his Turner water-colours, his medieval manuscripts, his own long shelf of published writings, it reminded her of the manifold interests and prodigious intellectual output of her cousin, lying muttering upstairs in his bedroom. *What has been can be again*, she reminded herself. She took up her position by the teapot.

Simon gazed down upon the crisp tablecloth, the blue and pink Staffordshire, the freshly boiled eggs and thinly sliced bread, the jam tarts from last summer's Brantwood berries. "You lay, as always, a lovely tea, Joan," he said.

They sat together at the small octagonal table as she poured out. The dark half moons under her eyes made her pink skin look more delicate than it was.

She brought the fluted teacup to her lip and then lay it down untouched. She was crying again. "I'm so sorry, sir."

Simon was a listener, and he waited.

"It's the china; when I took Coz that tray yesterday and he flung it at me, and it all smashed to bits against me and the door frame—and he loves this pattern so, he does, and will be so aggrieved if he ever realises that he broke so much of it." She shut her eyes against the memory, squeezing out more tears.

"I hope he lives to repent of that, and so much more," he told her, and smiled.

Despite his mild jest, his mind flickered a moment on the tin feeding cup with spout from which Ruskin was now being force fed; it was a long way from the delicate Staffordshire. Simon was exhausted too. Early next morning he was headed back to London, resuming his life and his position, facing the official reports to be read and opinions to be written. He could picture his desk now, its surface half obscured with pressing correspondence. Public health, sanitation—the care of and planning for the thousands and tens of thousands was his special faculty, and for the fortnight past he had been wholly absorbed with attempting to save the slight and overtaxed frame housing the labyrinth recesses of Ruskin's broken mind. His position was not unlike that of a scientific man who, long used to handling a telescope, had suddenly had a microscope thrust in his hands—the focal points and subject matter were that disparate.

Joan made him a plate of eggs and bread. The setting sun, low all day in its March transit, broke through the cloud cover for a moment. They both paused to gaze out the window before them. Simon regarded the lingering crusts of snow beneath the dripping shrubberies, and his eye travelled down the slope to the barely rippled surface of Coniston Water below, gleaming dully like liquid lead. He would have liked to have registered it as mercury, a quick-silver lake as furtive and fervid as his patient's mind when conscious, but Ruskin had been barely responsive all day and the lake looked leaden.

Joan spoke. "It's all this harrying of him, everyone wanting something; and his setting up of the Guild, and all the pains he's taken to make it legal so they might make a go of it; and that wretched Whistler taunting and gibing him with his hateful law suit. And I've—I've tried to protect him, tried my best, but he can be so very naughty and wilful, you know he can, sir."

Simon leaned forward and took one plump hand in his, but his voice was all professional demeanour. As tired as he was Joan required it of him, and he was not used to failing friends or anyone else. "Joan, no one could have proven more tender or faithful than you; no care more solicitous. There was nothing more you could have done. And—although its severity is great, this is not the first occasion."

"But at Matlock Bath in '71 it was inflammation of the bowels that made him—not himself."

Simon checked her as gently as possibly. "Mrs. Simon and I visited him during that time." He had discerned, as had Acland, another physician friend of Ruskin's, that the collapse Ruskin had suffered shortly after Joan's wedding was just as much of the mind as of the body, though both precipitated by the strain, he thought, of over-work.

Privately Simon had wondered if his cousin Joan's "leaving him" through her marriage had not also been a stimulus to the earlier collapse; Ruskin's aged mother was then dying and he was soon to be quite alone. There was, he thought, adequate fore-warning of a sensitive nature stretched to the limit, and then beyond.

"I think perhaps you may have seen in his past illnesses a harbinger of the shadow which has fallen on him now. And the letters he sent the week prior to this episode, perhaps even earlier…you read many of his letters, Joan, and would have seen the change in them."

"But his fancies so often get the best of him in his letters!" Her defence was feeble; she had already shown him a letter Ruskin had sent to his friend George McDonald the morning before this attack. It was a series of dashed exclamatory clauses, beginning "Dear George—we've got married—after all after all—but such a surprise!"

Ruskin's bride was none other than Rose LaTouche, dead these twenty months. McDonald, alarmed, had written to Joan upon receipt, only to learn that Ruskin had already plunged into the chasm.

They sat in silence for so long that Joan's voice when she spoke slightly startled him. "I've been ever so grateful for your coming, sir. We all are; my darling Coz too, if he could but tell you. You've been an unspeakable comfort to us. I only wish you hadn't need to go, but that's selfish of us, with all you've thrown over to be here."

She was struggling mightily to compose herself, and Simon felt how alone she was. "I am only sorry that I cannot remain longer. I am but a letter, or if need be, telegram away."

He was leaving Ruskin in the care of the local man, Benson, a young and able enough chap. Simon's diagnosis, with which the rural physician readily concurred, was morbid inflammation of the brain, leading to acute mania. *Acute mania.* Benson took notes like a stenographer as Simon paced the drawing room where their initial meeting was held. At last Benson hazarded a question. "Should I need help, sir, advice on any matter, could I presume to write you at London?" After being assured that Simon expected periodic reports, Benson nodded in relief, and offered, "I fear our Lancashire medical men would have but one opinion—'send him to an asylum.'"

Simon finished his tea. He must arise at dawn to catch the train, and wanted to write up his final notes and see the patient before then. His wife had cabled that there were rumours afloat in London that Ruskin was dead, and he needed to compose his press statement to the contrary.

"Is there anything more?" he asked her.

"Yes, sir, there is. It's—the accounts, sir." For the first time that afternoon, Simon tilted his head in puzzlement.

"Coz looks to all the payment himself, sir; the servants, the grocer, the butcher. Now we have the nurses to pay, and all the extra food costs as well." She blinked away welling tears. "I've no real money of my own sir, none, nor has Arthur. With Coz as he is, there's no one to pay the accounts."

Arthur Severn was what—a watercolourist—with not, Simon knew, two shillings of his own to rub together. He had made himself interesting to history by being Joseph Severn's son, and as the elder Severn was Keats' confidante and nurse in his final days in Rome, some dim lustre had settled upon the sloping shoulders of his offspring. Inoffensive chap, but ineffective too, thought Simon, and now fast in his own bed with sciatica while Joan faced all this uproar unsupported. Beyond this, if worse came to worst, who knew what fanciful causes or unexpected beneficiaries might be named in Ruskin's will, and Joan and her family forgotten? He had given her the Herne Hill property at London as a wedding gift, but she had no funds to maintain it on her own. She might fear being turned out of Brantwood, and perhaps left with nothing.

"Of course. I see. You must write at once to Mr. Ruskin's solicitors at London, petitioning them to instruct his bankers to release such funds as necessary to maintain the household around Mr. Ruskin in his infirmity. I will write my own letter supporting your petition."

He awoke to the fact that he carried over £30 in his pocket. Without being so indelicate as to gesture for it, he asked, "Have you immediate need? I always travel with resources, which I consider yours."

Baxter was alone in the bedroom with Ruskin when Simon entered for his final examination. The youth respectfully stepped aside while he measured the sleeping Ruskin's pulse and brought the lamp near to check his colour.

"I believe Mr. Ruskin will enjoy a quiet sleep tonight, Baxter," Simon told him as he relinquished the bedside. Certain household proprieties had broken down in the sick man's house, and certain boundaries had been temporarily breached. Not so with Baxter. He waited until spoken to to address himself to the physician.

"I'm happy to hear that, sir." Seeing that Simon was done, Baxter picked up a small canvas from the dressing table and resumed his seat at the bedside. He extended his arms and held the painting in front of his master's closed eyes. Simon had never seen it at Brantwood before this visit, but had glanced at it once or twice in the last two weeks. It was a copy of Carpaccio's St. Ursula, the lovely young martyr-to-be gently asleep in a pillared bed. He remembered it from the Accademia in Venice. Simon watched Baxter for a few moments as he held the painting. Ruskin had in recent years flirted with Catholicism, and spent weeks living in Assisi in a Franciscan monastery. This was perhaps more evidence of his late-in-life attraction to the early Church.

"Does Mr. Ruskin have a special devotion to St. Ursula?" he asked at last.

Baxter turned his head and looked up at him. "Begging your leave, sir, but it's her, sir. Miss LaTouche. She who's dead."

Rose LaTouche. Ruskin's lost will-o'-the-wisp. Simon had seen her socially once or twice, and known for years of Ruskin's frustrated love for the girl. Obsession might be the precise term. Two obsessives, drawn and repelled and drawn again together, and now parted in death. Or were they? He looked again at the sleeping face of St Ursula. Ursula died for her faith, he recalled, and seemingly so did Rose LaTouche;

she had every ear-mark of extreme religious devotion appropriate to a martyr. The visible sign to a physician's eyes was the perpetual self-abnegation that manifested itself in fasting. Simon knew of other cases of fashionable young ladies of society who voluntarily starved themselves, sometimes to the point of death, but Rose was no simple victim of vanity. He suspected her death indeed had been caused by the accumulative deleterious effects of self-starvation—he had heard that at dinner she oftentimes could force herself to consume no more than half a biscuit and a strawberry—but it was the intransigence of her religious views that had caused her, and those who loved her, so much grief.

He wished he had been less brusque when he advised Ruskin long-distance about Rose LaTouche's wasting illness; harassed with his attempts to contain a London cholera outbreak he had initially written it off as adolescent hysterics. From the descriptions of her ailments he expressed his extreme *a priori* scepticism of any actual disease, and even had suggested the female LaTouches guilty of "co-feminising twaddle." Not that Ruskin, poet and cloud-watcher that he was, attended to his words. That was one of the problems with Ruskin; he asked advice of everyone and listened to nobody.

Simon studied Baxter as he held the painting before his master's unseeing eyes. "You were with Mr. Ruskin in Venice last winter, were you not?" he asked.

Baxter again turned his head to speak. "Yes, sir, I was. From Brantwood last July to Venice through the winter, then to Verona on the way back, and then to London, and finally here again." There was some little pride in his voice as he related this route.

298

It would be neither appropriate nor discreet to question a servant about his master's behaviour. Simon was quiet, hoping Baxter shared the loquaciousness of his Irish brethren.

"I carried the professor's paints and kit for him, sir, each day that he went to the palace to copy the painting. And I heard him—speak to it, his copy, that is, sir, in his rented rooms. It's Miss LaTouche."

At Shady Hill on a recently passed Sunday night Norton sat at his desk to write to John Simon.

> *My Dear Friend*
>
> *Yesterday I had a most tender note from Ruskin. I had hardly read it when I saw in the paper a telegram announcing his serious illness. I felt that I had had his last words of love, & sweeter words for the close of twenty years affection could not be written. Tonight I hear that he is dead.*
>
> *I believe you will have written to me. If not, I pray you do so, tell me what you can of his last days.*
>
> *It is not all pain that the long fever of life is at end. But what a heart is stopped! Blessed is the peace of death!*
>
> *Ever your affectionate*
>
> *C.E.N.*

The night before Norton had refolded the slight letter from Ruskin and returned it to its envelope. The sweetest concerns and tender affections poured forth from his friend in the intimacy of their correspondence. Holding the envelope in his hand he raised his eyes to the windows of his study. It was the second day of March, and winter had a firm grip on Shady Hill's lawns, blanketed with snow. The wall clock read nearly five, and there was still light in the afternoon sky. It was Saturday. From the parlour he could hear his sister Grace, lately come to live with him, reading to the children, her voice low and patient amid their chirping enthusiasm for David Copperfield's adventures.

He had saved Ruskin's letter for last, and now turned to the newspaper, which he carried to the striped upholstered chair closest to the windows. The front page of the *Boston Evening Transcript* was dominated by the Eastern Crisis between Turkey and Russia. He read of the Turkish field army gathering in Gallipoli, and then a long piece about England's complications with Russia in the matter. His eye travelled with these cabled news stories to a small heading entitled "Personals" where he saw the line:

John Ruskin's illness is brain fever.

He read the cable report again. He turned his head and saw Ruskin's letter upon his desk blotter. He rose and went to the top of the cabinet on which yesterday's unread *Transcript* lay folded. He opened it standing by the cabinet and under the glow of the gas light scanned the front page where the foreign cables were printed. At the very bottom of page one was a single sentence:

John Ruskin, the well known writer on art, is dangerously ill from overwork.

On Friday night Norton had come home from Harvard where he had taught a class of nearly 200 young men about the treasures of Ravenna. He had had dinner with the children and with Grace—she not at the top of the table opposite him; her heart was too large and sensibilities too fine to sit in Sue's place—and then he had taken the children out for a moonlit walk to listen for the owl they had heard hooting the night before. He had retired to his study and worked on an article on Venice and Saint Mark's he was writing for the *Atlantic Monthly*. At half past eleven he grew tired and took himself up through the quiet house and to bed. All this without opening the paper. All this without seeing Ruskin was then, even then, gravely ill. Now on Sunday he had heard Ruskin was dead, one of the few losses left to him which could diminish his own life. He had long ago promised Joan that at Ruskin's death he would come and help her burn her cousin's questionable letters and papers. Mastering his grief he struggled to compose a letter to her about their great mutual loss. He was to suffer three days of misery before he found the report to be false.

Chapter Twenty-two

The Lamp of Truth

Whistler vs. Ruskin

In the High Court of Justice, Queen's Bench Division, Westminster

Monday: 25 November 1878

"I shall endeavour to persuade the court that the manner in which Mr. Ruskin has written of Mr. Whistler was absolutely calculated to discredit Mr. Whistler as an artist, and I might add, parenthetical to the action, as a gentlemen. The plaintiff must naturally suffer from this abuse in the public estimation, and perhaps his livelihood will be irrevocably damaged because of it."

At ten-thirty in the morning the room was stifling with coal-stoked heat and overpopulation. The legal teams of plaintiff and defendant in the action were numerous in themselves, and scores of followers of each camp had squeezed in behind them, leaving a small throng unseated in the corridor. Every chair and bench inside the courtroom was filled, and many were standing in any available and otherwise unoccupied territory.

John Humffreys Parry, Serjeant-at-law and Whistler's lead counsel, stayed a moment before the jury box and fixed his dark eyes upon the occupants seated there. He possessed the well-modulated voice of a trained orator, which combined with the natural solemnity of his face to arrest the court's attention.

302

"Mr. Whistler, an acclaimed and widely collected artist, is according to Mr. Ruskin—a personage no less than the Slade Professor of Art at Oxford—not only a 'cockney' and an 'impudent coxcomb', but perhaps most damning of all, approaches 'wilful imposture'. Is the vehemence and viciousness of this language calculated to spare the public, or scourge an honest artist? It shall be for you, our esteemed jury, to determine the appropriate damages for this injury."

Back at the table of the plaintiff, James Anderson Rose, Whistler's personal solicitor, looked beyond Parry at the twelve stolid property-owning Englishmen returning the barrister's gaze. Rose would not allow his own eye to linger, but as an art collector himself he doubted that there was a man amongst them possessing the necessary sensibilities to appreciate a talent as rare, original, and peculiar as Whistler's.

Rose owned a number of Whistler's etchings and believed wholeheartedly in his friend's artistic vision. He had more than once in the past come to the artist's legal and financial aid. A few of those etchings he had gladly accepted in lieu of past payment. Perennially short of funds, Whistler had urgent need for at least £1000 and had not been able to supply a retainer. In preparation for this action Rose, in his solitary moments, had been forced to consider how the entire costly legal team would be recompensed if they lost this case. Today Rose let no such notion of failure distract him. He sat quietly erect in his chair, clad in a waistcoat of superior cut but tastefully sombre hue. His movements of wrist and eye were minimal as he took notes with his slender gold-washed pen.

Parry turned from the jury and made eye contact with Rose, in which instant Rose conveyed his approval of the renowned barrister's opening remarks. Rose knew that Whistler, seated next him at the table, had leaned forward and Rose turned his head and with an understated nod assured his client.

There were, he had learnt from notes passed to him by his clerks, more than a dozen London newspapers represented in the room, and half that number again from the papers of the principal American cities, their correspondents all furiously scribbling with a stenographer's speed.

Not only was the main floor of the courtroom full. The gallery was brimming with fashionable young ladies, their tightly gathered skirts *á la polonaise* in demure aesthetic shades of nut-brown or moss-green. Rose had discreetly watched them file in and assume their places, and thought them more likely acolytes of Ruskin than of Whistler. Had they been presented with Ruskin's improving little volume, *Sesame and Lilies*, at an impressionable age, or, if he were mistaken, had they swooned over Whistler's likeness in the illustrated papers? Between the society element and the press contingent, Rose felt the entire atmosphere uncomfortably close to theatre.

Theatre or no, neither side had stinted in procuring counsel. Although Rose had written the actual brief, Whistler's case would be argued by John Humffreys Parry, Serjeant-at-law, the highest rank attainable by a barrister. Ruskin in turn had engaged London's most prestigious law firm, Walker Martineau & Co., and would be represented by Sir John "Sleepy Jack" Holker, a lugubrious Lancashireman and counsel of the British Crown—the nation's attorney general.

The courts had matched their hands. Lord Huddleston, the presiding judge, was nothing less than a baron; his exceedingly popular young wife "Lady Di" had even graced the proceedings this morning with her appearance in the gallery.

The legal point before them was a pretty one. Certainly Ruskin's words were ungentlemanly. Few would attempt to argue that they were not delivered in the form of an insult. But was the incendiary *Fors* passage *prima facie* privileged? Was not in fact the critic protected by his right to speak forthrightly on a publicly exhibited work, ostensibly placed there for criticism? And had not Ruskin displayed similar if perhaps not equal intemperance in past utterances in *Fors*? Whistler's team would have to prove actual malicious intent.

The first to be called was to be Whistler himself, and Rose hoped his client's more acerbic side would be held in check during the following examination and cross examination.

In the initial scramble for witnesses Whistler had suggested scores, from Prince Teck, the Queen's art collecting son-in-law, through a sheaf of prominent painters, sculptors, and art dealers. One after the next demurred the honour or were disqualified by Whistler's legal team. A few reluctant candidates had finally consented, only to send eleventh hour apologies that they had been most regretfully called away on pressing business. Leighton, Poynter, Tissot—even Whistler's old friend Joseph Boehm had forsaken him in the very breech. At least Frederick Leighton's excuse was allowable—he was at that hour down the Thames at Windsor, receiving honours from the Queen—but each refusal stung. By the eve of the trial only two artists had answered Whistler's call. The painter Albert Moore had agreed whole-heartedly "to take up the cudgels" on his behalf, but Rose himself had need to importune the Irish portraitist William Gorman Wills to speak for the plaintiff, as a special favour to his old friend Rose.

Most tryingly, Anderson Rose had not been able to conjure Ruskin to his own trial. Ruskin had initially been full of fight, even naming the prospect of defending himself in court "mere nuts and nectar," and this *volte-face* was unexpected. Ruskin had reportedly suffered some kind of collapse in the late Winter, but Rose had been made aware that he was resuming activity. After Ruskin's defence had three times sought and been granted postponements due to their client's ill health, Rose at last threatened subpoena to summon the man. Still Ruskin did not appear.

But for all Rose's misgivings he knew that over at the defendant's table things were little better. Yes, his not being able to examine Ruskin directly spared Holker the risk of the Slade Professor embarrassing his own cause. But Ruskin's own supporters had also failed to show themselves *en masse*. Despite Edward Burne-Jones' initial bluster—Rose had gotten wind that he had written to Ruskin that he could summon hundreds of ardent defenders—admiration for Whistler was such that not one other painter would stand for Ruskin save that symbol of the *bourgeoisie*, William Powell Frith, and Frith only under the legal duress of subpoena. It would be, it seemed, a trial that everyone wanted to hear, and no one wanted to testify at.

Frith's paintings were immense and crowded canvasses teaming with wholesome and recognizable specimens of the British middle class at public venues such as race courses or train stations being jostled by society toffs, prostitutes, gaming men, cut-purses, swindlers and wastrels of every stripe. A hundred little stories implicit in every incident, plainly offered up to any careless eye. Viewers recognised themselves, their betters, their inferiors. It was of course wildly popular work, held in disdain by both Whistler and Ruskin, and laughed at by collectors of discernment such as Rose.

Whistler was called, and stood with easy grace. All eyes were naturally upon him, and one could hear the silk-upon-silk shifting of the ladies in the gallery as they followed his movements. He was a striking figure, and strikingly virile as well; Rose had wondered if his client's very manliness hadn't proved disquieting to Ruskin.

Whistler advanced to the witness box as if it were an opera stall. His black boots were polished to a high lustre. The long cut of his charcoal-coloured coat flattered waist and shoulders, and his monocle was secured by a narrow ribbon of black satin lost in the silken folds of his chequered cravat. His silver-headed walking stick swung in his hand. Rose knew Whistler had just relinquished ownership of his new Chelsea house for non-payment of debts; the bailiffs had come and seized it but last week.

After a preliminary examination by Parry establishing Whistler's personal history, Parisian art training, and mention of many of the paintings he had sold, Whistler was passed to counsel for the defendant, Sir John Holker. Four of the painter's works, all part of the Grosvenor Gallery show, were in an ante-chamber to the court room. Only one had been for sale at the gallery, and as Ruskin had specifically mentioned the asking price of 200 guineas, the painting which had so exercised the critic was brought in and placed before the court.

Despite a life of privilege, Sir John had made his name convincing juries he was at heart and soul a common hearty Englishman, plain-spoken, without airs or fancies. He was in fact a collector himself, and Rose knew he had actually purchased a painting by a friend of Whistler's at the Grosvenor Gallery exhibition. A bear of a man, Holker managed to look almost rumpled in his gown at this early hour; the starched linen jabot about his neck was already limp. The white rolls of his horse hair wig contrasted sharply with his dark mutton-chop side hair. From his near vantage Rose could see beads of moisture forming on Holker's upper lip.

Holker paused for a moment before the easel, approached it by a step, retreated, and then appeared to screw up his eyes at the painting. The assembled throng watched him as he did so, some eyes straining in the gloom. The court's gas globes shed but feeble light upon the proceedings on this November day.

"Mr Whistler, would you be so good to tell us what the subject is of this painting, this—'Nocturne in Black and Gold'?"

Whistler did not glance at the work, but answered amiably enough. "It is my representation of fireworks at the Cremorne Gardens in Chelsea."

"You don't pretend it to be a view of Cremorne?"

"I should think the public would be very much disappointed in that expectation upon viewing." The audience laughed and Whistler smiled back at Holker. "It is my impression of the fall of fireworks—an artistic arrangement."

"Oh, I see. An 'arrangement.' And the musical reference?"

"It is a night piece, and the musical term "nocturne" serves well to identify those pieces of mine representing night." Whistler's erect carriage and general elegance of person made a strong impression upon Rose as he watched his client in the box. The amiability of his tone might go far to convince the jury that here was an honest and reasonable man, despite the popular presses' mocking portrayal of him as a self-promoting *bon vivant.*

"Certainly so," returned Holker. "Otherwise we viewers might have no clew at all as to what is being represented." The audience laughed again. "Although this 'arrangement' is indeed dark enough to have been extracted from a dustbin."

Light, Descending

Parry's "Objection, your Lordship," was met with agreement by Lord Huddleston and the request that Holker refrain from further prejudicial comments.

"I begin again. This 'Nocturne' is indeed dark, and appears to my untrained eye to be mostly black with a smear of green and a rather violent sprinkle of yellowy-gold. Is that correct?"

Whistler maintained the same amiable tone, but with a note of practical earnestness. "It is not. The painting contains every colour in my palette, with of course darker shades predominately, as it is a night scene."

"And for this you ask two hundred guineas?"

Whistler nodded. "I did. I have sold other paintings for as much."

"But is not two hundred guineas a stiffish price for any painting?'

"I should imagine some in this room might agree so." Whistler smiled at the resultant laughter.

Holker turned to regard the painting again. "How long do you take to paint such a painting as this one?"

"Two days. The first of actual work, the second to finish."

Holker's dense eyebrows rose and met in the middle of his furrowed brow. "Two days? You ask such an immense sum for two day's labour?"

Whistler paused for just a moment. "Indeed I do not. I ask it for the knowledge of a lifetime."

Applause was spontaneous from the crowd, and a smiling Whistler inclined his head to acknowledge it.

Huddleston brought the gavel down upon the block. "Any more outbursts of this nature shall compel me to clear the court room."

Holker had heard enough and passed Whistler back to his own counsel.

"You consider yourself to be a conscientious artist, who conscientiously forms his art ideas, and conscientiously works them out?" Parry's measured tone seemed nearly reverential after Holker.

"Yes."

"And your manner of working is rapid?"

"It could not be otherwise in my art. My system of harmony of colour and arrangement depends upon the freest and most rapid expression of my hand to capture the vitality of the subject."

"Thank you. I should now like to call William Michael Rossetti."

This was Whistler's third witness, and to Rose the most important. Rossetti was no artist himself, but a critic of some estimation, and younger brother to the poet and painter Dante Gabriel Rossetti. Both had been amongst the little confraternity who had once styled themselves the Pre-Raphaelite Brotherhood, championed thirty years ago by none other than Ruskin. That failed little band of dreamers, thought Rose.

Back in the late 40's the Rossettis and a few other acolytes—William Holman Hunt and John Everett Millais amongst them—had clubbed together in dedication to the ideals they saw expressed in early Christian art. Ruskin had stepped in at a critical early point and defended their work, and they had flung themselves around his neck as they earlier flung themselves at the feet of his writings.

The Brotherhood was collapsing of its own weight but the smash up came when Millais and Ruskin's wife fell in love. The trial for annulment due to Ruskin's 'incurable impotence' was still recalled after more than twenty years. Millais had then wed Ruskin's "wife" and produced eight children with her.

William Michael Rossetti had worked all these years at Inland Revenue and had remained solvent by doing so (there are few jobs more prosaic than tax-collecting, and Rose had wondered how the man's spirit had survived), yet he had never ceased his writing and reviewing of art.

"You have written upon art matters for quite some time," Parry began.

"Yes, I have written about both art and literature since 1850."

"And you are personally acquainted with both Mr. Whistler and Mr. Ruskin?"

"I am. I have known Mr. Whistler since 1862, and Mr. Ruskin a little longer."

"I should like to read to you an excerpt from a review you wrote for a journal called the *Academy*. 'Another contribution by the same painter is called 'Nocturne in Black and Gold: the Falling Rocket'...This is also extremely good...The scene is probably Cremorne Gardens, the heavy rich darkness of the clump of trees to the left, contrasted with the opaque obscurity of the sky, itself enhanced by the falling shower of fire-flakes, is felt and realised with great truth.' Do you recognize these words?"

"I do."

"And you still hold them to be true?"

"I do."

"What opinion do you hold as to Mr. Whistler as an artist?"

"Objection!" called Holker.

Lord Huddleston looked over to Parry. "Sustained. Please to remember that Mr. Whistler's abilities as an artist are not on trial."

"Let me ask rather: Are his works the works of a conscientious artist, one endeavouring to excel in his field?"

"They are."

Parry turned to the defendant's table. "Mr. Holker," he invited.

Holker rose and considered the 'Nocturne' once again. "Mr. Rossetti, we have established that this is a painting, that it is one you have commented publicly upon." He turned slowly to Rossetti. "What I should like to inquire of you is this: Is this a work of art?"

"Very much so, in my opinion."

"Because it startles?'

"No. Because it represents a particular intention. I do not say reproduce. I say represents. It represents the effect of night, water, trees and the dying embers of fireworks."

"And is not two hundred guineas a stiffish price for such a 'representation'?"

"I don't believe that my opinion on that should be relevant."

"I must insist that you offer it." Holker appealed to Huddleston.

The judge agreed. "As an art critic I should think that the cost of the wares you advise upon to be most relevant. Pray answer the question."

"I repeat, is not two hundred guineas a stiffish price for such a 'representation'?"

"No."

Rossetti's tone was so decided as to form almost a rebuke. There was a murmur from the assembled which only died down when it was clear he would speak again. "I should say instead it is good value." A gasp from the spectators was followed by the ripple of a titter.

"Good value! And so you yourself would lay down 200 guineas for it?"

"I have never enjoyed the means to indulge my love of paintings. Had I, there are very many paintings I should like to own, amongst them some of Mr. Whistler's."

It was now almost one o'clock. Parry had earlier argued that it was highly desirable that the gentlemen of the jury be able to see the work in question along with the other paintings Whistler had shown at the Grosvenor. Huddleston agreed, and during the luncheon recess the jury was sent to the nearby Westminster Palace Hotel where Whistler and Rose had had the paintings sent in hopes of this eventuality. Whistler's 'Nocturnes' were to Rose magnificent works of art, but he was well aware how challenging they were to those expecting a story, a moral, or the illustration of a famous scrap of poetry between frames. And of all the 'Nocturnes', Rose felt 'Nocturne in Black and Gold' to be the most challenging to the *bourgeois* onlooker. Viewing it in context with other, more conventional works, such as Whistler's portraits of Thomas Carlyle or the celebrated actor Mr. Irving might help the jury see the work in question as an artistic point on a continuum rather than the outrageous insult Ruskin described.

One escort from each side was permitted to join the jury on their viewing, and Rose sent his best young clerk, who reported back that the gentlemen had generally followed Lord Huddleston's instructions to look without commenting. "A bit of whispering, a few snickers," was what he said.

After court resumed Moore and Wills, Whistler's other witnesses, were examined, each attesting to their belief that Whistler was a fine, perhaps great, artist. "He has painted the air," Albert Moore told the court, "and that is a thing few artists have ever attempted, and very few achieved."

Serjeant Parry pronounced the case complete for the plaintiff, and it was left to the judge Lord Huddleston to remind the jury that the question to be settled was whether Ruskin's opinion of Whistler's work came within the compass of privileged communication. Was the review simply calculated to hold Mr Whistler up to ridicule, or was the writer expressing his honest and fair criticism?

It was the defendant's case now. Holker rose again from his table and lumbered before the judge, turning slowly before him, taking in the sweep of jurymen, spectators, gallery ladies, and finally the plaintiff's table. His eye rested a moment upon Parry without actually making eye-contact. He looked back to the jury and spread his large hands outward.

"With all respect to my learned friend Mr. Serjeant Parry, we hold the premise of this case to be a very minor matter, utterly unworthy of the court's attention. But I will recur to the point that the question to be put to the jury is whether or not the most respected art critic alive has the right to inform, instruct and if necessary warn the public from any works of art which that critic considers lacking a standard of finish and completeness that most reasonable men would deem obligatory in any painting pretending to be art, great or otherwise.

"Mr. Ruskin's language is strong, yes, for in matters of art-excellence he is an exacting master. He has in fact devoted his life to the discovery of the beautiful. He has written many highly regarded books and articles, and as we all know, has been these several years holder of the Slade Professorship of Art at the University of Oxford in just recognition of his erudition. He is an esteemed, nay revered formulator of taste, an honoured educator both within and without walls, and a pungent commentator on those aspects of art and art-commerce upon which he has turned his penetrating gaze."

Holker slowed and allowed his eye to rest on each of the twelve men in turn. "I ask you gentlemen, if Mr. Ruskin was not simply performing his duty as he saw it in speaking his honest opinion; and to consider that *if* these comments were in fact his honest opinion, whether withholding them would have made him neglectful of his duty to the public he has always attempted to serve and instruct."

A murmur of acknowledgment, if not of appreciation, rose from the crowd. But Holker was only beginning to warm.

"With this in mind, I ask you gentlemen to join me in an imaginary outing to the Grosvenor Gallery; time—last year. We shall perhaps begin our visit in the Gallery's dining room, where we partake of an artistic chop, served to us upon a plate of rare and ancient pattern. The wine glass we lift to our lips is of Venetian make." Holker mimed the act, and the crowd laughed appreciatively.

"We then proceed to the various gallery-rooms, hoping to see the new productions of Mr. Whistler, which we have heard made much of. We hear they are 'arrangements' and 'nocturnes', and therefore very likely are to be found some 'symphonies' and 'fugues'. But we cannot grow closer to them to satisfy our curiosity, for our view is foreclosed by very many artistic ladies in mediaeval millinery in raptures over the works before them. Can you hear them? 'How very pretty!' exclaims one, and adds, 'and it is a '*Nocturne*'!" 'How very remarkable,' says the next. 'And do you know what a nocturne is?' 'I do not,' sighs the first fair lovely, 'but it is such a pretty idea! Perhaps one day we shall be invited to one of Mr. Whistler's famous Sunday breakfasts, and ask him!' They go on to dispute the identity of the noxious insect with which the artist signs his work—'It is a glimmering moth,' cries one; 'No, a butterfly!' answers another. And so forth and so forth, until the ladies have exhausted their adoring chatter and moved on. Finally we are able to approach. We understand that the picture is supposed to be of Cremorne Gardens—which we heartily hope the ladies themselves have never visited. We look upon the painting. We have heard from Mr. Rossetti that this blackened smear is art. We do not see it.

"It is Mr. Ruskin's opinion that an artist ought to expend the utmost labour on his work, bringing it as close as he can to a finished and perfect state of completion. Does a blackened smear approach that ideal? My learned colleague has stated that Mr. Ruskin has ridiculed Mr. Whistler's paintings. Why then did Mr. Whistler place the work in question in a public exhibition where he knew it would be open to criticism? If he seeks his reputation in 'symphonies', 'arrangements', 'nocturnes', and such nonsense, he is nothing more than the coxcomb Mr. Ruskin has already proclaimed him to be."

The attorney general stared at the gentlemen in the jury stand, and his words slowed. "No one has ever before attempted to control Mr. Ruskin's pen through the device of a trial and jury. He has devoted his long life to instructing and criticising what he finds beautiful in art. Will you stay his hand now?"

Holker returned to his seat.

During this address the court had been rapt in their attention and wholehearted in their laughter at Holker's disparaging burlesque. Yet when Sir John had ended in such seriousness, faces fell and eyes widened to mirror his *gravitas.* Rose felt the jury to be right in the palm of the man's hand and was forced to grudging admiration.

Before he could shoot a look to Parry, Lord Huddleston leaned forward and addressed both tables. "It is now four o'clock, and the conditions of this court room might very well be termed 'nocturne'. The court will adjourn until half past ten o'clock tomorrow morning."

The following morning saw the continuation of Ruskin's defence. As the judgement was expected today, certain of the newspapers had sent multiple representatives, and reporters taking short-hand in rapid bursts in narrow notebooks were joined by sketch artists capturing the personages of the proceedings on soft pads of paper. Once again the fire of the coal heat was merciless. Lord Huddleston ordered the opening of a window, which, being defective, allowed the sight of only a few inches of smudged city sky above the blackened pane.

In this inhospitable environment the defendant's first witness, Edward Burne-Jones, was called to testify. He was a slight, pale haired, fair-bearded man with almost white skin which made the deeply ringed pale eyes more prominent beneath his domed forehead. The rigidity of his person as he approached the stand with his hands clenched at his sides made it abundantly clear that Burne-Jones was less than comfortable in the position he had found himself in. He stammered as he began speaking and Huddleston had twice to ask him to speak up. Rarely had Rose seen a witness less at ease, and he could tell by the glances and gestures from the defendant's table that Ruskin's legal team were attempting to reassure and calm the man.

After eliciting from Burne-Jones that he was an artist who had also exhibited in the Grosvenor show of the previous year, Sir John Holker eased into the deeper waters of his subject.

"Would you tell us what importance finish and completeness has in a work of art?" he asked.

Burne-Jones kept his eyes fixed on the attorney-general's face. "I think complete finish ought to be the object of all artists, and without it no work *can* be considered finished." It was clear to Rose the utterance had been rehearsed many times, and the witness exhaled visibly after getting through it without a stammer.

Holker nodded, and called for one of the exhibited paintings to be produced before the court. Two officers carried in a painting in a gilded frame from the judge's chamber, and placed it upon the easel to the left of Lord Huddleston. It was 'Nocturne in Blue and Silver'. Rose quickly turned and whispered into the ear of Serjeant Parry, and Parry stood to inform the court that the painting had been placed upside down. Amidst general laughter Rose glanced at Whistler at his right, and found that his friend was smiling with the rest of the court, but that his hands had fallen open in a gesture of helplessness upon the table top.

When order had been restored and the painting righted, Holker continued on with Burne-Jones.

"Now this is another painting named by Mr. Whistler 'Nocturne in Blue and Silver'. Would you kindly tell the court if you consider this picture to be a work of art?"

318

Burne-Jones scarcely glanced at the easel. He had been more discomfited by the painting being placed wrong way round than had its creator, and Rose imagined he was a man who did not think art should ever be laughed at. "It is art— but very incomplete. It is a beginning. A sketch, really."

"Does it show the finish of a complete work of art?"

Burne-Jones turned to the painting. It was a scene of the Thames at bluest twilight, that *heure bleue* in which water and fading sky merge. The foreground was almost completely of the waters of the great and still river. In the distant background arose the shadowy grey-blue forms of what Rose knew to be a steeple and some industrial smoke stacks; yet the indistinctness of these forms gave the impression of perhaps minarets or other exotic structures. The immediate foreground bore the suggestion of a few bare leaves nearest to the beholder, painted almost as if they were Japanese bamboo leaves. It was to Rose a stunningly beautiful painting.

"It is not a complete work of art." Burne-Jones kept on looking at the painting. "It—it is masterly in some respects; in many respects—especially the colour is exceptional and excellent. It is—a very beautiful sketch." As if suddenly aware he was over-praising a work he was meant to be damning, he corrected himself. "It is a beautiful sketch, but that is not sufficient to make it a work of art. It is deficient in form, which ought to be as important as colour."

Holker gestured to the waiting officers hovering in the doorway to Huddleston's chamber. "May we now have the Cremorne Gardens picture—the 'Nocturne in Black and Gold'?"

The embattled 'Nocturne' was brought out, and as it passed over the head of the jury actually bumped one of the jurymen in the forehead. The crowd guffawed and

Huddleston brought his gavel down on the block. Whistler still smiled at Rose's side, but had risen a little in his chair to see his painting so manhandled.

"And what is your judgement of this 'Nocturne'?"

Burne-Jones hesitated just a moment. "It would be impossible to call it a serious work of art."

"Could you tell us why?

"The subject, for one. It is not possible to paint night, and this is only one of a thousand failures artists have made in trying."

Holker allowed the term "failures" to hang in the air a moment.

"Is this painting worth 200 guineas?"

Burne-Jones spluttered a little. "Two hundred guineas? No, I will not say it is, seeing how much more careful work other men do for so much less."

Holker addressed Huddleston directly. "I should like to ask the court's indulgence and introduce an additional painting to the court, one painted by Titian and now owned by Mr. Ruskin, which may prove useful in settling questions of finish."

Parry immediately rose to object, but Huddleston did it for him. "I think this is going too far," the judge told Holker. "Counsel will have to prove the painting to be a genuine Titian, for one, and not counterfeit. I do not mean to conjure a laugh in my own court-room, but we all recall the recent situation in which a Titian was obtained and rubbed down to try and ascertain the secrets of the master's hand. On being rubbed down, red began to show itself, and the explorers grew excited that they had the secret in their grasp, when upon further rubbing the red was found to be none other than George III in military uniform!"

The courtroom erupted in laughter, but Huddleston, to Rose's dismay, waved the painting in. Both easels being filled, it was hoisted in the arms of two police officers who had taken their position to one side of the defendant's table. It revealed itself to be a half-length portrait of a man in golden robes, capped with the peaked *cornu ducale* worn by all Venetian doges, and set in a deeply carved golden frame.

To compare an Old Master such as Titian to a modern artist working in their midst was so patently absurd that the initial gasp from the onlookers was followed by a ripple of murmured disbelief.

For the first time Rose felt disappointment in the tactics, if not the strategy, of Walker Martineau. Would we next be comparing the Temple of Athena in Athens to St. Martin-in-the-Fields, or the Coliseum to the West End's Lyceum? The insertion of such a painting—one owned by Ruskin, no less—into a trial already laden with sensational-ism struck him as no more than cheap theatricality.

Holker returned to his witness. "Would you care to comment upon the painting now before you?"

Burne-Jones was eager to do so. "It is a beautiful example of Titian, a portrait of one of the doges; Andrea Gritti, I think. It is a most perfect specimen of highly finished work. The drawing is clear and fine, the modelling good, the flesh and gown beautifully rendered, the colour excellent withal. It is an arrangement in flesh and blood."

Rose felt Burne-Jones must be a little proud of this last allusion to "arrangements" and wondered if it too had been rehearsed.

"And returning to Mr. Whistler's work, what do you see there?" continued Holker.

Burne-Jones seemed not to anticipate this question at this hour. "I see signs of great labour"—surely Holker would regret him saying that, thought Rose—"and great skill. His colours are most beautiful—his moonlit pieces especially. But—I think he evades the greatest difficult of painting by not proceeding further with his work. He does not carry his pictures far enough. Difficulties in painting only increase as the work progresses; that is why so many of us fail."

Burne-Jones was whipsawing from one point of view to its opposite. He seemed not to be able to criticise Whistler without praising him, diluting all of his testimony with qualifications. Rose felt Burne-Jones had said enough about the excellence of Whistler's work to make Ruskin's published comments even more egregious. Holker and the rest of Ruskin's team could not be entirely happy with their witness.

Indeed, Holker passed over what was said and returned to the Titian.

"What is the value of the painting by Titian?" he asked his witness.

"That is a mere accident of the sales-room," answered Burne-Jones, the most sensible thing Rose had heard him say yet.

Serjeant Parry now examined Burne-Jones for the plaintiff. Burne-Jones tensed visibly as Parry approached him; unlike his questioning by Holker he could have no intimation of what he might be asked.

"If I am not mistaken, Mr. Burne-Jones," began Parry, "Mr. Ruskin praised your work rather extravagantly in the very same issue of his publication as he libelled Mr. Whistler."

"Libel has not been proved," objected Holker. Parry conceded, but Burne-Jones' pale cheeks flushed pink.

"Let me ask another question," Parry posed. "You are also a friend, I believe, of Mr. Whistler's?"

Burne-Jones' discomfiture was now so great that his stammering began anew.

"I *was*; I don't—don't imagine he will ever speak to me again, after today."

Parry made a little bow to indicate he was through with the witness.

William Powell Frith was now called, and after identifying himself as a member of the Royal Academy and the originator of such paintings as 'The Railway Station', 'Derby-Day', and 'The Road to Ruin' was asked by Holker to consider the merits of Mr. Whistler's paintings present in court.

Frith considered. "There is beautiful tone of colour in the blue one, but not more than you could get from a scrap of wall-paper or silk."

Someone in the crowd actually hooted, and Huddleston ordered silence.

It was now Parry's turn to examine the witness.

"Have you read Mr. Ruskin's work?"

When Frith assented that he had, Parry tried a new and bold tack. "We know that Turner is an idol of Mr. Ruskin," he offered.

Firth was quick to answer. "I think Turner should be an idol of all painters."

"And do you know the painting of Turner's, in the collection of Marlborough House, called 'Snow Storm'?"

"I do."

"Are you aware that it was once described by a critic as a mass of soap-suds and whitewash?"

Parry ignored the laughter from the crowd.

"I am not."

"Would you call it soap-suds and whitewash?"

It was Frith who now laughed. "I should think it very likely I should. When I said all artists ought to revere Turner, I meant before he went mad and produced works as crazy as those who admire them!"

"And yet Mr. Ruskin, on whose behalf you appear, is one of those who finds 'Snow Storm' very beautiful, and a great work of art."

Here Huddleston interjected, much to the chagrin of both Parry and Rose. "Someone described one of Turner's landscapes as lobster salad," he announced from the bench.

Eliciting more laughter from either jury or crowd was not his goal. Parry conceded the point and brought his questioning to a close.

Rose felt an upwelling of dissatisfaction, of near frustration, rising in his breast. He wished Parry could have better driven home the point that Ruskin had once defended an artist—the great but controversial Turner, no less—whose later paintings seemed similarly unformed, incomplete, and incomprehensible to certain viewers as Whistler's did now to Ruskin. It was not the legal point—that devolved upon whether Ruskin truly had wished to de-fame Whistler's character, and if he sincerely held the beliefs he had stated about his work would he have been in dereliction of his "duty" as a critic to refrain from saying so. And perhaps it was not precisely a *moral* point, yet Ruskin's impassioned defence of Turner's "soap-suds" was at least a point of historical fact, and Rose would have rather that Parry had made it.

By the noon hour nothing was left but the summations. A court porter stepped forward to the defendant's table and whispered in the ear of Sir John Holker. After a small stir Holker rose to announce that he must excuse himself, having just been called away on Crown business. The final plea for Ruskin would instead be delivered by Holker's younger assistant, Charles Bowen.

Rose and Parry exchanged looks. Bowen was competent, but conventional. Spared Holker's masterful theatrics, not to mention comic antics, the jury might be sobered enough to punish Ruskin's vituperative remarks.

Bowen was brief. He reminded the jury of Ruskin's greatness as an art-critic. He stressed that Whistler had exhibited his pictures in a public gallery and thus subjected them to criticism, which any painter ought to welcome as a way of bettering his art. He ended with a warning about freedom of speech. "May it be long that an English jury, regardless of any particular sympathy they may find for any individual, add a link to a chain which may fetter free comment and criticism in this land of ours."

Parry was left with the luxury of time. He moved slowly before the jury box and turned his solemn eyes upon each of the twelve men in turn, as if acknowledging their particular importance as individuals. He then addressed the court.

"I should like to begin with the observation that the tone that the attorney general has taken in this case has, if possible, added more injury to the original libel. He has attempted to ridicule Mr. Whistler's productions, and certainly succeeded in his sneering report of an imaginary group of ladies before his paintings to belittle both the intelligence of woman-kind and perhaps even the artistic abilities of the very many fine female artists who are so worthy of our regard."

There was spontaneous, if lady-like applause from several of the fairer sex in the gallery, and Parry allowed his comments to sink in as Huddleston hammered for order.

"Mr. Ruskin's defence is solely this: 'I shall say what I please and no one shall flinch at the touch of my lash.' Mr. Ruskin has not seen it proper to make the effort to attend upon these proceedings in person, nor to be examined before a commission, but we can assume from the defence offered by my learned colleagues at the defendant's table that he regrets and retracts *nothing* of what was written.

"I will not state that Mr. Whistler's career as an artist has been destroyed. But it has gone forth through the original judgement of Mr. Ruskin's in his own journal, through re-publication in other art journals, and certainly throughout the civilized world as the after effect of this legal action, that the great Ruskin believes Mr. Whistler's art— art considered by many to be beautiful and well worth the originator's asking price—to be worthless trash and an insult to the public.

"Mr. Ruskin may be great as a man, but as a writer, as a critic of the honest and creative labour of men, he has degraded himself. We contend his passage is personal and malicious, and was intended to harm Mr. Whistler and *has* harmed Mr. Whistler.

"It is up to you gentlemen to remind Mr. Ruskin that this is not the proper role of art-criticism, that he must make reparations for the damage done by him by defamatory and libellous statements, and to restore to Mr. Whistler the confidence of the art-buying public."

Huddleston adjourned for lunch. When they reassembled he would give the jury their instructions, and then it would be in their hands. Rose sat with Whistler at their table as the jury filed out and the room emptied. All through the proceedings Rose could sense Whistler's animal energy next him; the man was not nervous but his already high pitch had been turned up a key.

Several newspaper correspondents approached the table, shorthand tablets poised. Whistler had used the power of the newspapers to good effect over the years by granting interviews and inviting the press to his Sunday breakfasts. With his seeming willingness to live in the public's eye and his surplus of self-confidence he had been a favourite on the society pages.

It was Rose who had seen the crippling periods of self-doubt, witnessed the scraping down of nearly-complete paintings in despair; the desperate driven urge to start again to reach perfection. The pieces "dashed off" in a day or two stood in frank contrast to those upon which he had gone to the pillory for. Now Rose raised his hand to fend off the reporters and send them on their way.

Court reconvened at a quarter to two. Huddleston gave the longest and most contradictory and potentially confusing jury instructions Rose had ever heard. He pointed out that holding another up to hatred, contempt or contumely was libel. He stated that it was of the very last importance that a critic, having made up his mind about a work, be allowed to express it, and with unsparing censure if he honestly think it appropriate. He entertained the court with research he had taken upon himself with Mr. Johnson's dictionary on the terms "cockney" and "coxcomb." It was almost three o'clock before the jury stood and left the court.

Rose encouraged Whistler to go out for a smoke. He and Parry would be ready to send a clerk after him when the jury re-emerged. Rose congratulated Parry on the manner in which he had conducted the case, then returned to his end of the table. With Huddleston retired to his chamber, the noise of the court room ascended minute by minute. Parry sat paging through his notes, and Rose too looked into a notebook. Although he had just congratulated Parry, and had warmly reassured Whistler before he left for his cigarette, Rose felt grave misgivings and neither read nor wrote.

This court action was about far more than two pungent sentences published by a leading art critic about a younger painter's picture. It was not even a generational divide, as both Ruskin and Whistler enjoyed both young and old adherents. But an openness to the modern, to the art and ideas of today did play a part in it. Look what had happened——was happening now—with painting and music and literature in France, or in Germany. The eyes of the English public were being wrenched open. French paintings were now appearing at London, in galleries such as the Grosvenor, and Paris saw the Third Impressionist Exhibition last year. An underground channel was being carved steadily by the artistic currents of foreign visionaries such as Monet, Cezanne, and Tissot, and the *avant-garde* represented by the American Whistler. One day—soon—the thinning earth above that channel would give way and the torrent be released.

In the meantime questions of appropriate subjects for art came into it; the nature of beauty itself came into it. What was beauty? To fail to see the beauty in Whistler's landscapes was more than a failure of taste; it was a failure of imagination, a misprision of possibility. The subtle colouration, gauzy line-work, the very picture frames which Whistler designed and himself decorated, lured the sympathetic viewer to enter a *reverie* of his own. Nothing was blatantly told but enough expressed to invite a glimpse, rare and choice, of the elusive genius of the place he caught up in his brushes and breathed upon the canvas. Whistler's work showed there were many ways of seeing—just as there were many avenues of response to what was seen.

And—blast it all! What had happened to the Ruskin who so championed Turner, a painter whose depictions in his later work of steam and fog and rain and swirling sea made him the target of so much condemnation? Could the man honestly not see the similarities—not in style, but in intent— between Turner and Whistler? Or had Ruskin seen the kinship all too keenly, and been secretly indignant that any other artist might encroach upon the territory of his idol? Was that behind the charge of "wilful imposture" in the *Fors* review—was Ruskin calling Whistler a pretender to Turner's throne?

The minutes ticked by. Whistler resumed his seat by Rose. Maddeningly, the jury sent notes out twice for further clarification from Huddleston, and it was not until half past four that the door opened and all twelve returned.

The court was called to order, and the cacophony subsided as quickly as it had arisen. Huddleston looked across to the jury. "Are you all agreed?" he asked.

The foreman of the jury, a tall wiry-haired owner of a dry-goods supplier, nodded.

"We find a verdict for the plaintiff, with one farthing damages."

Huddleston brought his gavel down a final time. "I enter judgement for one farthing for the plaintiff, without costs."

The buzz of the crowd rising, speaking, beginning to move overtook the room. Rose stole a look at the defendant's table. Bowen could not conceal the momentary smile of satisfaction on his lips. Walker Martineau and Co. had performed admirably for their esteemed client. Whistler had hoped for £1000 in damages, and received but a farthing. And Ruskin, who could have been made to carry the entire onerous court-costs for both sides, was instead off with less than the cost of a postage stamp.

Whistler turned his head to Rose. "What…have we won, then?"

"Yes, the jury has found for the plaintiff." There was the grating of chairs being pushed back. Whistler sat motionless.

"But—only a farthing damages?"

Rose nodded. One farthing. A quarter of a cent. It was a contemptuous settlement, indicating the jury's disdain of the entire matter. Whistler's bill for the entire legal team would amount to over £200. There was now almost no likelihood of any of them seeing any of it.

"But—it is a victory."

Rose nodded once more. Whistler raised his head, expanding the space around him, drawing those now beginning to cluster around the table in. "It's a victory, a tremendous victory," he proclaimed. He turned from Rose. "I have triumphed; art has triumphed," he told the reporters.

The "award" had been a rebuke. Rose had never known anyone who could make victory of defeat as easily as Whistler.

Arthur Severn arrived back at Brantwood in a blinding snow. He had sat behind the defendant's table for the duration of the trial, taking notes and making sketches, and had been prepared to testify if called. He had further been charged with bringing into court Ruskin's Titian from its London home at Herne Hill. Now the task at hand was to inform Ruskin he had lost.

Severn was momentarily taken aback when he entered the study at Brantwood where Ruskin sat. The few days away made the physical change in the man since his collapse dramatically evident. Joan had said he had aged a full decade in those few months, but Severn had not fully apprehended this until he was out of the man's presence for a week.

Ruskin was sitting, thin shoulders hunched, in one of his father's heavy mahogany chairs, facing the fire. A shawl muffled his sharp shoulders, and his thickly slippered feet were resting upon a low stool. His beard—which he had been insisting he be allowed to grow long—was now compressed upon his chest beneath his lowered chin. His hands, so thin the blue veins were starting upon them, were wrapped around a china mug of some steaming liquid. The only aspect of the man not enfeebled was his voice; that rung loud and clear throughout the room.

"Verdict for the plaintiff? That coxcomb. That fluttering moth." He fell silent, only to resume with renewed vigour. "And my opinion—worth but a farthing? To credit my words as inflicting but a farthing's worth of damage!"

Severn could almost not stop himself at wondering aloud if Ruskin would have felt happier to have paid the full £1000, with court costs thrown in for good measure.

Ruskin swung his head back to the fire. His opinion so impotent as to be worth but a farthing? Where, and how to strike? Sunder the last tie that linked him to a blind and

331

ungrateful public! "And now it's to be forgotten?" he asked the flames. "I'll make them remember it, or my name's not my own!"

The following morning Ruskin resigned his Slade Professorship at Oxford, for

> *I cannot hold a Chair from which I have no power of expressing judgement without being taxed by it by British Law.*

Madness proved a persistent houseguest. Alone at Brantwood save for Joan and her family, seeing almost no one, Ruskin considered what had befallen him. He had gone headily and heartily and—he admitted—thrillingly mad. He was entirely surprised, and not a little grateful. Madness now marked him with another unique and superb distinction; he did not in his lengthy periods of self-examination recall his dead father's myriad black moods, his mother's intense peculiarity, or the tale of his paternal grandfather's gruesome demise. He saw no family link. He knew only that madness was eager to punish him for his sins against his parents and against his Rose, punish him too for the sins of his own flesh. Madness was a welcome castigator. Madness was as well a thief, grappling with Ruskin for his most cherished remaining possession: the splendid powers of his intellect, and he would not begrudge his victor.

Yet Ruskin regained enough bodily strength and tranquillity of mind to resume a small portion of his writing efforts, and even an eventual return to his forsaken Oxford professorship. His Slade lectures were as subscribed as always, but his brilliant idiosyncratic pedagogy crystallised into laughable eccentricity. In the exaltation of conveying his ideas

to impressionable undergraduates he did not notice that more
students came to smirk than to listen. Laughter became the
norm at his discourses, and he unwittingly played to it. One
day a discomfited dean sat in the back of the lecture room and
witnessed Ruskin as he ran, fully gowned, across the dais at
top speed, flapping his arms to the riotous approval of the
young men before him. He was demonstrating bird flight,
with Ruskin himself no longer bound to Earth's gravity.

He resigned again in an uproar over vivisection, took up
and discarded his monthly *Fors*, struggled to refine old works
on gothic architecture or the Greek gods, and formulate new
ones. His doctors continually cautioned him against work,
which was to Ruskin his water and air; there was no life
without it. But he had lost his ability to draw, it proved so
taxing to eyes and head that this great pleasure of recording
the seen world he must forbid himself. At Brantwood he
devoted more and more of each day to clearing woods,
hacking back invasive brush, or laying in the bottom of his
free-floating blue boat and gazing at the clouds above
Coniston Water.

One afternoon when approaching the landing steps
leading from the lake Ruskin was met by a large viper sunning
itself. It lay curled on the very step he must mount, a direct
challenge to his passage. He stared fixedly at the blunt nose of
the still creature. It had been a long time since he had seen
one. When he could hear anything above the beating of his
own heart he heard the steady whoosh of young Tommy
Davies scything grass in the upper garden.

"Tommy. Tommy," he called, focusing what strength he
could to call up to the boy. In a moment Tommy stood above
him on the grassy verge, resting the scythe on his shoulder as
peered down.

"Tommy. Come down. A serpent."

The boy jumped down, and all Ruskin could do was point at the basking adder. Tommy lifted his scythe over the adder and let it fall. With a start it slithered into the grasses by the steps, and at the second blow had coiled itself about the scythe blade, its chequered tan and black scales becoming a glittering coil of muscle as it avoided the sharp edge. Ruskin watched panting as Tommy swung and pounded the blade until the adder had taken a disabling cut. Ruskin found himself on his knees, grabbing a stone in his fist to crush the adder's head flat. He was not speaking to the bewildered Tommy as he viewed the flattened mass and cried, "The last lock of Medusa's hair!"

There was something revelatory and sacred about his madness. In madness he found himself thrust into all the dark places he had ever imagined, and into places of alluring and almost insuperable beauty. It was as though he had been found at last by another self who had been searching for him for years. He linked arms with Madness, and walked. Even when their paths diverged—which it did for months and sometimes years—he kept well in sight of Madness, not wanting to be left behind: the man knew something and Ruskin was always interesting in learning. But the more Madness spoke to Ruskin, the less he could speak himself. The final eleven years of his life Madness spoke for him.

Chapter Twenty-three

The Lamp of Sacrifice

Lancashire: Fall 1899

If only he could lie down in Coniston Water, he felt he should get better.

The wind whipping about him narrowed his blearing eyes to slits and blew his beard about his chapped and thirsting lips. The waters of Coniston were before and below him, and he stretched out his arms and pointed his mittened hands toward it. Down the slope he stumbled, tripping against bared roots and half-buried stones. Heedless. His ankle slipped within his shoe and the stone it turned against began to roll. He lurched sideways into the arching canes of a dog-rose. His mitten was torn off as the thorns bit his hand. He drew the naked hand before his eyes, his captive mitten lashing in the branch.

A bright drop of red was forming on the tip of his finger, and four more along the tissue of skin on the back of his hand. His mouth twisted. A rose! Ah Rosie-Posie! Her yellow hair and oval face were hanging there in those stripped canes. Rose, Rose, most angelic in beauty, most terrible in heart, a heart of thorn. Stripped and barren of your lovely flesh like this rose of its flower. He howled. Did he howl? The wind blew his tears across his cheeks before he ever tasted salt.

He blinked and raised his eyes across the lake to the hills. Great layers of slate- toned cumulous clouds smothered the rocky summit, his *Vecchio*, with streams of ice-grey cirrus clouds before them. Thick striations of clouds, one shifting over the next. Dots of black smoke arose, blossoming over hidden iron rails. He saw them spread and smear. No harm, no harm! A glint of late sun between cloud layers daggered his eyes, squeezing them shut. Shut he could still see the silvered waters of Coniston. Silver waters as Turner caught in his watercolour of the Grand Canal he cherished, no other painter had captured that; no, not his, given away now. Or did he still own that one? The Turners in the house, his life's study, God's joy, now speechless to him.

The stone his shoe had dislodged was rolling, bounding from hillock to hillock, bumping other stones, gathering speed. It fled before him down the slope to the lake. He abandoned his hung mitten and went after it. Mad, mad, and tired of Madness: Let's run him down to the water for holy baptism.

Fra Angelico was with him too, painting angels with peacock eyes upon their wing tips. Carrying baskets of roses red and white and pink. Fra Angelico, man reading in a cone of light: books sanctify.

St. Francis with my face. At Assisi in my cell. Outside the window is Coniston Water. I will lie down. Something comes across Turner's silvered water.

It is Rosie, Rosie in a boat rowing away from him. He will catch her, thrash arm over arm like a dripping Narcissus to her prow.

Harpies screeching, calling his name down the long hill. *Noli me tangere.* A woman in a dark skirt. Two men. Screaming, waving. Joanie. Joanie will save him.

finis

Book Group Discussion Guide

These questions have been created to spur discussion with others, or reflection within yourself. They are meant to enhance the experience of recalling what you have read, and how it affected you when you read it. The questions may also prompt consideration of how the meaning of the book might change or deepen with time. Following the questions is a list of important paintings mentioned in the novel.

1. How did John Ruskin's relationship with his parents affect his ability to go on and form normal attachments with others?

2. Ruskin repeatedly feels misunderstood, even abandoned, by those he cares about. Do you think this is due to his superior intellect, his personal timidity, the friction between his own values and that of much of 19th century culture, or his seeming inability to truly connect with others?

3. What advice would you have given him as he heads off to Oxford and his university career?

4. John Ruskin became famous at a young age–twenty-four–with the publication of the first volume of *Modern Painters*, even though he remained anonymous on its title page. Throughout his life he had a love-hate relationship with his fame, which he oftentimes felt was rooted in his lesser works, or in the details of his personal life. How is his disregard or contempt for his reputation depicted in the novel?

5. Ruskin appears to have been unable to physically express his love to a woman. Yet we know from his letters to Georgiana Cowper-Temple (later Lady Mount Temple, who does not play a part in this novel), that he was capable of sexual arousal and oftentimes satisfied

his own urges. Do you agree with the author's conclusion of why he did not consummate his marriage to Euphemia Gray?

6. Euphemia Gray–Effie–makes perhaps the most important decision of her life when she decides to leave Ruskin. Although she married John Everett Millais a year later and he went on to fame and riches, Effie was never again welcomed at court or in many of the homes in which she had once been a valued guest. What do you think of her choice to leave? Could she have handled it differently?

7. The circumscribed role of Victorian women made it difficult for intelligent and energetic women like Maria LaTouche to realise their full potential. As a married woman and mother she was fully occupied in running a fashionable household, and her elevated social class made it impossible for her to work outside the home except in a volunteer capacity. It was easier for a single woman, and one not "a lady", like Octavia Hill, to undertake and accomplish meaningful work. Compare this with the challenges facing today's working women.

8. The treatment of mental illness was in its infancy during Ruskin's lifetime. Today he would possibly have been diagnosed as having bi-polar disorder, or perhaps encephalopathy, and received psychiatric care and medication. Such treatment comes with its own costs and risks, however. Consider how such intervention may have changed Ruskin's life and work, for better, and for worse.

9. Rose LaTouche suffers from *anorexia nervosa*, stemming both from the desire to demonstrate her religious ardour through fasting, and the tensions she feels caught between her parents as they "battle for her soul". Were you surprised that Ruskin's physician John

Simon recognized this condition, and had seen it in other young women?

10. Which character, other than Ruskin, do you feel most strongly about? And why?

11. Do you think Ruskin truly loved Rose, and was capable of being her husband as he said he wished to be? Or would their marriage prove as disastrous as his first?

12. Which character would you most like to have dinner with? Which would you certainly not wish to sit down with?

13. The 19th century was one of tumult, with widespread revolution, war, and industrial growth. Into this mix came Charles Darwin's *On the Origin of Species* (1859), which made many question their faith in God for the first time, as it seemed to prove that the Bible was not infallible, at least when it came to the dating of the world. Consider John Ruskin's own spiritual path, from that of his parents' Evangelism, to his flirtations with the Roman Catholic rite, to his admiration for his friend Norton's Stoicism. How did the events in Ruskin's life lead him to his self-proclaimed "paganism", and his bouts of agnosticism? If mental illness had not claimed him, do you think Ruskin could have found spiritual peace? And in what tradition do you think that might have been?

14. In addition to being a biographical novel about a great man, this is also a novel of ideas. The most important of these is perhaps the conflict of Ruskin's dearly held ideal of a vanished, agrarian past in which handcraft is valued, and the frenetic pace of Industrial Britain with its crowds, pollution, and exploitation. Consider this conflict (or others that strike you in the

novel) and discuss how Ruskin attempted to further his goals even in the onrush of a technological age.

15. Another conflict in the novel is the idea of what constitutes "art". Ruskin favours the young Pre-Raphaelites partly because their attention to detail, meticulous nature of their observing skills, and historic subject matter remind him of the masters of the Middle Ages. Yet he considers that Turner reigns supreme, even when that artist's work was being derided as incomprehensible ("soap suds and white wash"); and much of Turner's later work looks similar to the atmospheric work of Ruskin's nemesis, James McNeil Whistler. This battle between historicism and modernity marked much of 19th century painting, sculpture, architecture, and music. How are these conflicts still playing out in 21st century culture?

16. What links the first chapter to the last?

Important paintings mentioned in *Light, Descending*, and where they can be viewed. (Images for most are readily available on the internet.)

Chapter One

Portrait of John Ruskin, age 3 ½, by James Northcote, R.A., Brantwood, Lancashire

Chapter Two

Juliet and Her Nurse, by JMW Turner, R.A., Private Collection
Mercury and Argus, by JMW Turner, R.A., National Gallery of Canada, Ottawa

Chapter Three

Slavers Throwing Overboard the Dead and Dying, by JMW Turner, R.A., Museum of Fine Arts, Boston

Chapter Nine

Isabella, by John Everett Millais, R.A, Walker Art
Gallery, Liverpool
The Girlhood of Mary Virgin, by Dante Gabriel
Rossetti, Tate Britain, London

Chapter Ten

An internet search for "John Ruskin Artwork" will
provide many examples of his work
The Dream of St Ursula, by Vittore Carpaccio, Galerie
Dell'Accademia, Venice

Chapter Eleven

Christ in the House of His Parents, by John Everett
Millais, R.A, Tate Britain, London
The Woodsman's Daughter, by John Everett Millais,
R.A, Guildhall Art Gallery, London

Chapter Twelve

The Order of Release, by John Everett Millais, R.A,
Tate Gallery, London
Portrait of John Ruskin, by John Everett Millais, R.A,
Private Collection

Chapter Thirteen

An internet search for "Elizabeth Siddal Artwork" will
provide many examples of her work

Chapter Fourteen

The Presentation of the Queen of Sheba to Solomon,
by Paolo Veronese, Galleria Sabauda, Turin

Chapter Fifteen

Val d'Aosta, by John Brett, Collection of Lord Lloyd-
Webber

Chapter Twenty

The Days of Creation, by Edward Burne-Jones, A.R.A.,
Harvard Art Museum
Nocturne in Black and Gold, by James McNeil
Whistler, Detroit Institute of Arts
Nocturne in Blue and Silver, by James McNeil
Whistler, Harvard Art Museum
The Derby Day, by William Powell Frith, Tate Britain,
London
Snow Storm, by JMW Turner, R.A., Tate Britain,
London

Author's Note

Why a novel about John Ruskin? In short, to take my decades-old fascination with the man and attempt to answer a few lingering questions as to his behaviour and motivations. It is only the sphere of fiction, however founded on established fact, which provides the scope for the well-reasoned imagining of the unknowable in a man's life. In the compass of the historical novel, solutions to unanswerable questions can be proposed, and the reader in encountering these solutions and examining their ramifications may find previously opaque behaviours or personalities resolving into sharp and even indelible focus.

John Ruskin died in January 1900. Six years later Ruskin was voted the most influential author of the Labour Members of the House of Commons, his books besting even the Bible, Dickens, Carlyle, and Shakespeare. His impact on such titans as Gandhi, Tolstoy, and Proust ensured that his ideas traversed national and linguistic borders, and his influence on artists, architects, and designers enshrined him as a sort of godfather of the Arts and Crafts movement. Yet his name and legacy rapidly fell into decline as the 20th century presented its own challenges, and it is only in recent years that new biographies, exhibitions of his own paintings and drawings, and a spate of stage and film treatments (mostly, alas, centred upon his ill-fated marriage) have brought the name of John Ruskin once again before the eyes of an inquiring public eager to learn more about this exceptional, exacting, frustrating, and frustrated genius.

Ruskin's life was so long and productive, his output so vast, and his opinions so self-contradicting that a sometimes ruthless selection of what (and in many instances, who) to include in a novel about him made for tough choices. Fine, and even exhaustive biographies of the man and his times are available, as are edited collections of letters (and he is said to

343

have written 40,000), as well as the all-important Brantwood Diary he kept as he descended into the punishing depths of the psychosis of 1877. Along with reading at least a selection of the man's own output and glorying in the beauty of his nature and architectural paintings these sources are a must in grasping the enormity of Ruskin's abilities, interests, and opinions.

But my goal was to create *a novel* to provide readers with no prior knowledge of Ruskin a portrait of his life, times, and contemporaries that would both hew to fact and make for compelling reading. The sort of liberties I have taken, besides the numbers of interests, passions, and friends left as it were on the cutting room floor (or indicated by only the slightest of mentions) also extend to taking an exchange of letters and dramatizing them as face-to-face conversations, turning diary entries into utterances, and presuming to enter the minds of the characters. Those deeply conversant with Ruskin will be certain to notice and lament the many glosses I was forced to resort to to imbue the narrative with the energy, variety, and propulsion that a novel must, in good faith with its reader, provide. I trust these same adherents will also note the very many instances in which I have taken the great master's words and interwoven them into the text in what I hope will be seen as a subtle enrichment of the whole.

For those wishing to plumb deeper waters, may I suggest a few of the primary and secondary sources most helpful to me in my research: *The Works of John Ruskin,* E.T. Cook and Alexander Wedderburn, in thirty-nine volumes (George Allen, 1902-1903, London) is the *sine qua non* of his collected writings, but his most popular books such as *Modern Painters Volume I, The Stones of Venice* and *The Seven Lamps of Architecture* are readily available in attractive paperback versions. *Praeterita,* Ruskin's autobiography (Everyman's Library, 2005), was begun in 1885 and is suffused with beauty. *The Brantwood Diary of*

John Ruskin, Helen Gill Viljoen, editor (Yale University Press, 1971), offers a unique perspective of a great mind teetering at the abyss of madness. *The Letters of John Ruskin to Charles Eliot Norton* (Houghton Mifflin, 1904) provides insight into their abiding friendship, intellectual jousting, and painful differences. *Dante Gabriel Rossetti: Family Letters Volumes I & II* (Roberts Brothers, 1895) presents the personality of the poet and painter and includes a memoir by William Michael Rossetti, the artist's brother.

Effie in Venice, edited by Mary Lutyens (John Murray, 1965), the previously unpublished letters of Effie Gray Ruskin, lifts the curtain on this vivacious and intelligent young woman during the fateful years of 1849 to 1852. *Millais and the Ruskins* (Vanguard, 1967) and *The Ruskins and the Grays* (John Murray, 1972) continue Mary Lutyens' exhaustive and fascinating study of the involved parties. *Rainy Days at Brig O'Turk* (Dalrymple Press, 1983) reproduces Millais' lively sketches from the Scottish working holiday of Summer 1853.

John Ruskin and Rose LaTouche, by Van Akin Burd (Clarendon Press, 1979) provides important background on Rose and her family, and includes Rose's diaries of 1861 and 1867.

Of biographies of Ruskin, the following were invaluable: Tim Hilton's *John Ruskin: The Early Years* (Yale University Press, 1985) and *John Ruskin: The Later Years* (Yale University Press, 2000); *John Ruskin: A Life* by John Batchelor (Carroll & Graf, 2000); *John Ruskin* by Frederick Kirchhoff (Twayne, 1984; and particularly useful for the insightful rendering of Ruskin's vast written output); *Ruskin: The Great Victorian* by Derrick Leon (Routledge & Kegan Paul, 1949; which despite factual errors and the overt worship of its subject, draws on valuable Leon family source material). Quentin Bell's *Ruskin* (Hogarth Press, 1963) is a short and piquant study, full of interest.

Other more specialised works on Ruskin from which I profited include *Ruskin's God*, by Michael Wheeler (Cambridge University 1999); *Ruskin and Oxford*, by Robert Hewison (Clarendon Press, 1996): *Ruskin and Turner*, by Luke Herrmann (Faber and Faber, 1968); and *John Ruskin: A Life in Pictures*, by James S. Dearden (Sheffield Academic Press, 1999).

Moral Desperado: The Life of Thomas Carlyle, by Simon Heffer (Weidenfeld and Nicholson, 1995) and Fred Kaplan's *Thomas Carlyle: A Biography* (Cornell University, 1983) provided the background I sought on the Sage of Chelsea, and the reading of Carlyle's *Sartor Resartus* proved an unexpected delight.

The Legend of Elizabeth Siddal by Jan Marsh (Quartet, 1989) examines that doomed painter and poet both as icon and artist, and the same scholar's *The Pre-Raphaelite Sisterhood* (Quartet, 1985) places Lizzie in context with the other "stunners"- talented artists and craftswomen, all.

Linda Merrill's highly readable *A Pot of Paint: Aesthetics on Trial in Whistler v. Ruskin* (Smithsonian, 1992) reconstructs the trial from scores of newspaper, magazine, and eye-witness accounts (as the verdict was not appealed, the court records were destroyed) and was the source for the chapter on the Whistler libel trial.

Finally, a few words of thanks. I am beholden to the many skilled and professional librarians who assisted me in my research, particularly those of The British Library; Houghton Library, Harvard; Margaret Clapp Library, Wellesley College; and The Cambridge Historical Society, Cambridge, Massachusetts. I am sincerely grateful to the administration and staff of the MacDowell Colony, Ledig House International, and Byrdcliffe for granting me residencies during which a substantial portion of this novel was written and revised. The peace, quiet, and natural beauty provided by these artists' retreats made it possible for me to harness five years of research and planning and produce the novel in staccato bursts of energy. My appreciation for my wonderful First Readers Jen Calder (truly a never-failing source of support and encouragement over six years' duration), James English, and Jennifer Joyce is unbounded.

CPSIA information can be obtained at www.ICGtesting.com
Printed in the USA
LVOW11s1946161215

466864LV00006B/783/P